Craig Thomas was e̶d̶u̶ llege, Cardiff, where he gained his M.A. in 196̶7̶. H̶e̶ the author of fifteen bestselling novels, including *Firefox* and most recently, *Winter Hawk*, *Emerald Decision*, *The Last Raven*, *All the Grey Cats* and *A Hooded Crow*, all of which spring from his interest in geopolitical tensions and conflicts.

Craig Thomas is married and lives with his wife and two tortoiseshell cats in Staffordshire. His interests include cricket, gardening and music, especially classical music and jazz. He is also interested in philosophy and political theory (his collection of essays *There to Here* is published by Fontana Press).

Acclaim for *Playing With Cobras*:

' . . . All the thrill of the chase, with an exotic, explosive background that fairly hisses with danger – like a cobra preparing to strike'   *Daily Express*

'Complex and satisfying'   *Mail on Sunday*

CRAIG THOMAS

PLAYING WITH COBRAS

HarperCollins*Publishers*

Lines from 'For the Union Dead' by Robert Lowell, published by Faber and Faber Ltd are reproduced with kind permission from the publishers.

Exerpt from `For the Union Dead' from *For the Union Dead* by Robert Lowell. Copyright © 1964 by Robert Lowell. Copyright renewed © 1992 by Harriet Lowell, Sheridan Lowell and Caroline Lowell. Reprinted by permission of Farrar, Straus and Giroux, Inc.

HarperCollins*Publishers*
77–85 Fulham Palace Road,
Hammersmith, London W6 8JB

Special overseas edition 1993
This paperback edition 1994
1 3 5 7 9 8 6 4 2

First published in Great Britain by
HarperCollins*Publishers* 1993

Copyright © Craig Thomas & Associates 1993

The Author asserts the moral right to
be identified as the author of this work

ISBN 0 00 647314 8

Set in Meridien

Printed in Great Britain by
HarperCollinsManufacturing Glasgow

for
Gethyn and Phyll

and for
Ed and Lynn

with love

'The old, most populous, wealthiest of earth's lands
The streams of the Indus and the Ganges and their
many affluents . . .

On the one side China and on the other side
Persia and Arabia,
To the south the great seas and the bay of Bengal . . .

Doubts to be solv'd, the map incognita, blanks
to be fill'd.'

Walt Whitman: *Passage to India*, 6

PRELUDE

'. . . it is perhaps only with him that
the real question mark is posed for
the first time . . . the hand moves
forward, the tragedy *begins*.'

Nietzsche: *The Gay Science*, V

Philip Cass nudged the Japanese 4WD out from behind the sight-seeing bus wheezing up the road, and slid carefully past it. The road dropped away to his left, into the smeared, scented darkness of pines. Pines loomed above, too, marching down towards the twisting, dusty track wriggling tiredly up towards Gulmarg. The bus, its asthmatic engine belching exhaust fumes, disappeared from the mirror as he rounded a twist of the road. Nanga Parbat, for a moment, hunched to the north, snow-peaked. The Kashmir Valley's orchards and ricefields, in the haze of late summer, spread out to his left then behind him as the road climbed and twisted again.

The smell of the pines. He sighed. Not long now, not much of such things left, unless he came back as a tourist. The steering wheel struggled in his hands against the potholes and stones of the road, before his vehicle levelled and confronted the old hill-station of Gulmarg. New ski-lifts against the sky, new hotels and bungalows beached amid grass and wild flowers. The sensation of imminent departure not only from Kashmir but from India suddenly hurt him, like emotions he might have felt beside a terminal sickbed. He passed two backpacked trekkers, utensils rattling at their shoulders above the noise of the vehicle's engine. Bright shirts and slacks on the highest golf course in the world. A necklace of tourists mounted on ponies emerged from the crowding pines. They paused to appreciate their first glimpse of the resort afloat in its meadow, with the Pir Panjal range pushing up to the south and the outriders of the Himalayas to the north, cupping the place in a great rock embrace. Cass smiled with something approaching bitterness. He spoke Hindi, Urdu, a smattering of Punjabi, could stumblingly read Sanskrit – all of which meant that his tour of duty in India was over and that SIS would probably send him to Washington or Moscow, where the last four years would immediately be redundant.

He tossed his head. He had another couple of months, why so sad already? He sniffed like a hound at the clean, sharp air. Delhi was still like a cauldron, even Srinagar behind him in the valley had been sticky, oppressive – but up here . . .

Up here was the real source of his melancholy, and it was human. Sereena. Waiting for him in her husband's bungalow just behind Gulmarg, perched on the edge of a cliff and facing north towards Pakistani Kashmir and the great mountain, Nanga Parbat. Sereena the Indian film star and the wife of the Minister of Tourism and Civil Aviation, V. K. Sharmar. He rubbed his hand through his breeze-blown hair as if embarrassed, grinning at the awakened sense of danger, the effrontery of their months-long liaison, the locales of their encounters in Delhi or here in Kashmir. The dangerous, exhilarating joke of it, the added earnestness that risk gave to their lovemaking. When he left India, he'd leave her behind, too.

The resort trickled tourists along its main street. There was noise from cafés, music blaring from open-topped cars and flung-open doors. Then he was climbing the short, winding, narrow track up towards the long wooden bungalow that once had housed, beneath elaborately carved eaves and in scented-wood rooms, memsahibs for each summer of the Raj. He slowed the vehicle and dragged on the brake, disappointed that she was not posed in the shadow of the verandah, then at once pleased in anticipation of her waiting for him in the minister's kingsize bed in the long, low-beamed main bedroom. The fan would be turning coolly above her, its arms waving in encouragement rather than reproach. He cocked his head, listening. The hi-fi was playing some of the American country rock Sereena

12

incongruously enjoyed; even as he preferred ragas and the sitar. She was, because of her status as one of the Hindu deities of the cinema, more Western than he, sometimes. She was in bed, then. It would all be done with titillating, cinematic cliché; the iced champagne, the silk sheets, the seductive underwear, the acted whore— everything. He smiled, rubbing his cheeks. He *was* in the intelligence service, after all; Sereena had merely changed his name to Bond, glamorising their relationship within the conventions of celluloid.

And, if it was a fantasy, then he enjoyed that too ... it was *every* man's sexual fantasy, after all. Experienced Asian beauty, exotic settings, the delicious-lubricious, the element of risk. Enough to make him all but rub his hands in anticipation.

Or remember that she'd become more than a fantasy, an appetite. Awkwardly, he had begun to love her. At least, to want to be with her, and to want not to end it. He climbed out of the vehicle and breathed deeply, slowly. He could just see the spray of a fountain at the rear of the bungalow. Jesus, it was close enough to paradise, every aspect of the situation. He dragged his overnight bag out of the 4WD and hurried into the cool, purple shadow of the verandah. Maybe, just maybe, he'd wangle another extension to his tour of duty ... trouble was, with Aubrey gone, there was no one who would just OK it with a slight smile. Pete Shelley was stuffed to the gills with pompous rectitude since taking over the Director-General's job. He might well not give him an extension –

Sod that for the moment, anyway. He called out: 'Sereena – it's me! The flight was on time.'

She must be teasing, some new game. Wanted him to go straight into the bedroom, be surprised by what she was wearing, or the way her body was posed in the bed or perhaps against the late afternoon light from the window, the mountains behind her. He hurried, dropped his overnight bag and cotton jacket on the living-room sofa. Scented woods, carved cornicing, heavy old furniture, deep, complex rugs. He plucked up a glass

13

of still-bubbling champagne from a small table, sipping it as he grinned. Sipped again, the drink's coldness tightening his throat pleasurably. A broken champagne glass crackled into shards beneath his shoe as he approached the bedroom door. He could smell, above the usual scents and incenses of the bungalow, the Chanel he'd bought for her last birthday –

He looked down at the broken glass beneath his feet. She was getting careless in her eagerness – perhaps she'd heard his engine note approaching and dropped it in her hurry. He stepped through the open door of the bedroom, rubbing his temple against a sudden dizziness. She was lying on the silk sheets – saried though, as if she'd flung herself on the bed in a modelling pose, her hair strayed out like a black cloud across the pillows. There was a great deal of blood, a great deal. It had soaked into the sheets and the pillows, there was even a splash of it on the wall behind the elaborate carving of the headboard. Blood everywhere . . .

The room whirled, even before he could vomit in horror, the smear of blood on the wall spinning like a firework, fiery in the slanting sunlight coming through the window . . . window, which was moving, circling the room, then floating above him as he fell into the darkness.

Window . . . He realised the opaque area of dull light was the window. It was unmoving, but not where . . . He was lying on the bed. The window was where it should be, if he was lying on the bed. Nanga Parbat's flanks were goldened as the sun began to go down. His hand and forearm, stretched out to where she would be across the bed, were sticky. His fingers – he wriggled them – were weblike, stuck to one another. His head lurched like a loosely-stowed cargo as he attempted to sit up and look at his – *red*? – hand – why red, *sticky*? Flies buzzed in the room beneath the revolving, slow fan. He turned. Her body was covered with them, feasting on the drying blood that covered her, covered the sheets – his hand, his shirt, the knife that lay

14

on the bed between them. He lurched across her body, waggling his arms, beating at the air around the flies, his head aching, his stomach revolted. His mind seemed pierced by a silent scream attempting to bully itself into his awareness. He stared at the gashes in the glowing, bloodstained sari, then at his reddened hands. He was stilled with shock, unable to move, his throat fighting back the bitter vomit he could taste. The flies settled on her again, advantaged by his paralysis.

The hi-fi continued its drool of country rock from the living room, the noise pressing against his throbbing temples. Then, gradually loudening as it approached from Gulmarg, the noise of the police siren drowned the music as Cass continued to stare, immobile, at the woman's body.

PART ONE

Casual Labour

'He has an angry wrenlike vigilance,
a greyhound's gentle tautness;
he seems to wince at pleasure . . .

He is out of bounds now.'
   Robert Lowell: *For the Union Dead*

ONE

the burning

'I can't oblige you – you see how I'm fixed,' Hyde responded mockingly, even though he had never intended it to come out as a flip excuse.

As if in disappointment at suspected compromise, the leggy Burmese cat walked away from him. The tortoiseshell, meanwhile, quizzically bent her masked features to one side as she sat outside on the sunblocked windowsill overlooking the scrappy garden. They were probably right to be disappointed. He had wanted to say, *You don't employ me any more. I'm a free agent. Bugger off, Shelley*.

Shelley was seated across the lounge, the unexplained videotape he had brought with him beside him on the sofa. The late summer sun fell across the carpet with the beginnings of reluctance. There was, seemingly, a third human presence in the room with them, even though the Burmese had joined Ros in the bedroom, where she was noisily packing. Aubrey was there, as usual reproving Hyde, on this occasion in fragments of the long, maundering, confessional letter he had written to Hyde only days after resigning from the Cabinet Office. The phrases flicked in Hyde's thoughts with the remonstrance of cuffing hands. *Only theories offer freedom of action. Other people offer nothing but endless obligations, the very opposite of freedom* . . . Aubrey, explaining why he had bent or broken every cardinal rule in order to pursue Paulus Malan to his death. Aubrey, to square his vigorous conscience, had been apologising for the predominance of personal motives over duty and the priorities of the operation.

Hyde shook his head and then rubbed his hands through his curling hair. He was instantly angry, recalling Aubrey – recalling *obligation*.

'I can't do it, Shelley,' he burst out. 'I don't have to do it. You don't *pay* me to do things like that any more. I resigned because of Aubrey. So, don't look for terminal boredom that'll make me do *anything* slightly interesting or dangerous.'

Even that hadn't come out as he intended. Obligation. As Shelley had already put it – assuming the irresistible force of any new D-G – he *owed Cass his life. Cass saved you in Delhi, put you on the right plane to the safe place. They'd have killed you, if not.* Because of the baldness of the statement, what he really wanted to say – *oh, sod Cass* – kept whimpering away in his thoughts, like a puppy dismissed for weeing on the new carpet; or like one of the cats caught stropping at the brocade covering of the suite. *Oh, fuck Cass* . . . It didn't work, not really, because in the darkness at the back of his mind Cass howled and whimpered like all dogs and cats.

'It's no *big* deal, Patrick,' Shelley soothed. 'What I'm asking.'

Shelley was there on his own initiative. The paint that emblazoned his name and new title on his office door in Century House wasn't yet dry. Director-General of the Secret Intelligence Service. Shelley could at last recite it to himself every morning as he looked out over the slate-grey river. Aubrey's dauphin had got the top job, but the old man must have pulled the last of the strings he held very hard to ensure the appointment.

To deflect Shelley, he said: 'How's the old bugger? I don't hear gossip any more.' *I'm an outsider.*

'What? Oh . . . Sir Kenneth.' Shelley smiled with genuine affection. 'I hear he's in Vienna, staying with Frau Elsenreith.'

'His only *old* true love,' Hyde scoffed. 'After that? Winter in the Bahamas – memoirs should be worth a bit.'

'I think he's happier than his former political mistress, at the least,' Shelley replied.

Probably true. Aubrey had waddled away overburdened with honours and praise.

In the bedroom, Ros was making ostentatious noises as she opened and closed drawers, shut suitcases. As if cued, Shelley murmured:

'What will you do with the cats?'

'What –? Oh, the cattery.'

'And you'll be gone . . . ?'

'A couple of months. It depends how long it takes Ros to sort out her uncle's estate.' A wardrobe door slid shut with an exasperated noise. Both cats had now disappeared from the windowsill, the Burmese having returned from the bedroom, inspected Shelley's trousers, then joined the tortoiseshell outside. The Earl's Court afternoon seeped the scent of petrol and dust into the bright room. Hyde shrugged. 'You see why I can't help.'

Ros clicked suitcase locks firmly shut, then, to Shelley's evident discomfort, her large shadow hovered at the door of the lounge. Discomforted, he was, of course, anyway. It wasn't acted, either. Not only did he no longer know how to ask, but he didn't really know the question he wanted answered.

Curious, Hyde murmured: 'What's on the tape? Snuff video?'

'Well – someone who appears in it *is* dead. May I put it on?'

Hyde shrugged, and Shelley moved towards the VCR beneath the TV set, inserting the cassette as Hyde felt himself burrowing mentally back into the room, noticing details – the glimpse of the tortoiseshell's features above the windowsill before it ran off, as if warned; then the slow slippage of the sunlight across the carpet, and the warmth it gave to the furniture and drapes. As if, he realised, he needed reassurance. Shelley flicked on the television set, using the remote control.

At once, a struggling mass of humanity.

'This is a film star's funeral, Indian style,' Shelley remarked drily, passing some photographic enlargements to Hyde. Hyde leant forward to take them. The screen showed the vast crowd from the vantage of a high window, as it seethed and struggled like the grubs in a fisherman's plastic box before being flung into a canal. Then, unedited, the scene was registered from ground level, amid the struggle for breath and glimpse. 'They seem quite keen,' Shelley added.

Hyde tossed his head and glanced down at the snapshots.

'Cass was giving *this* one?' he muttered.

'The affair had been in progress for some months.'

'I can't really blame him.'

Hyde glanced up from the spread snapshots to encounter the screen, where the camera swayed and wriggled through the pressing undergrowth of upraised arms and bent heads and waved scarves and handkerchiefs. He saw a distant funeral pyre – for a film star? In India, yes.

'That's the minister, her husband,' Shelley remarked, as Hyde watched a slick-haired and prosperous man circle the pyre. The soundtrack was poor, but the susurrations of the crowd, the collective orgasm of grief, was mounting. The sunlight gleamed into the camera for a moment, then the picture cleared. Foreign, hot, threatening, was how the scene appeared to Hyde – who allowed his senses to dictate, despite their catching Ros' exhalations of dislike coming from the bedroom. 'That's his brother, to his left.'

Hyde merely nodded. The minister, Sharmar – whom he recognised at once – was dignified and somehow aloof, despite the evident scandal of his wife having been murdered by an English lover. Perhaps the exigencies of the Indian cinema required decorum for a film star's burial, whatever the circumstances. Surreptitiously, he watched Shelley watching him watching the television screen. The husband's family gathered closer to the pyre, before the flames became too intense, while the crowd lamented in gusts of grief in the evening glow which managed to ridicule the flickers of flame from the scented wood surrounding –

He glanced down. *Her.*

'And Cass was giving her one, was he?'

22

'Apparently,' Shelley replied.

The crowd drew nearer to the updraught of flames from the pyre. The white-shrouded figure was further shrouded by blue and orange and the enveloping gleam of the early evening. The crowd seemed to press on like pilgrims towards an instantaneous miracle.

'What does *he* say?'

The afternoon, palely-English, reentered the lounge at the coat-tails of the Burmese, who had dropped like a large, dusky leaf through the open window. The scene on the television screen appeared exotically unreal.

'He won't say anything – that's the problem. Not to Head of Station or anyone else. He keeps – ' Shelley spread his hands in supplication and then added: 'Direct contact with D-G, or nothing.'

'I would have thought he'd be screaming for help.'

As the flames leapt higher and the nearest and dearest moved aside, the wailing and – yes, rage – of the crowd swelled like a chorus. Last night of the Indian Proms.

'He is, in a way.'

'And you think he *might* have something to say for himself,' Hyde challenged, 'but really you'd prefer to believe the salacious little story the Indian papers are reciting.' He grinned sourly. 'Go on, you would really, wouldn't you? No diplomatic immunity, just a sordid sexual quarrel that became very nasty in the final round – head-butting, whips-and-scorpions, buggery, then murder,' he goaded. 'What does Delhi say?'

'They're not surprised.' It was evident that Shelley had arrived at the rock in the road which halted him. Hyde vaguely recalled Dickson and the others.

'What would they know? Bunch of tossers, Delhi Station.'

Immediately, as if Hyde had mismanoeuvred, Shelley became supplicatory, his hands stretched outwards, forearms resting on his thighs, white wrists protruding from shirtcuffs, cuffs protruding from a light-grey suit.

'That's why I have to be certain, Patrick –' He grinned. 'Why I'm trying to blackmail you into assisting.'

'Because you can't trust those second-rate buggers? You should sort them out, *Peter*.'

The Burmese passed regally towards Ros – who had again become an unacknowledged shadow in the doorway, arms undoubtedly folded, chins defiant, nostrils wide. Shelley appeared to flinch back into his chair at what Hyde gratifyingly sensed was one of Ros' very best glares.

'Cass was sending back some puzzling material. He was playing things close to his chest,' Shelley announced cathartically, clearing his throat. The distance between him and Hyde was evident to both of them, as was the required favour that hung over them like a weapon. 'He thought –' He glanced towards the still-running videotape picture. Sharmar, the minister, was grief-laden upon some relative's whiteclad shoulder. His family crowded as if to hungrily eat grief or share its televisual benefits. '– thought Sharmar was engaged in something.'

'His excuse for bonking the wife?' Hyde mocked.

'Perhaps,' Shelley replied, disconcerted. 'We didn't think so. But we're not sure. People are inclined to disbelieve it now – in the circumstances.' He shrugged once more like a reluctant moneylender.

'What was it – this excuse for poking Mrs Sharmar?'

'Drugs. At least, that's the story. Sharmar owns great tracts of land in the Kashmir Valley. Cass seemed to think it was being used to grow the poppy. The harvest moves mainly in this direction.' He looked up from his hands. 'Before you say that isn't really the service's business, I'd just interpose that everything seems to be our business these days – for the want of our old objectives.' He smiled tiredly, appeared younger and as if he still stood at Aubrey's shoulder. It was a clever trick, if trick it was. 'Therefore, it's possible –'

'– Cass was set up.' Hyde looked down at the photographs on the sofa beside him, then up at the swimming, smeared images on the screen where the fire was dying down, as was the sun, and the crowd alone seemed vigorous — swelled with assumed grief and anger. 'Was he? Do you believe Cass? Or do you just want to make certain it *can't* be true? Sharmar's supposed to be our friend, isn't he? I imagine he would be, if he was making a fortune over here out of drugs.'

'I don't know — that's what I need to discover . . .' Shelley shrugged, as if a mild wave of nausea had shuddered through him. 'I don't want to sign my *first* termination order — a Black Page — unless it's necessary. I mean *really* necessary.'

In Cass' case, it meant slightly less than termination. Just being left to the mercy of local justice. No deals, no rescue.

Swallowing, Hyde said: 'I didn't know you *suddenly* became a psychopath. I thought you always were.'

'You mean the attack on the woman?'

'Did she say she had a headache?' He glanced towards the source of the indrawn breath at the doorway. 'Ros does it all the time. I haven't done her in yet.'

'Fat chance,' Ros offered, startling and embarrassing Shelley, but suggesting she was prepared to continue to monitor the situation.

'I'd like *your* assessment, Patrick.'

'Ask Aubrey to go — he's doing bugger all just now. I really want sod all to do with it. Why me?'

'Because you'll tell me the truth — at least as you see it.'

'So — JIC has Cass in the dustbin, and that makes *you* squeamish, so you come round here to do the same to me? You sure you don't want me to knock him off for you? Otherwise, you need an interrogator, not me.'

Ros' breathing was harsh. She did, after all, know almost all the routines and devices — so that she could, if it had ever happened to him, write to *The Times* or appear on *World in Action* and tell the truth in retrospect. She seemed annoyed with *him*; surprisingly.

'No, I don't,' Shelley asserted, as if he had only then reached

25

that decision. Then he blurted: 'Look, Cass sent word to me – bribed someone, I think, but it came via unsafe channels – *get me out – I didn't do it. They want my head.*'

'Doesn't trust Delhi Station? Paranoia – or good sense?' Hyde laughed. 'Got you jumping, though, Peter.'

Ros said, from the doorway: 'You're so bloody *childish*, Hyde!' She moved into the room with the span and deliberation of a treasure galleon, plumping herself next to Hyde as if to diminish him. 'What are you up to, Mr Shelley? You want *him* to talk to this bloke Cass. So – why? Is Cass going into the dustbin – a trial, long sentence, and then eventually he can serve it out over here, at Ford Open or somewhere nice? Is that it?'

'Gerald Ronson's old quarters,' Hyde smirked. 'Cass would like the two-inch pile on the carpet and the quality of the hi-fi. The Queen Mum might even come and visit him.'

Shelley shifted uncomfortably in his chair. Once more his hands came out of his sleeves in supplication. Hyde could not quite mock him. There was that trick of the genuine, that glimpse of the real, that Aubrey had retained and Shelley still possessed.

'I need to know!' he snapped. 'Sharmar, the widower, is the next leader of Congress – the country's next leader-but-one, maybe even the next leader. Cass is suggesting he's a drug-baron. Might I ask you to enquire as to the truth of the accusation, and perhaps help Cass at the same time –?' He glanced at Ros, then pressed on: 'Cass *insists* it's true – but he won't say *anything* to Delhi Station.' He clamped his fist on his thigh. 'I need to know! One interview – one bloody interview is all I'm asking – and we'll pay rank rates!'

'And a bonus, and expenses – you can pay our fares to Oz, while you're at it,' Hyde murmured. Ros, at his side, seemed to silently moralise.

'Patrick – find out what he has to say. It'll be a day, two days out of your trip – it's practically en route.' He rubbed a hand through his thinning hair. It was grey at the temples. Burden of office, Hyde thought mockingly. 'Unless I have something — anything — to show JIC, they may be prepared to go along with the current wisdom, which is that Cass be left to the mercy of Indian justice. Unless he becomes an *embarrassment* . . .'

'In which case, he might wake up one day to find he's hanged himself in his cell?'

Shelley nodded.

'The old order changeth — but do you think I want to change it *that* much? To see Cass off the end of an approved and authorised gangplank. If Sharmar wants it, if he insists — then HMG might just agree it be done. So — *now* will you bloody well go and see him and ask him what the hell is on his mind?'

Hyde clenched his hands on his thighs. The tortoiseshell — wisely, he thought — had withdrawn from the window overlooking the garden with a flick of ears and tail. The problem, the *real* problem — apart from his awakened curiosity, his reformed alcoholic's thirst — was that Shelley wasn't acting. He was genuinely bemused and reluctant. Sharmar was a powerful friend, a rising star. His actress wife was dead. He might want Cass to *pay* . . . if he wasn't a drug-producer, in which case the setup would have to end in Cass' neat death. A remorseful suicide, shot while attempting to escape — so sorry, sahib, these things happen.

Then Ros dug her elbow into his side, prompting compliance.

'So, JIC are prepared to let him go, turn the poor sod's diplomatic iron lung off?' Shelley nodded his head. 'And I just have to talk to him — report back?' Another nod. Ros nudged him impatiently, harder, as if it was nothing more than a child's game, a child's version of honour. *Dib dib dib* . . .

'Oh, ballocks,' he sighed. 'The things I do for England!'

She was still shaking as she stepped onto the deck of the houseboat, her hand quivering even as she waved aside the servant and passed into the sitting room. Her stomach revolted once more at the recalled images. A small child's legless body, an old man thrust through a window, glass-stippled and bloody, hanging across the sill – other things. A dead dog, noticeable because it had been flung onto a shop's torn awning. She glanced through the window as she noisily poured herself a large whisky and wiped at the sweat and monsoon dampness of her forehead and hair. There was a glow beyond the Hari Parbat fort, towards the centre of Srinagar, where fires started by the explosion and the subsequent rioting were still burning. She could faintly catch the noise of sirens – ambulances, fire-trucks, the police and the army.

She swallowed at the drink, coughed and all but retched, then stared down at her leg. The streak of blood caused by flying glass was muddied from the streets. She had run in the panic everyone had shared, fled the place in the torrents of rain from one of the last outbursts of the monsoon season. She continued to stare at her leg, her quivering tumbler at the corner of eyesight seen foggily as if through a cataract. The early evening sun splashed across the threshold of the houseboat's verandah and a kingfisher flashed through it.

A Moslem shop had been blown up, in a crowded market street, without advance warning. Hindu terrorists – that's what they would say, twisting the thong of tension tighter around Srinagar. The sirens wailed in the distance. Her cook's slight form appeared in the rear doorway for an instant, then flicked away. She lifted her head and stared at the intricate carving of the ceiling, then the panelling of the walls, the complex rugs, the old-fashioned English furniture. The room did not close around her, there was too much light coming into it through the net curtains, so that it appeared fragilely unable to protect her. She finished her drink and poured another before crossing to the telephone, on a table beneath the chandelier. A film set from the 1930s, the room repelled her now. As she picked up the receiver, she heard the cookboy padding barefoot along the catwalk that girdled the boat. From the neighbouring houseboat – one of her hotel boats – she heard the excited cawing of returning, unnerved tourists. Two more days of bombs and the bloody Foreign Office would be advising all the Brits to leave Kashmir! Business was bad as it was . . . Concentrating on stilling her index finger, she dialled a long-distance number and waited as the phone rang out, gripping her drying blouse across her breasts with her free hand, her hair, smelling of rain and fear, plastered to her cheeks.

He answered, and she blurted out: 'You bastard! You bloody nearly *killed* me!'

'What is the matter?' he replied, unbalanced. 'Are you hurt?'

'Scratch on my leg, I was luckier than a lot –! There are a dozen, two dozen *dead* –!'

'What would you expect?' he enquired levelly. 'Pull yourself together, Sara. It is all *necessary*, as you know, and as you believe yourself.'

'There were so *many* of them –' she began, swallowing bile and something else that clotted in her throat.

'Then there need be fewer in the future – fewer explosions. Now, pull yourself together. You did know this would happen. If you don't wish to see the evidence, stay indoors. Where you will be safer.' There was a distant, aloof concern, almost that of a doctor prescribing lack of stress and a stricter regimen to someone with a heart condition. *Heart condition?* Too late for *heart* now, she thought bitterly. She was angry with herself, heatedly so, because she appeared weak and stupid – *womanish*, having the bloody vapours!

'I – I might have been killed,' she repeated, cowed.

'I'll be there at the weekend, Sara. Meanwhile, be careful. I'm glad that you were not badly hurt. I must hurry now –' The phone rather than he seemed to pause, then the connection was broken. She put down the receiver with an angry thrust of the bakelite; unclenched her drying, creased blouse, saw another kingfisher flash across the sunlit doorway, and walked out onto the verandah, keeping in the shadow of the carved awning. Across the still water the vegetable and grocery boats plied with small, insignificant dips of oars, and tourists were poled under awnings across Nagin Lake and Dal Lake in gaudy shikaras. The glow from the city was fading like the sunlight. She looked at the hills cupping the lakes and the town and breathed deeply, slowly.

She should go across to the hotel boats and calm the bloody tourists, she supposed – before they tried to cross to her mooring and complain or ensconce themselves. In a minute, then – in a minute or two. There was a slight, fresh breeze off the lake, the putter of small outboard motors, louder now than the faded sirens, the cries of vendors and the responses of cooks and other servants; the cheekiness of cookboys. She avoided detailing any more of the human noises, since they failed to calm, drew her instead back into the crowded market and the first screams.

Instead she watched the boats as *boats*, as shadowy, silhouette cutouts, pieces of a mosaic or painting. Clouds persisted around the mountains, but wispily. The smell of drying grass. Lotuses clumped near her boat – there was a large, opened lotus-flower in a tall vase on the verandah table, alongside the two-days-old copy of *The Times*. She glanced at the foreign news, where she had opened the paper before her shopping –

Forget that. The headline, however, read – *Kashmir approaches boiling point* – and she could not, therefore, forget. A second, smaller headline – *New election probable*. Not in Kashmir or the Punjab, she acknowledged. But there will be an election soon. A quarter-column near the bottom of the page – *Bus massacre in Punjab*.

Savagely, she brushed at the newspaper, so that it fluttered over the rail of the verandah and down to the darkening water. It floated as if in threat towards the nearest clump of lotuses, which suddenly seemed to be the foam of pollution rather than a garland of flowers. She rubbed her forehead. It had become too real – much too real.

'You see the problem, don't you, Phil? I mean, it's all political from now on – not just murder.'

Cass looked up slowly, focusing on Miles' face, which flabbily betrayed a piquant sense of amusement, even a satiated revenge. As if Miles was responsible for his incarceration, the setup, the charge of murder and the demonstrating mob that surged and moaned every day outside the prison. Cass rubbed his unshaven cheek, which seemed deadened, like grafted skin from a less sensitive part of his body.

'Political, is it? Even if I didn't do it?' he sneered. 'I'm to be left in the shit, is that really it? Shelley and London are leaving me where I've been dropped – they don't like the smell!'

He tapped the cigarette Dickson had given him against the cheap tin ashtray that advertised Hindu beer. The prison warder stood at attention in baggy shorts and a peaked cap beside the interview room's door.

Dickson, less of a gourmand of Cass' situation, cleared his throat and murmured:

'It does seem to be the way things are moving, Cass. I'm sorry about it, Lord knows . . . I'm not getting much feedback or cooperation from London. Sharmar's playing the grieving husband for all the part's worth, and the FO really would like to make it up to him –'

'What with? A resurrection?'

'Your bitterness isn't helping.'

'Miles is enjoying it. It's helping *him*.'

'You're bound to be angry – but there's no *evidence* you were set up. Yours are the prints on the knife, there's no drugged drink and no trace of one, and there's the passing witness who heard your voice as well as hers . . . *before* the screams started.'

Cass glared.

'Then bloody get me out as a fucking murderer with diplomatic immunity – let's sort it out in London, for Christ's sake!'

Dickson shook his head gravely. It was the action of a dignified marionette, a hollow body suspended from strings. Dickson, as Head of Station, looked good at garden parties.

Miles scoffed: 'The best offer you're going to get, mate, is to eat your porridge here for a respectable time, then hope to get shipped back to Millionaire's Row in Ford Open prison after all the fuss has died down and Sharmar's forgotten about you.'

Dickson demurred by clearing his throat once more, then he said, leaning forward on his creaking chair: 'Cass, there was cocaine in your pockets. There were traces of it –'

'– up your nose, Phil.'

Cass clenched his hands into fists on the wooden table and snapped: 'You think coke makes you into a homicidal maniac? Someone *else* did it, I tell you!'

'Who? *Why?*'

'To stitch me *up*, bugger you!'

The room was hotter. From a high window, the pearly light fell wearily into the room, laden with dust. Cass rubbed his face once more, then gripped the edge of the table with whitening fingertips.

'Why would they do that, Phil? For poking his missis?'

'If there is anything, Cass – *anything*,' Dickson soothed, 'then tell us. Anything that justifies us making a special plea to Century House, reinvoking your diplomatic status. We'll get straight onto it –'

'What are you holding back, Phil?' Miles mocked him. 'That Sharmar bumped off his old woman, found you in bed together? London won't wear that. It looks much more likely that –'

'I don't care what it *looks* like, Miles, you dim little prick! I'm telling you I didn't do it. Get me *out* of here . . .' Dickson was embarrassed by the plea in his roughened, dry voice. Miles continued to smirk with evident, enduring satisfaction. Cass felt all optimism slump like a drunk against his ribs. Why the hell wouldn't Shelley listen? Send someone, or come himself? Fear sidled to his shoulder and he glanced nervously towards the warder. Staying in India – Christ, not like *this*!

He looked at his hands as if he could still see Sereena's blood.

What use was Shelley, anyway? SIS was being run by people Aubrey wouldn't have employed to make the fucking tea! Oh, shit, what a bloody mess . . . He looked up, avoiding the bland certitude of Miles' features. The interview room was hot. Flies had got in – as if looking for a promised carcase – and made the room small, noisy. They were hovering near the bucket that served as a toilet. He was alone in the cell, twenty-four hours a day. For his own safety. Almost anyone in the prison would knife the murderer of Sereena Sharmar, given an opportunity. He pressed his fingertips whiter around the edge of the table, confining the tremor of fear to his arms and legs.

Shelley was going to leave him in the shit. That much was obvious, the bastard. He couldn't tell Miles or Dickson what he knew, what more he suspected. They'd blab it around and then someone *would* come looking for him with a knife or an invitation to stage his own suicide. He shuddered, as if hands were on his sides and thighs lifting him into a noose. Jesus Christ . . .

Dickson stood up and said awkwardly: 'Is there anything we can send in for you?'

'Besides a hacksaw blade, of course,' Miles added.

· Cass ignored him, watching the livid, hypnotised disbelief and repulsion spread on Dickson's dignified, stereotypically-diplomatic features. Distaste mingled with the disbelief, and an incapacity to cope. Dickson had realised that he might, simply by assuming a soothing manner, have offered his hand towards something alien and malevolent. Then Dickson re-captured common sense, and seemed to disapprove Miles' remark much as he would have done a wind emission at the dinner table.

'Chin up, Cass,' Miles added. 'You'll get home – eventually.'

The guard let them out of the cramped room, and Cass turned greedily to the last of the cigarette. The smoke threatened to choke him, gagging his throat. His exhalations sounded fearful, ragged – God, they *were* . . . He began to shiver. Dickson's momentary admission of the nature of his supposed crime placed him in SIS' outer darkness. He *was* out there, beyond *any* pale. It had been so *clever*, the setup – so horrible and so clever. Who'd rescue a sex-killer, who'd speak up for him, who *wouldn't* let him go hang?

Therefore, the consequences were now political, diplomatic; a question of appeasement – *this* lamb to the slaughter.

He swept his hand across the table, as if to brush spiders or beetles from it. The tin ashtray rattled, with a pitiful little protest, into the corner of the room. He looked up, with a frightened glare, at the high window and its pearly light. It seemed that all India was rushing away from it, retreating.

He could see from where he was seated at his desk, if he looked out through the tall windows, all of Connaught Place and the hub and spokes of government. It was a dazzling pattern of grand buildings, dominated by the Parliamentary Rotunda, but it was called New Delhi – it perpetuated the Raj. *Oh, thank you, sahib, you will send Sir Edwin Lutyens here to redesign our city – thank you, sahib.* The Hindu had always been capable of thanking their oppressors, living as they did inside, and clinging to, some net-curtain Nirvana to compensate them for the unpleasantness of the present. When he looked down, there was little or no retinal afterimage of the city that remained stubbornly, ineffaceably British – the parliament, the war memorial, Parliament Street, Queen Victoria Road, the rectangular, tamed stretches of water and the neat, alien gardens.

On his desk were the first sketchy reports of the midair explosion of the Indian Airlines jet and the assumed deaths of more than eighty people. On the other side of his desk, his brother sat smoking a cigarette, patient and assured. Above them both, the traditional, British fans moved their huge arms stiffly against the soupy air.

As he looked through the windows once more, the sun, moving lower, illuminated the temples of Lakshmi, Kali and the Buddha, surrounding them with hazy gold. Then the Rotunda and the India Gate emplaced him firmly within the inheritance of the Raj. He gestured angrily at the report of the airliner crash, and said:

'*This* I could have done without.'

His brother, taller and slimmer in his chair than himself, smiled back. 'You must attend – you must be at the crash site. The publicity value is too great to ignore.'

'But there is a Party caucus tonight which I should attend, Prakesh! Some of those old fools are not to be trusted with decisions of any importance whatsoever!'

'Then you will have to trust me, V.K., to look after your interests –'

'If only that damned old Chopri would sign his letter of resignation –!'

'Our respected Prime Minister is hanging on to more than life, V.K. – but, brother, how could he sign? He's in a coma.'

'Then the President should call an election at once. Why wait for Chopri to die – or wake up just long enough to write his name?'

'Calm down, V.K. A few days, that's all – just a few days. Everything is proceeding very nicely. *You* get off to Punjab and look solemnly at the cameras. Leave the caucus to me.'

V. K. Sharmar looked down at his desk, his glance catching the personal letter of condolence from Peter Shelley that had been delivered by someone from the British High Commission an hour earlier. He clenched his hand and burst out:

'When I think of what that loose-mouthed woman may have told him –!'

Prakesh Sharmar clicked his tongue against his teeth in mild exasperation, then murmured soothingly:

'Whatever she told him, V.K., he has said nothing. Stop worrying. Cass is believed only as a sex-murderer –' Sharmar winced against his brother's casualness. 'You have that letter from Peter Shelley to prove the point. Do you think he would have written such a guileless letter if any word of what Cass thought he had begun to learn had reached London and been believed?' He gestured with a dismissive sweep, wiping a smear of cigarette smoke across his features before stubbing out the butt in an ornate wooden ashtray.

'But that *whore* could have told him so much!'

'Perhaps she did not – or Cass forgot to ask. Or didn't even believe what he was told . . . ?'

'Then we needn't have –?'

'Oh, yes, V.K. Sereena was too dangerous alive – in love with Cass. She was unreliable. On the way to recklessness.' Prakesh sighed and raised his eyes to the high ceiling, then glanced towards the windows where, Sharmar sensed acutely, all India seemed to press for admittance – or waited as a prize. The sunlight slanted across the room, and the temples and domes were oranged by the dying light. Prakesh insisted: 'We can be sure – after a week – that Cass knew nothing of any significance. He may have begun the affair to investigate you . . . he continued it for the pleasure it gave. His own people at the High Commission believe he is guilty. You heard the tape from their meeting with him in prison, V.K., what could be more reassuring than that? Shelley will be told Cass is a murderer.'

Sharmar nodded. 'Yes, yes –' He indicated the letter of condolence. 'Peter's embarrassment is evident here – oh, very well, Prakesh, very well!' Most of the buttons on the telephone console to his right were now lit from the pressure of calls which he had not answered. Perhaps Chopri had even died in his coma? Unlikely. They would have interrupted him and Prakesh had that been the case.

But there were urgent matters to be settled in Delhi. He did not need the inconvenience of inspecting the remains of an airliner and scattered bodies and luggage and metal in Punjab. Damned Sikh terrorists, they had no sense of timing!

'You're worrying again, V.K.,' Prakesh mocked, lighting another cigarette. 'That frown of yours. I can handle the caucus.'

'I am thinking, Prakesh – thinking. Not just about Congress, not just about the election. I am thinking that I would rather this man Cass never came to trial, here or in England, now or in the future. Do you understand?'

Prakesh Sharmar inspected his fingernails. Eventually, he said: 'An accident could be arranged easily enough – but not *yet*. Not for the moment. The timing isn't right just now. Cass is being watched. It's unlikely he will have any more visitors, other than his colleagues. So, when attention is lulled, perhaps then he can meet with an accident. One of Sereena's devoted fans, maddened by grief and a desire for revenge.'

'Good.'

'Now, go and make your press statement about this airliner. Put on your most lugubrious face, my dear brother, and forget about drugs and land deals in Kashmir – all those niggling little details Cass evidently knows nothing about after all!'

'Are you trying to irritate me, Prakesh? You think I would prefer it if she was still alive?'

'No. I know that's not true, V.K. You wished her dead from the moment of her first infidelity.' He spread his hands on the edge of the desk, as if it were a keyboard.

Sharmar stood up and walked to the window. The traffic was clogged along Parliament Street and into Connaught Place. His gaze followed the dusty lawns of Raj Path towards the arch of India Gate, then moved north once more to the hazed highrise blocks around Connaught Place. Domes and towers receded into the dusty evening haze beyond the modern blocks. The city teemed homewards.

It was true, of course. Prakesh could handle the Party caucus meeting – perhaps even more skilfully than himself, he admitted without bitterness. He would argue, subtly, quietly and without apparent drama or self-advertisement, the case for an election. Chopri's tired old heart would give out at any time, and an election would be expected, even if it was not mandatory. They must have the election, however – since now was the time when another and even weaker minority government would be

37

elected. And *before* the Janata fundamentalists become stronger than ever, strong enough to take power away from Congress. He rubbed his forehead soothingly with this thumb and forefinger. They had to have a minority government and a weak one with reliable partners. Only *then* did the strategy have a certain chance ... the time was right, *so* right —!

That much they had always agreed, and for that they had worked, getting a sick man like old Chopri in as PM, knowing the pressures would bring about the final collapse of his health and leave his office door open for ...

He clenched his hand against his temple, as if holding a gun to it – then rubbed his knuckles against the vein that throbbed there. Damned old Chopri, just like him to refuse to die right away!

As if reading his thoughts, Prakesh murmured: 'It will work, V.K. – it will. There is time for it to work.'

'Yes, yes!' Sharmar snapped.

Then the intercom buzzed and he whirled round, hurrying to answer it. Pray God the old fool is dead, he thought. Dead *now*.

'Oh, sorry to have got you out of the *shower*, darling!' Hyde grumbled into the telephone receiver as he lay back on the creased sheets and stared at the cracked ceiling. A large spider was patrolling the plaster, presumably in search of something to eat. Flies droned and circled in the room's hot, thick airlessness. The thin curtains at the window hung unmoving. 'Nice suite, is it?' He grinned in contrast to the sourness of his tone. Ros was installed in one of the largest suites in Claridges on Aurangzeb Road, south of the Raj Path. He'd wangled that out of Shelley to compensate for the seedy place he needed as a cover.

'Lovely. What's yours like?'

'A dump – listen to the noise.' He held the receiver towards the window. The decayed, dusty hotel was in the Paharganj

district, near the main railway station. 'Hear it?' he asked, forcing the hot bakelite against his ear. He was sweating, as if the
noise from outside was kinetic energy. It pressed against him, a
bellow of traffic and voices and animals. Unburned petrol was
thick and nauseously sweet on the air, visible as the dust.

'Christ,' he heard Ros murmur.

'Feel sorry for me, do you? Your bloody fault we're here —
I'm where *I* am, anyway.'

'Hyde, you could always have said no.'

'With the long moral face you were pulling from the doorway?
You must be joking.'

'When are you going to see him?'

'Tomorrow morning — if I can't get a pass, I'll have to buy
one. His cousin Pat has come a bloody long way, after all. He
should have got the letter from home by now, setting the cover
up . . . Listen, it's too bloody hot to talk. Just so long as you're
comfortable, darling, I can stop worrying about you. Have a nice
dinner — got the tablets? Don't drink the water, there's a sensible
girl.'

'I have been here before, Patrick. Before I met you. If I get
stomach trouble this time, it'll be you causing it, not India.'
There was a pause, and Hyde tensed against the anticipated
remark. As if aware of his dislike, Ros merely mumbled: 'Be
careful,' then, almost at once, 'See you, Hyde,' in her brusquest
tone and put down the phone.

Hyde studied the receiver for a moment, then rolled across the
creaking bed's sagging middle and replaced it. Then he swung his
legs off the bed and crossed the narrow room to the window.
Eighty rupees a day, fleas inclusive. Christ, what a dump — just
the place for someone like Cass' schoolteacher cousin, his closest
relative, to stay as cheaply as possible in Delhi. Just in case
anyone enquired after Cass' unexpected visitor . . . He rubbed
his hands through his hair, yawned, scratched his stubbled
cheeks, then thrust his hands into the pockets of his denims.
The flight, shoehorned into Economy while Ros lived it up in

Business Class, had been cool and noiseless by comparison with this.

Beneath the window, the narrow street between Main Bazaar and Panchkuin Marg moved with the slow struggle of a snake sloughing an old skin. People wriggled in opposing skeins and queues through each other and the dense scrapyard of vehicles and rickshaws – autos and the peddled variety – and old, fume-coughing buses. Spices and hot food scents penetrated the haze of petrol. Saris, grubby white shirts, the bright plumage of tourists, dhotis, turbans, the pyjamalike lenga trousers of bemused country people stunned by proximity, traffic and the sun. Inky, purple shadows. Out of one of them, a Moslem woman in an enveloping burka moved, her dark costume confronted by heaped dishes of spices in front of a shop – red, green, purple, orange mounds.

Hyde watched the street, fascinated and deafened, hands still in his pockets. He was detached, a spectator. An ex-field agent approaching forty, half a stone out of condition, reactions too slow for an endgame situation – for any operation, really. Pensioned off by his own choice, fit – just about – to be some Arab prince's bodyguard for the rest of his useful life. And someone to whom the most pressing question was whether Ros had some unconveyed idea of staying in Oz, once they got there. He suspected it – and was almost certain he didn't want it.

Eventually, wearying of the struggle of the street, its stink of ordure, sweat, petrol, dust and spicy food, he returned to the bed and sat beside the rucksack he had collected from the luggage locker at New Delhi station. He re-checked its contents merely to occupy himself before he waded into the breakers of the street in search of food. Apart from the pills and the alternative cover-papers and the maps and addresses, there was the gun. Heckler & Koch, as he preferred. Krauts make good, accurate weapons. Spare ammo, the knife, and the tablet – though not for him. Shelley was calling the tune, and Hyde understood the unspoken. If Cass proved likely to embarrass the service or if the Indians, intelligence or just police, decided it might be useful to take an abandoned agent apart to find out what he knew ... then kill him.

That was the bit Ros neither knew nor suspected.

home thoughts from abroad

Hyde shrugged himself back into the T-shirt blazoned with Mozart's profile that they had made him remove, then tugged on his denims. The body search had been polite, even delicate, but thorough. He zipped up the small rucksack – paperbacks, shaving gel, cigarettes for Cass – and then followed the prison officer along hot, wearying corridors, past blank doors whose peepholes stared at him with Cyclops' eyes. There was singing from behind one door, moaning from another cell, but after the streets the prison across the Yamuna River was orderly, quiet. The door of a small, cramped interview room stood open. Hyde saw Cass' grubby hands clenched together as if confronting a mean fire on the plain table, then the door was closed behind him. The officer stood beside it, at once impassive.

Cass' reactions were confused, muddy – relief, a sense of contrast between Hyde and himself, as if Hyde still bore the scents of the streets and the air on his clothes . . . and the almost immediate nervousness because it was he, *Hyde*, who was good at one thing above all – seeing people off the end of the plank. Cass was, irrefutably, aware of that possible solution to his situation. Immediately, Hyde said, holding out his hand:

'Phil! Christ, mate, I got out here as soon as I heard! You got my letter?' Awkwardly, as if slowly remembering behaviour, Cass nodded and mumbled a reply. 'A guy from the Foreign Office rang me at school. The secretary took the message 'cause I was teaching – 3W, what a bunch of spastics!' He sat down, adjusting the clear-glass spectacles with his forefinger, having released Cass' clammy, shivery grip. 'I had to check back with them – couldn't believe it, Phil! Bloody hell, matc, there must be a mistake –? How are they treating you, though?' His accent was somewhat Midlands, his tone breathless. He was amused by Cass' continuing suspicion as he assessed him, and recognised the erosions of shock and incarceration. Cass' face was stubbled, his eyes red-rimmed, his attention vague and selfish. A *civilian* going to pieces under pressure. 'This was such a cushy little billet,' he pursued sharply.

Cass' gaze flickered brightly with dislike for an instant, then clouded again, narrowing only on his fear of Hyde. His eyes inspected the table, as if fleas hopped and skittered on it. Open-eyed dreaming – Cass was in poor shape. Too poor to play the memory game the letter had set up?

At least hc didn't look ill-treated, just worn down from the inside. Hyde rubbed his hand through his hair and fiddled with the spectacles, then unzipped the rucksack at his feet. He pulled the paperbacks out and put them on the table, neatening them in a little heap with fussy movements. He pointed at the top of the pile.

'That's good, that one – sorry it's a bit tatty, I read it on the plane. I wasn't sure you liked Conrad –?'

'Yes,' Cass replied tiredly. Had he consented to the game or not? *Nostromo* – our man. It was supposed to reassure.

Hyde's finger tapped the spines of the books, one by one. Cass would be looking for *The Great Escape*, or another Conrad, *The Rescue*. Neither was there. *Our Mutual Friend* was, though, meaning Century House. He hadn't been abandoned – at least, not entirely. *All's Well That Ends Well* would have made him happier, but that was missing, too. Cass studied the titles of the books glumly, his head slightly on one side, his eyes staring. Jane Austen's *Persuasion* was at the bottom of the pile. *Tell me about it, it's in the balance but we want to believe you* . . . *Pilgrim's Progress* –?

Hyde reached down into the open-mouthed rucksack and fished out Bunyan's allegory.

43

'Forget this one,' he muttered, smiling. 'Remembered it was a favourite –'

After what seemed an interminable silence, Cass said quietly: 'Good of you to come, Patrick.' He was injected with the stimulant of the possibility of rescue signalled by the Bunyan. He might get out of this place, eventually. 'Bit of a mess, all this.' He spread his arms apologetically.

'You're not joking, mate! Uncle Peter's really down about it. I had to tell him, but no one else in the family. He sends his best –'

Cass blinked, and his gaze was clearer, more focused.

'I brought some pills, too –' Hyde began, and Cass sat bolt upright, stung and frightened. 'Left them at the hotel, though . . .' *Tell me as carefully as you can, tell me the truth, and there won't be any need for a cyanide pill . . .*

. . . if I believe you.

Cass swallowed audibly, a creaking, dry sound like that of old wood cracking.

'I don't – don't need pills. They're all right to me in here.' He looked at the patient, still warder.

'They mentioned drugs – you'd been taking drugs,' Hyde said, leaning forward across the table, his eyes round and surprised. 'You never touched drugs before –'

'You can – they're easy to get hold of here, Pat. Too easy. Grow the poppy everywhere . . .' He glanced at the guard and then seemed to surrender to lethargy and laid his forehead on his hands as they gripped one another on the table. He shook his head. 'I didn't know what I was doing,' he murmured, so softly that Hyde leaned closer to him, after shrugging at the warder, who seemed politely indifferent, staring at the opposite wall. If the room was bugged – it probably was, even though there was no sign of a video camera – Cass' voice would be barely decipherable. Good.

'Try to make the best of it, Phil,' he offered with studied naivety. 'It can't be as bad –'

Cass' words dribbled on.

'. . . Kashmir, mostly – top people own land up there, own the peasants to grow the crop . . . didn't think it would end like this, not her and me, that is. Not like *that* –' His voice had altered, and he looked up, his eyes wet, surprising Hyde. Cass rubbed at his eyes angrily, then at his loose, wet mouth. 'Christ, there was blood everywhere, but *I* didn't do it!' he snarled breathily. 'I'd never have . . .' He shrugged exaggeratedly. '*Would* I?'

Hyde sat stiffly, silently. It wasn't acted. Unless Cass was in the Gielgud class, his distress was real – grief hard as stone looked through the shivering cheeks and the welling eyes. Christ, the bugger had been in love with her!

'They – I mean, they're saying you went . . . you know, berserk. A quarrel –'

'*No.*'

Then he was silent. Hyde nodded slowly and Cass, sniffing noisily, understood and lowered his head onto his knuckles once more, sighing loudly. Hyde patted his forearm, bending forward. As if accidentally, he touched *Nostromo* with his fingers. Cass saw the gesture and swallowed wetly. *Our man.*

Cass murmured: 'Drugged – drink . . . woke up, she was dead.' His voice was barely audible. Hyde glanced at the door. If they were suspicious or interested, they'd be in before long to break it up – even tell them not to whisper. 'Husband owns . . . his family –' Cass sat upright suddenly, wiping at his face. 'Enough about me,' he announced. 'Feeling sorry for myself. Christ, thanks for coming, Pat – it's good to see you, even under the circumstances. Pity you had to tell Uncle Peter. Has he still got that allotment of his?'

After a moment, Hyde said: 'Oh, that – yes. You know what he's like. Up on it all the time. What he grows I don't know –'

'I do.' Cass lit a cigarette, the last in the packet, and crushed it in his fist, leaving the small crumpled ball on the table. Hyde said:

'I've got some more for you – bought them on the plane. Rothman's – like them, I remember.' The crumpled packet was Silk Cut. Hyde seemed disappointed.

Cass laughed. 'Thanks, Pat.' He smiled at the warder as he opened the pack of two hundred, then offered him one. 'Jawal here got the Silk Cut for me. Here, Jawal, one for you –'

'Thank you, Mr Cass.'

The warder moved back to his position beside the door, still smiling. Hyde took his hand from his pocket, leaving the crumpled Silk Cut packet inside. He then cleared the cellophane Cass had removed from the duty-free pack and thrust it into the rucksack.

Hyde relaxed on his chair as Cass smoked greedily, with a somehow greater, healthier appetite for whatever future he now envisaged.

'Is there anything else I can bring in – if they let me come back?'

'Some stuff at my flat – if they'll let you in.'

'Is there anyone I can see – at the High Commission?' Cass shook his head. 'Anyone else? Have you got a solicitor?' Cass nodded. 'He all right?' Again, he nodded.

Jawal coughed politely.

'Time's up, Pat,' Cass explained. He swallowed, and the skin over his jaw and cheeks tightened. 'Thanks again, mate. You're a good'un, coming all this way.' He stood up and thrust out his hand. There was a slight tremor. His shirt-cuff was grubby. 'Hotel all right?' he asked with forced casualness.

'A dump,' Hyde replied, grinning innocently. 'Still, I don't mind – in the circumstances. Look, I'll call Uncle Peter and tell him you're bearing up – and all the news. Blow the expense of the phone call, eh? And I'll see if I can get permission to bring a few things from your flat – what, clothes and that, eh?'

'Change of underwear – pity you can't bring the telly and the VCR.' Cass clicked his fingers theatrically. 'If you can get in there, see if I turned off the stopcock, will you?'

'Pipes won't freeze here, will they? OK, I'll look. I know people worry in – well, your sort of . . . yes. I'll come back tomorrow – OK?'

'Yes. Thanks again, Patrick – *thanks*.'

His eyes were sparkling wetly once more, and there was a catch in his voice. Hyde turned away and followed Jawal down the corridor as another warder appeared to collect Cass and take him back to his cell.

He hadn't killed her. Instead, it was drugs and Sharmar was involved at least as a producer and that was how it had begun. Then Cass had got careless because he fell in love and they'd had the opportunity to stitch him up. Sharmar – the Minister for Tourism and Civil Aviation, the next leader of Congress, and just maybe the next Prime Minister of India . . . ?

Interesting that –

– and worth killing one film star for, even if she was your wife, if it shut her up and banged up her boyfriend from British Intelligence.

Hyde was almost blithe as he stepped out into the blind sunlight of midmorning and looked across the brown river towards the hazy city that, even at that distance, hummed like a nest of insects.

Sharmar could have been – probably had been – a very naughty boy. Grinning to himself, he thrust his hands into his pockets, slouching beneath the smear of the rucksack across his back, beginning to sweat as he walked towards the nearest bus stop. He felt his knuckles touch the crumpled cigarette packet.

Read whatever Cass had written inside it on the bus, he told himself. Don't be impatient . . . then go to his flat, check for surveillance, and try to get inside. In the VCR, or on tape, hidden in the back of the telly, or under the sink. Something on Sharmar . . .

The wreckage was spread over hundreds of acres of farmland. Only the larger pieces of the fuselage of the medium-haul Boeing jutted above green wheat already springing up. The tailplane, like a great abandoned ploughshare, still evidenced the logo of Indian Airlines. Its scorched, sloping letters – IA – glowered like a message of great distress, a phonetic cry. Sharmar shivered at the idea. Glass crunched under his feet – or something did – as he waded through the new wheat, shaking his head lugubriously for the cameras, saluting Hindu and Sikh appropriately with the small hand-signals of sorrow and sympathy.

The flight deck lay on its side – like the broken egg in that Bosch painting, he thought; his imagination affected as if by some nervous tic rather than horror at the scene. It was hundreds of yards away, cordoned off, surrounded by the ants of the accident investigators and the police. Sikh turbans seemed inappropriately gay above the green wheat, alongside the wreckage.

'Yes, yes – terrible,' he must have murmured again and again. 'Such a tragedy.'

The domestic news services were already filled with speculation. Sikh separatists, was the consensus – and, no doubt, the truth. The plane had been en route from Amritsar to Delhi, and most of the passengers, it had been established, had been Hindu. Only months before, it had been buses, and a small suburban train. Only dozens dead. Now, it was eighty people, an entire passenger list – the innocent. The anger raged in his stomach. There was no space for guilt or reflection, only for the sense of outrage at the killing of –

People like that. The unwound length of a sari weighing down the new wheat, blue threaded with gold, and at the end of it a body. A young woman, broken like a rabbit dropped from on high by a hawk. He shivered, despite the heat. Always, he remembered that from his childhood, finding the rabbit, so loose as to be boneless yet its fur hardly ruffled. Staring up near the sun, he had seen the speck of the hawk that had been clumsy enough to lose its victim.

He paused a little past the body, where the field remained

untrampled and ungouged, and looked around him. Punjab. The granary of India that wished, with most of its unsettled hearts, to become Khalistan, an independent Sikh state. There were military vehicles on the nearest road, parked in a line, and soldiers near and about him. Martial law, even when it was only the dead they had come to see. TV cameras bobbed on shoulders like black water-pitchers through the fields and around the wreckage of the tailplane and the flight deck. V. K. Sharmar wiped his forehead, then his palms, on the grubby ball of his handkerchief. A helicopter, noisy as a wasp, droned high above the disaster site.

Then a pink-faced Englishman with wispy blond hair was beside him and he was staring into a shoulder-held camera. A microphone appeared. He did not catch the reporter's name, merely the initials that followed it.

'— BBC,' then, 'television news, Minister Sharmar.'

'Yes, yes.' He appeared, he realised, suitably abstracted. He *was*; it was no pretence.

'Minister, can you confirm . . . ?'

Sikh terrorists — oh, yes, quite certainly.

'Our investigations are proceeding,' he murmured. 'There are eye-witness reports of an explosion —' The reporter already appeared bored, he knew this much. '— and preliminary evidence that the explosion occurred in the main cabin. An item of hand luggage has been removed for forensic examination. All further speculation is merely that, at the moment.'

'No one has claimed responsibility, Minister? None of the separatist groups?'

He shook his head gravely. The object after all was terror, not publicity — to make the Punjab *untenable*, even under martial law.

'No. No one has claimed responsibility. We should not jump to conclusions —'

'Even in the light of recent atrocities, Minister?'

'I'm afraid that *I*, at least, as a minister of the government, cannot afford to speculate.'

He turned slightly aside, reassuming his sorrowful countenance. The reporter seemed compliantly bored, then the camera was at once beside him again as he walked forward with the senior army officer and the managing director of Indian Airlines. The microphone and the blond reporter, sun-pinked, thrust themselves in front of him.

'Could we do a short piece for tomorrow's main news on Prime Minister Chopri's health and your own future, Minister?'

Temptation for an instant that did not even reach his eyes. Instead, he scowled in affront.

'At the scene of this tragedy, I think that subject would be inappropriate. Now, if you will excuse me –'

He moved on towards the wreckage of the flight deck. This close, he could see the gouged earth and chlorophyll that stained its livery. Behind him, the reporter was performing his piece to camera which would introduce the careful, anodyne sympathy Sharmar had presented for a British audience. Strange that they referred to themselves as English while, more correctly, India had always known them as the *British*. The British . . . even *this*, this *here*, was part of their damned legacy to India. British India – Himalaya to Tamil Nadu, the mouths of the Indus to the mouths of the Ganges – had still only *begun* to fragment. This, in front of him now, this broken egg that had cracked off the main fuselage, spilling the yolk and albumen of passengers into the air – *this* kind of thing would happen again and again, perhaps forever . . . He clenched his hands in the pockets of his suit in rage. For the foreseeable future, into a new *millennium*, what had been *British India* would continue to tear itself to pieces!

'Yes, yes,' he murmured to the forensic investigators presented to him, the severed flight deck looming over them all. 'Yes, I understand – yes, of course . . .'

Sunlight glowed on the wreckage, glistening like dew on fragments of glass, plastic, metal, gilding the flank of the flight deck. The fields were dark green in the afternoon light. The attempt to make the scene innocent was at once illusory and touching. India, attempting to heal itself –

Ridiculous – poetry, he exclaimed against his thoughts. It can only be done by *effort*.

'Yes, yes,' he continued to murmur as he shook hands or listened with apparent absorption.

The cameras whirred nearer and the reporters gabbled into their microphones, louder than the flies that filled the wreckage and settled on dried patches of what had been human blood.

Cass' flat was in a low, modern block on the fringe of the Chanakyapuri Diplomatic Enclave, near the High Commission. Everyone lived either above or next door to the shop if they had diplomatic status in Delhi – and Cass' cover was diplomatic. He might, just might, need to go in, but it was under surveillance and probably bugged. The surveillance was discreet. It had taken Hyde an hour to establish its presence. On the other hand, here in a narrow street off the Chandni Chowk, he'd never have confirmed surveillance. The place was just a tributary pouring people into the main shopping bazaar, day and night.

Cass had scribbled two addresses on a sliver of crumpled paper Hyde had found inside the crushed Silk Cut packet. Contacts, though of what kind and quality Hyde had no notion. Unofficials – natives – who knew at least something about V. K. Sharmar's links with heroin poppies in Kashmir. He paused amid the evening crowd, jostled and buffeted by their slow, strong tide. Murmured apologies were a continuous hum. He looked up at the first-floor windows of a verandahed wooden building, crushed between a handicrafts shop and a grocer's. Below the first floor, a narrow, grubby window displayed shawls and bright cloth. A dog lifted its thin leg against the building, urinated and moved on, slipping awkwardly through the crowd's legs in constant anticipation of being kicked. Hyde scratched his head, then drew the tourist map of the city from his back pocket. The rucksack was jostled continually as it hung over his shoulder.

He looked up and down the street, not nervous, merely disorientated. Behind a long barrow untidily heaped with limp vegetables, he saw the face he anticipated. He had made little or no attempt to shake off the tail – it was his city, after all, not Hyde's. And it was idle curiosity, for the moment. He hadn't done anything other than visit Cass and tour the city, gawping and apparently unaware; fascinated. There were only two of them and they took it in turns to drive the battered Ford and follow him on foot. He thrust forward against the crowd and gained the shadows beneath the verandah. He bent to study the bright lengths and rolls of cloth in the shop window. Tourist buys Indian cloth for wife or girlfriend. The man who lived in a flat above the shop worked as a messenger – that was all the information Cass had minutely scribbled next to his name and address – *messenger*. The stairs up to the flat would be through the shop. Just so long as he wasn't followed inside, he'd have no problems . . .

He adjusted the clear-glass spectacles, sensed the little bulge of his stomach over his belt, the creased denims, the cheap trainers – reestablishing his cover, the harmless, bumbling teacher from the Midlands whose part was easy to play since it was probably close to his future . . . The sense of an operation refused to gather as closely about him as the flies did in the shadows near the shop window. Unconcerned with surveillance, he rubbed his hand nervously through his hair, as if expecting a current of static electricity to enliven unpractised instincts.

Two men are following you, and they know the old car-and-on-foot routine . . . you barely noticed, until now, how well they'd got their act together.

He felt a slight and surprising chill fall down his back like the slow descent of cold air from the opened door of a freezer –

He straightened, sighing audibly and shaking his head, even as the shopkeeper appeared in the narrow doorway and he was nudged towards the man by another push of the crowded street. He waved his hands, palms outwards, in embarrassed refusal of the sales-pitch, and shuffled away from the window, out into the evening light and the swimming motions of the crowd against their own mass, knowing more clearly now and with what intent the man on foot would have moved out with him.

He came to the corner of the street and its aquatic junction with Chandni Chowk, where the stream flowed more broadly and even slower. His skin tickled across his back and shoulders, reassuringly. The sun was an orange, muddy-haze ball behind the roofs of the bazaar, and Chandni Chowk was vociferous with insistence against the sunset. Gobbets of bright spices lying spread out – the smell was sharp under his hitherto unconscious nose. Shops and stalls, bullock-carts and buses and ancient taxis, into which the occasional Mercedes attempted to intrude, seemed to belong in a film set retelling some poignant-satiric tale of the Raj's last days –

Awakened.

He sniffed the air greedily, at once repelled and enlivened by the spices of ordure, crammed bodies, petrol and food. He controlled the twitches of muscles and nerves; ducked casually behind a stall of silk bales and balloons as the man on foot came into Chandni Chowk and at once betrayed nervousness – had he lost the subject? His head began to twitch and rotate more quickly. Hyde all but rubbed his hands. The old game. The Heckler & Koch was in the rucksack, a round in the chamber. But this wasn't even close to offensive action. He stayed pressed against a shop window where strips of unidentifiable meat stared at his back from the vantage of hooks. The battered Ford attempted, like a too-young salmon, to nose against the flow of people along the street, failing halfway through its turn out of the sidestreet. Hyde suppressed his grin of satisfaction. Then waited.

The man on foot began to move back towards the car. Hyde was in an alleyway now – the houses were shallow, there were noisome back yards, crowded alleys filled with refuse and rats and dogs. He found it, and began numbering back from the corner – there? No, next door, that one, where the eaves leaned drunkenly and wooden tiles had slipped like a minor avalanche. He shouldered the hanging gate aside and walked carefully across the strewn yard, where a child seemed as deposited as the rubbish sacks and the broken cardboard boxes.

He walked through an open door and into a narrow hallway of cracked linoleum over packed earth, his nerves twitching now. He calmed himself by touching the rucksack over his shoulder. Gun – old habits, old friend. He paused at the foot of a confined staircase, listening towards the shop and its customers and the breeze of street noise blown through it. He listened, too, towards the head of the stairs and a radio playing and the chatter of a small child. The voice of a man. Good, he was home from work. He stepped quietly upwards.

He'd seen Ros once, fleetingly, during the day, the bulkiest member of a party being towed by a tall, supremely beautiful Indian woman around the circumference of the Parliament House – while he had been dragging the two men around on another, more innocuous tour of the city, before plunging into Old Delhi like a nervous diver from a high board.

Now, it was nice to be back, even if it was only turning out for the Third Eleven in a limited-overs game. Enough evidence to get Cass off the hook, get Shelley interested in rescuing the poor sod –

– if there *was* evidence. He knocked politely on a thin plywood door at the head of the stairs. The radio or television was immediately turned down and the door was opened by a large, middle-aged Indian who was at once shocked at the sight of a white man, before he declined into practised cunning. It was as if he expected that sometime, somehow, *someone* would come and would have to be answered in a certain manner.

'You speak English?'

The man cleared his throat, as if assuming the language, then merely nodded.

'Oh, good,' Hyde said, fiddling with his spectacles, shuffling the rucksack, aware of the stairs behind him and his exposed back. 'You see I – I'm Philip Cass' cousin – well, half-brother, really . . .' He realised he was going through the motions *expected*. The noise of the street came through an open window somewhere behind the Indian, whose presence in the doorway had darkened because of the lowering sun. Hyde was suddenly aware that he was *expected*. Not feared, as he might have been by someone unofficial; but *anticipated*. Something was wrong and becoming *very* wrong. Hyde persisted with his cover.

'You see, Mr Banerjee –'

'I am afraid you have the wrong name – what address are you looking for, Mr – ?'

Time to leave –

'Oh – you're not Mr Banerjee? You see, my half-brother mentioned you, he said, in fact, that you were someone who might be prepared to act as a character witness.'

The Indian was shaking his head.

'Oh, no, I do not understand.'

'My half-brother, Philip Cass – he mentioned your name.' Hyde shrugged with disorientation. Fiddled with the disarming spectacles. 'You see, I'm only out here because of him – I don't really know my way around. Phil asked me to look you up.'

'I do not think so.' *Professional* dismissal. He was sure of it now. Sure the man was planted, *in place*. Poor fucking Banerjee, whoever he *used* to be.

'You're not Mr Banerjee – does he live here?'

'No Mr Banerjee here.'

They'd closed it off . . . Cass' contact was known to them, or had been dug up like any ordinary mole, and they'd put someone here in his place – Banerjee was on a rubbish dump somewhere outside the city, slowly decaying. But they'd sent a professional, and that meant the intelligence services were involved. So the tailmen were intelligence, looking for another

55

professional, not his assumed amateur . . . *But they'd acted to shut Cass out*, that was the point. *Minister* Sharmar had control. Not only of the setup – which was what it was now, for certain – but of the possible consequences. Anyone who might be coming round like the thin dog with the cocked leg, sniffing after the event. Hyde felt the adrenalin hurry through him like the dry, hot wind from a railway tunnel.

'Oh, I see. I must have got the address wrong, or the name.' Fiddling with the spectacles, shuffling the rucksack on his back, the stoop of the shoulders that confirmed the harmless anonymity of the caller. 'I'm sorry to have troubled you.'

The Indian dismissed him with a shrug, and Hyde at once turned away with an additional apology and began descending the creaking, narrow stairs. He heard the plywood door shut confidently behind him.

A man paused at the foot of the stairs, and the plywood door opened once more behind him. The man's gaze was beyond Hyde's shoulder, looking up, and then there was a glaze to the eyes – not dangerous. Hyde smiled innocuously at the man on foot who had been tailing him and the man moved aside to let him pass. He controlled his nerves and went out into the yard, where the child had been rescued by a magnificent young woman in a sari whose eyes fell as his glance moved over her. He slipped through the awry gate and huddled along the alley into Chandni Chowk and the crowd. The battered Ford's driver was at once alert, then was evidently calmed by a signal from behind Hyde . . . deep breath. He passed on, beginning to gaze up at the buildings, around at the still-massing crowds –

– shivering, nonetheless, from the aftershock of the encounter, which buffeted against him more palpably than the throng. The tailmen had responded to orders from the man occupying Banerjee's flat. They'd placed someone fairly senior there. Cass' contact had been identified and silenced – any family he might have had were also missing.

But *he* remained uncompromised. His fumbling, incoherent

sketch of a cover-story had convinced the man at the head of the stairs and wouldn't be scrutinised. He'd persuaded them that Cass had sent him in all innocence.

Hyde struggled through the evening shoppers, their noise and heat glutinously restraining him. He paused a number of times, apparently abstracted by stalls and shop windows. The battered Ford slipped farther and farther behind him, loitering out of boredom.

Sharmar wanted this buried deep. And, the deeper the hole, the bigger the guilt. The old adage in all probability applied here. And, for Cass, it was profoundly real. Shelley had better get Cass out – quickly. Sharmar was into drugs – growing, harvesting, refining most probably, even shipping . . . most likely along the Balkan lorry route through Yugoslavia. Neither Croats, Serbs or Slovenians stopped *that* traffic – there was a slice off the top for everyone. And Cass had blundered like a child into the game, and was right in the mire.

He rubbed his chin. Shelley had to get him out, or he'd be shipped home in a box.

Prakesh was standing beside the window in the last of the daylight as Sharmar hurried into the anteroom, closing the door on the Congress party caucus meeting from which he had been summoned. Prakesh's features were uninterpretable in the dusk. Beyond the window, an ornamental pool glowed and its fountain spray glittered in the last of the light. Sharmar hurried to his brother.

'What is it, Prakesh – what is it?'

Prakesh turned, smiling.

'It is *it*, V.K. That old goat, Chopri – he's dead. I've just come from the hospital.'

It was difficult to speak, for a moment. He stared beyond the pillars supporting the great dome of the rotunda's roof, beyond the pool, to the city stretching away into the darkness to the north. His breathing was noisy, as if attempting to blow words from his tight throat. The city blazed with lights. His hand moved like that of a nerveless old man, clutching at his brother's sleeve.

'Who – who knows? Who else knows?'

'His widow, the children. I hurried here from the hospital. It is advantageous for *you* to inform the President.'

Sharmar glanced towards the door he had closed on the meeting.

'What about –?'

'Call the President first – at once, V.K.' He hurried Sharmar across the room towards the littered desk and the telephone and all but thrust it against his cheek, then dialled the number for him. 'Very grave, V.K. – solemn sadness.'

Prakesh wandered to the window once more, his head cocked as if listening like a curious bird. V.K. paused, then was evidently talking to Namal Singh. Prakesh smiled. His brother was really so *good* at that kind of thing, fluid as an actor, a sinuous dancer of the personality, the adopter of masks and costumes that were always appropriate. Beside his brother, he knew himself to be clumsily arrogant, aloof, uningratiating. Merely the complete manager.

He lit a cigarette and stared out of the window at the darkened, broad paths surrounding the Parliament. A few figures, many of them slackly dressed tourists, the occasional more purposeful walk of a politician or civil servant. There would be much hurrying in an hour, perhaps less –

'I think you must announce it on the television this evening, Mr President,' his brother was saying. He rarely needed to be briefed. He found the words as he found the tone and the facial expression.

Prakesh looked down at his tightly curled hand. Not a fist clenched in threat, but a grip that was triumphant. The old women and the young and ambitious in the next-door room would not oppose V.K.'s elevation to the leadership of Congress. To persuade them to risk their possession of power in a sudden general election would be more difficult. They had to have one in the next six months, and by that time the Hindu fundamentalists would be much stronger . . . He rubbed his bottom lip with the fingers that held the cigarette, hardly attending to his brother's words. V.K.'s performance would be, as always, faultless.

Bharatiya Janata had a leader almost more persuasive than V.K., even more charismatic. A damned film star! Anand Mehta, heartthrob, action man, national dream-made-flesh. He could sweep V.K., himself and all of Congress aside. Prakesh smiled sourly, listening to his brother conclude his call to the President. Mehta wasn't as good an actor as V.K., but V.K. wasn't a damned film star, either!

He turned as his brother put down the receiver.

'Good,' he said, then: 'How is the caucus, the Party's mood?'

V. K. Sharmar waggled his hand, then shrugged.

'Worried – by Bharatiya Janata and Anand Mehta. Worried . . .'

'Then they must be made to see that an election now is less dangerous than one in six months' time. Are you ready, V.K.?'

'What –? Oh, yes.' Sharmar composed his features to solemn grief. Only his clenching and unclenching hands betrayed his sense of the moment. He took a handkerchief from his pocket and dabbed it as carefully as a makeup girl along his hairline, removing the slight sheen of perspiration. *Two* actors, Prakesh thought for a moment – it would be an election campaign between two consummate actors. Except that V.K. wanted to *do* while Anand Mehta merely wanted to *be*, to continue as adored as ever but on a larger screen. 'Are we ready?' Sharmar asked.

'Strike hard, V.K. – be very positive.' Sharmar nodded in acquiescence.

It was a risky strategy. Sereena would have been a great deal of help in the campaign, one film star offsetting another. But *that* would have been unthinkable. Had her affair with an *Englishman* become public, Mehta would have exploited it fatally against Congress. Dead, she might have the status of an invisible, minor deity, hovering over the Party. Mehta's own background was vulgar, murky, tasteless, financially often illegal. To exploit it to the advantage of Congress was, however, difficult. Hardly anything could dent Mehta – he was a living god of the screen. Only his political ineptitude could be used against him, and even then carefully and soon. They could not afford to wait until the beginning of the year for an election – it must be held before that star of Curry Westerns and cops-and-robbers fantasies became unassailable.

Sharmar was already at the door, his features suitably composed. Prakesh nodded, then crossed to his side and opened the door on the caucus meeting.

He sat behind the wheel of the Hertz-rented Ford and adjusted his tie and damp collar. The suit was uncomfortably warm, the Delhi night close and humid. Beside him, on the passenger seat, lay a briefcase, a further contribution to his cover. Hyde sighed, tuning the car radio to the BBC World Service and its hastily assembled voices discussing the death of Prime Minister Chopri. The well-lit, orderly street hurried with figures and limousines. Chopri's death had been a poked stick, stirring up the termite-mound of the Diplomatic Enclave.

'. . . of course Sharmar is the favoured successor – he and his family have the machine to manufacture the desired result,' someone pontificated in a light, trilling Indian voice from the radio. And the machinery to operate a drugs cartel, sport, he added silently. And have irritations like wives and British agents taken care of . . . *and* poor sods like Banerjee. 'I expect the announcement within a matter of hours . . .' the voice from the radio continued, lulling Hyde as much as the night and the purposeful, distanced hurry of figures and cars.

Cass' block of flats was at the end of the street. So was the surveillance car, a black Peugeot. There was a man on foot, too, patrolling near the entrance to the flats. He fiddled with his tie once more.

He'd called Shelley. Alison, the wife, had told him Shelley

wasn't home. Nor was he at Century House. This wasn't an operation, there was no board and no lines of communication. If he couldn't reach Shelley, there was no one else. Banging down the telephone in frustration, he'd switched on the radio, to pick up the news of Chopri's death. An hour earlier.

'– question of an early election?' someone posed from the radio.

'Possibly. Support among millions of Hindus is slipping away from Congress to the Bharatiya Janata Party and its charismatic, film-star leader –' Hyde switched off the car radio. Sharmar was about to become PM, was he? Cass' situation had become, as euphemism would describe it, *untenable*. And Shelley was out!

Hyde had slipped out of the hotel's rear entrance, through the noisome yard and its rubbish, wearing a sober suit. Hired the necessary car to deflect attention, bought the briefcase. If Banerjee was dead, so would be the possessor of the other name Cass had scribbled on the crumpled fragment of paper in the fag packet. Waste of time checking him out. Whatever material or product Cass had was inside his telly or VCR, or shoved up behind the sink, near the stopcock Cass had asked him to turn off. Get it, and he might attract Shelley's serious attention before Cass stopped waving and began drowning.

He raised the small, monocular nightsight to his eye and studied the entrance to the flats, where street-lighting fell silver through the branches of saplings. Activity, just the thing, diplomatic staff coming and going, busied with Chopri's death and its consequences for Congress, India – and most of all, their own piddling concerns and the guest-lists for immediate cocktail receptions and ambassadorial invitations and calls. A young woman emerged from the flats in the company of two smooth, ghost-grey young men and they moved towards a stretched Granada that drew up outside the block. A uniformed driver ushered them into it and the car pulled away, slipping past him moments later with tinted, diplomatic windows revealing nothing. Putting the nightsight in his pocket, he checked the toolkit in the briefcase. He slipped the gun into his waistband. Nodding, he opened the door of the Ford and got out, locking the car and walking with studied purpose towards the flats.

He passed the surveillance car. The man on foot was on the other side of the block. He felt tensed against the opening of a car door, a voice raised in question or recognition. The lights were bright at the entrance to the flats, so that even his back and shoulders might be familiar, recognisable. He paused, fishing in his pockets for a keycard he did not have. The foyer beyond the reinforced glass doors was empty. The entryphone invited and mocked. A keycard and a personal code number. Easy when you —

Ten seconds. He opened the briefcase, clutching it against his chest. Sweat was damp beneath his arms and against his sides. The humid air pressed like a soft, clinging towel. The image of the middle-aged Indian at the head of the narrow staircase, denying he was Banerjee, was very distinct. He raised his hand after closing the briefcase, to scratch his head, hover with some semblance of conviction.

The flat's doubtless been searched, anything there would have already been found . . . you should have gone via the solicitor, even the embassy . . .

'Thanks!' he blurted. 'Lost my bloody card or something!'

The woman, forty, precise, hurried and unsuspicious, nodded her thanks as he held open one of the doors for her as she left the building. She cradled a sheaf of files in the crook of her arm. Hyde closed the door behind him. Oh, easy when you know how —

Cass' flat was on the top floor, the fourth. He took the lift, chilly in the air-conditioning after the humidity of the street and the heat of his tension. The door of the lift opened onto a quiet, carpeted corridor — any office building anywhere; utterly anonymous. He heard a child singing beyond one of the doors, then an adult voice grumbled it into silence. For a moment. As he reached the door of Cass' flat, the singing began again. He smiled. The woman's arrival in the foyer had been more convenient than using the entryphone, pretending he was some diplomatic messenger looking for one of the names . . . entry, yes, but his non-arrival at whichever door he had selected would have aroused curiosity.

He looked down at the doormat, then along the corridor. There were doormats outside other flats. He knelt down, peeling the mat back like cut turf. Tut, tut . . . The pressure pad lay like an envelope left beneath the mat. Straddling it with his feet, he leaned gently towards the door; inserted the stiff plastic card, slipping it, forcing it . . . yes, it would go. He reached up, feeling along the top of the door frame. No wires. No sign of an alarm rigged from outside.

He employed the card once more, hearing the lock click back. Gently, he pushed the door open, studying the floor of the darkened hallway. No mat. He flicked on the pencil-thin beam of a torch he drew from his pocket, running the finger of pale light along the skirting. No sign that the carpet had been lifted, then replaced. He heard the child continue its nursery rhyme like a tape-loop and the predictable grumbles of its mother, and his own magnified breathing. Cass' flat smelt unused, already mildewed by the heat. He stepped through the doorway and shut the door behind him, locking it on the latch. The only sound now was that of his steady, loud breathing.

He flicked the torchbeam into a small bedroom, a bathroom, then he entered the main living room. The beam wiped assuredly over furniture, the television, hi-fi, bookshelves, a complexly patterned rug. They didn't use infra-red detectors in Indian alarm systems − legitimate or covert. Too hot. Here, if the flat had been bugged against intrusion by the people who'd tipped Banerjee off the end of the gangplank, then it would be noise-activated bugs and pressure-pads. Which way does the window look out? North-east, towards the illuminated wedding cakes of Parliament House and the Secretariat. Beyond them, the domes and minarets and towers of mosques and temples and forts jutted into their floodlighting. He needed to risk cross-ing the living room, which had to be bugged, to draw the curtains.

The thin beam from the torch preceded like the gently feeling enquiries of a blind man's stick. He avoided the rug, the chairs, the low table, a standard lamp set beside one curtain. Found the cord and softly drew the curtains. Then he flicked the torchbeam around the room's walls, skirting, corners, before he returned to the doorway and switched on the room's lights. Dimmer switch. He lowered the brightness. Kneeling, he peeled back the rug. Another pressure pad, its lead disappearing like a snail-trail under the sofa. Pads under the cushions, doubtless – don't sit down on the job, sport . . . He squatted on his haunches, absorb-ing the room. Where are the bugs? He looked up. Not in the lampshade suspended from the ceiling. He stood up and crossed to the standard lamp – hello, old friend. There'd be others, but perhaps not too many. Any hidden cameras? The furniture was functional, uncrowded. It hadn't been moved to accommodate sightlines or angles. He eased open the single sideboard. Nothing.

He knelt beside the television set, the VCR on a shelf beneath it, and felt its surface and angles and leads. Inspected his fingers. The TV hadn't been fiddled with – the dust on the back of the set only now disturbed. Opening the briefcase, he took the screwdriver from the toolkit and removed the back of the set, placing the breastplate-like board on the carpet beside him. Then he flashed the torch into the set.

Masking tape. Two miniature tape cassettes from a mini-recorder. Gently, he unpeeled the tape, grinning. He placed the tapes in the briefcase and judged the size of the video recorder. It would go into the case, no need to take it to pieces here. He unplugged the aerial and the lead and lifted the recorder into the briefcase. *They always pinch the video recorder, sir, first thing they go for.*

Stopcock. Was that just a general reference to the plumbing, or was whatever-it-was actually beneath the kitchen sink? He stood up, glancing around the living room. There were no photographs in the room. The place seemed self-contained, sufficient. Books everywhere, and an immodest collection of records and CDs. The sky had fallen in on a contented man. Pieces of jade, statuettes of Shiva and Parvati, the Lord Krishna, a bulging image of the Buddha. On a desk in the corner, opened books, notes, and a sheet of paper in a small electronic typewriter.

Shaking his head, he moved to the kitchen and switched on the light after lowering the blind. He opened the cupboard beneath the sink, and found the stopcock, then fingered his way along the copper pipework. He leant forward on his knees. The smell of detergent and the unemptied wastebin. He felt behind the belly of the sink. Masking tape. He tugged at it –

– too late realising that he had pulled away a fine electronic wire, broken a contact placed there just to be broken. No audible alarm sounded in the building or outside it. The wiring shook in his hand as he inspected it. He'd set off some alarm, somewhere –

THREE

diplomatic presence

Hyde switched off the kitchen light, as if to return the narrow room to a state of innocence, then stood hesitantly in the doorway of the lounge. The back of the television set lay on the fawn carpet like the shell of a dead turtle. *Put the bloody back on the telly or they'll ask Cass what was hidden there.* The idea's urgent clarity was its conviction. He hurried to the set, fumbling the casing and its screws into place, scratching his forefinger with the screwdriver, dropping one of the screws, snatching it up, pressing it home – then the second, the third, fourth –

– tightening it, he heard the noise of the lift from the corridor. *Oh, Jesus, not yet –*

He snatched up the briefcase. Then, swallowing, deliberately stood on the pressure pad beneath the bright subtle rug, scuffing the rug into shapelessness. Opened drawers in the sideboard, tugged books from the wall shelves and the bookcases. No time for the bedroom, it would have to do. The lift had stopped.

How the hell could they have responded so fast? He turned wildly towards the main window. Metal frames, lever-catches – no locks. He opened one window on the damply-clinging night air and looked down, then back towards the hallway as he heard the door handle tried. They'd informed the surveillance car and they'd been across the street like dogs out of traps. He swung one leg over the windowsill, clinging on to the briefcase with one hand, the other gripping the window frame above his head.

A key was tried gently in the lock, a small scratching sound as if a dog wanted to gain entry. *Drop the bloody case, the VCR doesn't have to work.* The briefcase fell dully onto a grass verge and was lost in shadow. He thrust himself over the sill, clinging to it as his feet searched for purchase on a jutting concrete sill above the windows of the flat below. He felt it through the toes of his shoes and let himself slide away from his grip, pressing himself to balance against the concrete of the wall. Pebble-dash scraped at his cheek and palms. Then he edged himself along the narrow outcrop towards the closest drainpipe. Above his head, he heard no sounds from Cass' flat. They were trying to catch an agent, a professional who'd been searching the flat, not someone who'd just waltz off with the video to flog it in Chandni Chowk tomorrow morning. They needed surprise, an edge. Reinforcements.

He tested the drainpipe. It moved – unsafe. Had to suffice. He looked down. A grass verge hard as concrete below him, shadow, a fall of light at the corner of the block, no one moving. He swallowed and began sliding as hurriedly as he dared down the drainpipe, hearing the small tears of screws from fixings, the grumble of metal against concrete. Dropped the last eight or ten feet, jolting himself.

Running footsteps – where the hell was the briefcase? He gripped it in the dark and thrust it under his arm. Then moved along the wall of the building until he reached its angle and the spill of light from the street.

Looking up, he saw a dark head leaning from the window through which he had escaped. Then a voice called with exaggerated and redundant caution. The running footsteps had halted. The man patrolling on foot was shrugging up at the man in the window. Go now –

He walked as steadily and unconcernedly as he could towards the streetlamps and the wide pavement and the neat saplings and the passing limousines, then crossed the street towards the rented Ford. He unlocked the door and got in, throwing the briefcase into the rear of the car. Despite the temperature of the night, his tension clouded the windscreen. Jesus. His hands slipped sweatily on the wheel. He started the engine and pulled away from the kerb. As he passed the surveillance car, he saw that it was empty, but one of them was standing at the glass doors of the flats, using an R/T. He glanced up at the passing Ford, and then ignored it as Hyde turned the car towards Satya Marg and the perimeter of the Enclave. Ahead of him, suspended but moving in the darkness, a light aircraft was coming into Safdarjang aerodrome. Then, heading in the direction from which he had come, a car at high speed. He grinned shakily. The backup was too late – just . . .

'Look, the sleek bastard's grinning all over his face!' Hyde snorted, towelling his hair as he slumped, bathrobed, into one of the cane armchairs that littered Ros' suite.

On the screen – Hindi newsreader's voice turned down – V. K. Sharmar was receiving the adulation of a crowd, waving his hands above his head, then presenting them folded time and again in the gesture of returned greeting which always appeared that of prayer or service. Apt in this instance. Garlands were placed around his neck, almost obscuring his broad, continuous grin. Unlike the late Rajiv, he did not remove them as soon as they bedecked him.

Ros' head appeared at the bedroom door.

'I thought your cover involved you keeping miles away from me,' she remarked.

'I heard there was some middle-aged biddy staying here looking for a toy boy.'

'*Toy*, maybe. *Not* a model steam loco whose clockwork's buggered.' She wandered forward into the suite's sitting room, wrapping a bright, sari-like housecoat around her and tying it at the waist. She tugged her hair to a semblance of order. 'You'd better bugger off into the bedroom when the waiter brings the breakfast up. I've got my reputation to consider.'

'He'll understand – you're Australian.'

'*Don't* make any observations that the amount of breakfast

68

you made me order won't arouse suspicion, on account of my size – will you?' She tugged at Hyde's hair, sharply. 'That's him, is it?' she continued. 'You think he killed his wife – or had her killed?'

'Had to be behind it.'

'Christ – they don't play about here, do they? Why, though?'

Hyde gestured towards the screen. The same image of Sharmar, in frozen, beaming monochrome, decorated the front page of the English-language daily, *Indian Express*, that had been left outside the door of the suite. *V.K. to lead Congress*, was a sober-enough headline, but it seemed to sussurate with adulation. There was a photograph of Anand Mehta on the same front page in a scene from his latest movie.

'Cass was a danger to him – the woman was a danger. Cass did start off by using her, after all.'

'Why didn't they kill Cass?'

'That might have aroused our interest. Though I doubt it!'

'Haven't got hold of Shelley yet?' Hyde shook his head. 'You can't get Cass out on your own – you're *not* going to try, are you?'

Ros' features were suspiciously concerned. Again, he shook his head. She stared hard at him for perhaps ten seconds, then nodded slowly.

'I haven't got the resources. And with the buggers at the High Commission telling Shelley there's nothing to worry his blond head about, I can't get hold of any. Shelley's either got to trade, or threaten. But is he going to do that to someone he used to be at Oxford with – I ask in all innocence?'

'Was he?'

'Weren't they all, darlin'?'

'There wasn't anything in that video recorder, was there?'

'I didn't have time to search through the tapes – perhaps they were what he meant? Though I didn't see a video camera anywhere. All I've got out of it is those two cassettes – a lot of hoarse breathing from Cass, a couple of voices mostly speaking

Hindi, Cass' jumbled jottings and meanderings. A lot of the stuff's got to be translated and I can't do it.'

'So? Apart from moving in here and trying to turn this into a dirty weekend, what *can* you do, Hyde?' She lit a cigarette and moved to the window. Beyond her, the morning heat made the scene indistinct, the towers of Connaught Place and the business area fragile and merely decorative in the haze; the government buildings and the Supreme Court were lightened, made less massive — galleys rather than great, monumental warships. The brown river was almost invisibly sand-coloured. 'Well, my bright, shining boy — what *are* you going to do?'

'If I can't get Shelley by the time I've finished my tucker, Ros*alind* —' Ros scowled at him and he grinned. '— then I'm off to see Cass again. I need to know more, in case.'

'In case of what?'

'In case they decide he's better off out of the way.'

'Would they — ?'

Hyde jabbed his finger towards the television. 'He's playing in a very big game. What's Cass to him, that he should weep for him? If Sharmar gets the slightest twitch because of Cass, then the poor bloke's going straight into the dark. *That*'s why Shelley needs to be at the other end of a phone!'

Ros turned back to the view from the window, blowing smoke across it, masking the slender minarets and towers beyond the office blocks. Then she said:

'How dangerous is this?'

'Not that much. My cover's still intact. Cass' diplomatic status could give Shelley leverage . . . ?' The observation became a question, and Hyde rubbed his chin. Ros' glance pounced on him with accusatory concern. He raised his hands, palms outwards. 'Not *that* dangerous. More a job of convincing Shelley than anything else. It's not going to degenerate into a punch-up — I'm just the wood-and-water joey in this. For once, I'm not left on my ace with the arse hanging out of my pants.' The colloquialisms were intended to diminish the situation. Ros' large features remained suspicious. 'Look, I'll go and see the poor sod *once* more, *get* something out of him to forklift Shelley out of his chair. OK?'

'Right. When do we leave, in that case?'

'Tomorrow – or the day after. Promise.'

There was a knock on the door. Ros was plucking at her lower lip with thumb and forefinger, ignoring the polite noise, even as Hyde nodded towards the door. She was staring at the front page of the newspaper.

'I don't like it,' she said. 'That bugger's got *everything* to lose.'

'Answer the door, Ros – I'm hungry,' Hyde said, grinning, as he disappeared into the bedroom.

Cass had become paranoid; sullen, grubby, withdrawn, his shoulders hunched like the frill of a carapace. Hyde rubbed his hands through his hair. The interview room was stifling, airless. Jawal stood deferentially silent beside the door. Cass had replied to his greeting and enquiries monosyllabically; he was disgruntled, fearful. Desperation had cultivated cunning.

Hyde leant forward, pushing more cigarettes towards Cass. 'Did you enjoy the Jane Austen?' Hyde asked. *Persuasion*. I'm interested, make it more convincing . . .

'What?' Cass' reddened eyes were ferally alert, like those of a rat caught by a sudden light. The mind behind them seemed to scuttle away from Hyde. 'Not much.'

'Pity.' Hyde controlled his quick anger. He had dressed as the Midlands teacher before leaving Ros' hotel, reentered his own hotel via the back yard, found that his room had not been searched. The awkward drawer of the rickety chest in the room had remained opened to just the extent he had left it. 'Pity,' he sighed. There was, as yet, no connection between the man in the suit at Cass' flat and himself. He'd been tailed out to the prison this time, however. The same blue Ford, the same team. 'Want me to bring you some more books, Phil?'

Cass shook his head, his hair flopping over his forehead in

greasy licks. He rubbed it back with one hand. Hyde quelled his impatience. This sort of thing wasn't his game. What the hell was Shelley doing, for God's sake? He still wasn't home – middle of the bloody night in London.

Clearing his throat, he murmured: 'You know, pity you can't have the telly in here, since you speak the local lingo. I've got one – but its only use to me would be with a VCR. But then, who wants to watch Indian films? A VCR would be useless.'

Cass appeared startled, then at once wizened with cunning, his eyes darting and hot with realisations and dangers.

'You – did the stopcock?'

'Already done.' Hyde stared until he perceived that Cass understood, then waited for him to weigh the implications of the information, hoping he would respond.

The silence continued. Hyde's temperature rose. His mouth was arid. He heard a large insect blundering slowly through the soupy air. Cass stared at the burning cigarette in his fingers, intent as if he had heard of the death of a close relative, Hyde thought. Shit. He's going to close up altogether. He's the *only* source of information now. He knows there's not much on those tapes, it's mostly still in his head.

Finally, Cass shook his head, and looked up at Hyde. His face was pale beneath the stubble, and drawn around what had become a very young man's eyes, expressing pique, adolescent defiance.

'Thanks for coming,' he muttered sullenly.

'I'm willing to help,' Hyde insisted. 'But really, Phil, I do need some information from you.'

'I've told my story too many times – *Patrick*,' he added. 'Too many people know my story.' He swallowed and his hands clenched together on the scratched table, stilling each other.

'That makes it all the more important *I* know.' Again, Cass shook his head.

'*No*,' he announced emphatically. 'Not here.'

'Tell me.'

The adolescent had vanished and the cunning, exhausted man had returned, with his rat's eyes. Cass' mouth was loose and wet, he smelt of dirt and fear, but his paranoid terror at being abandoned – even his terror of Hyde – silenced him.

'Uncle Peter – how do I explain it to him?'

'I'll tell him, when I –' he swallowed noisily. Hyde's throat remained dry. 'I get out of this place. Don't want to go over it now, not *again*. Not here.'

'Christ, Phil – don't be so upset!' Hyde urged. 'It might help, you know. You say you didn't do it –?' He glanced towards the guard. Jawal seemed uncomprehending. Was there any point in this furtive half-dialogue any more?

Except that it might keep his own cover intact – and keep him alive.

'Phil,' he murmured, leaning forward. 'I *understand* the chip on your shoulder. The High Commission doesn't seem to be doing much – but if *I* could talk to someone in London, create a stink at *home*, then things might get better. But, I'd need to be able to convince them with something. You know, what really happened, what you were doing there . . . ?'

Cass prodded his own chest, as if inviting attack. The small room now seemed further diminished by the tension within him, the clash of desperation and paranoia. The prodding became a feeble tapping, as if he were attempting to transmit in a morse code he had largely forgotten. Hyde felt the perspiration as a line across his forehead. Cass opened his lips, but said nothing.

Hyde persisted: 'You don't want to spend more time here than you have to, Phil – you need help. *I* need help with London.' Cass was shaking his head. 'Uncle Peter was a bit shocked – you having a mistress, an affair. You know how old-fashioned he is in some ways.' Hyde searched for some word or idea that would act like a cattle-prod. No good frightening Cass, he'd already done that to himself. His paranoia at least prevented him from asking about Banerjee. No good just coaxing him. He'd already lost interest, perhaps even forgotten he'd smuggled the two names to Hyde. Everything had hinged on the tapes and whatever else –

– hadn't really. Cass had collapsed of his own accord. Caved in. Abandoned, isolated – expecting to be cheated.

The cunning was back in his eyes, as was the palsied, ceaseless shaking of his head. He pointed to his chest, then to the door, still silent. You bloody stupid bastard, Hyde thought, and said:

'You're *wrong*, Phil – *dead* wrong.' The head continued with its palsy and the eyes glittered with held-back tears. The room, the prison, were as small as the enclosure of Cass' temples. Hyde had to make him believe they *had* to get him out, that they knew he had a great, priceless secret. He wasn't really in touch any longer, merely crawling towards the mirage of an oasis. 'Phil.' Nothing short of shock therapy would awaken Cass. Strangely, he was safe inside his terror. His secret was keeping him alive. Hyde stood up.

For a moment, there was a new horror of being abandoned in Cass' eyes, but it faded almost immediately. A weak and cunning smirk possessed his mouth. Jawal opened the door.

Hyde went out into the corridor, tugging the rucksack onto his shoulder. Cass' silence pressed at his back like the fear of a terminal illness. The stupid, *stupid* bastard . . . but there was no vigour in his condemnation. Cass had retreated to his only place of safety – the den of his secret. He'd been alone too long. Nothing had been done for him with enough *urgency* –!

Right, *Uncle* Peter – be there, on the other end of the line.

The security guard seemed disdainful of him, the effect of his appearance combined with the scent of the tandoori meal he had bought and eaten at a stall near his hotel. His lips were probably still stained from the food. It was a pleasant little confrontation at the gate of the High Commission on Shantipath, the porticoed Edwardian building looming behind the uniformed man. He trumped the guard's reluctance with his ID card, drawing it from the lining of the rucksack with a small flourish. Midday pressed down on them, hazily burning.

'Now you know,' Hyde remarked with a smirk designed to irritate.

The security guard's disdain seemed unchipped. Having presented his ID, he had declared himself one of a species thought extinct; a coelacanth brought up in a fisherman's net, a dinosaur bone excavated on the site of a new office block.

'I want to see Dickson – now.'

The guard, stiffly refusing to perspire in the glass booth parked beside the open gates of the High Commission, picked up a telephone. Behind him, in the grounds, a fountain was displayed in a peacock's tail by a momentary puff of breeze. Dark privet hedges, English lawns being continuously watered. The place seemed more archaic than his ID card. Shelley would be peeved by his self-declaration, but there wasn't time any more. The midday editions of the English language newspapers were speculating with what seemed worshipful, obsessive ferocity on Sharmar calling an early election. Photographs of the new PM, the President, the dead Chopri and the magnetic Mehta littered the newsstands. There wasn't time now for a quiet chat, a teasing-out of Cass' story. Shelley had to promise the Indians whatever they demanded for Cass' transfer to London – or for a transfer to diplomatic custody, pending his trial.

The guard put down the receiver.

'With a certain reluctance, you're to be let in,' he announced.

'So kind.'

He crunched along the weedless gravel drive towards the marble steps up to the main doors. Another puff of hot breeze splashed droplets pleasantly from the fountain's spray against his arm and cheek. He all but rubbed his hands as he mounted the steps and passed the raised eyebrows of another security man. Then he paused.

'Where's Dickson's office?'

'*Mr* Dickson's office is on the second floor. Room 221. You the new punkah-wallah?'

'Your bovine mate at the gate told you who I am.' The foyer was as cool as its marble, less frosty than the security man's glance. 'Cheers.'

He climbed the grand staircase. Whitehall-among-the-Darkies, the Raj lives, OK? He turned and reached the first floor, then climbed to the second, passing secretaries and attachés and even cleaners who regarded him with the same blank incomprehension. Long windows overlooked the careful, ordered gardens around the Commission. India remained at a respectful distance beyond an imitation of Sussex. Delhi, to the north, squatted patiently in its own heat. He checked the numbers on the doors, and when he reached 221 simply opened it and walked in, sniffing loudly to announce his presence in an amalgam of haste and mockery.

'Mr *Hyde*?' a youngish woman asked, rising from her chair behind a desk. He nodded. She moved hesitantly from the desk towards the other door in the room. Air-conditioning grumbled against the enormity of its task and a small fan on the woman's desk turned with a bemused buzzing noise. 'I'll see if he can see you now –'

Hyde passed her at the door, opening it on a larger office that was scented with cigar smoke. He recognised Dickson behind the desk, haloed by the light from tall windows. Other embassies, mirror-images of the High Commission, echoed away in the windows' perspective. A game of mirrors. Dickson was immediately angry, bridling to a squatting position above his chair, hands gripping its arms. The other man in the room may have been Miles, or another of the SIS complement. It had no bearing. Dickson nodded at the secretary, who remained behind Hyde, then lowered himself into his chair and immediate imperturbability. His features composed themselves diplomatically; aloof, certain, half-amused.

'Hyde, isn't it?' he asked, the slightest trace of Edinburgh in his voice, his mistrust evident. The other man grinned, even mockingly held his nose.

'Who's the monkey?' Hyde asked, nudging an elbow towards Dickson's companion. 'You're obviously the organ-grinder.'

'Miles — Hyde . . . Hyde — *Mr* Miles. Your senior, I'd say.'

'You mean he's reached pensionable age?'

Miles scowled.

'Why are you here — or needn't I ask?' Dickson remarked equably, gesturing towards a leather chair after Hyde had dragged it closer to the desk and sat down. 'We were a little puzzled when Jackson at the gate rang through, saying he'd got someone with one of *our* type of ID cards down there.'

'Right scruffbag, he said,' Miles offered.

'I heard him, and he didn't.' He slapped his hands on the edge of the desk, and said: 'I haven't got time to waste. I want fully independent use of the Code Room now, full signals with Shelley. No one else, just Shelley.'

'I was about to ask who might have sent you into our neck of the woods. It doesn't seem necessary any longer, does it?'

'Or have you just run out of traveller's cheques, Hyde?' Miles sneered.

'Look, neither of you are any good at this stuff. I've had it from the best, Sir Kenneth of sainted memory. Now, stop pissing about and give me the key to the Code Room.' His voice was level, even amused. He realised that he was enjoying himself.

'Did the D-G send you — why?' Dickson asked.

'That's it. Watch your arse, it might be on fire. You don't know *what* authority I have, do you?'

'You're not here about the Cass business, are you, Hyde?'

'Someone has to be, Miles — you don't give a stuff, that's obvious. Look, Dickson, you're Head of Station. Just get me into signals with Shelley. No skin off your nose.'

A giant fan windmilled above their heads. The room was comfortable with cigar smoke, leather, bookcases, rugs — the view from the window of a safe, surrounding diplomatic world. Delhi was a good posting for anyone – for the SIS personnel, it was a glimpse of Nirvana. It had made Cass careless and soft; and endangered.

'You don't believe Cass' story, do you? I took you for a cynic, not a soppy girl.'

'Miles, why don't you piss off?' He only then turned to Miles, and added: 'If I was Shelley, I'd want to know why you *want* to believe Cass killed the woman.' He turned to Dickson, squinting into the noon, pearled light from the windows. 'Both of you.'

Dickson's face narrowed on the acid of Hyde's tone, then he said equably: 'All – *all* the evidence points to that fact, Hyde. We've been over it, again and again. Hence our report to Shelley. You've got *other* information?' There was a tiny tremor of worry in his voice.

'Cass is a *mate* of his, sir,' Miles offered with obsequious sarcasm. 'I doubt very much whether the D-G sent him out here. We'd have heard –'

'Will you put me in signals with Shelley or not? I haven't got time to waste.' He paused, then something about the room, its occupants or the hermetic view from its windows angered him. He caught the scent of perspiration and fear and the prison interview room from his clothing. He clenched his right hand into a fist and banged it down on the desk. Dickson's cheeks flinched. 'I haven't got time to waste on you pair of wankers! Sharmar *framed* Cass – or someone did on his behalf. Sharmar, in case you don't read the papers, is the new Prime Minister – Sharmar is into heroin. Cass *knows* – at least, Sharmar thinks he knows! QED – Cass' life isn't worth a fart after a vindaloo! Now, do I get into signals with Shelley or not?'

Dickson's features glowed with affront. Miles' face had whitened as if with flour, and his eyes moved with a fierce cunning that reminded Hyde of Cass. Hyde saw him nod at Dickson from the corner of eyesight. Collapse of less-than-stout parties. Parties were as much as they were good for, these buggers who'd been prepared to hand him over to Harrell and his *Carpetbaggers* the last time he was in Delhi. Just as they were prepared to let Cass go into the dark now. And Cass had saved him from Harrell, smuggled him out of the airport under their noses . . . he owed Cass a bit of outrage on his behalf and half a chance to go on living.

As if mind-reading, Miles sneered: 'You owe Cass one, don't you, Hyde? He saved your skin a couple of years ago.'

'Just remember whose side *you* were on, Miles. I didn't hear that Harrell got the Congressional Medal of Honour post-humously – did you?'

Dickson stood up. 'I shall report your manner, Hyde. I am effectively your senior – you know the rules. This is *my* bailiwick. However, I'd be interested to observe the D-G's reaction to your claims that he sent you out and that Cass is innocent of murder. I think we can accommodate you.'

'Good!' Miles appeared relieved, and then angry that he experienced a sense of relief; angry mostly against Hyde – perhaps even against Cass. It had been so easy to ignore Cass, even enjoy his predicament. Even Shelley only wanted to be *sure*, just in case something blew up in his face. Bunch of fucking time-servers and cocktail-party spies. 'Let's go, then.'

Clearing his throat, Dickson announced like a butler at a door: 'Jim, would *you* take Hyde down to the Code Room – and *stay* with him, please?'

'Sir.'

Miles hurried after Hyde through the outer office. Hyde glimpsed a flash of amusement at Miles' heightened colour and evident haste on the secretary's face. Then they were passing the tall windows with their view of the gardens and formal, regimented hedges set out for a chessgame that had been assumed to be eternal. Alices, all of them, unaware they were about to stumble upon the Queen of Hearts behind one of the hedges. Miles and Dickson were as stupid as anyone who had

ever Rajed it out here. Sharmar was going to have Cass killed —
— and he had to convince Shelley . . .

. . . not easy.

Miles, at his side on the staircase, exhibited an edge of fretful
anxiety and a contempt for Hyde that was masked by caution.
He was handling a wild animal. The business of the High Commission passed them with careful accents, wearing white shirts
and bright blouses. Then they were in the marbled, pillared
foyer, and Miles nudged him towards a narrower set of stairs
leading down to the building's basement.

'Shelley's not going to like you calling him,' Miles offered.

'Too bad,' Hyde murmured casually. The air was cooler and
musty in the corridor they entered, the walls cream-coloured,
drab and unornamented.

'Things are changing rapidly. Cass is a bloody great *embarrassment* now,' Miles insisted. There was a shirt-sleeved security man
seated on an upright chair at the end of the corridor, beside a
blank door. Hyde saw the shoulder holster beneath his armpit.
'Sharmar's PM now. Big Friend status — and did you know that
he was at Oxford with the D-G? Quite pally they were, I believe.'

'I knew.'

'The boat isn't going to be allowed to rock, Hyde. You ought
to realise that. Not for Cass, anyway. Sending you, mind — I'd
have thought that was to do Cass in. Sure you got your orders
right?'

Miles' broad pink forehead was greasy with perspiration as he
exuded gratuitous well-being, as if after a satisfying meal. He
was no more than an inch taller than Hyde. The temptation
to headbutt the obsequious, crowing little pillock was all but
irresistible. Especially because there was an element of truth
in his supercilious confidence. Hyde clenched his hands in his
pockets.

'What's the matter with you, Miles? Home comforts been
withdrawn until you lose weight, or something?' He turned to
the security man, who was on his feet. 'Get him to open the

door, will you?' Miles wasn't certain, but his confidence was enraging. Most of the man *did* believe Shelley would hang Cass out to dry, just as Dickson evidently did.

'Rogers, open the door.'

'Yes, Mr Miles.'

The Code Room was like an exhibit in a theme park museum. Secure Room for Cold War Purposes, c.1960–1990. A bored young man with a designer stubble climbed languidly to his feet as the door was relocked behind them. Plastic coffee cups and old newspapers littered his desk. The screen of his most immediate VDU was turned away from him. He had been reading a paperback on the English Civil War – probably doing an Open University degree on the quiet. Hyde felt like a maiden aunt inspecting dust along mantels and table-edges.

'This is Geoff,' Miles said. 'Hyde here wants full signals with home, D-G personally.' Geoff seemed as much bemused as impressed. Hyde's name evidently meant nothing to him.

Cass had gone the same way as Geoff – private study, a nice little billet, very little to do.

'Mr Hyde –?'

'Don't bother with the *Mister*,' Miles smirked.

'Just get on with it, sport. I want high-speed voice contact. Get it set up. Should take you two minutes, if you're in training.'

Hyde wandered away from the banks of equipment and especially from Miles. Geoff was already signalling London, while Miles idled his way through a days-old newspaper he had found on one of the work stations. Then he remembered Cass' face, during the first encounter. The bemusement, the stunned horror of any hostage, any victim. Why me? *How* me? Knowing he was trapped in the nightmare, while people like Miles smirked and then ignored him and read old newspapers. It was as if Miles had, indeed, held the English tabloid up as a deliberate insult. A ghastly footballer with vacant eyes and his tongue protruding grimaced at Hyde like something from Bedlam. Cass *was* in Bedlam, his appalled, horrified sense of innocence like a

81

torment, more violent and incarcerating than the prison. *You overweight bastard, Miles*, he thought.

'You through yet?' he snapped at Geoff, hunched at tape-spools and a microphone. Geoff glanced round, his features filled with alarm, as if his competence had been challenged by a remote, aloof professor. 'They're getting Mr Shelley down to their Code Room now – er, Mr Hyde. Won't be a minute,' he added with a tepid grin. His fingers dabbled nervously near the high-speed tapes.

Hyde drew a typist's chair towards the central console. High-speed voice transmission and reception was old-fashioned now – and redundant, by and large. It was associated with operations and urgencies and men and women's lives – and the past. It was quick, covert, almost romantic. He experienced a mild tension merely confronting the electronics. Then a light came on near Geoff's sallow cheek and the tapes whirled, momentarily stopped, rewound at the same speed, then began playing. Shelley's voice, prim, hurried, slightly breathless.

'Patrick? Why have you broken your cover and involved the High Commission? What's wrong?'

The other tape deck waited for Hyde to speak. Voice-activated, no buttons to press. Hyde leant forward almost eagerly towards the microphone. The air-conditioning's soughing was the only sound in the room for a moment, except for Miles' turning of the newspaper's pages. Beside him, Geoff's face wore a childish, uncomprehending excitement.

'Cass needs to be got out soonest. He's in poor shape, he's *innocent*, and he has a story to tell.' He nodded, and Geoff transmitted his words. The tape noise was the brief rush of wings of an unseen bird. Shelley's tape began working almost immediately. Hyde felt his own excitement.

'Who's with you there?'

Hyde's tape seemed to spit back his reply. 'What the bloody hell does that matter – I'm the one who saw Cass.'

A few moments later, into which intervening silence Miles

had dropped a snigger like a pebble; 'This business has taken on a different dimension, Patrick. I have a full report on the Sharmar family from Delhi Station on my desk – I have a long fax from Sharmar himself. It's been analysed, of course – the distress is quite affecting, very genuine. Sharmar has been deeply grieved by his wife's murder. He is not, however, vindictive. Cass will receive justice.'

The voice had become more impersonal than the machinery rendered it. It seemed to echo out into the corridors and rooms of the embassy, and have nothing to do with secrecy; it had become diplomatic.

'Cass is *innocent* – he *didn't do it*,' Hyde enunciated with cold anger. 'Sharmar is in the heroin business.'

'We checked all that,' Miles offered snickeringly, with assumed boredom. 'Cass disagreed with us, went off on his own.'

Then Shelley, before Hyde could reply: 'Cass might just *want* you to believe him, Patrick. There's no corroboration. Sharmar is a force for stability –' Again, the words seemed directed beyond Hyde, out into the legitimate air of the High Commission. Having been absorbed by Shelley from other corridors and vaulted rooms in London. Cass' features did not need to return to fuel Hyde's corrosive anger, though they were there in the dark at the back of his head. '– as PM and leader of Congress, he is now in a position, as a staunch friend of HMG –'

Hyde gripped his microphone. 'You sound like a bloody Foreign Office communiqué, Shelley!' he snapped. 'Just because you were up at Oxford with the bugger, that doesn't make him squeaky-clean. *Howard Marks* went to Oxford, and *he* had his hand in the drugs till! Get Cass out of prison – get him here, into diplomatic custody to await trial. Don't leave him where they can reach him.'

Eventually, Shelley's tapes stilled after rewind, and began to play back soothing assurances.

'My room for manoeuvre is limited. But we have reassurances regarding Cass. Just so long as he pleads guilty on a reduced charge of manslaughter, even diminished responsibility –'

'I don't believe I'm hearing this, Shelley.' Hyde heard his own breathing rustling like hoarse autumn leaves around the foam-capped microphone. Heard Geoff's embarrassment signalled through his fingertips on the desk; heard Miles' theatrical, dismissive sighs.

Heard Shelley.

'– fundamentalist parties getting in because of a scandal involving Sharmar. To put it bluntly, Patrick, the game has gone beyond Cass in the past forty-eight hours.' Beyond me, too . . . Hyde watched his hand curl and uncurl on the grey surface of the desk, like that of a child constantly wishing to inspect a bright insect it had caught. Cass wasn't going to fly away, there was no open hand here. Shelley had paused in the basement of Century House, expecting another outburst. He continued: 'Tell Cass that everything will be conducted through normal channels. Tell him –' It must have been embarrassment that provoked another pause. '– tell him there's nothing to worry about. That he's in no danger.'

'Tell him the committee that sat all day and most of the night in Whitehall don't give a shit about what happens to him as long as he keeps his trap shut,' Hyde offered cynically, and waited. Miles was behind him now, as if looking over his shoulder at a letter he had difficulty in composing; a letter explaining to parents that their son was missing in action. *Missing through inaction* . . .

Shelley's absence the previous day had been at that bloody cookery school in the Foreign Office where they concocted elaborate sauces to disguise the flavour of rotten meat. The Foreign Secretary and his smarmy Permanent Secretary and probably the Cabinet Secretary had all signed Cass off.

And there was no Aubrey to cut through the crap, not any more. It was all assessments, weighings; the Foreign Office's futures market. Sharmar was flavour of the month, and Cass was a nasty smell from the drains.

'Patrick, I understand your – concern. Tell Cass simply to plead guilty when offered a lesser charge. We have certain assurances –'

'He'll be killed trying to escape, Shelley – is that what you'd *like*?'

'Thank you for your help in this matter, Patrick. There's nothing more you can do. If you'd like to leave matters in the hands of the High Commission . . .'

Hyde stood up abruptly, thrusting his hands into the pockets of his denims. He snatched up the rucksack from the floor, and glowered at Miles, who found the outcome immensely satisfying.

At once, Hyde barked: 'It's in your hands, Miles. I'm dumping it all on *you*.'

He allowed his face to be inspected. Miles' gaze crawled on his skin like the sensation of moving ants. Shelley was reprimanding Hyde for breaking cover, but only Geoff and Miles were listening now. He jerked open the door of the Code Room, and slammed it shut again on Miles' parting:

'Have a good flight, Hyde. Enjoy retirement –'

Hyde passed the security man, bestowing a meaningless glare, then mounted the basement stairs to the foyer. Coolness, elaborate cornices and ceiling roses, great, intricate chandeliers. The export department of the Foreign Office. He went through the doors and down the marble steps to the gravel drive. A small flock of black Mercedes limousines was waddling sedately in through the open wrought-iron gates. He had hardly noticed the red carpet spilling down the marble steps. He stepped onto the grass as tinted, unrevealing windows slid past him. The High Commissioner was on the steps. Hyde had noticed nothing in preparation inside the place as he had stormed through the foyer. Business as usual, Praise the Lord and pass nothing more dangerous than the port decanter.

The security man at the gate seemed, by his expression, to lift him in mental fingertips and deposit him like a speck of ash on the other side of the High Commission's walls. As he paused, the embassies and consulates receded from him like great, secure ships in line astern, marshalled for some meaningless review. White and cream, basking like walruses in the early afternoon.

You just didn't do it . . . it could be me, he thought. You didn't leave agents hanging out to dry because it was *politic*. You just didn't do it – and if Shelley didn't understand that, then he understood *nothing*!

'Don't come the old soldier, Hyde,' Ros warned as he threw the rucksack across the sitting room of her hotel suite. He was shivering suddenly, because of the air-conditioning or because of the journey on the crowded, sweating bus; or because Delhi had clamped upon him like a straitjacket, heat and noise imprisoning him as certainly as Cass was incarcerated. He poured beer into a glass with shaking hands, and gulped most of it in a single swallow. 'What do we do now, Hyde? Never mind the tantrum.'

He glowered at her, rubbing his free hand through his dust-dry hair then across his stubbled face, before pouring himself a second beer snatched angrily from the minibar.

'Oh, bugger off, Ros! I've had it up to *here* –!' The flat of his hand chopped at his forehead. 'They're leaving the poor sod to drown in his own vomit!'

After a moment's silence, Ros asked: 'Better now?' Her features fluttered with a muscular tic, and her brown eyes were dark with premonitions. 'You're not giving it up, then?' she said quietly. Then her effort at calm erupted, and her slim hands slapped her thighs and she burst out: 'Why *you*, Hyde? Why do *you* have to care so bloody much?'

Hyde's gaze roamed the sitting room, glancing across the windows onto the alien city. On the table were curling sheets of paper covered with Ros' hastiest handwriting. The mini-recorder sat there, too. As he'd asked her, she had transcribed the contents of the tapes from Cass' flat.

'About Cass, you mean? I don't, really. Except it might have been me, some time, any place. They're just ditching him because the Foreign Office doesn't want Sharmar's nice white suit to get stained.'

'You can't do anything.'

'Maybe not.' He'd lost the tail in the crowded streets, leading them the old dance through crowded alleys and across vast, governmental squares and into the main bazaar. Dropped them one by one. If they knew anything, they knew he was professional. But then, they could have guessed that already. They had no way to Ros — they'd be waiting at his hotel. 'Christ, I don't know what to do, Ros! But no other bugger's going to try — what's on those tapes? Cass' bits and the other bits in English?'

'Liquorice allsorts. Some names, places, dates . . .' The information seemed dragged from her, as if she were being interrogated and was already guilty of betraying colleagues and friends. 'Look, Hyde, I don't want you to go on with this — let's get out of here. Let's just –' She hesitated, her feet shuffling against each other. Then she violently smoothed the full, flower-vivid skirt, and added: ' – get out of here, get on the plane and carry on . . .' Her voice faded, as if something inside, rather than Hyde's eyes, cautioned her.

He waved his arms dismissively as he crossed to the window. Then he turned to face her.

'I am pissed *off* with that attitude, Ros! Not from you, from Shelley and Century House and Whitehall! The *big* picture. It's all *bullshit*, when it comes to it. Diplomacy means don't rock the boat, policy means doing sod all to upset anyone.' He waved his arms again, as if raging at the city beyond the window. He couldn't see the river from here, only the solidly complacent ships and wedding cakes of government. 'Cass is like John McCarthy and Terry Waite and Jacky Mann and all the others — stuffed by a bunch of *bandits* and abandoned by a bunch of wankers wearing Old School ties!' He turned back to her once more, leaning heavily on the table, his knuckles curled hard on her transcription of Cass' tapes. 'Nobody gives a *toss* about *one* poor sod with the shaft stuck up his backside!' He licked the spittle from his lips. The table trembled beneath the pressure of his outburst. 'Cass didn't kill the woman, he was set up for it. Sharmar is into heroin, but that doesn't matter if you've recently become Prime Minister of India and went to Oxford with Peter-bloody-Shelley! They'll kill Cass now, just *because* Sharmar's got the foreman's job at last. Cass is on the way out and no one wants to hear the bad news!'

He turned away from her, poured himself another beer, and faced the far wall of the sitting room as if exiled there for mis-behaviour.

Eventually, Ros murmured: 'Are you sure you're not making this your grand exit, Hyde?'

He turned, enraged, then felt the violent frustration lessen. He said, quite calmly: 'No – I don't think so . . .' Shook his head after a brief pause. 'No, I'm not making it my cause. Any more than any other cause. Sharmar's dealing in filth and now he's hoping to run India. Should I be *pleased*?'

'No. But you're usually just a complainer, not a campaigner.' She raised her hands in almost comic defence. 'OK, I apologise.' Hyde saw accommodation of a kind, however reluctant, and said:

'You're always on bloody marches, signing petitions, making covenants all over the place. This is just charity on the move, Ros – *practical* charity.'

'They're on to you!'

'Not quite – not completely.' He grinned shakily. 'Look, now isn't the time to show you the size of the gap someone like me needs to slip in and out of things.'

'What can you *do*, you stupid bugger? I saw you when you came out of Tadjikistan, mate. *Remember?*'

'And getting blind drunk to forget and not sleeping because of the nightmares – I know, Ros. As to what I can *do* . . . there's nothing in those transcriptions that'll convince anyone?' Ros shook her head reluctantly. Her hands fidgeted in her lap and along the edge of the table, as if they were attempting to dig her out from beneath some fallen weight of soil.

Hyde crossed to the table and sat down.

'Let's see what there is, then. Something — some links, clues . . .' He shuffled the sheets busily, then slyly looked up at her face. 'Are you in, Ros?'

Eventually, she shrugged.

'I'm not leaving you here on your own, mate — not bloody likely.'

He smiled at her, but she tugged her hand quickly away from his as he reached for it.

'OK, then — let's see what we've got . . .' His finger began tracing across Ros' handwriting, his head nodding as he did so. Then he murmured: 'Order some sandwiches or something, will you? More beer.' Her shadow moved on the page as she got up from her seat. He sensed her tension, and her compliance. She'd be getting angry soon, too. Her voice on the telephone to room service faded to the buzzing of an insect.

His hand, curled against his chest as he leaned over the page, was happily clammy. The tracing forefinger occasionally smudged Ros' handwriting.

He picked up a felt-tip pen and began linking material, taking it into the bedroom when the lunch order arrived, bringing it back to the table immediately the uniformed waiter had been tipped and had left. Cass had used the tapes as rough notes, nothing more, bits of breathless speculation and snatches of interview and passed-on information. He noted the name of *Banerjee* — late and lamented, poor sod — and of someone called *Lal* . . . the other name on the crumpled piece of cigarette paper. He hadn't checked Lal — perhaps he should. Ros placed a plate of sandwiches beside his hand and a glass of beer. He nodded his thanks.

There were two other voices, neither of which was identified, neither of which Cass had mentioned — their words were in

Hindi, anyway. The city beat against the window and his cheek, strong as the sunlight. It was the sense of the cool, ordered Diplomatic Enclave, however, that irritated his skin like a rash, rather than the towers and minarets and office buildings. That and the Lutyens Raj now to be controlled by a drug producer. A woman's name, curiously English – no one Cass knew . . . ? No. *Sara*. He scribbled on Ros' pad. *Sara Mallowby. Kashmir – houseboat hotel. Srinagar*. Had Cass been mixing the white sugar and the brown –? No, he didn't know her, not from his first comments. He'd sent whoever *Lal* was, up to Kashmir . . . oh, yes, Lal was the *reporter* – on what, who for?

He heard the cork of a wine bottle being removed, and liquid falling into a glass as if in a slowed-down recording. Almost at once, it seemed, Ros was refilling her glass. His glass was empty, so was his plate. The afternoon was older beyond the window. Eventually he underlined the name of the newspaper, which seemed like the freesheet Delhi equivalent of the *National Enquirer* – no, it appeared to be some radical rag that preferred to work from scandal rather than ideology. Lal had . . . yes, gone up to Srinagar on Cass' advice, to check on Sara Mallowby – when? Two months ago . . . dead end? He sipped at another beer Ros poured him. Sara Mallowby owned some houseboats on Dal Lake. Sara Mallowby –

Shit . . .

He stifled his grin. Crossed to the rucksack and drew out a map, crackling it open as he returned to the table, then spreading it like a cloth. The city intruded at that moment, its afternoon haze deceptive. He bent over the map. Cass had been found with the dead woman . . . there. The resort outside Srinagar. His finger jabbed on Dal Lake's blue smear on the map, while his thumb stretched towards Gulmarg. Sharmar's bungalow –

– shit again . . . Because what he had read was once more under his hand, pierced by the tip of the pen. Sharmar *knew* Sara Mallowby. Sharmar had hosted a party on one of her –

Feverishly, he snatched up the recorder.

'Which tape was this on – about the woman Mallowby and Sharmar?' He looked down. 'Tape two, counter mark one-seven-four – the one that's in here now – yes.' Ros remained seated, forking the last of her salad and sipping her wine. He ran the tape back to the counter mark. He wanted to *hear* Lal's words, not just read them.

'. . . recognised one Pakistani general . . . another of them was the Sikh leader, Khushwan Singh . . .' He let the tape run as if cold water were running against his beating temple. 'The Englishwoman is Sharmar's mistress, I am sure . . .' Finally: 'I will keep the pictures, Mr Cass – they may be useful to *us* – indeed, they belong to us . . .' He switched off the tape and sat heavily down, sighing. Grinning, which became chuckling.

'Oh, shit – what a bloody neat arrangement. They're *all* in it, the Pakis, the Sikhs and the Sharmar family. They're *all* shovelling that shit into Europe – and a different sort of shit all over Cass!' He clasped his hands behind his head as Ros waited with an expectant face. He swallowed carefully, so that she would not remark his guilt, then he said:

'You know Kashmir, don't you, Ros? Know Srinagar and Dal Lake quite well. From your old hippy days . . .'

God forgive me, I'm not risking your life, he thought. Say yes, Ros – please . . . I'll join you just as soon as I've found Lal, wherever he is. Oh, Lal – what a tale you can tell. Ros, say *yes* – I promise I'll watch out for you.

It sounded hollow, as if he were promising into a tunnel that had opened ahead of them.

FOUR

in harm's way

'You are certain of this, Colonel?'

The light of the afternoon fell heavily across the room. The heat was almost kept at bay by the air-conditioning. Prakesh Sharmar rubbed at his cheek below the earpiece of the telephone, where perspiration threatened. His office overlooked Connaught Place and its receding ripples of the modern which stretched out like a whirlpool that might, eventually, suck in the old city and the Red Fort, the temples, mosques and stupas. Every spoke of its wheel was labelled with numbers and the birth-name of Radial Road.

He listened to the colonel in Intelligence with what might have been consternation. It was tight-reined still, but the sweat seemed to break out like little signals of fever around his throat, across his forehead, behind the ear pressed to the telephone.

'The man's name is Hyde?' he repeated. 'He is a British agent – *resigned*? Then what, I ask you, Colonel, is he doing interfering in our business?' It was as if he expected a reduction in price on some item in a bazaar, and he despised the tone of his voice. 'Yes, yes –' he said urgently, the scribbled words on the pad heavily underscored, the whorls and loops of indecision curling away and around the Englishman's name – Australian, the Colonel was explaining . . . 'Yes, yes – I know of Sir Kenneth Aubrey. I also know, Colonel, that he has retired from British Intelligence! You assume that this man Hyde was the thief who broke into Cass' apartment –? You do . . .'

Connaught Place, revealed again as one of his assistants

92

moved away from the broad window on the sixteenth floor of a building owned by a foreign bank, was ringed with high, modern buildings and thronged with crowds as he carried the telephone to the window. To the south, the government buildings and then the Diplomatic Enclave were all but lost in the heat haze. For a moment, it was as if the scene – or just perhaps the altitude of the office – made him dizzy; he was disorientated between the irreconcilable images of India that forced themselves upon him.

'Yes, then,' he admitted to the colonel, the scene and himself, 'the man must be taken care of at once. If you are certain of his identity, and therefore he has masqueraded as a relative of Cass, he is here for some other purpose.' Perhaps, we should not have taken Peter Shelley for the fool he appeared to V.K. at Oxford . . . ? 'No, I think as soon as is practicable. And the other matter – Cass – they must not meet again. That can be taken care of today. Thank you, Colonel. Goodbye.'

Prakesh put down the telephone and then returned it to his desk. He lit another cigarette. It was amateurish, he instructed himself, a case of just-in-case. It was nothing to do with Aubrey, nothing important. The colonel would understand that it must be made to look accidental –

He'd seen Ros onto the Srinagar flight, watching her in a detached way. A fat white woman, travel bag hitched over one shoulder, walking through the Departures door, which slid back like glass lips to swallow her. Then the sense of her on the other side of the glass and her large figure diminishing along the moving walkway suggested her danger and his guilt. He was – *could be* – risking Ros' life, and that was unforgivable –

But he needed information. Shelley would make no move against Sharmar because they were up at Oxford together! Sharmar was untouchable – he grimaced. His eminence was a matter of policy, and Cass – and even himself – had become an embarrassment.

Hyde sighed and stared at the ceiling, listening to the radio news in English and the newest atrocities in the Punjab and Kashmir. He was uncomfortable. Ros was flying into a war zone. The Pakistani army, the woman newsreader's voice informed him, was strengthening its positions along sections of the Cease-fire Line that amputated Indian Kashmir from what they referred to as Azad – free – Kashmir. Sharmar was on the news, of course, soothing and promising. The evening slid across the cracks in the ceiling as if investing a tumbled landscape viewed from a high satellite. A tiny lizard in search of insects followed the dusk across the ceiling.

He'd reentered the hotel without encountering surveillance. If the room had been searched, it had been expertly done. He felt unsettled, itchy to move on, find an even more anonymous hotel somewhere in the Chandni Chowk. But Ros and Cass weighed; restraining him like bonds. He needed to find Lal, the reporter for a scandalous radical rag, wherever he had gone. He was not at home – but his family didn't behave as if he'd been arrested. He'd hovered near the house on his way from the airport. It wasn't under surveillance – didn't *they* know about Lal? A young woman in traditional dress and an incongruous knitted cardigan had left the house and returned with shopping. A child had played in front of the house. It was either a clever come-on, or it was innocent.

He had to get up to Srinagar and Ros soonest. It was a crazy imperative to have created.

He rolled off the bed and twisted the cap on the bottle of Evian water – the one with the French-applied seal that distinguished it from the fakes that induced immediate gut-ache. Sipped the tepid liquid. The travel bag was packed. The Midlands teacher was ready to leave, bill paid. He wandered to the window. There was no way *he* could get Cass out, unaided. It would require pressure, leverage. *We know you're a snowman, a horsebreaker, V.K. – sorry about it, but would you let our man out in exchange for our silence . . . ?* In exchange for *mine*, Shelley. *This chap Hyde threatens to tell the papers if you don't let our chap go . . .*

Hyde grinned and watched the changing of the guard in the hot, crowded, inkily-shadowed street below. His phone call to the rag Lal worked on had produced a *Mr Lal is on holiday* response which was almost certainly untrue. Another phone call had proven it was. A woman's nervous answers, abruptly ended. Lal was on the run, or in hiding. Tonight, he'd make certain.

There they go. Even the surveillance men seemed animated by an Indian courtesy towards one another as they changed duties . . . old team wandering off, new team more alert, selecting new shadows and doorways and innocent occupations. He watched the outgoing team slide away through the crowds –

– coming back. He raised the Evian bottle to his lips with slow, calming deliberation, even as he stepped slightly further to one side, out of sight but still able to monitor the street. The three men who had been watching the hotel had doubled back, reinforcing the new surveillance team. Six of them now –

He looked down at the sweatshirt he was wearing, as if to accuse it of ineffectuality. Its blazon for some real ale made in the Black Country had become a transparent mockery of a disguise, like the dirty trainers and the denims. He had been seen through. His forearm, tilting the bottle to his lips, was stringy with the muscular tension of his grip; the skin quivered as if on entering a cold store. His ears caught the first of the sirens and the men below him moved immediately. He'd be arrested and the inevitable drugs, or some unlicensed weapon, would be found in his baggage – anything to put him in the cell next to Cass for long enough to make the right decision about the burial plot.

He placed the bottle of water on the rickety table with exaggerated care. Pulled the gun from the travel bag, slid a round into the chamber, then tucked it into his waistband, pulling the sweatshirt loosely outside it. Returned for an instant to the window. The siren was muddy, its noise struggling through the crowd. There was one man left on the street. There'd be another at the rear of the hotel, perhaps two. The others would come bolting up the stairs and through the door of his room within —

Time to go.

There were two uniformed policemen in the evening street now, close to the surveillance man.

He opened the door of the room, slinging his travel bag to comfort on his shoulders. The corridor creaked with his steps and with heat and age. Noises of radios from rooms, like the radio he had left on in his own room; the murmur of conversations. He leant over the balcony. Swift, purposeful voices from the hotel desk. Only seconds now. The back exit through the kitchen was out. He returned to his own door, then moved to the end of the corridor and climbed the last rickety, twisted flight up to the attic rooms where the staff slept. Bare floors, paintwork all but vanished, the smell of a urinal despite the open skylight above the tiny-waisted passageway. He reached up. Low ceiling, low skylight. He gripped the wooden frame. The wood powdered and his fingers were gritty with old flaked paint. Just strong enough. He pulled himself up until his head was through the skylight and the evening struck as hot as the hotel passageway against his cheeks. He levered his body through the gap, pushing back the skylight, struggling like an exhausted swimmer on the shore of the sloping roof. His feet came through the opening and he clung to the wooden tiles, his chest thudding against the roof.

He crouched, and closed the skylight. Hardly the world's greatest bluff. Looked around him. Two big-eyed children were watching him, squatting beside a narrow cage in which pigeons chuckled. A goat munched some dry and yellow grass on the flat roof of an adjacent building. The low sun made him squint against its red glare. The occasional television aerial, the odd petrol-tin or cardboard shack erected on flat roofs to house relatives from the country, friends, dependants. Chickens being fed with corn scattered by a woman's hand which glowed with bangles in the sunset.

He reached the edge of the roof. He could cross other roofs, but it would be like moving through open country, and already the curiosity of the roof-dwellers was aroused because he was white. He looked down into a shadowy, noisome alley at the side of the hotel. A sacred cow wandered along it, defecating complacently. A cart with a broken wheel lay on its side, there was the smell of decaying fruit, rotting flesh, and a thin, nosing dog. And two forms slumped in boarded-up doorways which might be those of beggars. Or the dead.

Hyde lowered himself over the edge of the roof until his feet rested on a window ledge. He slid himself down, balanced against the weight of the rucksack, until he squatted on the windowsill like a tame monkey. The darkened room appeared empty. He lowered himself to the next storey, squatting again to regain his breath, then to the ground floor –

Lost patience in a surge of panic aroused by voices on the roof, and dropped the last eight or ten feet into the slither and stench of the alley's mud. He stumbled, righting himself against the bare breezeblock of an outside wall. The smells from the hotel kitchen –

– and then his temple recognised the impression of a gun barrel pressed against it as his neck cringed from the hot breath of the policeman whose triumph was a shiver that communicated itself to Hyde's body.

Cass looked up, slow even to be startled, as they entered his cell. The very last of the sunset was barred redly against the opposite wall. They had arranged themselves on either side of him before he could swing his legs off the cot and sit upright. Two of them in suits. There was no prison officer, no Jawal or any of the other faces with which he had become familiar. His mouth tried to form a protest, but that was difficult because they were almost deferential as they pushed his arms into those of his jacket – just like a couple of express tailors. Their grip on his arms as they marched him from the cell and then along unexpectedly deserted corridors was firm, unshakeable – yet weirdly polite.

He couldn't struggle against them, as if it would be bad manners, a social inelegance. Even though he knew they were removing him from prison on Sharmar's orders, and that those orders certainly, irrefutably, encompassed his murder and the disposal of his body.

Shot while trying to escape . . .

Had he hesitated for another moment after his body recognised the gun and the triumph of the man who held it, it would have been too late. Instead, his hand pushed the gun up and away, the involuntary shot deafening him. His assailant hadn't turned his head away and his large brown eyes were blinking and unfocused. Hyde head-butted the man, and he staggered back, leaving the gun in Hyde's hand, his palm and fingers pained by the barrel's heat. As the Indian collapsed onto the ground, holding his broken nose, Hyde turned away without glancing up at the roof and the source of the cry of alarm, skittering along the alley. He turned into another, narrower backstreet where washing draped between the houses on either side as if to cover the embarrassment the filthy alley represented. Then, after another corner, he blundered into a crowded, violently noisy street – and immediate obscurity. Safety.

Flame roared at a cooking stall, the scent of the food overpowering. He brushed against men, women, a progress of apologies amid the crowd's shallows and sandbars. The sky was blue-black above the awnings and verandahs. He glanced back occasionally, but no individual could have been distinguished in the veldt of faces, and the grass of the crowd did not sway or disrupt with the purposeful movement of a hunt.

Slowly, with increasing certainty, he made his way to the railway station. The porticoes of a temple confronted him after the narrow streets and the press of Paharganj. The square before the station seemed alien within the walls and courts and twisting streets of the old city. Something British-oriental. Above the railway station, the crescent moon already gleamed amid warm stars.

In the main concourse, he reached the left-luggage locker and opened it. He removed a travel bag, more affluent than the faded rucksack, and thrust the rucksack into the locker. The new set of papers, clothing, money – a second gun – were all contained in the travel bag with its fashionable logo. He was, he admitted with cynical amusement, about to go upmarket. He required a better sort of hotel, one out near the Interstate bus terminal – a room with air-conditioning and a TV, as befitted the name in the passport and the clothing in the bag. He looked around him, locating the cloakroom. Better change now and put the old clothes in the locker, and appear at his new hotel clean-shaven – what was the cover? Journalist?

The cloakroom was clean, the water that leaked into the basins slightly rust-stained but hot. He began shaving, the travel bag at his feet, the mirror clouding from the water, its temperature stilling, comfortable. Indians moved in and out with grace and humour; Westerners with hurry and purpose and slight but evident disdain, suspicion of the plumbing. A victim of gastro-enteritis groaned in a cubicle, cursing the country and its back-wardness. Hyde grinned at the mirror. They tell you to bring the tablets, not to drink the water, no ice in your G and T –

He ducked his head and washed the remaining lather from his cheeks and throat. When he looked up, he realised they'd found him.

Expected him, rather. They knew enough to know that the SIS method had always been left-luggage lockers for guns, papers, changes of identity and clothing. Or Dickson or some other bastard at the High Commission had *supplied* the information – just for a laugh.

The man reflected in the mirror was tall for an Indian, lithe, well-balanced and at his ease. Hyde continued to lave his face with the soapy water in the washbasin, watching him from beneath half-closed lids. Through the slight misting of the mirror, he seemed prepared to wait; confident. He was reading a copy of the *Illustrated Weekly of India* with apparent interest. Nothing was overstated.

The gun would be in a shoulder-holster. He was right-handed as he lit a cigarette before returning to the magazine. There was the bulge of an R/T in his pocket. Its weight drew the jacket down over the bulky silhouette of the holster. He'd have summoned assistance. Slowly, carrying the travel bag, Hyde crossed to the row of roller-towel cabinets on the far wall; tugged down the towel and wiped his face carefully, methodically. They must have Cass already – maybe they'd even done him in? Not necessarily. Taking him into their own custody would do for the moment. They might want to know what he'd told Hyde, whether Hyde might be believed, not quite trusting the Old University tie. But these boys were quick and they were good.

They would be – they were working for the bloody Prime Minister of India.

He'd have to make a move for the door. The Indian was waiting for assistance but ready to act. He wouldn't let him run.

Hyde finished drying his face, sniffing loudly. He picked up the travel bag and wandered as innocently as he could to the door. The Indian carefully folded the magazine and laid it on a chair beside him. His hand began moving towards the inside of his jacket, as if reaching for a wallet or comb. The travel bag drew level with the man, feeling like a dog straining at the leash in Hyde's hands. Then the bag leapt at the man's groin, making him wince, expel breath, making his hand hesitate, want to move to the area of the sudden pain – for long enough. Hyde hit the Indian across the throat with the flat of his hand to silence any cry. Hit him twice in the stomach with quick jabs, then once to the side of the head as he doubled up. Before the first raised voice of alarm or protest, he had vanished through the door into the main concourse, his eyes ferreting in the crowd for recognition, gestures, movements, for R/Ts clamped to cheeks like poultices, for guns.

Nothing — not yet. He hurried between bookstalls, food vendors, the detritus of beggars and passengers returning to the countryside and the tourists debouching into the deceptive familiarity of the station. He glanced back once. A railway official was entering the cloakroom, but there was no crowd yet, and no security men or police thrusting their way through the gawpers.

The night air was as warm as a cloak, making him sweat at once. He must go to ground. Dump the travel bag, get another one, then find a better class of hotel —

But they were good and they were quick and they knew exactly who he was and why he was in Delhi . . . and they doubtless knew he was on his own, without legitimacy. Killing him wouldn't cause a ripple, never mind waves —

If Ros ignored the last sultry smoke from one of the fires started the previous night during a minor riot of Hindus through a Moslem shopping area, then Dal Lake was as beautiful as it had ever been when she was eighteen. The water was still and pearly beneath a slight mist that would burn off in no more than another ten minutes. The shikaras of traders slipped in and out of the mist, startling the occasional duck into flight from clumps of reeds. The mist magnified the songs and murmurs of other birds. Last night's rain pearled in droplets along the carved roof of the verandah at the front of the houseboat. There was, as yet, no scent in the early morning that was not sweet. Breakfast was not yet cooking and the woodsmoke from the boiler had nothing to do with human beings, belonging instead to the scene and to memory.

The early '70s. Her youth. Pot and idleness and sex . . . before she became the fat white woman. She had spent almost three years, on and off, in Srinagar and other, more remote bits of Kashmir. Without a single regret. Recalling her father's unyielding hatred of what she — pretended? — to have become and his apoplexy at her wasting her dead mother's money . . . Now, even all that was long gone. She did not need marijuana or

101

anything else to clear her head of her father, as she had in those long-gone days. Pot, idleness, sex — she smiled cleanly for a moment before the nerves returned at the thought of him. She must recommend it to Hyde . . . but she had hardly completed the thought, when she remembered what she was here to do —

— and Sara Mallowby had just appeared at the square, roofed front of her own houseboat, thirty yards of water away. The woman stood with casual, inbred elegance, slightly pigeon-toed. She saw Ros and waved. Ros returned the gesture as Sara Mallowby called, clear as any of the birds or vendors:

'Good morning. Sleep well?'

'Yes, thanks,' Ros replied, clearing her throat.

The muezzin calling the faithful to prayer . . . in *Hyde*'s mosque, where *all* the worshippers were to be regarded with suspicion. It was as if the lake, the hills surrounding it just emerging from the mist and the mountains climbing beyond, all vanished. The illusion that had been herself at eighteen vanished too. She hadn't ever really escaped into Kashmir from Melbourne. She had still had to confront her father and quarrel so violently with him that the next time she had seen him his face was staring sightlessly up at her after the embalmer's work. Nothing she had ever said had touched him. She had always been the *disappointment* registered in her father's hard, forensic glance.

Hyde's work. She stood up. She had the houseboat to herself because it was early in the season, *and anyway*, as Sara Mallowby had explained as they had struggled her suitcases across the causeway to the houseboat in the wobbling light of the Englishwoman's torch the previous night, *I'll be lucky to see any return this year — people won't come to a war zone, will they?*

Am I doing this because I'm still grateful to Hyde for noticing me? she had wondered, crossing the little causeway behind Sara Mallowby. Because he made me not as plain as Dad always remarked? She brushed the thought aside. Hyde wanted to know about the woman —

– who moved with leggy grace along the shore from her own causeway to the one connecting Ros' houseboat to Srinagar. Behind the boat, the moored cookboat was active and the boy was padding along the catwalk, tugging down the awnings against the sunlight now leaping like a tiger across the lake, so that great claws of gold appeared on the water, having thrust through the remnants of the mist. Sara Mallowby's low shoes clicked on the planking of the houseboat. Ros took off the shawl – reminder of cool nights in Kashmir and a former life – and went through the sitting room and the narrow passageway between the bedrooms to encounter her.

Sara's hand flicked through her long hair, brushing its gold away from her face. The sun caught it for a moment, illuminating it like fire catching at straw. Ros envied her carriage, her waistline – her sophistication. Sara reduced her to her father's dumpy, plain daughter in a silent moment, even though the Englishwoman was engaged in a burst of orders and repartee with the cook and his wife. Then, consciously remembering her role, she allowed Ros to precede her back to the verandah and the noise of the lake lapping against its wooden steps. Even so, Sara sat first, crossing her legs, brushing her hair once more away from her fine cheekbones, smoothing her full skirt. *Memsahib*, Ros thought, her guilt making her vindictive rather than merely envious.

'Good – I'm glad you slept. I think it's for early mornings like this I *live* –! But you – you said you'd lived on a houseboat on Dal before?'

Sara Mallowby watched the fat Australian woman as she nodded in reply. Her face was moonlike – gentle but plain, like so many women in middle-age. She was the pretty girl's fat friend and flattering mirror at school. Sara stretched.

'You mentioned you knew Srinagar. Last night, when you arrived –?' she said.

The Australian woman nodded again, her gaze roaming beyond the houseboat, over Dal Lake and the mountains and temples and great clumps of reeds and water-lilies.

103

'A long time ago.' The woman seemed displaced, uncertain now that she had returned to somewhere that might have only ever existed in her imagination – or youth, which was much the same species of illusion. There had been hundreds of Australians, English and Americans in Kashmir, cluttering Srinagar and the lake and the villages and towns or scattered like ash over the hills, back in the late '70s when Sara herself had first come. This woman had been fleeing – what? Her plainness, the unbelievable dullness of most of Australia? 'I stayed, off and on, for almost three years. My misspent youth . . .' The woman's smile was striking; warm, almost beatific. Beneath the moon face and the extra stones in weight badly concealed by the loose, flowing frock, the woman was either currently happy or had at least recently known happiness.

'Didn't we all,' Sara replied drily, a sting of dislike evident like a slight headache. 'Old times –' Her sigh quavered and fell below the genuine, becoming a false note. The woman seemed not to remark it.

Old times. Perhaps it had been a better place when the litter of hippies still lay in the streets and on the lake's margins. Better that than the increasingly stifling Moslem atmosphere of the Kashmir that hated, and was hated by, the central government . . .

. . . better than V.K.'s schemes and stratagems for a different India.

Better than seeing the broken and bloodstained bodies after the atrocities of each night – which V.K. allowed, by restraints on the army and his strategic contacts with Kashmiri separatist groups. Because greater and greater turbulence made Kashmir ungovernable and thus easier to let go when the time came. She rubbed her forehead. It was information she now hated being privy to; there was no lingering glamour of the covert, of the emanated power of the men who met on her houseboat. Conspiracy had become an exercise in sense-deprivation; the technique of an interrogator. It maddened her. Why else would she feel so eager to talk to this fat woman from London, seeking obliquely for news of a place she loathed, a country she had abandoned almost twenty years before? *Old times.*

Bloody V.K. had arranged another of his damned meetings with the Pakistani generals and the Sikh and Kashmiri leaders for that weekend —! To plan, arrange, decide — to caution and control. Only *so* much violence, only *so* many dead. Cold, brutal and clever. As clever as the drugs that founded the family fortune of the Sharmars and helped control the separatists. High-risk strategy — *in which I don't believe any more —! Cri de coeur*, darling, she told herself at once. Too late for that much honesty.

'It used to be a much more relaxed place,' she observed. 'And more peaceful.' The latter bitterly.

'I almost cancelled,' Ros said. 'Didn't even want to come as far as Delhi, then I thought, what the hell —?' She shrugged. 'I suppose I didn't really believe it. Is it that bad now?'

Sara pointed towards the smoke, which had begun to flatten like stretched grey cloth on the morning breeze.

'Last night wasn't too bad. But you noticed the soldiers at the airport?' Ros nodded. The woman seemed to be wandering in a landscape of the past on which the contemporary hardly impinged. That must be why she had continued her journey; these events were only as real as newspaper reports. 'We haven't had any trouble here. But there's only you on this boat and a couple of elderly Americans now on that one — there, the pink and green one. The others left yesterday.'

'How many boats do you own?'

'Four — oh, and my own, of course.'

'You fell in love with the place, too?'

Sara almost wrinkled her face, as if at an odour or the touch of something slippery. Then felt appalled that she had dismissed her own past so easily. 'Yes,' she replied as if in a foreign language, 'I suppose I did.'

The cookboy appeared in the doorway onto the verandah, the

day's menus in his hand as innocent as his smile. Sara said, before he could speak:

'We'll have the French breakfast, Hamdi,' hardly glancing across for Ros' acquiescence. 'Tell your father *not* to overheat the croissants and not to burn the toast. Coffee?' she aimed at Ros, who nodded at the English word amid the evidently incomprehensible Hindi. The cookboy nodded gravely, then vanished beyond the curtain. Pots rattled only moments later signalling comprehension of her orders.

'You evidently did – fall in love with Kashmir, I mean?'

Again, the woman nodded. It was as if she were visibly regressing to awkward adolescence before Sara's gaze. She was leaning gauchely forward, big hands clasped together on her knees, attaching herself through a sense of inferiority and her own plainness to someone more languid and assured.

Ros watched the woman watching her. It was so bloody *easy* to play the part expected of her – plain, dull, naive, mawkish. Sara Mallowby appeared entirely satisfied that she *knew* her and, in knowing, could afford to dismiss her. There was no mote of suspicion in her eyes.

The woman was tense, resentful, and bored. The voice, beneath the clipped drawl, was quavering and uncertain, like voices Ros had heard before, on the Samaritans' line she periodically manned. Like many voices on that line, except the few who had already abandoned all forms of self-deception and defence, it betrayed a person lumbering around a darkened, enclosed space filled with alien furniture, where nothing was familiar. The woman was already worn and eroded behind habit and manner. None of which Hyde would have noticed, of course.

'How was London when you left?' Sara Mallowby enquired as she leant back in the wicker chair, which creaked gently like the small noises of the houseboat against the water.

'Sticky and full of tourists. Do you ever go back?'

She shook her head. 'Not for years. I prefer New York if I

must have the manmade – or Delhi at the right time of year. Sometimes Tokyo.'

'At times I wonder why I still live in London – what with this here.' A faint police siren sounded above the voices of hawkers in shikaras which made finlike trails on the lake. The siren gradually faded. Ros shivered. 'You know what I mean –'

'Yes, I suppose so.'

The breakfast arrived, served by the cookboy and his father. For the memsahib, Ros thought, the proprietor; Sharmar's mistress, hawsered and roped to the shore of Dal Lake as certainly as her houseboats, and as rudderless as they were. A kingfisher flashed in the rising sun. Sara Mallowby's eyes were caught and held by it as if by some imagined alternative, or even a dream. Ros carefully pretended not to notice the swift, dismissive shake of the Englishwoman's head, then the rough brush of her hand sweeping her hair back. Recomposed, she seemed to stare out from above her high cheekbones as if over some fortress wall. The chains mooring the houseboats to the shore of the lake glittered. The roof of the Hazratbal Mosque gleamed against the backdrop of the mountains.

Ros picked up a small plate, helped herself to a croissant. The cook poured the coffee.

'London must have changed a lot – tell me,' Ros heard Sara murmur. She wiped a flake of croissant from the corner of her mouth before replying. One could begin to sympathise with her –

– and Hyde had said, Watch out for that. That's like pointing a gun at yourself . . .

So she smiled as mawkishly as she could manage.

Lal's house, of which the first and second storeys were let out to relatives and assorted tenants, was on Desh Bandhu Gupta Road, north of Main Bazaar in Paharganj. Less than half a mile from the railway station, the point at which the stone of his assault on the Intelligence agent had created the ripples of the search for him. He had found a middle-priced hotel on Ashoka

Road, ten minutes from Connaught Place, booked in, tried to rest – not easy – staring at the bruise spreading on the flat of his hand. He had had to get up from the bed and scout Lal's house twice during the night – an incontinence for action. There were police cars threading the streets, foot patrols, other cars with greater purpose than homegoing or early appointments. No one had stopped him. He was a man in a fashionably shapeless summer suit, loose tie, clear-glass spectacles. A respectable Westerner.

Now, as dawn streaked the sky above the street with pink clouds, delicately coloured and trimmed with orange and gold as roses might have been, he was opposite Lal's narrow house once more. It was imprisoned between a rambling guest house and a tiny mosque. The refuse cart was grinding its jaws outside the guest house and the traffic was already thickening and darkening the air. Further along the road, tapes and the first crowd of the day enclosed the filming of some rubbishy Indian cops-and-robbers movie, screeching cars racing each other along Desh Bhandu and down into Main Bazaar. Hyde had wandered past the filming and the applauding crowd, as he approached Lal's house. It had the necessary earnestness of all movie productions everywhere in the world, and the same unnecessary result.

He had phoned again, in another voice. Lal was not at home, he was *away on assignment*. To his newspaper, he was *on holiday* still.

Then there was the other phone call he had made, before he had picked up the early edition of the *Times of India* and read of Cass' escape from custody. The phone call had resulted in demands as to his identity, a regimented secrecy which had disturbed Hyde. The newspaper had been explicit. *Murderer of Sereena Sharmar escapes*, bellowed the front page. The photograph of Cass – a bad one – had been minuscule by comparison with the glamour shot of the dead film actress. There had been a statement by V. K. Sharmar, and assurances from the Chief of Police. Prison officers were being disciplined for their abominable laxity with regard to a dangerous criminal. Cass' persona was established. When his dead body – drowned, suicide, otherwise discovered – turned up, the case would automatically be closed.

The article was designed to tell him – *him* before the rest of humanity – that it was too late, that Cass had been rendered unreachable. Then to tell Shelley, as a friendly warning and confirmation of his worst nightmare, that Cass *had* done it . . . then to tell India so that there was nowhere Cass could go or be safe.

While they got rid of him.

But they'd want to know – wouldn't they? – what Hyde knew, what Cass had communicated, why Hyde was there, if he'd been sent by Shelley . . . before they killed him? And, if that was to be prevented, then Lal – bloody vanished Lal – would have to come out of the woodwork. Hence, the *urgency*. He'd rung Ros late the previous evening to give her the new hotel number, the new name. She hadn't made contact with the woman, apart from signing the bloody register – he'd checked.

The sky lightened to a washed-out blue, and became less distinct, as the sun dropped heavily into Desh Bandhu. Window blinds had long opened like mouths in the façade of Lal's house and the pavements were already crowded. Lal and his extended family lived on the ground and first-floor front. Faces at the windows, the activity of women. He had asked at a shop on this side of the street, the grocer Lal's wife used. *Yes, Lal's mother, her mother, an aunt, three children, a grandfather* . . . and then the other residents, including a solitary white man who was regarded with tolerant contempt by the shopkeeper. One of those whose head had died years before, courtesy of some permanent drug trip, but who still shambled between the house, the nearest cinema, a bar, and the local mosque, having exchanged an adopted Buddhism for the certainties of the Prophet.

It was after eight when Lal's wife emerged from the house in a violent green and gold sari and a flash of arm jewellery, and turned west along Desh Bandhu. The grocer's description was close enough for Hyde to casually unfurl himself from the wall against which he was leaning. *Haven't seen Lal for years . . . used to work with him before I got transferred back to London. Heard he lived around here . . .*

The same cover would suffice for the wife. He moved like a matador through the traffic to the other side of the street, forty yards or so behind her. Lata. Hyde quickened his pace to overtake her.

The woman paused outside a shop selling locally made clothes. She seemed intent upon men's shirts, and her attention was a small betrayal. Hyde arrived at her side – and startled her, even though he appeared, deliberately, as no more than another window-shopper. She stared wide-eyed into his face. The phone calls enquiring about Lal – the newspaper report of Cass' escape? He closed his hand on her slim, bangled wrist.

'Lata – it is Lata, Lal's wife? I *remember* –!' The little charade was boring and pointless, but necessary to prevent her inviting attention and suspicion from people around her. Did she speak English?

'Yes,' the woman fumbled. 'I do not know you – sir.' It was dropped at the end of the protestation like a curtsey, a racial memory.

'Dave – Dave Holland. No? It's been a long time. We only met briefly . . . I used to work with Lal. Got sent back to London – now out here again. Came to look him up, thought I knew you, you haven't changed –!' Her suspicions remained, but he was now a nuisance, someone who had blundered on a secret, who might cause embarrassment. Good – she knew where Lal was. 'You don't remember me at all, do you? Be honest with me –' His smile was at its most ingratiating. The last vestiges of suspicion disappeared from her fine-boned features, from the huge brown eyes. She shook her head, intending a smile that did not quite break through a small cloud of nerves.

'Mr – Holland? I am so sorry, Mr Holland, but I do not remember. You worked with Lal?'

'Yes, years ago. Before he got onto *Conscience of Delhi* . . . in fact, I was hoping we might work together again. Generous expenses, you know. I could do with local help, you understand? When could I meet him? Is he at home now?'

She glanced fearfully back along Desh Bandhu, shaking her head vigorously. His smile continued, inappropriate and necessary in the atmosphere she had so changed. He was still holding her slim wrist, and sensed the quiver of her arm.

'No, no – he is away, on an assignment. I – he cannot be reached, I am sorry . . .'

'Oh. When will he be back, do you know?'

'He did not say. I will tell him, when he returns. Perhaps you have a telephone number, Mr Holland – ?'

She had remembered the lessons Lal must have drummed into her.

Hyde shrugged reluctantly.

'I suppose so. Don't let him leave it too long. Soon as he gets back –'

'Yes, yes,' she replied urgently, as if she was late for an appointment. Hyde stilled the tremor in his fingers. After a moment, he released her wrist. She snatched her arm away, then her body almost at once, to continue her journey. Then she looked back, nodding. 'Yes, I will tell him, Mr Holland, I will tell him.'

Hyde watched her go, then turned away and slowly crossed the road. She glanced back a number of times, on each occasion more satisfied that he presented no danger. Eventually, she hurried on, oblivious once more.

By that time, Hyde was tailing her on the opposite side of Desh Bandhu, moving coolly, assuredly, through the crowd, weaving between stalls and barrows and sacred cows and ill-parked cars. He was certain that she was on her way to Lal, dragging him unsuspectingly behind.

*

Ros disliked the manner in which she felt she must be imitating Hyde – or, perhaps, the manner in which she was no longer Sara Mallowby's Samaritan at the end of a telephone line replete with intimacies. She was actually spying on the woman. Spying . . . Hyde always referred to himself as an *agent*. She was not an agent, there was no pay cheque and pension scheme to alleviate the sense of unpleasantness and intrusion she experienced, as she trailed the market streets of Srinagar with the Englishwoman.

Especially since she had begun to notice . . .

Sara Mallowby was supervising the purchase of supplies for her four houseboats, for the coming weekend. There was, firstly, the amount, then the selection or variety, and finally the Moslem element. An Urdu-speaking woman accompanied them, together with a Hindu male who seemed to be some kind of head chef and who resented the woman's presence, even though he deferred to Ros as a paying memsahib. A tight flowered cap on her head and a loose, long cotton blouse, her trousers tied at the ankles, the woman was evidently Moslem, passing brightly against the brick and wood of the houses in the narrow streets. Ros knew enough to recognise Urdu – and halal meat ordered at one shop where the butcher's wife wore the full black burka to conceal her form and a chador scarf over her head. Ros had glimpsed her passing across an open doorway at the back of the shop. But the colour of the meat, the language of the customers, were both omnipresent. Was Sara Mallowby expecting strict Moslems, a group of them?

The air was sultry, like a hangover of the retreated monsoon. The narrow streets pressed their crowds against her, and there was a smell of old burning in the atmosphere and a fear of more fires to come. They had passed a patch of dried blood around which insects vainly noised at the corner of the street in which Sara now argued, through the Moslem woman, with the halal butcher. She was evidently known, and respected – the butcher was enjoying the haggling, the selection of meat, the attendance

112

to the ceremonies of slaughter. Ros caught the scent of slow-leaked blood – or an image of it in her mind – and pressed her hand against her lips, swallowing hard. She wanted to distract herself from her thoughts at a papier-mâché artist's shop across the street, but remained obedient to Hyde's strictures. Ingratiation and observation would sum them up. As a compromise, she stared out of the window of the shop, vaguely seeing a grain dealer's sacks beneath broken window-frames and the scorching of fire across the whitewashed brick of the building. Then a woman in spotted robe and headdress squatting outside a greengrocery with a huge basket of carp from the lake.

Eventually, Sara Mallowby had finished with the butcher and, smiling apologetically, guided Ros back into the noise and smells of the street. Which still hemmed her in like thoughts of Hyde and what she was engaged upon. *Pakistani generals*, Hyde had said, repeating Cass' information. *Strict Moslems*.

. But it was the amount of meat and vegetables, fish and fruit, that was being ordered when business was slack and no one else occupied the houseboats except herself and the elderly Americans . . . and the *dislike* she felt at the ease with which suspicion came! She smiled disarmingly at Sara as they paused outside a greengrocer's. A rickshaw loaded with produce brushed past them, heavy as a wagon. Srinagar was laden with odours, depressing her. Making her guilt seem enormous. She shook her head, puzzling Sara, but not inviting suspicion. It wasn't the bloody Samaritans, she admitted. Hyde said Cass had been framed, he was in danger – and she had bloody *agreed* to act as Hyde's bookie's runner until he could get here himself! Oh, Hyde, you bugger, you'd better not have thought of me as just the *bloke* for the job –

'Yes,' she murmured, admiring papier-mâché vases and dishes in a greasy shop window as Sara pointed them out. She manned a telephone at the Samaritans, she helped at an animal rescue centre, she had joined Amnesty International, she wrote letters

113

when she couldn't march or protest in person – and all of it was because she was an optimist who didn't really believe in human wickedness! Hyde had accused her of that, and now it stabbed like indigestion, created by her suspicion of Sara and a gaping hole where a shop had been bombed days before. Flies around a dead dog which no one had bothered to remove, its body broken by the blast. 'Yes . . .' she repeated, so that Sara Mallowby glanced narrowly at her. 'Sorry . . . headache,' she explained weakly.

She *was* naive – at least, not a cynic. That was the problem. They turned into a broader street with cleaner, well-lighted shops. The cloudy noon pressed down on the street, but not as formidably as in the narrow gash of the town they had just left. She wanted to help, the world was redeemable . . . unlike Hyde's world, which was peopled by enemies rather than fellow creatures. That was what she hated about his work – and what she was now asked to do. To pounce upon impressions as if they were facts, to interpret moments as if they were God-given and set in stone; to condemn people on a glance or whisper or facial tic.

It would have been so easy, of course, to have dismissed everything Hyde wanted and suspected – and deal only with Sara's upper-middle-class patronage and uneasy compromise with Srinagar – if it was not for the two men. The one outside the greengrocer's as she had looked from the window of the butcher's shop, near the woman with the basket of carp; and the other paused against an old scorching on a whitewashed wall, his head and shoulders darkly haloed by the mark of the fire. Both men had fallen in behind them soon after they had walked the causeway from Sara's houseboat and had trailed fifty yards behind along a new street of lakeside shops deserted of tourists. Sara had promised souvenir shops, but had concentrated slavishly on groceries and meat. But that hadn't been the problem, even though she recognised she had tried to make it such. The problem had been the two men.

They followed, paused, began again in rhythm with the shopping expedition. And they were tall, hook-nosed, suited. Dark-eyed, arrogant. She was afraid to ascribe a country of origin, but could not but think of Pakistan once they were ensconced in the Moslem butcher's shop. And then could not forget the fanciful identification. The men were watching them, but seemed to be their bodyguards. And so Hyde's world closed over her like water, and she was drowning in suspicion and twitchy nerves and tension. The men were still behind them as they avoided donkey carts and rickshaws and fume-belching buses in one of the main shopping streets. Halal-bled carcases in one window, Benetton sweaters in the one next to it; perfumes and spices, Amex symbols and Urdu. She glanced back from a pause outside a leather shop, where made-to-measure suede coats were being offered at 500 rupees and shoes at less. Italian advertisements induced. Get your genuine copy here . . . The men had stopped, one of them smoking a cigarette, the other unfolding a newspaper, perhaps forty yards behind them. There was little effort at concealment, no effort at disguise. She turned, suddenly, to Sara –

– whose eyes were looking beyond Ros, back towards the men. Her eyes narrowed for a moment, then she relaxed. *Fat, dim woman*. Ros had been dismissed.

But Sara knew the men were there – *expected* them to be there.

'The quality never used to be very good,' Ros offered, nodding at the leather shop's window and displayed goods. 'Fell off your back or your feet in the first cold snap – is it any better now?'

Sara laughed exaggeratedly, also shaking her head.

'Not often. If you're serious, I can get something *good* made – but not here.' She moved away, and Ros followed dutifully.

The street opened ahead of them, and there was a glimpse of mountains, and of the lake carved into a slice by the buildings at the end of the street; a wedge of still, gleaming cake rather than water. Then the street closed about them, quivering as if in a heat haze, before beginning to crumble and bulge outwards. The two buildings had begun to collapse into the street as the pressure wave and the first flying glass struck against them and they still hadn't heard the noise of the explosion –

FIVE

reportage

Lal's wife glided past the tiny mosque and entered her house. From the opposite side of Desh Bhandu, Hyde watched her disappear through the narrow doorway, then glimpsed her pass across one of the windows a few moments later. She paused and bent to kiss an old woman who was presumably either her mother or Lal's. Then the bright sari flitted from the window. The early afternoon sun was like a pressing hand in the busy street and the petrol fumes stirred in the light, hot breeze as visibly as a mist.

Hyde had lost Lata Lal in the lunchtime crowds, in a narrow, twisting street near Chandni Chowk. The Fatehpuri Mosque had glowered down on his frustration, and a cinema's blazons and queue had mocked him. The woman could *not* have suspected she was being followed, it had to have been an accident. Whatever, the result had been the same – she had eluded him when, he was sure, she was close to Lal's hideout. Cars passed, ancient Hindustan Ambassadors looking like old Morris Oxfords, belching fumes, horns continually irritated against inevitable delay. The occasional Mercedes or other imported car, old buses jammed with passengers, bullock carts and rickshaws clotting at the slightest obstacle or opportunity. The waving of arms was a semaphore of distress and anger; part of the ritual of driving in Delhi. Hyde bit into the last of the samosas, savouring the curried vegetables in their pastry triangle. He'd bought them from the cookstall ten yards beyond the alley corner where he had taken up his loungeing surveillance, awaiting the wife's return.

117

His hotel had been checked. His cover passport had been taken away by the police for examination, so the desk clerk had informed him. It wasn't worrying – the passport would withstand any examination, and besides he had a second should he need to use it – but it meant that the search for him had been stepped up, had become urgent; while he was no nearer Lal then he had been that morning.

He wiped his mouth on a paper napkin and deposited the paper plate in an overflowing bin, then moved further along Desh Bhandu. There was no surveillance of the house, so far as he could tell, but the torpor of the early afternoon heat was twitchy with his nerves. He slid around a legless beggar, dropping some rupee coins into his bowl; they rattled ominously, like the first drops of a thunderstorm's rain on a corrugated roof. The situation was too open, too unprotected. He needed to talk to Shelley, even though he knew the pointlessness of such a conversation. Shelley would, in all probability, have swallowed the official story and order him out of Delhi – all expenses paid.

In the midday edition of one of the English language papers, he saw his own photograph – the passport photograph of the scruffy, anonymous man who had posed as Cass' Midlands cousin. Suspected drug smuggler. Rich that, coming from V. K. Sharmar and his brother. He passed a newspaper vendor. Sharmar stared at him from the front page of a Congress-allied evening paper, his expression slightly surprised, as if he had recognised Hyde as he passed. The same photograph, with an English headline, struck him so much that he paused. Sharmar – a reported speech. *We are a nation of entrepreneurs held down by our outdated nationalised industries and institutions* . . . the state banks, the state businesses. *Other parties represent the past – Congress is the future.* Go for it, sport. The big lie. Maybe the bastard even meant it –

– and if he did, then his own life, that of Cass, Ros' safety . . . all meant *bugger all*. Because the apostate who wanted to get back into the church was ruthless with his past and anyone who lived as a reminder of it. Sharmar had made a fortune in a not very nice but certainly not unusual manner, for India and Pakistan, but now it was a loose cannon on the deck which could crush him against the hull of his own ambition.

Fanciful . . . he already knew his life wasn't worth a damn, so why fill in the background?

He drifted back towards the Lal house. Would the woman see her husband again today – even tomorrow? How long could he hang about? How long before Sharmar, his brother or one of the police or intelligence high-ups they controlled stumbled on Lal's name – a snapshot of Lal with Cass, the recollection of some copper keeping an eye on the radical rag and its employees who remembered an Englishman . . . ? The Lal house's shutters were being closed by the old woman, who threatened to burst from her sari and obligatory, alien cardigan. The shuttered façade seemed final, and pricked memory concerning Ros. He was wasting his time in Delhi and he'd placed her in probable danger. He looked at his watch. Nearly two. He'd give it until evening. That night he had to be on a plane to Srinagar –

Headlines against the wall behind the news-stand, surrounding the grizzled, lined features of the seller. *Bombs in Kashmir, rioting in Srinagar*. The possible price might, at any moment, become too exorbitant. You pillock, sending her up there . . .

He must ring Shelley – get some action –

It was settled, agreed. That much was obvious to Prakesh Sharmar as his brother emerged from the party caucus, waving the draft manifesto for the election like a flag. In V.K.'s walk there was the strut of success and the sweep of ideas communicated. And a gleam of distance in his eyes as he saw Prakesh – who turned aside at once from the Intelligence colonel to move towards his brother. The manifesto would be titled *Golden Bridge*, the path to the next century. It was indeed grandiose, but necessary.

'It went well?' Prakesh murmured, his concerns with the

119

colonel remaining uppermost. Behind V.K., the senior Congress party members were filing out of the Cabinet Room. Prakesh checked their expressions as if calling their names and their futures. They were persuaded, even enthusiastic. The meeting had gone *very* well. 'Good, good –'

V.K. was looking over his shoulder, as at a small cloud on the horizon. His firmament had expanded and he filled it like a visiting god, Prakesh realised. He was seized by his own ideals, by a sudden, urgent purpose of good works, of *change* and the incessant business of government.

In less than an hour, V.K. had a meeting with senior representatives of the IMF, to attempt to unfreeze the next structural adjustment loan of perhaps three billion dollars. V.K. would be arguing, together with the young, clever economic advisers they had gathered into their fold, that their indebtedness was a better risk than the horrendously large debts of every country in South America and many in Africa. The loans would come – especially since the manifesto offered entrepreneurialism, privatisation, the setting free of the economy and measures against endemic corruption –

– and *there* was V.K.'s sudden distaste for his brother and for the Intelligence colonel who had drifted to a corner of the anteroom. Endemic corruption. The legacy of the family fortune. The expansion of their father's little plots of poppies designed to make their fortune. How else might a middle-caste, middle-income Kashmiri become Prime Minister of India? The Nehru dynasty had been Kashmiri, but they had had money – and the Sharmars would have remained farmers and clerks forever, without the heroin. Nehru had been a *pandit*, an intellectual, educated. Only money could have placed V.K. where he now was and would be – perhaps – for the next decade . . . and their only resource, their *cash crop*, had been the heroin poppy.

Which was now so inconvenient!

Prakesh shook hands with passing caucus members, his enthusiasm imitating their own. Firm gripping of hands, nodding, the few enthusiastic clichés, the assurance of success. V.K. adopted a more backslapping style, but the hand was laid upon the shoulderblades more as a form of blessing, Prakesh noted, than had formerly been the case. V.K. had grown into his role, but now the past threatened like insects at a broken screen, poised to invade his new and future kingdom.

Then the room was empty, except for himself and his brother and the colonel. As if the man's presence stung him, V.K. burst out:

'It could all end in ruin, Prakesh!' *Mea culpa*, as Catholic priests, with whom both of them had had some contact when schoolboys, would have claimed. V.K.'s hands made a putting-behind gesture, the putting-away of the past.

'It will not, V.K. – it will not,' he soothed.

'Has this man been found?' Sharmar hissed, taking his brother to the window so that they looked along Raj Path together towards the India Gate; the perspective of power.

'No, V.K. – it is only a matter of time.'

'Has he gone to Srinagar – Cass was in Srinagar!'

'No, he has not gone to Srinagar. Our people are in place, there are more than usual precautions at the houseboats –'

'I wish I did not have to go –!'

'You must, V.K. You must continue to deal with these people . . . no, not just in the old way, but the violence must be controlled. Only *you* can ensure that there is just sufficient violence and not too much.' Prakesh squeezed at the expensive shoulder of his brother's suit. 'This is a small matter, V.K. It is being *handled*.'

Sharmar looked into Prakesh's eyes quizzically, and Prakesh despised the weakness he saw in them. He masked his reaction as he murmured:

'The man Lal is still in Delhi. We have someone at that rag he worked for. If Hyde approaches the newspaper, he will be found. Lal's house has been watched. Hyde has not appeared there – as yet. As to – the family *business*, V.K., how could you be in a position to lead the country into the next century, without it? We were not the Nehrus. We had to have money. There was only *that* way –'

'That damned woman! Why did Sereena ever get herself involved with Cass?'

'She was a whore when you married her, V.K. – for the sake of your political career . . .' His brother flinched under the quiet whip of words, then subsided into nodding. 'As you were rid of her, you will be rid of this man Hyde. You *are* the PM, V.K. – unreachable now. *You* do the work you must do – I will do the rest of it.' He sighed theatrically, holding his brother's sleeve.

'Yes, yes. The Pakistani generals are necessary. They must hold back at the Ceasefire Line while Kashmir goes into decline – they must prevent the hotheads in Islamabad from taking advantage. Yes, I must go up to Srinagar and placate them over again.' He leaned forward fiercely. 'But, the drugs, Prakesh –! If anyone found out, I would have to resign. Not just the fundamentalists – the West, America, the IMF and the World Bank. The moral tones in which they would condemn me!'

'Be damned to them, V.K.! I am your brother. We are family. Do you think I would let this happen now?' Sharmar seemed reassured, stiffened – just like a straw doll, Prakesh thought, with a metal rod thrust into it in place of a backbone. 'The manifesto is agreed. You call the election next week, surprising the other parties and that damned film star who is your only rival. I *know* the stakes are the highest, V.K. No one knows that better than myself. Except you.'

'Thank you, Prakesh. But what did Cass tell this British agent?' He smiled disarmingly. 'Just this *last* question,' he added.

'So far, we have got nothing out of Cass. But it won't be long. The prison officer who was present is frightened enough to be telling the truth. He says nothing was said, nothing was passed –'

'Then I won't worry.' V. K. Sharmar looked at his watch, consciously ignoring the retreated presence of the colonel.

Staring instead along the broad Raj Path, scanning the offices of government. 'Better bring in our experts!' he announced heartily, the past forgotten like a dream.

V.K., Prakesh observed, had awoken into his future. He was still in the present but winking in and out of it like a star, really existing in the time after the election; the remainder of the decade and beyond. 'You have no need to worry, V.K.'

They embraced briefly, and then Prakesh, nodding to the colonel that he must exit and wait until their conversation might be concluded, went to a set of doors leading to another anteroom. Prakesh thought of the *corridors of power*. But he knew that the real power was in *rooms*. The occupation of rooms by right, the coming into them as into an inheritance. That was power.

And power was also the colonel and his people, the ability to mobilise steam hammers to crack betel-nuts, to take a huge machinery under control to destroy mere mosquitoes. The man Hyde would be found, and anyone else who might, or might not, be a small obstacle to ownership of these rooms. Lal, for example; a smell from the drains, nothing more.

He smiled as he opened the double doors on the eager young faces of their economics team, some of whom all but bolted from their chairs to begin the changing of India. The slight danger, which periodically unnerved V.K., was to him, enjoyable. A spice. India was, above all, famed for its spices. His smile broadened, to welcome the new recruits into an inner circle.

As the young men filed past him and the colonel slipped into the room they had occupied and sat himself like patient machinery near a tall window, Prakesh Sharmar nodded to himself. V.K. could take on the great work, he would deal with the little problem. A couple, even a few, deaths –

– all that was required.

Ros stared at the gash along her left forearm in the same mood of disbelief as when she had come round in the devastated street. Now, hunched in a cane chair on the verandah of Sara

Mallowby's houseboat, there was further incredulity at the tall man's words, spoken in Urdu, and Sara's contemptuous, pained reply.

'The woman is – *nothing*. It is *not* important – do you understand me?'

He was one of the two men who had formed their bodyguard or prisoners' escort. The other had been blinded in one eye by flying glass. This one, standing between Ros and the afternoon light, his arms working like the blades of a windmill, was protecting –

– an area. Not people, just the place. Ros knew she was *the woman*; inconvenient, possibly dangerous. Then she caught *others*, and the respectful tone. Superiors. Others were coming, Ros was an object of suspicion. Beyond the carnage in the street, the moans of the injured and dying, it was Ros that concerned the tall Pakistani.

A doctor wound a careful bandage around the cleaned and stitched gash along her arm. It puckered like an elongated smirk, as if taunting her memory with the explosion, the bloodied forms on the ground and the helpless screams and waving limbs of the injured. *This* place was alien now, unnerving. Who were the *others* – his superiors? The tone of respect was more immediate than the rusty dribble of Urdu she was able to recall from twenty years before. He had left his companion lying blinded and screaming in pain in the street, commandeered a taxi and driven himself and Sara back to the houseboats. Sara had, despite her own shock, ordered him to remember Ros. She nodded her thanks to the silent, efficient doctor, who moved away. He was watching the tall Pakistani carefully, awaiting his dismissal – with a nod that came almost immediately.

As she pretended ignorance of Urdu and lack of interest in Sara's clipped conversation, she was aware of guests on the other houseboats. The turban of a Sikh on the one next to hers, a bulky, self-important figure posed with binoculars on another. The binoculars seemed trained on Sara's boat, and she realised that some of the tall man's gestures might have been made in the direction of that boat, that man. She shivered.

'All right?' Sara asked with surprising concern, disconcerting the Pakistani. Kashmiri Moslem would explain the Urdu. Though he was *official* in some way, a man used to the currency of orders, discipline. And enough of a stranger to Sara, even though permitted on her boat, to convince Ros that he was not Indian. 'All right, Ros?' Sara persisted with an effort that strangely suggested guilt.

'What –? Oh, yes, thanks . . . Sorry, just a bit dazed still, I expect. The arm hardly hurts at all.' The man watched her with gleaming eyes, at a loss as to how to deal with her. 'God, what a bloody awful thing –!'

'I know,' Sara murmured. She was leaning back against the brass rail that surrounded the verandah, one arm stretched behind her as if trailing her fingers from a punt. 'God, I know.' She was staring at the Pakistani with a hard glare. Then, jerkily, she stood up, and swayed as if dizzy, before holding out her hand to the man. 'Thank you very much for your help. We were very lucky you were there, just at that moment.'

Moonface, moonface, Ros instructed herself, holding her bandaged arm with her hand, seemingly slightly giddy herself as she stared at the lake. Sara's face had been full of instruction to the man; she knows nothing, she's not a problem. It had all been there, and in the pressure of her grip on the man's hand. Finally, he nodded in acquiescence. Ros controlled her relief as the man turned away without again glancing in her direction. Moonface – play dumb. He passed through the curtain towards the rear of the houseboat and the causeway to the lake shore. Sara at once relaxed. Ros swallowed carefully. The dull, plain-girl charade had succeeded. Suddenly, Sara was shivering, rubbing her bare arms as if a cold breeze had sprung up, dispelling the hot afternoon.

'*You* all right?' Ros asked. Sara's features at once bridled against sympathy.

'Yes,' she replied sharply. 'Fine.'

'I see some more guests –' She gestured with a movement of her head.

'Some kind of business meeting, I gather. They've just asked for a meeting room and dinner.' The explanation was pat, tidily clear. 'Bit of a nuisance, actually, but beggars can't be choosers.' She smiled, confident that the thin fiction was accepted. Shareholders' meeting of Poppies for Export, Ros thought. 'They're staying in the area but this is good *local colour*, or something. I didn't take a lot of interest.'

'Bit of an intrusion.'

'What? Oh, yes – it'll have to be my boat. Biggest sitting room –' She laughed. 'I shouldn't say that to paying guests, should I?' Then her features clouded almost at once, as if she was staring – but where? Not across the glittering water towards the tall Pakistani and the man on the other houseboat he had now joined, and with whom he was engaged in an urgent, deferential conversation. Not even towards the meeting soon to occur on her boat . . . Towards something further away; an instruction against laughter that had been issued a long time ago. Sara sighed. 'Scraps from the rich man's table – that's all there is in this business until things settle down. You're sure you're all right? I wouldn't blame you if you left.'

It was not an enquiry or a nudge.

'I might stay close to the lake,' Ros replied. 'I *was* enjoying myself.' She settled back into her cushions as Sara's cook solicitously brought coffee. Sara nodded him away. 'Yes, please,' she added to Sara's gesture with the silver coffee pot. 'Lucky that chap was there, and recognised you,' she murmured, eyes half-closed.

'Yes.' The noise of coffee slight as that of a shikara moving lazily through the water. The birdsong was muted in the heat and the mountains were hazy and distant. Sirens wailed from the town. 'Yes.' She passed Ros her cup.

'My backside's going to be black and blue,' Ros announced,

shifting uncomfortably in her chair. 'Too much weight to bounce,' she added. Then she stood up, shakily. 'Could I use your loo before I drink this?'

'Of course. Same location as your boat. Excuse the mess.'

'Ta.'

Ros forced unreliable legs to move her through the curtain, along the short passageway and into the large, ornately panelled sitting room. The furniture was Edwardian rather than the usual '30s or '40s copies, the drapes heavy at the screened windows. The wood was richly scented. A long dining table occupied half the room, a suite of big chairs and a sofa gathered heavily around the long, inlaid coffee table. Crystal glittered in cabinets. A few oil paintings on the panelling – English landscapes or French ones, Impressionist in execution. They might even have been valuable.

Get on with it –

She knelt heavily by the dining table, as if a bout of angina had doubled her up. Her head rested on the tablecloth that diamonded the centre of the table. She searched with her fingers, then transferred the small metal object from her hand-bag to the underside of the table, tucking it adhesively into the inner side of the table's carved fringe, a polished pelmet of flowers and birds. One of the birds stared at her with bright suspicion. Then she rose to her feet like someone with arthritic joints. Done –

She had brought the bug, hoping to plant it, not anticipating its almost immediate use. Hyde had told her where, how – and how to monitor what it picked up.

And told her to be careful –

As she thrust herself, quaking, towards the bathroom, she tasted sweet, fearful nausea rise at the back of her throat. If they found it, they'd *know* at once –

The Overseas Communications Service office on Bangla Shahib was under surveillance. It had taken him a wasted hour to be

127

certain of it. On Market Road nearby, they were watching the Post Restante. Tightening the noose, or hauling back on a dog-lead he hadn't until then noticed. Were they following him, rather than just waiting for him to fall into their arms? Once or twice, Hyde had thought so, catching suspicious movement like grit at the corner of eyesight. But his instincts wouldn't confirm how close they were.

He had decided he could not go back to the hotel, now his passport had been taken for scrutiny. They might just think of putting someone in the hotel lobby to wait for him. If he went back, it wouldn't be until he had flushed Lal out.

The Telephone Office on Janpath, which ran south from Connaught Place towards Raj Path, was opposite a hotel, and the banks of telephones, though near the broad expanse of the main window, were masked by the hawkers and stalls selling the overflow of India's garment export trade at knockdown prices. And the Tibetan refugees selling carpets, the trinket stalls, the junk jewellery . . . It had taken a great deal of careful time to decide that the Telephone Office was clear of surveillance, then to enter it and place his call to Shelley at Century House. Insecure phone – tut.

He loosened his tie further, wiping his forefinger around the dampness of his collar. The heat in the streets was stifling, the air-conditioning suddenly chilly, even if inefficient. The perspiration sprang in cold droplets along his hairline. It was taking too long, they were too interested in finding him, they held all the cards. He watched the broad glass like a crowded movie-screen for the first signs of intent against him. The gun pressed into the small of his back as he perched on the narrow, folding seat in the telephone booth. Shelley's new secretary was having difficulty in interesting herself in his call, seeming resentfully puzzled that he should have the office number.

'Just tell him it's good old Patrick – telephoning from Delhi, will you, *dear*? What . . . ? He's only being briefed at your time in the morning, dear – nothing he can't break off from. Please do as I ask – *dear*.' The venom calmed his itchy nerves. For a few seconds. 'Shelley?' he eventually blurted out, aware at once that the tone was stretched thin – aware that Shelley, too, would be mindful.

'What is it, Patrick?' he heard asked urgently.

'Cass' escape. Don't believe it.'

'I – must,' Shelley eventually replied. 'I have been given assurances. It's become official, Patrick. The truth.' Shelley's clipped constraint was enervating, at once wearying him. Bright bales of cloth and brighter finished garments were wielded like matadors' capes beyond the window, almost disorientating him. 'You understand me?'

There was reluctance in the voice, a flinch against any accusation Hyde might make. Hyde understood. *Nostromo* was being abandoned. *Without a net*, it had been called – or *Kiss of the Spiderwoman* if you felt anything for the agent who was being disowned. It had happened, though not with Aubrey. The old man would never have –

'I understand,' he replied woodenly.

'Everything points to Cass' guilt – of murder, I mean.'

'Yes, doesn't it? He didn't do it, though.'

'You believe he's been removed?'

'He has. Article of my faith – *Pete*, old mate.'

'But you have no contact – ?'

'No.'

'Then give it up.'

'No.'

The pause was filled with the hypnotic, calming swirl of clothing beyond the window, the glitter of jewellery, the somnolent, surging passage of the constant crowd. Finally, Shelley murmured:

'What can you do?'

'Not much.'

'Delhi Station would be of no help, I'm afraid.'

'That bunch of tossers? I wouldn't ask them to look after

my Auntie Glad. Listen, Shelley – will you use *leverage*? In an *exchange*?'

Another lengthy pause, then, tightly and small-toned: 'Yes.'

Hyde sighed with relief. The old vacillator had come down, finally, as he usually came down, on the right side. Shelley wouldn't lift a finger until there was leverage, something to use. Shelley arrived at the good by way of the broad avenues of career and pension, knighthood and high office. Aubrey had always travelled the narrow path of loyalty, personal probity. More overgrown, harder on the feet, but quicker to action.

'Good. I'll get it for you.'

'Usual *Schedule D* strictures apply.' You're on your own if anything goes wrong. No trades, no official status. 'You think they *are* running drugs?'

'Cass does.'

'Hard to believe – almost impossible.'

'Sure. But they were boys from the village, not the Nehrus or the inheritedly rich. They needed a fortune, and now they've got one.'

'They weren't *quite* boys from the village.'

'Still two generations too close to it – for India.' Hyde relaxed. Shelley had given his word. He would keep it.

'You *can* get something?'

'I hope so. One chance. But quickly or not at all.'

'Then, I'll instruct my secretary to deal with you more respectfully, and man a line for you with someone who'll understand cryptic remarks and your misplaced sense of humour. Right, go quickly and in safety.'

Hyde put the phone down. The imitation of the old man's grave and theatrical concern was intentional, deliberate. I mean what I say. He watched the window, the foyer of the Telephone Office, the row of heads bent or raised, impassive or emotional, along the line of glass-sided booths. No one was interested in him. He looked at his watch. Four. The glass of the window was slightly tinted towards the top, like a car windscreen. The smoky effect was a line of threatening cloud along his horizon of action. He left the hot, enclosing booth, shutting the glass door behind him, then reopening it for a small, plump, saried woman to enter. Ringing Bradford? he wondered. Or Southall?

The cramped, ramshackle façade of the offices of *Conscience of Delhi* was farther along Janpath. He'd call in, see if he could talk to someone who'd worked with Lal, might know or suspect where he was.

What you really have to do, sport, is to flush his wife out, good old Lata Lal who threw off your tail. Con her into going to Lal – today.

Easier said than done . . .

Janpath boomed with noise. Cycle-rickshaws, taxis, old Harley Davidson four- and six-seater auto-rickshaws on their usual routes. Long Mercedes and American limousines, ancient cars tottering like the fragile aged on the pavements. Hands in his pockets, he nudged his way through the crowd. It was impossible to spot a tail – all but impossible to maintain one. A crowded bus debouched its passengers through one door, devoured a new queue of them through another. He passed jewellery shops, statues of the Buddha crammed into niches, beggars, lame dogs, the screams of parrots from a petshop. Then crossed the broad street at the next junction towards the narrow front of the decaying building that housed the radical freesheet for which Lal worked. His hands clenched in his pockets. Lal had – and had kept – information. Lal wasn't a dummy. He had to be found before others found him, and his wife had to accustom herself to a lodger from Intelligence who waited like a spider for seekers-after-Lal to innocently turn up.

He enquired at the reception desk. Behind a flimsy, temporary door, he heard the babble of the newspaper staff. One of the windows had been boarded up, too, which probably indicated someone had attacked the newspaper offices recently.

'Dave Holland – that's H-o-l-l –' The girl seemed insulted,

and her handwriting hurried to overtake his spelling. Then she picked up her telephone and dialled an extension, speaking rapidly in Hindi almost at once.

As she put down the receiver, she said: 'Someone will come to answer your enquiry, Mr *Holland*.' Upper-caste girl with a social conscience? Not prepared merely to decorate an Air India office or a bank counter while she waited for her marriage to be arranged. She indicated a dusty plastic-covered bench, and Hyde sat down near a large tear in the material and two cigarette burns.

He waited for fifteen minutes, increasingly aware of the narrow corridor in which he sat, the cool, distant girl behind the scuffed desk, the front door, and the inner door behind which was a layout he could not begin to imagine – should he need to bolt that way. Then a short, slim young man, bespectacled and sharp-glanced, came through the flimsy door and studied him as he approached, hand extended. Hyde took the cool grip for a moment.

'Dave Holland,' he persisted. 'I'm looking for Lal. He and I have worked together in the past.'

'You are a foreign correspondent?'

'Right. Press Association. I need a runner –' It was intentionally demeaning to Lal and *Conscience of Delhi*. The young man duly bridled.

'I don't think Lal is looking for such work.'

'I'd like to ask him. Generous expenses, all that. Where is he?'

'He is – on holiday.'

'Lata says he's on an assignment.'

'You know Lata?'

'Used to. Which is it – assignment or holiday?'

'Whichever you prefer, Mr Holland.'

'Look, I'm not trying to make trouble – just offer the guy a job. Is that a crime?'

'No. I'm afraid that Lal's whereabouts are a matter for the newspaper.'

132

A young woman in Western dress, accompanied by a man of around thirty in grey slacks and a white shirt, came through the inner door and edged past them. The girl looked sharply at Hyde as the Indian mentioned Lal's name.

'– coffee break,' Hyde caught from the girl before they went outside and the street's noise bullied in. Hyde shrugged.

'OK, I don't want to spoil a good story. Sorry to have bothered you.' He looked around the narrow corridor with undisguised superiority. 'Just tell him I called. When you talk to him. I'll call again.'

He waved a hand loosely and drifted back into the street. His shoulders sloped casually, his hands were in his pockets. He saw the girl in the cream suit and the shirtsleeved man forty yards or so along Janpath. They had paused at a stall selling fruit. The girl had been almost stung by Lal's name. She might know where he was.

He hurried after them as they turned into an ice-cream parlour decorated in black and white, patronised by bodies in Western clothes with loud voices. Hyde saw the girl wave to various tables, then she and the man sat at the window. The Indian waitress who took their order, might have been uniformed for McDonald's. The girl saw Hyde at once as he entered the tiled, chromed room, its fan turning slowly as if mixing the air into a paste rather than cooling it. The air-conditioning struck chill after the street. He approached their table at once and sat down, holding out his hand, which neither of them took.

'Dave Holland. You two work for *Conscience of Delhi*, right?'

'Obviously,' the girl replied, her eyes warning her companion. 'Who are you, Mr Holland?'

'Press Association.' The girl seemed to disbelieve him. 'Look, I've worked the Delhi beat before, now I'm just back after a spell in the UK. I worked with Lal – you know Lal. I just wanted to look him up, offer him some work. Can't get hold of him anywhere.'

The girl held up a cigarette and the man snatched out his lighter. Hyde banished amusement from his face. The crowds flowed sludgily past the windows in the late afternoon light.

'He's not in the office. At the moment.' She brushed lustrous dark hair away from her heavily made-up cheeks. Her huge eyes were highlighted by makeup and the curve of her nose. 'Don't know when he'll be back.'

Hyde turned to the man. 'Look, last I heard Lal was doing some work with a pal of mine, Phil Cass –? Name mean anything?' It did. Would they admit it? The man glanced at the woman, who glared at his incontinence of expression. 'Phil Cass? He and Lal were onto something in Kashmir. Some government scandal – the sort your paper revels in. Do you know anything about it?'

'Are you looking for ready-made headlines, Mr Holland?'

Hyde grinned. 'Not quite. Sharp question, though. Look, Phil Cass has passed stuff to me before now, stuff he couldn't hand on or wasn't being given the prominence – listen, you do *know* Cass is British High Commission, yes?' The girl evidently did. It didn't matter now, his risk of exposure. Risk was inevitable, the foot on the accelerator. 'OK – Phil had me fired up with some dark hints about government high-ups and Kashmir, right? I come out prepared to take up the story, but no Phil and no Lal. I can't find either of them.'

The man was prepared to trust him, that much was obvious. The girl *might* have delusions of grandeur, a sense of the big story. He wasn't sure. Neither of them seemed other than wary of him. They were clean, in that sense. The man said, with the woman's voiceless permission:

'Can you describe Mr Cass?'

'What?' He grinned again. 'Oh, Phil – how much do you know about him? Six foot, fair hair, the skin under his eyes is crinkled like crepe paper – you know what crepe paper is? Speaks Hindi like a native – sorry. Been posted out here for about three years

134

now, went to school –' The woman's glance allowed him to pause. Then she said suddenly:

'We know what Mr Cass is. Do you? *Are* you –?'

'Not in that game, love. Phil was a spook. I got that impression a long time ago. Glad we agree. So – where is he?' He leant forward conspiratorially as he said it. The woman's eyes flickered with something that might have been success, as she said:

'Your NUJ card?' Clever girl – the trouble was, she was too clever. Hyde produced his wallet, then the crumpled NUJ membership card.

'Sorry about the state of it.'

The girl didn't believe the card. It was suddenly a situation that required containment – simply keeping these two at that table until he could exit. The man hadn't graduated to this level of the game, he was just what he appeared to be. But, the woman –

The man blurted, satisfied: 'The police raided us a week ago. They searched Lal's desk and locker, asked questions about him –' The woman's rite of passage to indifference was momentary, but there had been an instant's hard, squinting glare, as if into the sun.

'What were they looking for? Did they find anything?'

'They took a lot of material away, Mr Holland. We lodged a protest, produced a vigorous editorial –' And the woman couldn't have given a stuff, apparently. Oh, yes – she knew the game as it really was. One move to the bog and I'm off, sport. She'd be ringing police HQ or Intelligence at the first opportunity. And she knew what he looked like, his present cover. He prompted the man, even as he watched the woman's eyes watching the windows of the ice-cream parlour. The gun in the small of his back was present in an insistent manner, like someone calling loudly for a debt that was outstanding. She wasn't yet sure. She obviously hadn't a good photograph of him, she hadn't recognised him. Was just suspicious.

'What do you think Lal was working on?' Come on, catch the

scent – *you* could get in on the act, the London expenses.

The man shrugged. 'Something involving the Sharmar family, I believe. I'm not sure –'

'But you don't know *where* Lal is now?' The man shook his head, attempting cunning and honesty in a single, awkward moment. He didn't know, bugger it . . . nor did the woman, that much was obvious. It was becoming a waste of time at a great rate of knots. 'Shame. And Phil's done a runner, too. They must be together, wouldn't you think?' he asked, turning to the woman.

'I didn't know Lal's business very well,' she managed. She lit a second cigarette, but her disguise of calm and haughty indifference wasn't as convincing this time. 'The police were very interested –' The radical journalist had to emerge now, or her cover was snapped. 'He could be dead.' The man shivered. 'Or imprisoned. It happens here –'

'Do the Sharmars go in for that kind of thing?'

'How would I know? Perhaps Lal does?' The contempt was undisguised for a moment. 'I hope not,' she added perfunctorily. The man was nodding in more fervent hope.

'OK, thanks.' He stood up quickly. 'I'll keep looking.'

'Have a coffee,' the woman offered. He shook his head.

'Must dash.' And bloody how.

He turned back after his plunge into the tide of the street. The woman was already on her feet and making her way towards the row of helmetlike phone booths at the rear of the ice-cream parlour. Hyde allowed himself to be drowned in the crowd, taking him instantly away from the man's gaze.

Right, darling – you're the inside-job on the paper, but you don't know where Cass or Lal can have got to. You know me, though. Time to get on with it, then. Back to Lal's place and get the wife stirred up. Some message, some sudden intrusion of danger into the woman's imagination that would drag her out, send her rushing off to where Lal was hiding –

*

It was him, Ros thought, her confirmatory nods making the night-glasses wobble, causing the small, tight group of men crossing the short causeway, to dissolve as if behind oil. Then she stilled her head and the men's faces reassembled in the grey half-light of the binoculars. It *was* V. K. Sharmar, and that was his brother, Prakesh, if their newspaper photographs were anything like. Bodyguards, presumably, around them.

She took the glasses away from her eyes to rest them for a moment, as the Sharmars entered at one end of the tunnel of Sara's houseboat, evidently to emerge at the other end, where a group of men were knotted in quiet conversations on the verandah. The moonlight silvered the lake and the carved wood around her. She pulled the shawl closer around her shoulders and breathed deeply – but softly, as if the bug was capable of two-way transmission and they might easily hear her breathing. The recorder was at her feet as she rested against cushions in the darkest shadows of her verandah, its tape sighing regularly as it turned. The headphones lay in her lap ready for use. Voice-activated, Hyde had explained. Just leave the tape on, it'll collect the info . . . don't listen if you don't want to. She put on the headphones and was startled by the greetings exploding from them. Yes, *Prime Minister*, was an instant reply. It *was* the Sharmars.

Half an hour before, the setting sun had still gilded the water and drawn the mosquitoes, and she had been nervous of appearing on the verandah and attracting their notice. Now, the mountains in the distance were ghostly with moonlight and the lake appeared as if that silvery light was melting into the water, staining it.

Sharmar and his brother passed through the sitting room and beyond the range of the bug, which was picking up no more than distant murmurs now. She raised the glasses. Yes, there they were, amid a tight group of Pakistani Urdu-speakers and a small knot of turbanned Sikhs; perhaps no more than eight – maybe nine, if she hadn't counted in one of the houseboat's servants.

She shivered. The temperature was falling, but it was more than that. She looked down at the recorder at her feet. It was working again, but in the headphones it was only the casual intercourse of security men and orders to the servants. She left the equipment where it lay and retreated into the houseboat, picking up the telephone from its ornate table against one wall. The old-fashioned black bakelite was now a tourist attraction. She felt her body decline into the armchair with heavy tension as she began dialling the number of Hyde's hotel. Talking to him would be enough – she didn't need him there, not yet, she was coping. Even if her fingers did drum out more than mere impatience as she waited for the connection to be made through the slow Srinagar exchange. *Holland* –

'Mr Holland's room, please.'

There was a pause, and the woman's light voice and practised manner were replaced with a peremptory and demanding bark.

'Who is this calling, please? Mr Holland is not available at the moment. Who is this, please?'

She stared, horrified, at the receiver, brandishing it in the air like a rat she had caught attempting to bite her in her sleep. 'Who is this, please? Why do you wish to speak to Mr Holland? Can I take a message for Mr Holland?' Then she thrust it away from her, back onto its rest. The voice had flickered in and out of politeness and threat, cover and reality.

Oh, dear *Jesus* – the bloody police! They knew who Hyde was, they . . .

. . . had Hyde –

The room swirled, as with drunkenness, changing its proportions and form. She could hear her heart in the silence.

Eventually, the room slowed.

Knew – but didn't *have*. They'd have been less eager, a lot more cocky, if Hyde was in their hands. But he'd been Holland for a day, no more, and they knew who Holland really was.

Her forehead was cold with perspiration and her arm throbbed with adrenalin and the stitches. She couldn't warn him, she had no means of contacting him. How could they know about him? Her chest heaved, as if she were being asthmatically assaulted. Her heart sounded louder, yet more feeble and uncontrolled. Jesus, they were waiting for him to turn up at the bloody hotel —!

'Ros?'

She heard the call before she heard the footsteps end their passage across the causeway from the shore. Sara Mallowby's voice.

'Ros? Can you stand some company? *Ros?*'

Ros stared towards the verandah and the recorder lying on the planking of the deck and the night-glasses resting where she had left them.

lord of the dance

The urchin had been easy to find, easier to coach after the lubrication of bright, high-denomination rupee notes. He was already, at perhaps twelve, undersized and beyond small change. Huge-eyed, their darkness almost entirely cataracted with cunning and street wisdom, except where there was concern for the even younger sister who accompanied him and the three-legged dog that had attached itself to them. Ros would never, in a million years or fear of her life, have been able to exploit them. *Employ*. It sounded better.

The message was simple and seemed to cover all anticipated objections – just so long as Lata Lal had met Cass, knew as much as Hyde believed she did, it would work. *Mr Cass has come to me. Do not call, the telephone is intercepted. We are being watched. Be careful. Bring money.* Yes, son, it's crooked. The boy probably wouldn't have done it if he couldn't feel it was criminal, something to boast of later.

After returning across the street, the boy winked at him in the quick dusk, his teeth gleaming bright as his eyes as he passed him. In another moment, he and his sister and the limping dog had disappeared down a narrow alleyway and turned out of sight. Hyde put them out of mind and concentrated on Lal's house; the lights gleaming through the shutters on the windows, the slow passage of time being marked by the door not opening. The thinner crowds offered no chance of missing someone slipping through that door – there was no easy back entrance, he'd checked that. The drug-aged hippie returned from one of his shambling journeys and let himself into the house. The father of the family from the country appeared at one unshuttered window and called to a passer-by he knew. Lata Lal was *not* taken in, was not going to come out –

Half an hour, and darkness, the soft night flaring with sodium lamps, electric bulbs, candles and butter lamps. She's called Lal, he told himself, again and again. She knows it was a bluff . . . Forty minutes. A woman smaller and more rotund than Lata Lal emerged, carrying a shopping bag and a child slung in a tiny hammock across her breasts. The woman from the country. He all but started after her, especially since he had not seen the door open as a crowded bus passed, only seen the woman close it . . . but she wouldn't be undertaking the journey for Lal's wife, carrying her youngest child. Forty-seven minutes –

She was on the doorstep, furtive, it seemed to his stretched nerves. She turned the way she had gone that morning, her face scarved as if to conceal her identity. Hyde crossed the street and fell in behind her, twenty yards back. There was no evidence of other purposeful movement on either side of Desh Bhandu as he passed the tiny mosque and the first of the shops. Ahead of him, her bright-scarved head bobbed and wended through the shoulders of the crowd. Then she turned into Qutab Road. As Hyde reached the corner, the lit windows of a train flashed along the tracks towards Old Delhi station. The line was raised above the brow of houses and shops and the lights of the train made the scene strangely wintry, despite the warmth of the night. Hyde closed to ten yards behind her as she hurried across the street in a surge of pedestrians loosed by a change of traffic lights. It was the same route as before. She wasn't aware or even suspicious of being followed, since she never looked round. The delay might have been the money, or a lack of nerve – anything. Hyde clenched his teeth. Her house wasn't being watched – he was certain of it. Almost.

He'd done as much to change his appearance as he could.

Walk, posture, taking off the jacket of the suit, cigarettes – anything he could do that wasn't makeup or dye that needed an expert. A new tie, red braces. An absolute prick, he admitted, catching sight of himself in a dingy shop window where lizards, snakes and frogs lingered in glass tanks too small for their comfort.

He hurried after Lata Lal, feeling his teeth grinding together in increasing tension, his jaw begin to ache with the pressure. He was fifteen yards behind her as she climbed the steps of a wooden bridge that crossed the main railway tracks as daringly as if over a chasm, fragile and unlit in the night. Still the same route. Her pace had increased. The smell of food from a stall perched precariously above the descent to the other side of the tracks, the exhalation of steam and smoke as a train passed beneath, a vast adapted Russian or American locomotive hauling packed carriages. Already, there were passengers on the roof. He paused to remark its passage, watching sidelong the way he had come. Amid the pedestrians, there seemed no one interested in him. If the operation – if operation there were – were big enough, he'd never see them, they'd waste manpower handing him back and forth between front and rear tails like a ball. Too late now –

He hurried down the steps and caught up to within ten yards of the woman. The train's sparks, lights and smoke moved away into the night as they turned north, then quickly east into Chandni Chowk. His teeth gritted again. It was here he had lost her that morning, at this junction of the Chowk and three other crowded streets. Almost at once, in the darkness and the pools between the sodium flares and the lights from cafés and shops, he thought he had lost her again. Immediate rage of frustration. Then he realised she was still in sight, he was merely dazzled by the lights. The Fatehpuri Mosque gloomed over her. He closed to six or seven yards behind her – he'd hung back too far that morning, the bazaar had been too crowded. Books, jewellery, parrots filled the windows of the nearest shops. Stalls crowded the pavements as if suggesting fraternity with more legitimate businesses. He pressed on behind her, past a cinema queue, past the ugly, garish hoardings. One of the films of Anand Mehta, the new leader of the fundamentalists. A cops-and-robbers spectacular. Above the cinema's entrance, two huge, badly-painted, idealised Indians – Mehta and his leading lady – embraced passionately. It might, a year ago, have been Sereena Sharmar . . . then he realised it was –

– and that he had lost Lata Lal.

Oh, *Jesus* –!

Mehta and the woman's stylised, high-coloured portraits stared down at him as he stood, hands on hips, as if to indulge a bout of temper as the queue shuffled into the interior of the dilapidated cinema. A sitar and tabla boomed, together with a high-pitched Indian voice, from a loudspeaker, unseductive but effective. Sereena Sharmar seemed to mock him, her broad red lips pressed against those of her co-star. Where the hell had she gone? His head twitched angrily to and fro –

– so that she passed all but unnoticed in front of him, oblivious to him, beyond the pay-booth and into the cinema. He stared after her in an effort to convince himself, as if following her was impossible. Then he lurched to the cashier's window, ahead of good-natured protest, paid in loose change and pressed into the flock-papered, red-lit interior, past the betel-nut sellers and hawkers and the saried usherette, into the hot dark.

Lights sprang up for the interval. The cinema buzzed like a hornets' nest and the whole audience seemed at once on its feet, engaged in another element of the ritual of cinema-going. He watched in a moment of calm that was little more than orientation. He had Lata Lal in sight as she swayed down one of the sloping aisles then paused in confusion.

Then she looked up towards the balcony. She seemed the only still figure, besides himself, in the auditorium. The screen flickered with pale images of Indian products. In front of it, she was posed in stylised, intense bewilderment.

Hyde realised, as her head began turning almost mechanically,

143

like some searching, unimaginative radar dish, that this was the meeting place – that she expected him to meet her . . .

. . . but the summons was Hyde's. Lal wouldn't show up. He didn't know his wife was here. He wouldn't show –

'You must be just a little bored?' Sara asked in a desultory tone. 'Sitting in the dark, listening to your Walkman.' Ros saw her smile in the moonlight, her face tiredly paled by the silvery night as it reflected from the lake. Rose looked down guiltily at the recorder and the headphones she had bundled onto the cushions.

The glasses were under her chair.

'What –? Oh, no . . . time to think. You know.' Hyde had said once, on one of the few occasions he indulged in description, that *running for your life was the easy bit. Sitting still and telling porky pies to save your skin was a lot harder.*

God, I hope not, Hyde, I really hope not . . . 'Time to think.'

Sara arranged herself on one of the chairs with unstudied, languid grace. The upper classes must be born with suppler bones –

'Is that why you came? Running away?' she asked. There was an edge to her voice as she touched intimacy then withdrew herself like a child's hand encountering a new pet with teeth.

'Not really . . .' *Making up a cover story as you go along is the worst . . .* 'Well, yes, I suppose so,' Ros added confessionally. Sara leaned forward with what might have been eagerness. 'Just a bit sick of things. At home – wherever that is.'

Sara was silent for a time, brushing her hand through her hair, then she said:

'You came to find yourself the first time – lose yourself the second, mm?'

'Something like that.'

'Some man, I suppose? Tell me if I'm prying –'

'No, it's all right.' Ros settled in her chair, her bandaged arm across her lap, her other hand against her forehead with spread fingertips. She could feel a tremor in her legs and hear the palpitation of her heart. 'Not fundamentally, I suppose – not really his fault.'

'You had someone? A long time?' It was as if she was an anorexic of the emotions attempting to swallow what had become alien to her. Ros was puzzled by the woman. She seemed to have been hollowed out from inside, not just worn. 'Men are buggers,' she added, glaring across the moonlit water towards her houseboat. There was an edge of fear in her voice, quarrelling with contempt.

'He wasn't so much of a bugger,' Ros replied, thinking of Hyde and amused at the pretence. The one thing she did *not* share with her younger self who had first met Hyde was the fear of losing him. She was sometimes – perhaps too often – his mother or his elder sister, but he needed her in all sorts of ways. Even if it had taken years for her to believe it. 'He was a clerk in an office. Not very exciting, but he was a decent bloke –'

Her voice broke, aware that they knew Hyde's new cover, were waiting for him at his hotel, that she couldn't warn him. The sudden rush of renewed awareness made her shiver. Her response was misinterpreted.

'Sorry,' Sara muttered. 'Being on one's own makes one just a little insensitive. Wounds still not healed?'

'Just about.' She gestured with her hands at the bulk of her body. 'Can't blame him, can you? Not much of a catch for any bloke, even a clerk, am I?' She sniffed loudly. 'Don't worry, I've been through the self-pity stage. I only came away while the estate agent tries to sell the flat. I don't think it would be a good idea to go on living there, for either of us.' Again, her voice had caught. There was something cathartic, however, in maintaining the pretence. Her fears for Hyde could be channelled and disguised. 'You said men are buggers – you sound as if you've been handed the shitty end of the stick, at some time?'

People don't notice you when it's themselves they're talking about . . . That wasn't Hyde, that was the Samaritans. It helped now,

145

though, in a way that Hyde would appreciate. Sara began staring at her low-shod feet shuffling on the planking of the deck. Near the concealed night-glasses.

Across the water, the murmur of voices, the subdued lighting of Sara's sitting room showing through the drawn curtains and the mosquito screens. The night was turning chilly. Ros thought she could hear the slow, interrupted susurrations of the tape.

'I've rehearsed the story so many times – for shrinks, lovers, guests, it sounds very pat now, and rather dead.' Sara's smile was ironic, bitter. She brushed angrily at her hair, sweeping it away from her face. 'I wouldn't want to hear it if I were you.'

'Anyone in particular, or just men in general?' Ros prompted.

Sara grinned. 'I did warn you.'

'You did. *Men are buggers*, you began . . . ?'

'How were you with your father, Ros? I ask everyone that. Hoping to find out I'm not a freak, I suppose –'

'Don't ask about the old man!'

'Ah, but the trick is – did you fail him.' Sara observed, her eyes gleaming, her hands picking at the stuff of her full skirt. 'Or did he fail you?'

The lights dimmed quickly, and Hyde squeezed onto a narrow, hard aisle seat three rows from Lata Lal. She seemed similarly disorientated by the communal sigh and the ensuing silence as the film's credits began to roll, superimposed upon a shot of a speeding car. It might have been the movie he had seen being filmed in Desh Bhandu early that morning. The woman hovered against the technicolour images. Latecomers passed across the screen, eager to be seated. The auditorium's temperature rose with feverish anticipation. Dustbins and a fruit stall were sent careering and spilling by the impact of the car, to the unalloyed delight of the audience. Lata La remained standing. At a loss.

Hyde knew he wouldn't get her out of the house again on any similar pretext – it was blown for that night. Blown for good. The hotel was effectively barred to him, his only option was Srinagar. Imperative, not option. Ros couldn't be left on her own any longer. His guilt and sense of her danger nagged more than a decaying tooth, continually present.

The appearance of the movie's hero, played by Anand Mehta, immediately swinging a fist at a scowling, scar-faced Indian, was greeted with a sigh and a great cheer. Sharmar could lose the election to this celluloid hero . . . he'd have to, wouldn't he, *you* can't do anything about bloody Sharmar. At once, Sereena Sharmar – welcomed with almost mystical, revelatory responses from the audience, entered, to rush into Mehta's arms. Sharmar shouldn't have had her killed, she was an election asset . . .

Lata Lal hovered on the edge of another aisle seat, four rows in front of him. She was hunched, her shoulders stiff with fears and dislocated nerves. Sereena Sharmar and Mehta continued their embrace. Cass had had an affair with *her* – lucky sod. Yet it was weirdly unreal, looking at a dead woman on the screen, relating her to Cass and to heroin production and to the woman in front of him, and Ros . . . He hesitated for a moment between the unreality of the appalling movie and the unreality of the situation he had muddied and let slip.

Then Lata Lal got up and hurried up the aisle, to the curiosity of a few patrons before they at once returned their mesmerised attention to the incredulities of the screen. Mehta was swinging from a rope which had been let down from a high window – Christ, I couldn't manage half that without drugs. Sereena gazed enraptured from the window at his spinning, descending figure. Vote for a real hero. Hyde got up and scurried after the woman, who had already reached the heavy curtains on her way to the foyer. The usherette seemed offended that he was capable of walking out.

Lal's wife had paused again, then she began climbing the narrow staircase to the balcony. Hyde followed. If Lal was here, if he was only *here*, he kept repeating. She couldn't just be changing her seat, surely. He swallowed the lump of hope that had risen into his throat. He passed a toilet's odour, then paused at another curtain through which she had slipped. Behind it, a cramped, uncarpeted staircase. He glanced at the splay of light, smoke-roiled, from the projection equipment, then down at the screen, where Mehta, to the evident absorption of the audience, was engaged in another fist fight. Probably beating up Sharmar –

He closed the curtain behind him and ascended the stairs as he heard the sigh and click of a door shutting. In the light of the single weak, dusty bulb, he had momentarily been aware of a gleam of light surrounded by darkness through the open door. The projection room? He reached the door and edged it open a couple of inches. The whirr of the projector, the murmur of voices. A door closing at the other end of the projection room, cutting off the light of another weak bulb. He could see the outline of two heads, smell food. He eased himself into the hot dark of the room. The two outlined heads turned incuriously towards him, and he was surprised by their lack of interest and continued silence. The narrow staircase behind him was vivid in his imagination, then the staircase to the foyer and the corridor to the street, all as if he had walked into a trap. Was that the delay before Lata Lal left her home? That she had been acting on instructions, that the setup had to be put in place?

He opened the other door and slipped through it. A grubby corridor with a door at the far end. The smell of another toilet. The door claimed *Manager*, in English and Hindi. He touched the gun in the small of his back, as if at a talisman, then knocked and quickly opened the door. Lata Lal looked round at him, afraid, while the Indian who was presumably the manager of the cinema rose to his feet in mid-gesture – waving his arms in denial or panic or both. The other man had a gun in his hand and paused in the act of shouting at Lata to waggle it fiercely and amateurishly at Hyde. Christ, it was just like the bloody movie!

The woman's expression was one of recognition and immediate fear. The two men appeared sufficiently alike to be brothers. They had been sharing a curry when Lata arrived.

'Oh, my stupid wife –!' the man with the gun cried out in English, as Hyde raised his hands to the level of his shoulders. 'Who is this man? He has followed you here, you silly woman!'

The manager's forehead was greasy with the situation. Lal's face was vivid with consternation, anger, a growing sense of the gun. Amateurs killed out of panic. Lal would be aware of the room as narrow, cramped, of Hyde's form as something between himself and the door. Hyde waggled his hands.

'Lal?' he said quietly. 'You don't need the gun, Mr Lal. I'm a friend of Phil Cass. You know Phil . . . I'm a mate of his – *really*. And we need to talk – I just came to talk.' On the manager's desk, beneath the debris of the curry, lay the evening paper. 'You must have read he escaped, right? I don't think he did. We *need* to talk.'

The woman was making the room edgy now, she and the manager. Lal himself seemed like an actor off-set, not playing his part, divorced from the imagery and plot of whatever he had been doing with Cass. Just a freesheet radical who knew how serious the police could become, now he'd had hiding-time to think about it. Looking for money or a story, he'd found the shitty world where people disappeared, were no longer a joke but had become a threat to the powerful.

'What damned trouble have you brought me *now*?' the manager protested, glaring at Lal. 'Oh my brother, you have been a damned bloody *fool*!'

'Be quiet, Prem!' Lal snapped back. 'He is alone. You are alone, friend of Mr Cass?' The gun waved, not quite with a life of its own, but nor was it entirely subdued.

'I'm alone.' There was no satisfaction, no edge of nerves that suggested they had only to keep him immobile for a matter of minutes before others arrived. He hadn't been led into a blind alley. 'Can we talk?'

He moved forward very slowly, almost deferential to the gun, and gradually drew a chair from the wall and placed it

149

innocently beside the chair on which Lata Lal perched. He placed his hands, fingers spread, on the table.

'Can we talk, Mr Lal? There isn't a lot of time –'

'What do you mean?'

Hyde raised his hands in innocence. 'For Phil Cass, there's not much time. That's what I meant. They've removed him from prison, he didn't escape. You didn't suppose he had, did you?'

Lal shook his head. 'He would have contacted Lata.'

'Or *me*, Mr Lal.'

'What kind of friend are you to Mr Cass?'

'The kind he needs. Are *you*, Mr Lal?'

Ros sat on, staring at the moonflecked ripples on the lake as they reached the hull of the houseboat and gently touched it. Sara had finished her second whisky and excused herself – to *supervise the servants. These people require extra deference.* Ros listened to her footsteps, quite clear against the hum from the town and the night-noises from the reeds, crossing her own short causeway in the silence after a passing car. Their conversation had been as hypnotic as the landscape under the moon and the noises of Srinagar.

The problem had been absurdly simple . . . Christ, don't I know how simple. Her father, carrying the burden of exposure of his shady business deals by a left-wing Labour MP, had collapsed into self-pity and feet of clay and eventual decline to the moment of suicide. War hero, magistrate, kind father, all gone in an instant. The instant had been England as well as a shotgun cartridge. The easy partnership in property development, the easy money, the easy guilt when the frauds and the exploitations had been illuminated by one self-righteous torch. Sara Mallowby had left England in the late '60s and had never been back to what had become a place without heroes. A place that destroyed heroes. And because there had been no one to turn to, no other close family, no husband or lover. And spent more than twenty years blaming England, politics . . . and her father for not being a continuing hero in unpropitious times.

Enter Sharmar?

Eventually, yes . . . Sharmar, another hero. Dominating, attractive, charismatic, uxorious. Sara had fallen in with him, fallen *for* him, been taken up by him. And had eventually discovered the nastiness under the stones. Ros guessed that she knew it all, or at least most of it, and feasted on the past as a means of dieting with the truth in the present. Sharmar was an idol she couldn't afford to let fall.

Shaking her head, she absent-mindedly picked up the headphones and slipped them over her hair. The tape had wheezed only intermittently during the last half-hour, while the group of men appeared once more on the verandah of Sara's houseboat, breaking off the discussion she had not overheard.

Walkman . . . She smiled. It was well enough disguised. Good job Sara didn't want to share her guest's taste in music. Then, at once, the brief exchange between Sara and the voice she knew to be V. K. Sharmar's mesmerised her. She recognised an excess of guilt as Sara confronted her lover. Their voices were punctuated by her own sharp breaths, heard from beyond the headphones like the cries of a distressed bird somewhere in the lakeshore reeds.

'You seem worried – tired – ?' Politic sex, a stroking operation.

'No, it's nothing.'

'What is the matter? Where have you been?' Diplomatic nostrils and the scent of trouble.

'It's nothing. I need a drink. That depressing woman –'

'What woman?'

'The one on the boat, the one I told you about.'

'Who is she?'

'No one, I told you. How's your meeting – ?'

'Sara, never mind about the meeting.' Political nerves heightened by the situation and declining into suspicion. Pouncing on it. 'Sara, what has upset you?' The stroking gesture again.

151

Ros stared across at the other houseboat from the shadows of her verandah. She was intrigued, fascinated, just as she was by glimpses into Hyde's world whenever he came back, shagged-out from wherever his orders and his own personality defects had taken him. Her own danger struck like melted ice, hardly cold.

'Oh, nothing. You know me.'

'Yes. I do. This woman has been upsetting you, that much I understand.'

'No, she hasn't —! Thanks.' Ros thought she detected the clink of ice, but that had to be her heightened nerves. 'Oh, she's a sad case —' Thanks, darling. '— oh, how long are these people going to be here, V.K.? Can't you get rid of them tonight?'

'Perhaps. You've been talking to this woman?'

'Not about you. Don't be stupid, V.K. — sorry.' The last word was hurried, as if he had glared at her, even raised his hand. 'Just about old times . . . the long-dead past. I'm tired, V.K.'

'Yes. You're sure about this woman? You seem upset by her presence. Can't you get rid of her?'

'She's *paid*, V.K.' An audible sigh. 'She *is* peculiar, though.'

'How?'

'Perhaps it's just a clever person inside a fat body.'

'How clever?'

'Just insight, V.K. Just insight.'

'Into what?'

'Anything she turned her attention to, I shouldn't wonder.' The extra drink had made her mocking, and as rebellious as a teenager. You profoundly silly *cow*, Ros added. 'Goodnight, V.K. Tell them not to make a noise as they leave, would you?'

'She'd better be watched, Sara. Just as a precaution.'

Snatching off the headphones in no measure diminished her sudden, uncontrollable fear. Her coat of bluff, which had been so warm around her as she talked to Sara, had vanished.

Dal Lake spread out friendlessly before her, and the town's murmur was like that of a disturbed wasps' nest. And Hyde's

152

hotel was being watched and she couldn't warn him – couldn't tell him about her own situation, closing over her head like deep water.

'I will not stay, brother.'

The manager got out of his chair, shiftily afraid and very sensible, and motioned Lata Lal to accompany him to the door. Lal laid his free hand on hers and nodded.

'I'm quite safe with this man, Lata. I do not think he means us any harm.' He smiled at Hyde. 'Anyway, he is alone. As stupid –' His features darkened quickly, as if dyed. '– as Mr Cass, walking about unprotected, thinking they can blunder in anywhere!' His eyes glittered. 'As stupid as I have been, my wife, in bringing us all to this!' The gun ground at the cartons the curry had come in, at the sheets of the evening newspaper and the ledger in which Lal's brother had been entering the receipts for the afternoon. Old-fashioned cloth bank bags on the desk.

Lata Lal held her husband's hand imploringly as her brother-in-law waited at the door with undisguised impatience. He held it slightly ajar, and the gunfire from the movie intruded, startling Lal and unnerving his wife.

'It's all right,' Hyde soothed. 'It won't take long. I'll have come and gone before the big picture's finished.' He grinned disarmingly. Lal nodded his wife's dismissal.

As the door closed behind them, Hyde said: 'Thanks. For believing me.'

Lal, surprisingly, put down the gun.

'Lata said someone approached her this morning. Mr *Holland*?' Hyde nodded. 'I thought so. Mr Cass told me that journalism was often a disguise for – his friends. I wondered – indeed, Mr Holland, I hoped –'

'I'm here. The entire US Cavalry – and I mean *entire*. What I *can* do for Phil Cass is to acquire leverage. Understand, Mr Lal? *Evidence*. You have some.'

'You are certain of it?'

'Oh, yes, I'm certain. It was your story, after all. Once Cass had picked the bones out of it, the rest was yours.'

'I warned him about that woman, Sereena Sharmar!'

'Trouble was, he fell for her.'

'Yes, I realised that. I was more cautious from that moment, Mr Holland. Of necessity.'

'So? What have you got?'

'What have *you* got?'

'A couple of tapes Cass had hidden in his flat – which led me to you. The other bloke – I forget his name – he's disappeared. Not like you, though. I think he's dead –'

'I – had heard that, too.'

Lal hesitated now, and stared frequently at the gun, then at Hyde, then at the cracked and peeling walls of the cramped office. Even at the curry's remains. He did not seem lost, simply miserly with what had created his predicament and which might still save him. Why spend it on Cass or Mr Holland? Hoard it until it *had* to be spent –

'It's now,' Hyde said, startling Lal. 'It's now. This is the last chance for Cass – and for you, if you're thinking of bargaining with the Sharmars. The lady down there on the screen is *dead*, Lal. Even you don't believe Cass killed her, do you?'

Lal shook his head.

'I don't think it was possible for Mr Cass –'

'Neither do I. So, where do we go from here? You point the gun at me, and I leave. You shoot me and I'm dead. And so is Cass, and so, probably, are you.'

'The British government will save *me*?' Lal asked scornfully.

'*I* will.' Keep your hands on the table, keep smiling, let's have utmost sincerity in the eyes, shall we? '*I* will,' he repeated. I will, too, if I can. But that isn't good enough for belief. A little cinematic heroism is what is required. Believe me, Mr Lal – come on, *believe me*!

Eventually: 'Very well. I was beginning to hate this place,

154

anyway. My brother has the most awful films here, week after week!' He smiled, but touched the gun's butt.

Hyde sat back on his chair. 'Good. That's settled. Can't say I'm sorry.' Conspiratorial grin. 'They're into drugs, correct? Their whole fortune is founded on drugs. That's what you two found out.'

'We found *evidence*, Mr Holland. We had photographs – of Prakesh Sharmar in the middle of a poppy field, for example. Of V.K. and his brother with high ranking Pakistani officers and government officials from Islamabad – with Sikhs, too, it is true, but the Pakistan connection is the important one. That is how it was smuggled out of Kashmir, with the connivance of the Pakistan army. On its way to the West.'

Lal was proud, and afraid, of what he had done. It had been a radical adventure, *Boys' Own Paper* in an honourable cause. Biggles and Algy exposing corrupt politicians instead of just tapping Orientals and Germans on the jaw.

He continued: 'People who would leave each other to die in the gutter, under any normal circumstances, were embracing like brothers in Srinagar –'

'Where?'

'On V.K.'s mistress' houseboat, Mr Holland, where else? Regular meetings, which we both eavesdropped upon.' The fear had dissipated now in the glow of the righteous goal. 'I have the tapes. Much of what *I* discovered I did not tell Mr Cass. It would have made him too afraid. You see, at first, the woman was useful. Then he became attached to her, and I was no longer able to trust him completely. He began to want to save her.'

'He would.'

'There were land deals, of course, buying more and more acreage to grow poppies – but that is a small matter beside the smuggling itself. It would bring them down, all of them, Congress and V.K. together.' His eyes glowed.

Srinagar . . . Christ. Ros . . . on one of the woman's bloody houseboats!

155

'Where — where would they have taken Cass, do you think, Mr Lal?' The tone was ingratiating, congratulatory.

'To Kashmir. Srinagar. The lake maybe, or one of the houses V.K. and his family own in Kashmir.' He shook his head. 'How much can you do to help?'

'Depends on what you can do to help me.' He tapped his palms lightly on the edge of the desk. His features were bland with confidence and alliance. 'I have to know — *have* — everything. I have to have it now, if I'm to do any good.' Lal was already shaking his head, and the glint of fear had returned to his eyes. 'You haven't got a government you can go to —' He pressed. Neither have I, he thought, all he'd got was Shelley. '— I have. I need proof, to be able to guarantee your safety and that of your wife, brother and anyone else — as well as Cass. I have to get him handed over.'

'Then what will happen to the material I have collected?'

Jesus, the *Sun* or the *News of the Screws* will pay you for it, Hyde thought. Think big, Lal.

'Your story would be worth a fortune in London. Look, it won't be used publicly by my people. It's still yours, in that sense. You'll have made copies?'

Lal hesitated, his forehead creased, for a long time. Eventually, he said: 'I must have time to think about it, Mr Holl —'

'There isn't any time *left*, Lal!' Christ, he had to get to Srinagar and Ros tonight. '*Cass* is in their hands, it's just a matter of time before he tells them where to find *you*. He knows about your brother, I take it?' He did. 'Then get off your arse, get me the stuff, and then lie back and think of all the money the rags will pay you in London, or New York! Now, do it, Lal!'

His reaction must have been subliminal, almost like capturing a moment ahead of the present. His anger was at what he only now seemed consciously to hear. An alarm. Not quite outside, but in the cinema itself. A continuous, old-fashioned ringing. A bloody *fire* alarm.

Lal heard it, too, and appeared wizened as if by the onset of heat and flames. Hyde was already hearing the first distant bells of fire engines thrusting towards the cinema through crowded streets. He rose, hands resting on the table, weight poised – hand on Lal's gun.

'Get the stuff.'

Lal's brother appeared in the doorway, for an instant.

'You must get out now, brother. Lata – I have sent her down the back stairs to the street. I must supervise, and be legitimately evacuated. Hurry, my damned fool brother!' Then he disappeared, his footsteps running along the corridor back towards the projection room. The murmur of the audience, an angry, disappointed hum at first, was now becoming a swell of panic. Hyde crossed to the window, holding Lal's gun by the barrel, and peered down into Chandni Chowk.

Police cars, their lights whirling above their roofs, and the first of the fire engines. A cordon of police and tapes pushing the crowd back, creating a bottleneck into which the audience would be funnelled to be checked. They knew that neither Lal nor himself would come out –

The cordon spread outwards, but there were more police, sifting the audience roughly as it panicked into the wide street. He turned to Lal, who seemed stunted by disbelief, then hurried along the corridor and through the deserted, silent projection room. There was a muffled bellow, as through a megaphone, from the auditorium, and the sound of whistles and orders. He peered, on tiptoe, out of the open flap of the projection window. The lights were on and there were torches sweeping the rows of seats. The noise of boots thudding on strips of carpet and on stairs. They'd be here in moments.

Then he smelt it – the smoke. The bastards were going to have a real fire, one they started. We don't need to interrogate you, sahib, we just want you out of the way, or panicked like a forest animal into our arms. Either way, you're done, sport –

The smoke's scent intensified. He hurried back towards the manager's office. He couldn't go down into the auditorium,

157

probably wouldn't be able to use the fire escape. They had the place sealed off – and now they had it alight.

The office was empty. Lal had gone, neatly, simply, completely. And Hyde realised where. He dragged open the narrow door he had thought must lead to a lavatory, and found behind it a narrow, twisting flight of concrete steps. Lightless, silent. He sniffed.

The fire was approaching. He felt his skin warm and shivered, but that was only imagination. Outside, the sirens of more fire appliances were bullying through the streets. Trapped in the crowds, as he was trapped – oh, *shit* . . .

He closed the door behind him and began climbing the stairs towards the roof of the cinema. It did feel hotter – it *did*.

dark area

There was still no sign of smoke, but it was as if the fumes were already in his head and lungs; choking him, making thought obscure. He dialled the number, watching the door of the manager's office. Lal's gun was on the desk near his dialling hand, a round in the chamber, safety off. This was bloody daft. He had heard Lal moving about in which must be the roof space, heavy-footed and secretive. He had returned to the office – to make a phone call. His action, as much as that of Lal, was stupid beyond belief.

If he didn't call now, when would he? Later would be too late to organise an exit for himself and the man whose stumblings above him settled tiny flakes of plaster on his hair and shoulders and the littered desk.

He rendered his name to the secretary like a threat – then got whoever Shelley had manning the all-hours line.

'Hyde – I want a Dark Area. Understand? Blanket coverage by Delhi Station, active from this moment. Two in the dark. *Two*. Got that? What – location? Tell them a cinema's on fire on the Chandni Chowk. I'm inside –' His nostrils dilated. He could smell the smoke. There were no noises outside the office – yet. The staffer manning the line was clinical, detached – as required. 'No, no ingress. Tell them to wait, then move. Get Miles – say the field agent asked for Miles to command.' He replaced the old-fashioned, heavy receiver with a grimace. The smell of smoke was stronger now –

Wrong composition. He sifted it. The clever bastards, they

were using smoke canisters, just to fill the auditorium and make it look good. *After* the search, the flames. They'd burn the place down if they couldn't find him and Lal, just for the sake of verisimilitude. All the searchers needed were masks and breathing equipment. He strained to listen, but they were being cautious because they had the time. No one was hurrying. He moved to the door and shut it behind him before climbing the lightless stairs towards the roof. Lal had ceased moving, had burrowed into some corner behind inflammable rubbish and believed himself secure.

'Lal?' he whispered hoarsely as he reached the top of the stairs. 'Lal, you pillock, where are you?' The gun was in his hand, his own VP-70 still thrust into his waistband in the small of his back. He listened back down the stairs. Nothing yet. 'Lal, stop playing games!'

There was a small door into the roof space — which was obviously cramped, as only part of the roof sloped. It was mostly flat. The sirens and the noises of the crowd were loud through the thin walls, the broken skylight —

— through which a beam flashed, glaring yellow, stabbing like a finger on an ant. The roar of a helicopter drowned the other noises — he could feel the slightest breeze from its rotors. They'd be putting police down on the roof, or just waiting, marksmen dangling their legs out of the open doors of the chopper like kids sitting on a sea wall at high tide, until he and Lal raised their heads through the skylight or broke through the rotting roof. Neat, encompassing.

'Lal?' he called more loudly as the helicopter's growl threatened to drown his voice. 'Lal?' He pushed at the tiny door, through which Lal must have crawled, unless he was already on the roof —? No. They'd be calling down to him, or shooting at him if he was up there.

He crawled on hands and knees into the roof space. Through dozens of collapses and erosions of the lath and plaster, the helicopter's searchlight seeped and poked. There were patches of damp, and the ceiling between the joists across which he slowly crawled creaked and murmured at his passage.

'Lal – listen, you stupid bastard, they're going to set fire to the whole place! I smelt the smoke before I came up here, for Christ's sake!' There was a whimper of protest, as from a kicked dog, from the darkness away to his right. He turned towards it. 'Lal, I can get us out. I've made the arrangements. It's all laid on. Just come out and let's get moving before we get torched!' There was no need to inject panic, it had already taken up temporary residence in his voice. 'Come on, you bastard! Get off your arse and let's get out of here!'

He still could not see Lal, but could all but smell the man's fear, his retreated self in its den behind what looked like packing cases and old cinema hoardings propped against the far wall. Utensils rattled as Lal shuffled in terror. This had been his bolt hole – still was. Hyde realised, with a sick certainty, that Lal had no intention of moving. *All* safety was here, where he had spent maybe a fortnight or more above his brother's office, emerging for meals like a squirrel in a hard winter. The bad weather's only just beginning, Lal . . . but Lal wouldn't believe that. He was protected, crouched in there behind the garish images of men and women embracing and fighting. The helicopter's searchlight insisted through the roof.

Where the hell was the stuff? In there, behind the leaning, crazed hoardings and the cardboard boxes?

'Can't you smell the bloody smoke, Lal? You'll burn to death if you stay here!'

He *must* be able to catch the scent by now. He wouldn't recognise smoke canisters. He must want to live, or he wouldn't be here in the first place!

Hyde heard the scrabbling of what might have been a large rat, but it grunted with effort and clumsiness like a human in the dark, and then a hand touched his arm and clung to it. Lal's terrified features were caught by a glance of the searchlight. Lal was shivering as he knelt beside Hyde. In his hand he held the straps of a rucksack, then held up the bag as a pitiful offering.

'Come on – keep close to me.'

'Which way can we get out?' Lal began. 'They have a heli-copter on the roof.' *I know they have*, don't ask awkward ques-tions. The smoke was acrid in his throat, as it seeped up through cracks in the plaster of the ceiling below his knees and through the tiny door into the roof space. 'How can we get out, Mr Holland? How can we get out?'

The smoke was thick on the stairs, billowing wearily in the rays of light from the helicopter. They'd be coming any moment, with their frogs' masks and soughing breaths. He turned back to Lal and saw the glitter of terrified eyes. Then Lal must have knelt on the plaster of the ceiling between two joists, and it broke away from beneath his weight, revealing a jagged section of the office below – the littered desk and the strip of threadbare carpet in front of it. The chairs where he and Lata Lal had been seated.

Lal cursed and shuffled. More plaster fell, showering the desk, opening up the office and making the roof space lighter. Hyde could see Lal staring as if transfixed down into the room.

'Come on!' It was as if the joists and plaster beneath him had turned him to stone. Lal seemed unable to move. The rucksack was hanging limply from his grip, down into the office. Santa's fucking sack and he's stuck up the bloody chimney! Sweat streamed from Hyde's forehead and from beneath his arms; a sweat of panic and rage. '*Come on!*' he screamed at the immobile Lal.

Then there was a frog staring up at the hole in the ceiling, and a second, two-legged frog behind him. Both of them had guns. And there was only a moment of shock before the guns were raised towards Lal, who seemed newly afraid of the appar-ition of the security men in breathing apparatus. Hyde made a lunge towards the hand holding the rucksack, but they had already fired twice, both bullets hitting Lal. He slumped forward, deadweight, then toppled through the hole in the rotten joists, tumbling onto the littered, plaster-strewn desk – to roll to stillness at the feet of one of the men who had shot him. The rucksack obligingly obtruded itself by lapping against the man's legs.

Lal was dead and they had everything he had. Everything . . . Hyde couldn't move for the shock of enraged disappointment. The searchlight's streams of light filtered into the cramped space where he knelt, its fingers touching his shoulders as if to arrest him.

The black tube of the Minimodulux night-vision module attached to the SLR camera tapped in nervous accompaniment as she attempted to steady it on the windowsill of her bedroom. Her fingers were damp with perspiration. The image intensifier tube was less than eight inches long and weighed no more than three and a half pounds, yet it felt leaden. She heard the footsteps of the police officer Sharmar had instructed to check on her, crossing the planked causeway from Sara's boat to the shore. Her tension invested the camera and its surveillance lens. The motor whirred, startling her, as if a weapon had accidentally discharged. The Sikh and the Pakistani were together at the blunt prow of Sara's houseboat, posed as if they understood they were being photographed. They were almost the last of Sharmar's guests to be caught by the night-vision tube and the shutter's click – then she would be done.

The footsteps along the shore were masked by the last of Srinagar's nocturnal activity. In a moment, they would sound on the causeway to her boat. Ros blinked away the perspiration that coldly blurred her vision.

She dragged the camera and the Minimodulux back through the window and slumped onto her bed, the betraying apparatus seeming strange and unmanageable in her quivering hands. The first footstep sounded on the planking at the back of the boat, sharp in the gleaming, still night. *A routine check*, she had heard Sharmar instruct – the brother, not the Prime Minister. *Check her papers – say it's for her safety. Get her to think of leaving.*

With what seemed a huge effort, she untwisted the image intensifier from the camera and fumbled a harmless, commercial daytime lens onto the body of the SLR. Folded it, in rhythm to the approaching footsteps, into its case. Surely, he'd wake the cook, wouldn't he, or the cookboy, and pause to explain himself? The Minimodulux lay phallically, full of threat, on her wide lap. The footsteps halted. The sound of the police officer's voice, then the cook's voice. *The memsahib is asleep*. Her terror made her want to giggle at the archaic form of respect. The policeman was not to be deterred. Ros clutched the tube against her breasts, as if intending to flee with it as with some prized possession from a burning house. One of the cats –

Christ, Hyde –!

She blundered across the bedroom, its furniture indistinct in the moonlight filtering through the mosquito screen – banged her right shin against a chair and stifled the exclamation. Then feverishly opened the bedroom door as the door to her left was tapped politely. She lurched across the narrow corridor and dumped her shivering body on the edge of the bath, still clutching the tube against her. The knocking sounded again, a little more peremptorily. The cook's murmur still protested her innocent sleep, which the policeman brushed aside. She stood up, her legs weak, and placed the tube on the lid of the toilet. Bending forward, she felt nauseously dizzy. As quietly as she could, she lifted the top of the cistern and placed the Minimodulux into the tepid water, replacing the lid gently, holding her breath, a terror of perspiration bathing her. Then she sat down on the edge of the bath once more. She stared down at her clothing, hanging in creases and folds. She hadn't changed, she was supposed to be asleep, her light had been out for nearly an hour –!

Christ . . . She held her forehead with her hot, damp palm, and forced her lips to move, rehearsing sound as she cleared her throat. The words seemed farther back than the sweet taste of nausea. She was shivering, and clutched her upper arms with her hands, arms folded tightly across her breasts.

Eventually, after the knocking had occurred once more: 'Yes? Who – is it?' A thin, reedy voice, like an actress playing the radio part of a child. 'I'm – who is it?'

'Ms Woode? I am from the police. It is a routine matter. May I come in?'

'Wait a minute – I'm busy. Hang on.' She had managed to shape her fear into something that approximated irritation. She stood up and deliberately flushed the toilet. Realised, as the cistern noisily emptied, that the Minimodulux tube was audibly moving against the vitreous china. As the flushing noise faded, and the cistern began to fill, there were small, distressed tappings. She stood, frozen, her hand having turned the cold water tap in the basin.

Cold water –

She dabbed the cold water on her face, rubbed at the wetness with a thick white towel. Smoothed her creased frock – *frock*, Christ –! She pulled the bathrobe from its hook behind the door and tugged off her dress, throwing it over the bath. Then she struggled into the too-small robe and tied it across her middle. Untidied her hair as she walked to the outer door and unlocked it.

'Yes?' she snapped, expelling nerves in the pretence of annoyance.

The police officer was dressed in a lightweight suit, was slightly taller than herself, and prepared to be deferentially pleasant – for the moment. The cook hovered apologetically behind his shoulder.

'I am sorry, Ms Woode. I am Inspector Dhanjal, of the Srinagar police. I am ensuring the safety of visitors to our city, in view of the circumstances.' His English was polished, carelessly displayed like a family's accumulated objets d'art. He wasn't any ordinary Kashmiri copper . . . drugs? The stitch you up with an illegal substance kind of copper? Ros quailed. She'd heard Sharmar's brother give his instructions, but the conversation had moved about the room like a weak radio signal, wavering into audibility. And there had been a murmured babble from the other guests. 'We would not wish anything to happen to any of our foreign visitors,' Dhanjal added.

'Thanks for the concern,' Ros bridled. 'Does it mean you have to disturb me at this time of night?'

Dhanjal raised his hands apologetically. 'I am sorry for that. Your arrival has only just been processed. I'm sorry. But I would like to ensure you are safe here. Could we call it a security check, perhaps?'

Search. Christ, Hyde – you owe me for this bloody lot!

'I feel safe enough.'

'But – an expert eye, perhaps?'

'The town seemed quiet, tonight.' She was holding onto the door. The bloody cistern hadn't finished filling up yet! 'Is there any cause for alarm?'

'Perhaps not.' His eyes were becoming suspicious, glinting in the moonlight. The air cooled her body beneath the bathrobe, tautened the skin on her cheeks. 'Nevertheless, we of the Srinagar police –' Blow that for a tale, mate. '– would feel happier if we had made a security check on our visitors. Especially those in such isolated positions as this.'

Just let the bugger in, Ros – just let him in. It was as if Hyde was prompting her. It even sounded like him. He's getting suspicious, he thinks you should be more frightened by rumours and bangs offstage.

'Yes. I see. Come in, Inspector.'

She held the door wide for him and he squeezed past her. The cook shrugged another of his interminable, silent apologies, and departed towards the cookboat. The lights of Srinagar were a hazy, deceptively peaceful glow. As she turned, Dhanjal was already checking the windows of the lounge, having switched on the lights. At once, there were small explosions of insects against the mosquito screens.

Ros followed him into the lounge. He was determined to make a search, that much was evident.

'Are Ms Mallowby's boats a special target, then?' she asked, disconcerting Dhanjal, who looked up from an apparent inspection of a window lock. Beneath the window, Ros' handbag yawned. The fingers of his hidden right hand had played over it, she guessed.

'Oh, no, I would not wish you to think that.' His English was suddenly more stagily Indian as he, too, deceived. This is going to cost you, Hyde – real money. She seized on the idea. It's adding up, Hyde. Fifty quid for the Cats' Protection League. 'It is wise to be sure, however.'

'OK. Pity you had to wake me up, though.'

'The bedroom windows, please?' He put down the telephone. 'This way.'

With a trepidation she could not entirely suppress, she opened the door to her bedroom.

'Ah, I'd advise you did not sleep with the window open, Ms Woode,' Dhanjal said at once, turning to her. That's another fifty for the Samaritans, Hyde, she announced to herself. In a strange way it calmed and distracted, enabling her to appear off-balance and nervous in a way that was free of guilt and professionalism – which he would be looking for. I *am* a bloody amateur, she told herself.

'I won't.' He closed the window for her. 'Just used to fresh air.'

'In London?' He shook his head. 'Ms Woode, I really do not think that this houseboat is very secure, though it pains me to slander Ms Mallowby.' He smiled. 'But, I would suggest a move to one of the larger hotels – for your own safety.'

Was he there to threaten, or inspect? Suddenly, Ros did not know, and was unnerved. Bugger fifty quid handouts, she calmed herself. This is *really* serious. Two hundred quid for Famine Relief . . .

'I – I take it I can choose?'

He had moved out of the bedroom, having glanced through the window across at Sara's houseboat – and seemed satisfied

167

at the safety of distance. Glanced, too, at the camera, then disregarded it. An unspecialised Japanese 35mm SLR – which it was. *Now.* She controlled her breathing, but felt a tremor in her flesh that made her wrap her arms more closely about her.

Dhanjal peered into the bathroom, hesitated – so that she hovered at the brink of panic for what seemed minutes – then withdrew his head. Then he marched through the lounge once more and opened the doors onto the verandah. He stood with his hands on his hips, staring at Dal Lake like a visitor.

Then he bent and picked up the recorder, turning it in his hand like a nugget of what might only be iron pyrites. The cord of the headphones dangled from the recorder. Smiling at her, he picked up the headphones and pulled them over his head. Ros watched with assumed, taut passivity. He listened for a moment before switching off the recorder. Then he inspected the cassette inside.

'I am, perhaps, too young to remember,' he murmured. Cheeky bastard.

The meeting had declined into huddles and coteries. Some members had even left. She had concealed the tapes in her suitcase and substituted *Blood on the Tracks*. This Kashmiri didn't like Dylan – but felt that Dylan fitted with the image he had acquired of her.

A concept of innocence, of middle-aged prologue to pathos and decline. Fat white woman. Hyde, it's bloody two hundred and fifty to the NSPCC if it's anything!

Dhanjal seemed satisfied; mystified, and irritated that he had been despatched on a pointless little exercise. His self-importance made him intolerant, impatient.

'Thank you, Ms Woode. I would heed my advice, if I were you – but I can do nothing to force you, of course. Good night.'

With a great effort, Ros closed the door slowly behind him, then leaned back against the perfumed wood of the corridor's rich panelling, head lifted to the carved ceiling. Oh, my God –! Oh, my sainted bloody Aunt –!

Hyde, you'd better get here tomorrow – I can't stand any more of this. No more of it. Charity donations or not, *get here!*

Hyde ducked aside from the ragged, gaping hole in the ceiling, uncertain that he remained undetected. The two men in the frog-mask breathing apparatus still had their guns drawn. They seemed mesmerised by the body of Lal lying amid the plaster, his head at a strange angle, the light palm of one hand twisted so that it appeared about to accept a furtive remuneration. They were drawn to the rucksack, which had obligingly spilt folders of snapshots at their feet. Had they seen him? They'd flinched back at Lal's fall, after they'd shot him, and now one of them was kneeling beside the body. He could hear the artificially loud pumping of their breathing inside the masks. There was a leak of dark blood across a wedge of fallen plaster, near the feet of the man who remained standing.

He decided they hadn't seen him. They were in no hurry now, he recognised, peering forward down into the room, balanced on his haunches, hands taking much of his weight. Their magnified breathing was more immediate than the noises of sirens and the continuous, disregarded din of the fire alarm. The helicopter's rotor noise had retreated too, filtered out for the sake of survival.

Feet were dropping onto the roof above him, regular small detonations. The chopper was dropping two – three? – men onto the roof to link up with these two below –

Noise of an R/T, from the room. English rather than Hindi. Official language. He leaned forward, like a monkey about to leap from one branch to another. The snapshots, Lal's papers, the other contents of the rucksack, were spread on the littered, plaster-strewn desk, and were being relayed to whoever had command outside, or in the chopper.

'– the man Lal, confirmed, sir . . . yes, the material is very interesting, sir.' The tone was authoritative. These two, and the men on the roof, must be elite troops. Either army commandos or Intelligence. 'Yes, sir – we'll bring the bag and leave by the roof. Sir –'

Hyde watched, appalled at the idea that they would climb the stairs, pass his hiding place and leave by the door onto the flat roof. He might hide over *there*, in a still-dark corner . . . Forget it, he admitted, as he saw the man with the R/T draw a wedged, bulky pistol from inside his black windcheater and aim it at the sagging sofa. Flame glared at once, dazzlingly bright. A flame-cartridge pistol. He had turned his head away, but his eyesight was flaring with solar images. The acrid smell of the charge, the smoke from the sofa which would choke him –

They'd start other fires now, burn the whole place down. His vision wouldn't clear. The two men moved through smoke and flame and the sunspots on his retinae out of the room towards the stairs. The fumes from the sofa were scratching at the back of his throat. Without conscious decision, he had closed the small door through which he had crawled to find Lal, and listened now as their footsteps climbed towards the roof. R/T voices crackled like flames. They were hurrying now, the rucksack prize enough, the burning cinema a rather definite kind of insurance against having overlooked anything. The roof door banged open, then closed again on the bellowing of the helicopter.

He clasped his handkerchief over his mouth and nose. The whole of the roof space glowed like the interior of a small furnace, and the smoke and fumes rolled upwards. The office was burning a bloody treat. There was nothing left up here, nothing he could see. Lal had had everything in the rucksack, everything that was going to make him rich. His body was obscured by smoke, licked at by flames. Hyde's temperature soared.

The helicopter's rotors moved away into the night, leaving the noise of the alarm and the sirens of fire appliances and ambulances. They'd left, assured of an irrefutable certainty – if the Englishman was inside, he was dying or dead already.

He opened the door. The staircase was blind with smoke. He coughed retchingly against the fumes, more dense now. His lungs felt hot. Something exploded in the office below. He eased his way up the stairs, hand sliding along the wall, and kicked open the door to the roof. He staggered out, his body overwhelmingly relieved yet flinching against an anticipated flurry of shots from someone they might have left on the roof. He dragged air in, his head spinning, his lungs bursting.

Flames gouted from skylights and gaps in the tiles where the roof sloped, like a line of flares laid for the night landing of a small aircraft. He hurried to the edge of the roof and looked over the parapet. His eyes ran with tears, and he brushed them away. The side alley was taped off and empty. He saw firemen passing its opening onto the Chowk, the snake of hoses, the gleam of a ladder reflecting hot flame. There was no drainpipe, no fire escape. He was trapped on the roof, as they had anticipated. He looked up wildly. The lights of the helicopter as it retreated were no bigger than the warm stars. They were bloody certain. He glanced around the roof. There was no escape.

He felt the panic rising. Nothing rational was going to get him out. The panic had to do it or nothing would. He stared at the roof across the alley, and at the barrenness of the cinema's roof. No ladders, no planks, nothing he could use . . . distance? Too much.

Alarms and sirens were louder, phantasmagorical. A part of the roof, a whole raft of wooden tiles and joists, fell inward, leaving a volcanic hole through which the fire erupted. Most of the pitched part of the roof had gone, sliding with a terrifying laval noise down into the bowels of the auditorium. The flames glared over him and he was enveloped by smoke. He was gasping and coughing as a shift in the slight breeze moved the fire closer to him. The concrete beneath his knees and feet seemed to be hotter.

He looked longingly across the gap of the alley to the other, smaller roof. It wasn't flat like that of the cinema, but sloped with ill-fitting wooden tiles. There was no lip of guttering. He could see two skylights set like eyes, seductive and mocking. The

171

parapet was a couple of feet high, he'd have to jump onto the parapet and thrust himself off, land flat – it was impossible, but what was the alternative . . . ?

Do it.

He backed away from the low parapet, walking steadily, sensing the heat against his back, feeling his temperature climbing inexorably –

He ran, head down, the parapet jogging towards him. He was as helpless as if he was in a car rushing towards a collision. Images of flame, images of pain and broken limbs, the swallowing sensation of falling, the parapet under the arch of his foot, the last stride and thrust from a powerless leg, the moment above the alley, and then the collision.

The breath was forced out of his body, his chest and stomach ached, his knees were stabbed with pain, his hands hurt as they slapped against the wooden tiles – tile coming away in his right hand, left one loosening, hands scrabbling, his body slipping, so that his feet and ankles were over the edge of the roof, then his shins and knees –

Right hand holding, holding –

– left hand scrabbling, come on, you bloody useless *thing*, get hold of something . . . breath impossible to draw, the blood pounding in his temples, left hand, left hand – legs waggling over the alley, pointlessly seeking purchase against air –

– left hand holding, right hand climbing, stomach and crotch shrugging themselves further up, back onto the roof . . . right foot holding against a gap where a tile had been dislodged.

He lay there until he was certain that there were no noises from the alley other than those funnelled from the Chowk; until he was assured he had broken no ribs or limbs. Until the first ragged gasps had become breathing that was recognisably human. The sirens had died like the anticipation of a crowd that had been watching him. Behind him, another section of the roof of the cinema collapsed and he was bathed in brighter, fiercer light from the fire. There were sparks in the breeze landing beside him, on him. Smell of singed cloth and hair. He beat at his head with one hand. Licks of flame leapt from the wooden roof on which he lay spreadeagled.

Slowly, carefully, unable to suppress a grin that felt like a rictus after cyanide ingestion, he climbed the roof, wriggling his way up like a crippled lizard. He reached the nearest skylight and heaved it open. Old paint flaked. Below him was darkness. He crouched, then lowered himself carefully into the musty scent. A roof space littered with boxes and junk. His feet touched joists and he released his grip on the frame of the skylight. Balanced himself, hearing his breathing magnified by the musty silence, then fished in his pockets for the cigarette lighter whose lid clanged open like a steel door. The wobbly flame was little more illuminating than the reflection of the fire, but he saw the joists –

– and the hatch from the room or stairwell below. Opened it, listening to the gurgle of a water tank and the rusty whirr of a bat. The glow of the fire through windows revealed an office. He dropped into the room.

Then he hurried. Three flights of stairs, the offices and corridors becoming progressively better decorated, more Western and proclamatory. The ground floor was a travel agency.

Through the windows, he could see the play of hoses and the scamper of fire-fighters and the taped-back crowd in the Chowk, the scene played upon by an orange light. He made for the rear of the building, his elbow aching, splinters in his left hand, his knees raw, chest aching with each breath – *no* broken ribs, he reminded himself. He smashed a small window when he found the door locked. A narrow yard, an open gate, then an alley. He paused for a moment, then brushed at his clothes. Pockmarked with the singeing of sparks, greened by the old wooden tiles. You'll do – in the dark, anyway. He coughed again. His throat was raw from fumes and smoke.

Where would they be? On the Chowk – Miles wouldn't have the imagination to look round the back. Casually, after checking the pistol – he'd lost Lal's gun somewhere – he followed the alley until it junctioned with a crowded street, then made for Chandni Chowk. Paused at the corner. The police had long since completed their check on the cinema audience, who had melted into the absorbed, gabbling crowd held back by tapes. Fire appliances and police cars and ambulances littered the street. Glass exploded somewhere in the direction of the cinema.

He waited for ten minutes.

The young man who approached him furtively even glanced at a photograph – presumably of Hyde – before making contact. He seemed more concerned with his form of address than with anything else.

'I – Mr Hyde . . . *sir*?' Was he a sir? Did he have any rank? Hyde saw the young man's eyes bemused by the total significance of his question.

'Don't worry about it.'

Surprised, the young man said: 'Lowell – Hyde.'

'Lowell,' Hyde replied, luxuriating in the nervous shiver of relief that possessed him. 'Where's Miles? Let's get on with it.'

'This way.'

Two more fell in with them as they walked along the Chowk away from the cinema, where the blaze seemed to be slowly falling into the grasp of the fire-fighters. A pall of smoke hung over the street and the smell of burning cloth and wood clung about them. Dark Area. The relief was stronger now, its effect making his legs rubbery and ill-moving. The aches of his impact with the roof nagged. Lal's death – *the loss of what Lal had!* – was a hangover of frustration and anger.

Lowell opened the door of a black, stretched Granada parked two blocks away from the cinema. The street was crowded, its occupants moving, pausing, shopping with strange normality. Hyde glanced behind him, as if to assure himself of the reality of the fire. Miles' features glared up at him from the rear of the Granada.

'Get in!' he snapped. Hyde grinned contemptuously. 'Where's the other one? *Two* in the dark, you claimed.'

'He didn't make it.'

'Come on, for God's sake – don't waste any more of our time!'

'All right, keep your drawers on, Miles –'

He bent to climb into the rear of the car. Sitting beside Miles was an Indian in an expensive grey suit, his hands calmly resting, palms down, on his thighs, his interest in Hyde apparently minimal.

'Come on, Hyde –'

'Who the hell is *he*?'

'You don't need to know. The deal's done, Hyde. You're on your way within the hour – and good bloody riddance! You're guaranteed –'

'This is supposed to be a Dark Area – that doesn't mean black faces, Miles. What the hell have you done?'

'How the hell else could we have done it in the time?' Hyde was aware of Lowell, the others. 'It's a *deal*! You'll be –'

'You prick, Miles! You think Gunga Din here –' The Indian's face was pinched. '– is just going to see me off the premises? You *pillock*!' he raged, appearing absorbed in the confrontation, aware of passers-by stopping, off-balanced by his raised voice. Miles' features were puzzled, then enraged. 'You made a deal with Intelligence because you're too bloody idle to organise a Dark Area!'

'You'll be in London tomorrow morning, Hyde – out of my hair! Get in the bloody car!' He was already looking over Hyde's hunched shoulder towards Lowell and whoever else had closed in behind Hyde.

'Tell him where I'll be,' Hyde snapped at the Indian. Calculating eyes alive, mouth a narrow line, a sense of preparation. His people wouldn't be far away – he wouldn't trust Miles either. 'In the morning – bottom of the bloody river!'

'Get him in the car!' Miles barked, but Hyde slammed the door before the order was complete. Miles rocked back in his

175

seat, staring at the hand he had rescued before the door closed on it. The Indian's hand was reaching for his door handle. Hyde's elbow caught Lowell's soft midriff, before he turned and saw the other two of them hesitating as Lowell buckled over, retching.

Hyde moved into the crowd at once, then into the first side street off the Chowk. Dark Area my arse! Miles just wanted the horse manure removed from the street and thought the Indians, nice polite chaps as they were, on our side and all that, would help him put Hyde on a safe flight out of Delhi, back to London. What a dickhead –

He slipped and minced through the thinning crowds without looking back until he reached the Mukherji Marg, north of the Chowk. Heading for the railway station, they'd assume. Having to get out under his own steam. He thought he saw one bobbing head, then a second moving radarlike to locate him. The black Granada, too, ploughing through the crowd as if across a muddy field. The Indian Intelligence officer was out of the car, so was Miles, both of them angry as they bundled themselves in the direction they knew he had taken. He hurried away along Mukherji, then crossed the street towards a rank of decrepit taxis – a few black hackney carriages, ancient Ambassadors, the revenants of old European cars. He scanned the railings of Mahatma Gandhi Park, the portico of the railway station, the town hall. Picked out Lowell, still delicately clutching his stomach, another face he recognised, two purposeful Indians, and the Granada.

Then he bent into the first old taxi at the rank.

'Safdarjang Aerodrome – no haggling, I'll pay what's on the clock.' Twice the price, but then, twice the eagerness.

'Certainly, sahib – into the back, sir!'

Hyde climbed in, raising dust from the ancient upholstery. The Ambassador pulled chuggingly out into the traffic, heading west before it turned into Shradha Nand Marg, paralleling the main railway line towards Connaught Place. He took out his wallet and removed the scrap of paper on which he had scribbled the pilot's name. A two-Cessna operation called Krishna Air

Taxis, flying anywhere – for a price – out of the aerodrome near the racecourse and the polo ground. They'd be watching the trains, Indira Gandhi airport, the bus terminals, but they might not be alert to a small plane taking off from the aerodrome.

Might not. If he was quick.

It had seemed more certain when he'd booked the flight to Srinagar that morning, as a backup. It had seemed much more certain, then –

Ros lay in the darkness, the headphones of the recorder against her ears, her body half-propped on pillows. Her position suggested an uncomfortable sense of hospital, of invalidity, to her frayed, worn nerves. The illuminated dial of her travelling clock showed three-fifteen. Only the Sharmar brothers remained on Sara's houseboat, and awake. She had not heard Sara's voice since she had dismissed herself from Sharmar's presence hours earlier. V. K. Sharmar showed no interest in joining her in bed.

She knew what they were doing. Arranging India's future. Carefully sustaining and controlling the violence in the Punjab and Kashmir, so that both might be surrendered without national outrage at some unspecified time in the future, after they had won a general election.

They had to compromise; they were afraid of Moslem fundamentalism, and the power of Pakistan. They would buy Pakistan's friendship, buy peace with the Indian half of Kashmir . . . because the Soviet Union had shattered into pieces and India's most powerful ally didn't want to hand over money and weapons and support any longer. Couldn't afford to.

What wearied her more than any other element of the situation was the see-saw of relief and tension she experienced. It was listening to the Sharmars as they talked and drank, and waiting for them to finish – or to mention herself. That was it, that anticipation and its disappointment. Being free of suspicion yet aware that suspicion could be expressed at any moment –

Three thirty-two. It was voiced.

'Dhanjal seems convinced. I do not know –' Prakesh Sharmar.

'What?'

'The woman on the next houseboat.'

'Why are you so concerned?'

'Because of what we are *doing* here – because we are here, the others are here.'

'Is she anyone official?'

'I do not know. She will be watched, brother. I *know* she should be watched.'

'Very well, then,' V. K. Sharmar replied wearily. 'If you think so.'

Ros snatched off the headphones, as if they would transmit her coarse, sharp breathing to the Sharmars. Her heart palpitated with great, rapid thudding noises and she pressed her hand against it. It wasn't better knowing – it was worse, much worse.

It was as if her heartbeat was an echo-sounding device to locate metal objects at great depth, where the tapes were, the location of the recorder on the bedside table, the Minimodulux night-lens, the camera, each little tub of exposed film. Knowing that it would take less than a minute for a trained man to find every piece of evidence.

Not knowing where Hyde was – *if* Hyde was, any longer.

She was shivering. Her entire body was chilled and trembling. She had to leave. Had to get away – in the morning – before they *knew* about her.

PART TWO

Full Employment

'Stand now with thine enchantments,
and with the multitude of thy sorceries,
wherein thou hast laboured from thy youth;
if so be, thou shalt be able to profit,
if so be, thou mayest prevail.'

Isaiah: ch. 47, v.12

EIGHT

doubt and certainty

Even the static of the code room seemed musty to Miles as he shut the door behind himself and Dickson. Shut it on an image of the High Commission's lawns glistening with the first of the day's constant watering, the sprays turning slowly like dancers' skirts. Hyde was more alive to him with the door shut; the absolute *shithouse* –! Dickson was enraged at him for losing Hyde, releasing his grip on the loose cannon. As for Shelley – who knew which way Aubrey's protégé would jump on anything! Shelley could start handing out armfuls of manure, piling it on . . . That bastard Hyde – the deal was *done*, for Christ's sake. There was no setup, it was a plain tit-for-tat, a favour. No questions asked, no names, no pack-drill. Hyde would have been on the plane to London by now, in sodding Business Class, too, if he hadn't bolted into the night, cocking up a perfectly well-organised Dark Area and making *him* look a wanker in Dickson's eyes and maybe in Shelley's, too – oh, *sod* Hyde!

He eventually murmured: 'Sir? Better get it over with, I suppose –?' He realised his grin was sickly, undernourished. Dickson's features were momentarily contemptuous; then the eyes within the diplomatic Noh mask became more calculating.

'Yes – Jim.' There was a hesitation before Dickson pronounced his name, as if he were close to having forgotten it.

The room was empty, apart from themselves. Miles checked the equipment, which had been brought to readiness for full Signals with Century House. He felt hot – yet it was the thought of Hyde that was raising his temperature, rather than his

181

anticipation of any discolouration of his record. Yet perhaps it was better that the bastard had gone haring off. It gave him and Dickson another opportunity to insinuate their disbelief in Cass' story and his innocence. If Hyde chose to believe otherwise, so what.

It did not calm. That was just knowledge. Instinct continued to hate Hyde and raise his temperature accordingly. He wiped at his damp forehead as Dickson seated himself with some ceremony in front of the main console.

'Ready, sir?' Miles asked. Then added: 'Hyde can't really *believe* in Cass' innocence, can he? I mean, Cass was talking rubbish from the start. He was having an affair – *and* he did the woman in after a frenzied quarrel – ?' Even to himself, it sounded as if he were rehearsing a cover story. Dickson, however, after narrowing his nostrils momentarily as at a sudden, unpleasant odour, appeared mollified; the structure of the story, the account of their behaviour and attitude, seemed to satisfy him.

'If the D-G wants any more than we can offer – Jim,' he announced in a warmer tone, 'then he'll have to find Hyde for himself. Or Cass – if the man ever turns up. Very well, Jim, let's get on with it.' The slight impatience was a gesture of confidence.

Perhaps it would be all right. After all, what could Shelley do to them? He sat down beside Dickson. And what, on his complete tod, could Hyde do to upset *any* apple-cart? The bugger had probably started the fire in the cinema, anyway, just as the police suspected . . . not to mention a body they'd found inside. Shot to death. Hyde was a berserker, trying to pay an old debt. Off his trolley –

He switched on the microphones, readied the high-speed tapes. The needles twitched at their breathing in the silent room.

Hyde was just bloody paranoid, that was it – all of it. The needles quivered more violently at his exhalation. It was easy to hate the bastard, hard to remember he wasn't important any more. *Nobody*'s star pupil –

*

He had little need of Hyde's file. He *knew* Patrick's psychological profile, service record, peccadilloes, shadows and lights, relationships – everything – almost by heart. To have sent for the file would have implied consideration or reconsideration, neither of which was necessary. And the file would *not* provide further illumination.

Peter Shelley thrust his hands into his pockets and stood at the broad window overlooking the Thames, turning his head from the watercolours and charcoals framed on the buff walls towards the river, glinting with morning sun. The leaves along the embankment hinted at yellow. The air-conditioning purred as if pleased at remaining necessary. Shelley removed one hand and brushed at his hair, then clutched at his narrow chin. What the devil was Patrick playing at now?

Perhaps he'd *over*-prodded his indebtedness, so that he was determined to find something – anything – that would get Cass out safely.

Both hands were again in his pockets, as he nodded sternly towards the river. It must be the answer. Hyde believed this fantastic story about the Sharmars because he must. Driving himself forward with it.

No assistance, hands off, he'd agreed with Dickson and Miles half an hour earlier. Accepted their assurances, which were his own, that the Sharmars were not guilty and that Cass was. How could he believe otherwise, for God's sake? V.K. a drug-dealer? How could there possibly exist any *proof* that V. K. Sharmar, Prime Minister of India, was actively engaged in the growing, refining and smuggling of heroin? Cass must be wrong – and because he was wrong, he was guilty of murder. *Quod erat demonstrandum* – inescapable logic, the one inextricable from the other.

And Patrick was a convert, a zealot after his new faith.

Must be . . .

The Foreign Secretary, the whole of the Foreign Office, was behind Sharmar. Big-friend status. Coming man, right policies, man of the future, just what India needs, what *we* need in India

. . . The whispers seeped along the corridors of the Foreign Office and through Whitehall like a chorus of breezes. Gentle zephyrs, no rough winds shaking any darling buds, not in the Sharmars' case.

Q.E.D. again, then. He was answerable to the Foreign Secretary and could not go against him. So, Patrick was mistaken, abused – just like Cass.

And on his own –

Shelley glanced at the wide desk and its banks of telephones. Then back towards the river and the slow patrol of craft on its wrinkled, glittering light. *Proof?* Even proof would hardly be able to dynamite current thinking into new channels on the subject of V.K. Without proof, nothing whatsoever could be done. If Patrick wouldn't come out when the chance was provided, then there was nothing he could do for him – nothing.

And if what Delhi Station reported was the literal truth, that Hyde had killed an Indian citizen and was being hunted by the police . . . it was a bloody mess all round. If Patrick would only get out of there, it might be smoothed over . . . which meant, if only Cass were dead. It was a bitter, rather shaming thought, but it was a consummation rather fervently to be wished. Whatever was going on, and whatever the truth, Cass' demise would be a clean fracture. If Phil Cass was dead, and Patrick learned that fact, then he would get himself out of Delhi and away. And take Ros with him – the image of her niggled like a splinter beneath some mental nail.

He sniffed. He had erred, it was true, in sending Hyde, in giving the slightest credence to Cass' story. Otherwise, the pressure of the facts was irresistible. Even Kenneth, who was not at his elbow with an admonishing look, would have had to have seen that. Phil Cass killed the woman in some sort of frenzied argument, and the rest was convenient fantasy. A dream that wouldn't persevere in a bright morning –

– must be.

*

184

She had set out, in a hailed shikara, with a deliberate bravado that had now evaporated. She had crossed the lake through the clinging, chill mist, as if engaged upon some covert enterprise, towards the Nishat Bagh, the Garden of Delight, on the eastern shore. Now the sun was out, the shawl she had clutched about her in the stern of the narrow shikara was dry as it hung over her arm, where her stitches still pulled. On the lake, hearing the noises of waking birds and the cries of vendors and the unseen, slow dip of oar or pole, the shawl had clung as damply as the mist. As the mist dispersed, the mountains had lumbered, alien and high with menace.

None of her admonitions, her self-ridicule, could recapture the initial bravado. Not while she knew she was being followed.

If you can't sit still, then go for a walk. Nowhere quiet. Hyde again, tossing scraps of tradecraft from his dangerous table. Where the hell was the bugger? Terraces, water, dark lilac hedges, flowerbeds, amid which the scene in the now hot morning air was sickly, clinging like too much perfume. Ros paused to take photographs, admire a lattice-windowed pavilion, a fountain erect in the windless air. Dal Lake was diminished, yet she could make out Sara's small group of houseboats like the shadow of a detached retina at the corner of eyesight. Nanga Parbat, the vast mountain, was reflected in the lake. Shikaras and other craft plied the water like insects.

She rubbed her arm where the stitches plucked like a sudden chill. There were two of them. Sharmar must have sent them after her, and Dhanjal probably controlled them. She had seen neither face before – they might be local police. Birdsong littered the bushes and paths, bright plumage flashed into shrubs and trees. The colours of the new flowers were hot, alien, real only as a backcloth against which she posed, out of place. And alone. In her capacious shoulder bag, were the tiny tapes and the tubs of film. She could not risk taking them to be developed – though what else was she to do with them? What *use* were they? She had not dared approach the airport or even call to book a flight. There was an army presence there.

She'd bloody done the bloody job, for Christ's sake —! So, where *was* he?

She felt dizzy, as if her eyes had let in too much of the hot light and the dazzle from the lake and snow-capped peaks. Her broad hand pressed hotly against her forehead. She felt nauseous with fear — not because of the two men who hung back as if respectful or without orders, but because she hadn't heard from Hyde. Because she knew they knew who *Holland* really was — because they must have him; knowledge which had forbidden sleep.

Ros stumbled to a wooden bench and slumped heavily onto it as a sense of all his absences rushed against her like a bully. Sitting offered no relief. The place and its few tourists was autumnal and lonely, the birds mocking. The Sharmars and whoever else had been on Sara's houseboat had gone. She must recover the bug, but hadn't the nerve or any idea how to accomplish it. But that was a pinprick, like the small protests from the new lips of healing skin on her arm. It was Hyde's danger, and its likely outcome, that churned in her head and stomach.

One of the two men following her passed idly by, all but unnoticed. He seemed content at her lack of occupation, alert to the bench as a possible place of contact. With whom, for Christ's sake? The bugger was dead or incarcerated . . .

. . . it was hotter, brighter it seemed, when she finally looked up, wiping her eyes clear, steadying herself on the arm of the bench spotted with bird droppings. With a vast effort, she moved her body onto boneless legs and forced herself to walk towards the gate in the high wall surrounding the gardens. Gravel rustled beneath her flat shoes. Her full skirt clung around her thighs and her blouse constricted her breathing. Ahead of her again was the lake, the purposeful mountain occupying the northern part of its mirror, the small clutter of insects on the far shore that were Sara's houseboats black in the light.

At once, there was a shikara, but she was reluctant to get into it, as if the water churned betrayingly. Then she stepped in and sat down heavily. The boat rocked. The small Indian in a ragged shirt and shorts seemed amused at her bulk, but she had no energy for either resentment or self-mockery. The shikara, poled with a long, knobbly tree branch, slipped out onto the lake, and she glanced behind her, just once. One of the two men was hesitant on the landing stage, then he, too, climbed into a narrow boat which was poled after her in slow pursuit. The slowness of it suggested inexorability, the plod of something she could not avoid or escape. She clutched her arms about her knees, and the strap of the shoulder bag slid to her wrist, as if to suggest its being snatched by another's hand. She shivered. The mountain seemed to press closer, the dark beetles of the houseboats became larger, brightly coloured, like boiled sweets in the sunlight. Then they were low buildings, eerily floating. Kashmir was sullied by the dread of what must have happened to Hyde.

The shikara behind her own glided past as her boat bumped against the steps of her houseboat, its prow knocking as if to alert someone who might be waiting for her. She paid, the tip effusively accepted, and clambered aboard. The narrow boat slid away, now pursuing her pursuer. Srinagar seemed unnaturally quiet. She paused, dizzied again. She must get out of the place, back to –

– well, *where?* London? To Shelley –?

The cookboy looked up from washing pans, his smile gleaming. Ros ignored him and passed into the cool gloom of the houseboat. The scented wood was sharp to her heightened senses as she all but saw Dhanjal or someone else unfurl themselves from a chair in the lounge –

– empty. Her breathing was loud in the silence. Only motes moved in the sunlight strained through the net curtains and mosquito screens at the windows.

The bedroom door opened. She turned with huge reluctance. '*Christ –*' she breathed. 'Where have you *been*?' she accused him.

187

Hyde was shocked by her appearance, the signs of strain and tension around her dark-stained eyes, quivering on her mouth. She backed away from him, waving a hand as if to ward off his advance. He grabbed the hand, then her body, which shook against him in mingled relief and anger.

'All right?' he asked insensitively.

'No, I'm *not* all right!' she burst out. 'You've put me through the bloody mangle, you bugger!' The two statements balanced each other, the first angry, the second relieved welcome.

'Sorry.' Her body went on shuddering against him, her eyes and mouth wet against his cheek and neck. He swallowed residual guilt, controlling his own quiver of relief. She was all right. In a bad way, but *there*.

When her shaking had diminished, he sat her in the large settee and perched on its arm, stroking her hair. Her hand rested on his thigh, clamping it firmly as if to test the flesh's reality.

Then she said: 'You stink.'

'Morally or physically, darling?'

'Probably both.' She sniffed. 'Your clothes will do for the moment. I thought you were —' His hands paused on her head, squeezing the back of her skull. She was warned into habitual silence regarding his risks.

'Just think of the size of the gap. I got through it. Not even really close.'

Then they were silent, his silence enforcing hers. Until eventually, she was, by the relaxed pressure of his hand on her hair, allowed to ask: 'How did you get here?'

'On the boat?'

'The lot.'

Ros' debriefing. He could permit that. Only scars, limps, or an uncontrollable shudder required the nastier details. He was exhibiting no physical symptoms of another brush with his diseased world. She'd be satisfied with a timetable, his travel arrangements.

'Light aircraft out of Delhi – last night. Then a taxi. I got on board from a shikara or whatever they call them, after having a look at the other houseboats from the lake. Not much doing –'

'Not any more, *no!*' she snapped. 'You missed the bloody *party!*'

He suppressed the shiver that threatened to accompany a memory of Lal's body lying on his brother's office floor amid plaster debris, of the frog mask looking up at the gaping ceiling, and the heat and smell of smoke.

'Any good – the party?'

She wasn't ready yet. There was a residue of unused anger and fear.

'I've been *followed*, Hyde –! They're interested in me. I heard it –' She glanced at her shoulder bag, then at the Walkman lying on the table. 'I heard them talking about me, Hyde!'

He started brushing her hair, but the set of her head seemed to resist the gesture as patronising, uncomfortable. Yet she did not shake his hand away, instead she calmed slowly, her hands greeting and reassuring one another in her lap. Oh, Ros, I'm sorry –

Then: 'No one's searched this place.'

'You'd know, of course – having just arrived?'

'I know. Who's interested?'

'The brothers. They were both here last night. Gone now. A copper called Dhanjal has been around. Said it was routine. It wasn't.'

'There's no one out there now – unless you brought them back with you?'

'One followed me across the lake. There were two of them.'

'It's OK, then – for now.'

She turned her head and looked up at him. 'Are we getting out?' She attempted to suppress the plea, but it was nakedly in her eyes.

189

'What have you got?'

She swallowed in distaste, her eyes flaring angrily before she closed them with pseudo-cunning. She'd seen the way out. Her information was good. She believed he'd be convinced enough to get them out at once.

'Drugs. The easy bit.' Then she asked quickly: 'Did you get anything?' He waggled his hand.

'Yours is what we've got. Anything about Cass?'

'Not that I heard. He must be dead, mustn't he?' she hoped.

'I don't think so.' Her disappointment was evident.

'He's bound to be dead,' she insisted, her cheeks white, her eyes clown-dark in her pale face. Her fingers hurt his thigh. 'They're bloody everywhere, ahead of everything. They'll have done him in – won't they?'

It was strange – stupid to be disappointed, but he was, for a moment – that she felt no spell of safety around her now that he was with her. His monumental sense of self-preservation did not communicate itself to her. Only getting out would help. She was more worn than he – a lot more.

'They could have done. I'll listen to the tapes, though,' he compromised.

She pleaded silently for a moment, then snapped: 'Get back in the bedroom. I'll order some breakfast.'

'Ros, I have to listen to the tapes – have to be sure.'

She glared at him. His presence had meant only escape, not safety.

'This is a *fucking* mess, Hyde –!'

He spread his hands as she halted at the door.

'I can't help that, Ros – I shouldn't have involved you, but it's done now. Shelley and everyone else are being played as a gang of mugs, Ros. Sharmar's flavour of the month. There has to be something on tape or in the snaps you've taken, something I can *trade* for Cass, if I can't find out where they've got him –'

'*Why?*' she all but wailed.

'Because I can't leave him, if he's alive – not if I *know* he's here. I can't uninvent Cass.'

She did not reply, merely turned and left the room.

It's out of control, V.K., Sara had said when he had been brought news of the atrocity, the bus that had been bombed. *You have to make an announcement, bring it to an end* – now. He had shaken his head as much in horror at the event as in attempting to refute her demand. The gesture had further angered her, her hair falling across her face as she bent to her toast and coffee and deliberately ignored him and Prakesh as they prepared to leave for Bandipur.

To be flown by helicopter to witness –

– *this*. Beneath the vastness of Nanga Parbat, with Wular Lake's great expanse below the town, this devastation. The morning sun reflected in a million shards of glass, the scattered bodies, the trails of hosepipes. And, central to it all, the wreckage of the crowded bus that had been lifted and flung onto a bus shelter, so that it lay on its side like a scorched, dead lizard of gigantic size.

The noise, the faces of the survivors, the cries of the wounded and the police had maddened him like flies or Furies. So that he had retreated from the medical teams, police, fire officers, his security guards, even Cabinet colleagues who had managed to reach the event before it lost its news value. *The Prime Minister was visibly distressed by the scene*, the newspapers could claim. He sat slumped, with only Prakesh, on the hard bench of a deserted waiting room, through the shattered window of which the wreckage of the bus was visible, were he but to lift his head and turn it through only a few degrees.

He did not.

. . . *bring it to an end*, she had demanded. He could not answer her, since he would have had to say, *Not yet. Closer to the election*, and earn a withering contempt, vivid and unspoken. He curled his hands tightly on his thighs. Fragments of glass glittered amid

191

the dust on his suit, as if it had remained suspended in the air like bright soot, only to fall on him as soon as he arrived. He could not even protest that it had been no more than agreements with the Sikhs and the Kashmiri separatists who had done this, and with Pakistan – it wasn't planned or funded. He was only trying to bring some control, some lessening . . . a sense of slippage, not chaos. He was not to blame for *this*! *Yes, you are*, she would have answered implacably.

Prakesh stood at the window smoking a cigarette, apparently able to look with equanimity across the littered desolation outside. V.K. glanced away from his shadowed form against the light and the wreckage.

Two opinion polls – *only in damned Hindu papers!* Prakesh had snapped back at him above the roar of the helicopter's rotors – put him slightly behind Mehta and his party, the Hindu fundamentalists. Another poll in a government newspaper put Congress and Bharatiya Janata neck-and-neck, and in personal terms he lagged two points behind Mehta, the bloody film actor! How *could* he now make any announcement about the future of Kashmir or the Punjab, with Mehta and his hangers-on calling for retribution and more emergency measures to protect Hindus from Moslem extremists. Of course it could not be done – not yet.

He feared, too, that it was out of hand, that those people with whom he had met only last night had known in advance of this atrocity, that they welcomed it, their impatience battening on his promises like vultures on a carcase. He shivered, attracting the attention of his brother, who studied him sardonically.

'What is it, V.K.?' Sirens wailed behind Prakesh's words; women and men mourned behind them. *Bring it to an end* . . .

'Those – *people*,' he managed. 'Do they want the army down on them once and for all?'

'They can't control everything, V.K. They are trying. It would be worse without your intervention, without the future you have held out –'

'You make it sound like a bonfire of waste paper out there, Prakesh!' he stormed.

'Keep your voice down, V.K.'

V.K. swallowed, lowering his head. 'Will they be satisfied *now* – for a time?' he asked in a small voice.

'Fifty dead, sixty more injured – I imagine so.' He studied his cigarette carefully, then continued. 'I imagine so. The Sikhs have had their airliner, the Kashmiris their bus –'

'How can you be so callous?'

'I was going to add – and they have made you attend both spectacles, to remind you of your promises. I think they want you to win the election, V.K. They must want that. There'll be no hope from Mehta. Things will be quieter after this.'

'First it was Sereena –!' he blurted.

Prakesh turned on him. Even with his face in shadow, his eyes burned.

'*You* wanted Sereena dead! From the first moment – don't shake your head, it is true! – the first moment you discovered she was playing you for a cuckold with the Englishman! Ever since you began to believe she had slept with Mehta when she played Sita to his Rama in the bloody television series!' He had moved closer to his brother, bent forward, the cords in his neck as visible as ropes, his voice a whispered bellow that cowed V.K. 'Or was it when she played Parvati to his Shiva, or moll to his gangster or trollop to his hero in a dozen other movies? When was it, V.K., that you *first* wanted her dead?'

His shaking head was inadmissible denial, a form of perjury, and he knew it was such.

More softly, Prakesh murmured: 'Sereena would not have won you enough extra votes to take hold of all India, V.K. Only *you* can do that.'

'But, Mehta –?'

Something V.K. would have identified as contempt in anyone else's glance flickered in Prakesh's eyes for an instant, then was replaced by a smile, the bestowal of confidence.

193

'Mehta? When things have died down, you can make your announcement. Promise India her *future*. Mehta will never surrender Kashmir. You can surrender it, and win the votes of everyone in India who is sick of murder. So long as the timing is right . . . in a while. Not just yet –'

Sara's features were contemptuous in his imagination for a moment, then he was able to dismiss her. She did not understand strategy, necessity –

'Find that Australian, Prakesh. How did they let him get away from them? Are we surrounded by incompetents?'

'He was to be handed over, in all innocence, by the British. It was all agreed. They had no suspicion – he did, however. Such people are paranoid. It will not be long –'

'That woman – at Sara's – she's Australian. Are they connected? Is it coincidence?'

'I'm having it checked. In London, at the woman's address. We have their names. I should hear this evening. If so, then we can expect him in Srinagar, no doubt.' He smiled, then added: 'And now, your press conference . . . ? It is time you made an appearance. Father of India must be –'

'I understand, Prakesh,' V.K. replied waspishly. 'I may not be in the movies, like that damned Mehta, but I know which part to play when the cameras are pointed at me!'

Despite his confident tone, his commanding anger, he quailed at his glimpse of the ruined bus as he rose from the bench and brushed at the dust and glass fragments on his suit. The glass pricked and roughened his palms.

Hyde looked at his watch, glancing almost guiltily away from the notes he had transcribed from the tapes. Eleven thirty. Time, time – no that wasn't the bone sticking through the skin of his concentration. He was guilty because he had finally admitted that the Sharmars knew precisely who he was – *what* he was. Patrick Hyde, of Philbeach Gardens, Earl's Court, London. They'd have found out from Miles and Dickson if from no one else. And therefore, they'd know by now, or very soon, precisely *who* Ros was.

He clenched his hand on his thigh, the clutched felt pen marking his denims. He sensed Ros' presence in the lounge press demandingly against the wall of the houseboat's second bedroom, where he sat hunched over the tiny recorder and the miniature tapes, as if fiddling with scale models of something real. He wore the headphones with one earpiece askew, listening for the noises of the cookboy or anyone else. He heard beyond the confines of the boat the sounds of Srinagar, the location of transport – the airport. He had to get Ros out. She had to leave legitimately – now.

The tapes were interesting. The photographs, when they were developed, might be even more incriminating. There were references to drug money, to the distribution of funds which could be damagingly interpreted . . . and the other thing, that Cass had not had any idea of. The Sharmars playing for the future of India . . .

. . . and they might even be right, for God's sake, to let Kashmir and the Punjab go independent, linked to the rest of India only by economic ties. V. K. Sharmar's big idea –

Big, dangerous idea, because there was enough on the tapes to confirm links with Kashmiri and Sikh terrorists. Enough to bring Sharmar down like Lucifer. And the bug that had picked it all up was still on Sara Mallowby's houseboat, just waiting to be found by someone flicking a duster along the underside of the table . . . Hyde shivered.

What about Cass . . . ?

He pressed the Play button and adjusted the sweat-damp earpiece over his left ear. It was *so* incriminating Shelley would merely have to wave it under Sharmar's nose and the smell would make him faint. He'd surrender the family fortune, never mind Cass . . . of whom there was still nothing –

– get out then. Forget him. Get this stuff back to London, stick it in the post, for Christ's sake, and leave before they arrange your disappearance!

And yet he could not. Not even with Ros' tension like an invisible tremor through the boat. Not even with the risk of being stumbled upon, nor the danger of a dark-skinned, polite man from the Indian High Commission calling at Philbeach Gardens, having inspected the electoral register, just to confirm that he and Ros were —

Not even for that. Until he *knew* they'd done the poor bastard in, just like Lal and Banerjee. The tape rolled. He wanted, he admitted, proof that Cass was dead, out of the way, unrequiring of concern, time or effort. One word — he'd missed nothing so far — one word that said *kaput*, one dismissive verb in the past tense in reference to Cass. Then he'd get Ros on the first plane out and himself —

Right, then, this is the last of the tapes, there's no more than twenty minutes of stuff on it. Hurry it up . . .

. . . the unvoiceable — be dead, Cass. I have to save Ros. Be —

He was alive, then . . .

Almost robotically, he rewound a short section of the tape and adjusted both earpieces. Cass alive, in stereo. A half-caught, brief report by Dhanjal to Prakesh Sharmar, late the previous night, the buzz of politics uninteresting as mosquitoes at one of the mesh screens in the background, the occasional rise in volume of V. K. Sharmar's reassurances. Hyde listened intently, feeling the shirt dampen under his arms and perspiration spring coldly along his hairline. He rewound the tape once more.

Alive, then — and uncommunicative, just. But *soon*, Dhanjal promised like a procurer, to Sharmar's evident pleasure. Cass was in bad shape. It would be difficult for him to be rescued, hard to move him if he was got out. He let the tape run on, but there was nothing more. Prakesh Sharmar moved away into the political murmuring. Dhanjal's voice vanished from the room.

Hyde wiped his forefinger along his hairline and inspected its wetness, then rubbed his arms after switching off the tape. He retained the headphones. They kept out — almost — the sense of Ros and the immediate future. The *decided* future. The polite

Indian on the front steps of the house in Philbeach Gardens, inspecting the list of tenants' names. *R. Woode. P. Hyde.* Asking Max or his girlfriend, who occupied the ground floor – *ah, Mr Hyde and Ms Woode are in India . . . on their way to Australia – together. I will call again . . .* Reporting direct to Sharmar or his brother, who would report to Dhanjal.

He breathed carefully and slowly, removed the headphones, unplugging them from the recorder and stowing the recorder and the phones in the travel bag alongside the tubs of undeveloped film and the other tapes. Then placed the travel bag in the wardrobe after zipping its mouth tight. Ros *had* to go, today. The evening flight, at the latest, to Delhi, and then back to London with the tapes and film. See Shelley, be safe.

He straightened, as if from hard physical labour, his hands cradling his back, his face raised to the carved ceiling. Exhaled. It had to be done, she had to go.

She was frightened enough, after all –

He opened the bedroom door and stepped into the corridor, almost colliding with Sara Mallowby, who was entering from the stern, as Ros' shadow darkened the passageway, her form motionless in the lounge doorway.

The Englishwoman's eyes were suspicious. Hyde dropped his shoulders slightly in embarrassment. His smile was deliberately slow and uncertain, puzzled yet aware of incongruity.

'I – er . . .' he stared at Ros rather than Sara, turning away from the tall blonde woman. 'I'll – see you, then . . . uh, thanks for – you know . . .' He shrugged. 'I'd better be off –'

He willed Ros to see his posed form as that of a semi-stranger. Her face was stunned and pale, her body awkwardly still.

'Sara –' Ros began and Hyde hesitated, his hands aching with tension. 'Yes . . . *Max*!' Hyde winked at her, even though she had grasped at her tenant's name too eagerly, plucking it from memory rather than acquaintance. 'Yes – um, thanks, too.'

Hyde waved with a small gesture.

'Excuse me.' He passed Sara, whose face was sardonically amused. Beaut. Just keep up the pretence, Ros – where we met, et cetera. He stepped onto the rear deck, to the shock of the cook, then crossed the planked jetty towards the shops along Houseboats Boulevard. The traffic seemed senselessly loud and the scents of the middle of the day oppressive. He glanced back once, then began to hurry, the inventory of what he needed unrolling in his head like the hard copy of computer-stored information. Ros weighed on him as heavy as the sunlight. The woman was Sharmar's mistress, she was on the payroll. And Ros was frightened and disorientated.

And Cass was alive. That was the worst news –

NINE

brief encounters

'Sorry to create embarrassment,' Sara Mallowby offered, her mouth sardonic in expression as soon as the words had been uttered.

Ros shrugged and attempted a grin. 'Doesn't matter . . . I – I was hoping he wasn't going to hang around, anyway. You helped shoo him off.'

She gestured Sara to the settee and held the door handle for a moment, steadying herself, before moving into the room behind Sara.

'Where did you meet him?' Sara enquired, arranging the full, brightly flowered skirt around her long legs.

'Oh – the cocktail bar of the Oberoi. I wasn't keen, to tell you the truth –' Her tension was beginning to become absorbed by the fiction, and the amusement of belittling Hyde – however much it was like laughing at fear in a dark house. 'He tried chatting me up . . .' Her hand movements conjured at her body, as if to make her bulk vanish. 'He just knocked on the bloody door last night like the Sheik of Araby, full of eastern promise!'

Sara laughed without suspicion.

'And you didn't turn him away.'

'It was charitable, wasn't it?' Ros responded with studied lightness. 'Coffee – or can we share lunch?'

Sara hesitated, then: 'Lunch would be fun. Shall I organise it?'

'Please.'

Sara rose from the settee and left the room. In another moment, she was talking to the cook in Kashmiri. Ros' hands fluttered at her face, then she calmed them in her lap, laving them together. She was so much inside the fiction that she felt her cheeks flush. Then Hyde's absence chilled her, together with images of the Sharmars, Dhanjal, the Pakistanis and Sikhs on Sara's boat. Sara was *dangerous*, she told herself. Why had she come? What did she want?

Lunch stretched ahead of her like an obstacle course, a place of menacing pitfalls.

He'd seen Sara Mallowby leave Ros' houseboat, watching from beneath the awning of a shop whose window spilt furs like frozen streams, bright leather handbags lying amongst them like pebbles. Her movements had been languid, unsuspicious, but he had not dared return to the boat. Then, an hour later, Dhanjal had called briefly on Sara and, on leaving, had paused to study Ros' boat before getting back into his Japanese 4WD. The vehicle's driver was in police uniform. Guiltily, he had begun trailing Dhanjal through Srinagar, the houseboat becoming ever more isolated and unprotected in his imagination as his Land Rover followed the Subaru out of Srinagar and up towards the hills.

Now, in the afternoon's light and warmth, he brought the Land Rover to a halt at the edge of Gulmarg . . . knowing that the bungalow a few hundred yards away belonged to Sharmar, and that Sereena Sharmar had died in it.

Cass must have been brought back to it . . .

He looked at his watch. A little after four. The sun had ignited the lower sky, so the valley burned and Srinagar seemed little more than debris amid the fire. Dal Lake gleamed like a blank window. The flanks of Nanga Parbat glowed to the north. Gulmarg was crowded with trekkers and tourists, with large cars and wealthily dressed children. Ahead of him, the track was a pale, dusty parting in the vivid grass leading towards Sharmar's bungalow, outside which the Subaru and its driver sat impassively.

His mind inventoried once more, as if he was again a child checking obsessively the means of his own safety and reassurance . . . switching off lights six, seven, eight times, walking only on the edge of the rug, pressing the door again and again to ensure that it was shut. He had Ros' ticket for Delhi in his pocket, bought at a travel agency. The Land Rover had been easy to hire, the Sterling Mk 5 sub-machine-gun and the old but operable smoke grenades even easier. No one wanted addresses, credit card numbers in the Srinagar backstreets. The binoculars had been bought in a tourist trap. He studied the bungalow through them. Nothing at the windows or the door. Two men loitered at the rear of the bungalow, amid the fountains and trees.

It would have to be tonight.

He had trailed Dhanjal north to Lake Wular and what he knew to be the Sharmar estates. From there, then, the heroin began its journey, probably west on the first leg to the border with Pakistan. Too close to the Cease Fire Line to be used by tourist traffic – by anyone without passes, authority or influence. Dhanjal was evidently keeping a managerial eye on the family business. A truck was being loaded as Hyde watched. Then the policeman had headed south towards Srinagar, until he had branched off and climbed up to Gulmarg. Hyde did not need to see Cass to know he was there. Scene of the crime.

He studied the bungalow for another hour, as the sun slipped down towards the valley, obscuring it in gold and fire. A late afternoon breeze prickled his bare arms. He saw two more men, but no sign of Dhanjal or Cass. Cass was being turned inside out, imploded on himself in the effort to discover *who, what, how much, when* – and *who is this man Hyde?* It didn't matter now – unless they'd taken the use of his legs away from him and caused him to be incapable of movement. The noiseless bungalow presumably had a cellar or they'd never have taken Cass there; he would have been somewhere more secure.

Having to render Cass the extreme unction of a final bullet would solve a great many problems . . .

The bugger was going to have to walk, even run. To that he could make up his mind the moment Hyde dragged him off the cot or out of the chair in which he found him. Ten past five – time to get back. The shadows were longer, the sun low, Dal Lake's mirror spotted with the flyspecks of places like Ros' houseboat. Lights were already pricking out from Srinagar.

He hoped Ros had had the sense to pack in preparation.

'Cass is alive, you berk – and Sharmar's been a *very* naughty boy. When I call you again, *be* there.'

Hyde slapped the telephone back onto the receiver. The voice of Shelley's wife, Alison, on the answerphone. *You have reached the Shelley household. I'm afraid –*

You're afraid, darling? What about the poor bleeding infantry – how do you think we feel? He glared at Ros, whose whole frame had shuddered at the suggestion of violence that his replacing of the receiver had promised.

'That's that, then,' he said, shaking his head. 'Another two hundred quid on a night at Covent Garden, or whatever that tosser is doing with his time!'

The windows of the houseboat's lounge were dark, the room itself goldenly dim with the light of a single table lamp. Ros stood up stiffly and began pacing the room, her shadow thrown towards the windows and to Sara Mallowby's houseboat. He kept out of the light, hunched on the settee.

'What now, then?' Ros suddenly demanded, turning on him as if he had tried unsuccessfully to steal up on her.

'We're getting out.'

Her relief was immediate; and immediately qualified.

'Without Cass?'

Slowly, Hyde shook his head. 'No.'

'We could –' But she could not continue. He had told her where Cass must be held, what they must have been doing to him. She clenched her hands against her breasts like doves, angry at her empathy with a man she had never met, the un-regarded debt he had accumulated in Hyde's name, even her own. 'How can you get him out?' she protested.

'That's the easy bit. Out of India –? I'll need Shelley for that.'

'He's not answering your calls, haven't you noticed?'

'He will. When you tell him, show him.'

'Me? I'm not going anywhere on my own, Hyde! I tried it once before and ended up in this bloody mess!'

'You're going to have to. I've –' *Got all my work cut out looking after Cass*, was what he wished to say, but saw that she under-stood. 'There's your ticket, on the table. There's time to make the flight –' She shook her head. 'You've got to go, Ros – for Christ's sake, you have to let me do my own thing here!'

'*When* you've got Cass. Not before.'.

Part of her wanted to escape as easily as waking from a nightmare. Nothing, however, would persuade her to leave him until circumstances permitted or forced her. He spread his hands.

'OK – since you're in, there are rules. If I'm hit, you disappear – *understand?*' He emphasised the point by pressing his hand on the arm of the settee as if squeezing unsupple flesh, to hurt it, to knead it into feeling. 'You just go away from wherever it happens. Also, if I can't move Cass, then I may have to – do the vet's job for him. Understood? That's non-negotiable. He might be too far gone for anything else.'

He listened to her outraged breathing for a few minutes, all but heard her tension thrum in the panelling. Eventually, she sniffed loudly, and announced:

'What a *filthy* bloody job you've got, Hyde.'

'Too true.' He picked up the nightsight from beside him on the settee and sidled to one of the dark windows. 'Too true.' He felt a thrill of nerves, the rush of adrenalin. He was about to

203

attempt to repay his debt to Cass in his best currency, physical action, his gold standard of professional skill. The anticipation was satisfying, and Ros had begun to move to the edge of his mental field of vision.

Through the nightsight, he saw grey figures moving behind the uncurtained windows of Sara's houseboat. A long Mercedes was parked at the end of the jetty, and there were two policemen beside it, smoking, engaged in amused conversation. He returned his attention to the houseboat and saw Sara and Dhanjal, as if mimicking the two policemen – except that he recognised the postures of bullying and outrage. They were quarrelling.

'Get the recorder and the headphones, Ros,' he murmured. Her bags and the suitcase she had brought up for him lay neatly on the bed in the main bedroom, as if awaiting a hotel porter. He heard the zip of the travel bag drawn back like a blade being unsheathed from a heavy scabbard. When she handed it to him, he plugged in the headphones and switched on the recorder. The tape moved, the voices tinnily reaching him. A distant play transmitted from a country thousands of miles away.

'Then *describe* him to me!' Dhanjal.

'He was ordinary. So bloody *ordinary*!' Sara replied. 'A nobody who picked her up –'

He swung the nightsight towards the Mercedes. The two policemen were inattentive, relaxed. The Land Rover was in the underground garage of one of the better hotels.

'Ros – get the bags ready.' He could see the lights of late shikaras, hopeful for tourists or sales, shimmering across the lake like fireflies.

'What?'

'Ros, just do as I tell you. Just what you *need*.'

'What is it –?' she began, but then hurried from the room.

Through the headphones, he heard himself accurately, if disparagingly, described. Dhanjal's murmurs were as precise as if

204

he were studying a photograph to match it to the woman's words. Ros returned to the lounge with one suitcase, the travel bag and his own small case.

'Too much?' she asked, her voice breathy with an exhilarated fear. He shook his head.

'Go and attract the closest shikara – do it quietly.'

'There's a light – Sara showed me.'

'Don't attract her attention.'

'Who's there with her?' Her breath was warm on his scalp and cheek. Her hands touched his shoulders for reassurance.

'Your boy Dhanjal. Quick, Ros –'

On Sara's houseboat, the woman continued to dribble out her description of him. And the fact that he had left at once – *no, she hadn't seen him return* . . . Give me credit for a little skill, darling. Was she sure –? Yes – she hadn't seen him again. *He's just a tourist. She can hardly afford to be choosy, can she, Inspector?* Arrogant female. Hyde swallowed nervously.

Come on Ros – hurry up with that bloody shikara and let's get out of here.

'Prakesh has received a report on the man you describe – at least, someone very like him. He's a British agent. He and the woman live together in London – Earl's Court? Do you know it?' Dhanjal asked with mocking anger.

V.K. was confident that he appeared at his most solemn and statesmanlike; a father figure, wise, tolerant – yet now deeply angry, like a god with his recalcitrant people. On the monitor screen, the images of carnage succeeded one another. On the desk, jutting as it were from beneath his formally folded hands, his speech waited. The airliner disaster, the bus station atrocity . . . earlier horrors, even the attack on the Golden Temple in Amritsar . . . army violence in Kashmir . . . rioting, the Tamils –

The sequence was brief, hardly more than two minutes, but it had taken weeks to compile. Its use had been intended very close to the election, but the party's inner caucus had agreed that it should be used well before the nation went to the polls. They had been persuaded by the latest outrage and the calm they suspected would follow – except from Mehta's fundamentalist camp. The exact timing had not yet been decided. This was merely a rehearsal. *A new headline image*, Prakesh had said. The bus station at Bandipur. The sequence rolled back, inexorable as a blood-soaked tank track, through the post-Imperial history of India, to culminate in rioting and murder in monochrome. 1948. Independence – from what? British India's ways and irreconcilables hung about the new nation like a shroud, tormenting her . . .

He would speak as the father of the nation. That, they had decided. The speech would probably be rewritten another dozen times, tinkered with obsessively after that, the images on film juggled, honed, choreographed. As father of the nation, he would ask the people – *is this what you want? Is this really how you see India and yourselves?*

It was a risky strategy – the highest of risks. Mehta wanted this kind of India, one full of dead bodies and old hatreds; self-mutilation, abject, passive suffering. Mehta played with a strong hand of cards – history. But *he*, V. K. Sharmar, offered the future, which was the greater risk . . .

. . . yet they might believe. Soundings were promising. People were almost as tired of murder as they were of poverty. Would they come with him, into the future, or would they choose a movie star and all the other old, weary clichés?

It was very perilous.

Prakesh had hurried away, leaving the Party's studios almost an hour earlier, his features determined, angry. Why? Because of the *other* danger, the one that could bring them down? The greatest risk, that the British agent could not be found, that he would find someone to listen to his story –

His stomach clenched with nerves, as if the broadcast were about to begin in earnest, to be seen by hundreds of millions.

The images had reached the riots of 1948, the country the British had *created* tearing itself in two.

He felt frightened and enraged.

The shikara landed them near Dal Gate, where the glow of Srinagar threw the houseboats along the boulevard into comparative darkness. Hyde paid the owner, tipping him generously, then the shikara was poled silently out onto the glimmering silver mirror of the lake, creating a lengthening scratch on its surface.

'Where's the Land Rover?' Ros asked, her whisper hoarse and exaggerated. Traffic all but swallowed her words.

'In the garage of the Broadway –' He waved his arms. 'On Mandana Azad. Know it? It's not far.' He was squatting on his haunches on the jetty, watching back the way they had travelled, the patrol of traffic along the boulevard, the gleam of shops, the briefer, more discreet lights from the ranks of houseboats.

'What is it?'

'Just watching my back.' He sniffed sweet, unburned petrol on the cool night air, and the scent of open-air cooking. 'Just making sure . . .' He held the small night-scope to his right eye. Grey night, off-white ghosts of people and cars, the lighted windows of the houseboats like a retreating audience of white, square mouths. He found Sara's houseboat, then the one Ros had rented and the long Mercedes – policemen suddenly alert. A figure was waving its arms at them from the jetty to Sara's boat, then they were running towards Ros' boat, tiny figures with bent elbows then freed hands holding what had to be guns.

A siren, nearing, the springing on of headlights along the boulevard. 'Time to go,' he murmured, straightening.

'Are they on to us?'

'They are, my one and only – they are.'

He hefted the travel bag onto his shoulder and picked up the suitcase in his left hand. He was aware of the gun in the small of his back, beneath the cotton jacket. Ros, carrying the smaller

207

suitcase, followed him into the thinning crowds along Azad Road, noise and imbibers spilling gratingly from the garishly neoned clubs and the gleaming hotel foyers. The body of a dog in the gutter, a beggar hunched into a shop doorway. Superstitiously, Hyde scattered coins near the gaunt figure without pausing. His face was grateful in the light that illuminated jewellery behind a security grille.

They entered the Hotel Broadway's carpeted foyer and crossed it to the lifts. Casually dressed tourists, uniformed police, suited, wealthy locals. Then the lift doors closed and opened again on the petrol-scented, dusty air of the underground garage.

'Goodbye to all that,' Ros murmured, shivering despite her heavy sweater.

Hyde grinned at her, realising the expression unnerved her. Too feral, too close to that of an animal scenting prey.

'It's all right, Ros,' he reassured. 'Over there, beyond the pillar.'

Two Mercedes, a Jaguar, a small red Porsche; European saloons and older Indian cars, a few 4WDs. The Land Rover – he bent and looked beneath it, checked the bonnet. It was undisturbed, still locked, its contents unriffled. He dumped the suitcases in the rear, away from the tool box which contained the guns and the locker containing the smoke grenades. His hands hesitated, as if he had come to the wrong vehicle, then he realised that Ros' presence was disorientating him. She hovered like someone waiting for a door to be opened for her, a door to safety or sleep.

'OK?' She nodded, but was not. 'Look, Ros,' he began reluctantly as she climbed into the passenger seat, he remaining beside the driver's door, holding it open. 'I'll take you to the airport now.' He checked his watch to avoid the glare she directed at him. 'You can still make the flight.'

She shook her head, struggling not with his suggestion but with everything in her that wished to acquiesce with it. Then she shook her head more decisively.

'Not without you.' She had decided; he was her responsibility. 'Let's get on with it.'

He knew they must. If Dhanjal was convinced Sara had seen him, that he had been on Ros' boat and had only now vanished, then the city would be cordoned, the roads checkpointed. The police patrols would be increased, and the army woken and forced into its uniforms and vehicles. Anticipating the immediate future, he realised how normal the streets had seemed; without incident, as if Srinagar had exhausted itself, sated on recent violence. The police and army would have no distractions, they could concentrate wholly on him and Ros.

He climbed into the vehicle, fishing the ignition keys from his pocket, gripping the wheel tightly for a moment, as if settling himself into his seat like someone disabled.

'OK. Get that travel bag from the back and sort through the tapes and film. Split it in two – half for me, half for you –' He swallowed, flinching against her realisation of the implications of what he had said.

She did not reply, merely twisted her bulk in the seat and reached the travel bag onto her lap, unzipping it loudly in the garage's silence –

– broken by the firing of a car engine, which made her shudder, and drop the two tubs of film she held in one hand onto the floor of the Land Rover.

'Shit,' she muttered, bending forward to retrieve the tubs.

Hyde watched the small Nissan draw past them, driven by an Indian, a woman innocently in the passenger seat. His gaze followed it towards the ramp up to Azad Road, its headlights glancing off the concrete wall, then fading –

– appearing to return. Headlights enlarging, bucking along the concrete from a still-concealed car . . . which became a police car, nosing down the ramp into the garage as if sniffing like a trained dog. Ros straightened up, holding the two tubs of film like a small consolation prize, and, as Hyde glanced sideways, her face changed as she saw the blazon on the approaching car.

Automatically, she dropped the film into the bag and zipped it hurriedly shut. The police car's engine growled off the walls of the underground garage. Ros' hand hesitantly reached towards his arm, but then withdrew itself.

The police car stopped thirty yards away, almost rubbing flanks against a mudstained Japanese 4WD. Both policemen got out of it, their doors slamming shut like echoing explosions in the garage. Hyde held Ros' arm and pulled at it until she imitated him in sliding down in her seat. Delicately, he opened his door, tugging at her sleeve to indicate she was to remain in the Land Rover. The two policemen had already completed their inspection of the Japanese vehicle and had moved routinely and together to the car parked next to it. Procedure.

He shook her sleeve, then slipped out of the vehicle, closing the door to behind him. The policemen's heels clicked echoingly. He resented the sluggishness of his senses, the almost clumsy movements of his body. It must be Ros, acting like a kind of moral multiple sclerosis, insinuating the ailment of ordinary sensibility. The policemen's heels continued to click, pause, click, their voices murmur. He eased himself onto his back and slid under the Land Rover, crabbing beneath it until he reached the passenger side. He climbed upright against a BMW. Cassette tape cases littered its rear seats, nestling in the cobralike folds of a Burberry scarf. The hotel restaurant must be full . . . The two policemen had begun a return journey towards their own car, inspecting in little darts and rushes the scattered cars in the garage.

Hyde waited, then skittered on his hands and feet in a caricature of a frightened cat towards the door of the lift. The majority of the cars were parked near the lift, and he remained unseen. Then he stood up, and began walking abstractedly across the garage as if towards a distant car, oblivious of the police car and the two uniforms – who had come to a halt to observe and discuss him. He noticed them, even nodded in the vague, supplicatory manner of a stranger in a strange land. They nodded politely back. He passed on, towards a dusty grey Peugeot that he might have hired from Avis or Hertz, aware that they were still watching him. Then he sensed the moment when they lost interest, before he heard the more rapid click of their heels and the acquiescent murmurs of their mutual boredom and agreement that they had fulfilled their instructions –

– another glare of headlights froze them, as if they were the hunted, and the long black Mercedes that had been parked at the end of the jetty nosed sharklike and implacable into the garage. The policemen, ten yards from their car, remained immobile in the limousine's headlights as the vehicle slowed.

Almost at once, Dhanjal stepped from the rear of the Mercedes and they hurried to him, saluting with a deference greater than mere rank required. Different organisation, close to the Sharmars ... Dhanjal was even more interesting, much more dangerous.

He was interrogating the policemen in Kashmiri, as if to exclude them from the caste of the educated and powerful who continued to regard fluent English as a letter of credit. The policemen shrugged, even at attention, snapped back answers, shook heads. Dhanjal, tall in his well-cut suit, stood with his hands on his hips, inspecting the garage. Hyde glanced towards the Land Rover, and could see no sign of Ros. He crouched behind the bonnet of the Peugeot, his right hand poised behind his back. The police radio crackled and one of the policemen made as if to answer it and was stilled by a gesture from Dhanjal.

It was as if the man *knew* he was in the right place and that he was in time.

Then, as if to confirm Hyde's creeping anxiety, Dhanjal began walking across the stained concrete floor towards the Land Rover. He must have asked them which vehicles they had not inspected. Hyde slipped from behind the Peugeot to the concealment of a rough pillar, then to a hotel minibus, then to a dusty Hindu Ambassador ... Dhanjal continued his leisurely patrol towards the group of vehicles amid which the Land Rover was parked. Hyde was close to the doors of the lift –

– as they sighed open and laughter emerged, tugging an obese Indian behind it and a woman whose legs were uncertain and whose figure was trapped inside gleaming lurex, as if she had been wrapped tightly for the oven. Dhanjal was distracted, the couple surprised into stillness. The doors clattered shut and the lift sighed away. Dhanjal approached the ill-matched, perfectly-mated couple, then halted and nodded in recognition. The obese man in the dinner jacket called Dhanjal's name and rank, drunkenly amused. Dhanjal explained – Hyde heard *drugs*, they were speaking in English now, and the obese man snorted in derision, as if Dhanjal had lost face. He and the woman, propelled now into movement and giggling by the man's tug on her arm, made towards a large American limousine. Dhanjal watched them, then shrugged in irritation and hurried towards the Land Rover and its satellite cars. He glanced into the BMW, then turned to the 4WD, trying the door handle –

His footsteps in the trainers were dull thudding noises that required time to interpret correctly. Too much time for Dhanjal and the policemen, now engaged in conversation with Dhanjal's driver. Hyde's right foot hit the bonnet of the BMW and felt it flex like a disapproving cheek as Dhanjal whirled away from Ros' appalled face at the passenger window. The Indian's expression all but matched hers for an instant before Hyde struck Dhanjal across the side of the head with the pistol as he cannoned into the man and crushed him against the Land Rover. As Hyde hit him again, Ros' face was almost alongside that of Dhanjal, her expression suggesting that she was Hyde's intended victim. Dhanjal slumped to the concrete, curled like a damaged crab. Running footsteps, shouts.

Hyde rounded the Land Rover and thrust himself into the driving seat, slamming the door behind him. Ros' breathing and his own in chorus. The engine caught and he put the vehicle into gear, the tyres screeching as he accelerated towards the two policemen.

Ros' scream of protest, surprised faces, bodies flinging themselves safely aside.

He careened along the side of the Mercedes as he dragged on the steering wheel, the driver's gun hardly emerged from his jacket. The tear of metal sharp as a scream. Then the Land Rover was bolting up the ramp towards the street. He bucked over a speed-restriction bump set with gleaming cats' eyes, then the flimsy arm of the barrier brushed the roof, unable to raise itself in time to avoid the Land Rover's stampede.

A screech of brakes, the wobble of a cycle rickshaw as he swerved to avoid it, then the glaring tunnel of lights of Azad Road, the quick card-riffle of restaurant and café and shop façades before the telegraph office blurred behind them. A queue at a bus stand, then the wide street bore right towards the market and a narrow bridge over a tributary of the Jhelum. The road to Gulmarg. He'd have to bluff them after he crossed it, before they had the centre of the city haltered in a bag.

Behind them, the police car stumbled as if blinded by the lights out of the garage and swung violently as a drunk to pursue them. Ros, beside him, was stiff-bodied, silent.

And with him, whether he wished it or not.

The responsibility for Cass was a debt, a single occasion. Not her, though. The obligation was too great, too continuous; part of him.

'The damned man was *here*, Dhanjal!' Prakesh Sharmar raged. His own anger buzzed in his ears like the noise of the engines of the family plane which had brought him up from Delhi. Summoned by a *confident* Dhanjal! 'He was here and no one realised it!'

Dhanjal occupied a corner of the houseboat's lounge, his long fingers itching through the contents of the suitcase Hyde and the woman had left behind. Her clothes, in the main, some men's clothing. A pristine white bandage decorated Dhanjal's scalp and forehead like an unearned medal.

213

Prakesh strode about the room, the fingers of his right hand extending and closing, as if he were attempting to reckon a complex sum and take hold of something physical at the same moment.

It was not complex – it was absurdly simple. One man to be silenced – and the woman, of course. Hyde was a British agent – or had once been. Shelley must have sent him, not entirely convinced – although now, from the manner in which his people in Delhi were behaving, Shelley *was* convinced. So, it was remarkably simple, so simple that Dhanjal had managed to make a complete damned *curry* of the whole business!

He turned to Dhanjal, whose features immediately assumed a composed, earnest apology, a sheen of loyalty and self-criticism.

'Where are they now?'

Dhanjal said, hesitantly: 'They cannot have got far. We have the registration of the Land Rover, we know where he hired it. We have –'

'You have *nothing*!' Prakesh stormed back, striding about the room. Then, silkily: 'He must be found and eliminated, Dhanjal. That is your only priority, my good fellow. He has to be eliminated. He must be here because of the man Cass. Do you agree?'

'He can't know where he is.'

'You're certain?' Dhanjal nodded. 'Why?'

'The man must have arrived last night. The woman has been watched since you and V.K. gave the order –'

'You didn't see him arrive, even with the woman under surveillance.'

'He was in Delhi, wasn't he? He couldn't have been here before early today.'

'Quite. So, he doesn't know where Cass is – the woman couldn't know?' Dhanjal shook his head. 'Very well. But you say the woman was entertained on Sara's houseboat? What was our English rose playing at, Dhanjal?' Dhanjal offered neither word nor expression. Dumb machinery, awaiting instructions. Prakesh felt his anger direct itself at Sara Mallowby. That

214

unsacred cow. 'What measures have you taken to apprehend Hyde and the woman?'

'Army and police units. The centre of Srinagar is sealed off. The hotels, good and bad, are all being checked, the houseboats, everywhere they might attempt to hide. The airport is closed to them, the railway station, the buses and the roads. They cannot get out – Prakesh . . .' The name was offered with the greatest respect, like a title; and as a litmus test of favour or displeasure.

'Very well, Dhanjal, very well . . .' Prakesh's anger had been redirected. Dhanjal had been over-confident. He had known Hyde was a British agent, and therefore he should have been a great deal more careful. Just as Sara should have been.

Why was the woman here? he wondered with a sudden urgency. She came up to Srinagar before Hyde, she must have come with a purpose, not as *cover*. Then what has she done, what has she learned –? He felt himself inflate with rage. That damned Sara Mallowby, always feeling sorry for herself, bitter even when V.K. had taken her up, aloof and so bloody *British*! She could have said *anything* –

Damn V.K. for enjoying the kind of patronage she dispensed in bed, the covert humiliation with which she always seemed to treat him – and himself to an even greater degree. Undisguised dislike. Unless V.K. exercised power over her, dominated her, she had always seemed able to ignore him entirely.

'Come with me, Dhanjal – Ravindar.' He added the given name as a small token. Dhanjal gobbled it as eagerly as a hungry dog. 'I want to talk to our hostess.'

They left the houseboat and crossed the jetty to the boulevard. The shops had closed, and the place was strolled only by a handful of people and a few cars. As he had told V.K., the Kashmiris had subsided into quiet. There had been no incidents in Srinagar for two days, and no threat of any. The air smelt of the lake and the mountains, not of smoke and ashes. He knocked violently on the door of Sara's boat and immediately opened it, hurrying through the corridor and into the lounge.

Sara Mallowby was seated languorously – it was the only manner in which he could describe her pose, for that was what it was. Her elbow rested on the arm of the chair, as if she were engaged in inspecting the tumbler of whisky; as if she had anticipated his entrance and upstaged him. He could almost visualise her in some Memsahib's long dress, high at the throat so that it tilted the head back in surprised disdain. She was so damned British he wanted to strike her.

Frighten her, rather . . .

He had left her not fifteen minutes before. The whisky was refreshed, the level in the bottle apprehensibly lower. He did not frighten her, he realised as Dhanjal slipped into the lounge of the houseboat behind him, deferential and stereotyped. She was V.K.'s whore, and that gave her an unseemly, and now, he thought with satisfaction, an unfounded sense of self-assurance. She could be hurt. She could be pricked and she would bleed. What had she told that bloody Australian woman in one of her half-drunk bouts of confidence?

'The woman is the *mistress* –' He emphasised the word. '– of a British agent. An intelligence agent. Does that surprise you?'

'A *spy*? Do we still have any?' she mocked.

We. We *British*. We stealers of an empire and we runners-away when things get difficult, leaving you *wogs* to get on with it. The British legacy . . .

'Yes, you do. Apparently.' He felt chilled with anticipation. 'What did you and she talk about, Sara?'

'This and that.'

He moved two steps closer to her. She turned her head as if to welcome a blow, but really so that she could exhibit his unimportance.

'What *this*, exactly – and what *that*?'

'Why? Does it matter? I didn't commit any sins of indiscretion, Prakesh, if that's what's worrying you.' She smiled and flicked her hair aside, again as if inviting him to strike her across the face.

He took a further step closer to her and she continued to ignore his presence, sipping meditatively at the whisky as if she still enjoyed it rather than found it necessary. Necessary because she slept with his brother, or because she suddenly found it inconvenient to be privy to their strategy?

'Sara, the woman was sent here, ahead of the man you discovered on her houseboat and conveniently ignored –' Her eyes flashed with contempt. '– obviously to spy on you, V.K., myself, even Dhanjal for all we know. She would have been eager for information, she would have probed.'

Sara snorted in derision. 'I think I would have noticed any *probing*, Prakesh. She was an overweight, middle-aged woman who was desperate –'

'She was not!' he shouted, losing all sense of control. 'She has lived with this man for years, Sara! He is her *lover*! She is sane, well-adjusted – *happy*.' His voice had become softer. 'She is not the sad, pathetic creature you described earlier. Perhaps that figure of pity is yourself? What did you tell her?'

The whisky trembled in the tumbler, as if a breeze had passed across its surface, but he could not divine the motive, whether anger or apprehension.

'Not me,' she replied, tight-lipped. 'Whatever would *I* have to complain of, Prakesh? Except the poor business I'm doing at the moment because of the uncertainty – the atrocities.'

Dhanjal shifted his feet as if having stumbled upon an embarrassing struggle for temporary advantage in some endless marital conflict.

'Exactly. Yet you drink.'

'I drink because I enjoy it, Prakesh. *And* because it contains an ingredient for forgetting.' She smiled, folding one long leg over the other, then smoothing her skirt. She sipped again at her drink.

'Then you told her nothing?' he asked, baffled, his anger returning.

Sara shook her head. 'Not likely, is it, Prakesh? By the way,

Ros, my lover, the Prime Minister, is a drug producer and is engaged in . . . Finish the sentence yourself, Prakesh, I'm going to bed.' She swallowed the whisky and made to get up.

Enraged, he lunged forward, his hands gripping hers on the arms of the chair, his face thrust towards her.

'Do you think I am some sort of idiot?' he yelled. 'Some bloody *cookboy* you can treat like dirt whenever it suits you? A bloody Indian servant who must be watched in case he is making off with the knives and forks, memsahib?' He saw the spittle from his words on her cheek, saw the flinch of genuine fear in her eyes, felt her hands struggle under his grip. 'You bloody bitch! You may please my brother in bed, flatter his vanity, but I am not your servant! You will answer my questions politely, you will listen to me, you will sit in that chair –' He backed away with a lurch that might have been that of a drunk. ' – until I have finished with you.' His voice was hoarse, he felt heated and clammy in his suit, his collar tight at his narrow throat.

He lit a cigarette and stifled the initial cough it provoked. The fear in the woman's eyes had faded, but it remained in her voice as she said:

'I won't mention this conversation to V.K.' It was a threat, a bloody threat!

'Do as you like,' he snapped at her. 'Meanwhile, where do you think the woman has gone?'

'Has she disappeared?'

'For the moment.'

'Why do *you* think they came here?' There was something businesslike, controlled and commanding about her now which he tried to dismiss but which made her quite formidable. It reminded him of her early enthusiasm for their ideals *and* their tactics, the dangerous strategy of allowing violence in order to control it. She had enjoyed power then; secret power. 'Well, Prakesh? You had a great deal to say just now.'

'To find the man Cass. That is who Hyde has been seeking. In

Delhi and now here. Did you tell them anything – did the woman ask?'

'The woman did not ask. If she is connected with the man, then she's his cover, nothing more. You have my word on that.'

Prakesh Sharmar sat perched on the edge of the table, his hands gripping the carved, pelmetlike wood that fringed beneath it. Birds, flowers, vines curved and flitted beneath his restless hands. Trees, leaves, branches, flowers, small animals. He had always admired the old table. *Indian* craftsmanship merely bought by the British, not inspired or made by them.

'I can, can I? Can I be certain you were always sober, on your guard – ?' She tossed her head in contempt.

Birds, flowers – the petals of a wooden lily, the beak of a wooden hoopoe or bulbul, its stiff wings . . . He fingered the table as if poring over a work of history, some national epic. Fanciful –

He looked down at what his fingers had dislodged and which had fallen onto the polished floor near the fringe of a rug. He bent swiftly, outraged yet triumphant, and picked it up. Held it out to Dhanjal, whose face paled, then towards Sara.

'And what is this bloody thing doing in your lounge?' he screamed, his neck taut, his lips wet. 'This is a *bug*, the kind that *spies* use!' The woman's eyes darted, her face gratifyingly ashen. Her fingers played at her lips. 'That woman who was so innocent, so *pathetic* – put it here. When? They have overheard everything! You stupid, damned woman, they know it all!' He lunged at her, striking her across the cheek, then danced away from her as from an opponent in a boxing match. 'They have everything on tape, because you were taken in by that woman. You believed her as stupid and innocent as she wished to be thought!' Sara cowered in the chair, all masks removed and somehow boneless. Prakesh whirled on Dhanjal, shouting: 'You – get up to Gulmarg and have the man Cass killed! Do it now! Kill him and bury the body. *Then* find the other two and dispose of them. Do you understand? *Kill* them!'

As Dhanjal exited, Prakesh at once turned to Sara. He pounced forward on the balls of his feet and struck her twice across the cheek and mouth with his open hand.

hill station

'All right?' he called out softly. The whisper was almost lost in the static of laughter and music floating up from a long, low bungalow perched on a grassy outcrop below the track on which the Land Rover was parked.

'Yes!' She realised there was too much relief in her voice.

Hyde's head and shoulders thrust themselves above the vague edge of the track, where the slope fell away towards the lights of Gulmarg. His slight figure loomed like a shadow against the big stars. Then she could hear the exertions of his breathing and his hand scrabbled on the passenger door. He was grinning in the darkness. She touched his face momentarily and he did not resent the gesture.

'Done,' he murmured. 'How many have you seen?'

'Two more. That's five.'

'Six. There's one inside all the time, by the look of it. They're jumpy. I didn't see Dhanjal – he must be back in Srinagar.'

'Where's the bug?'

'Corner of the living-room window.'

'Did you see – him?' She saw Hyde shake his head vigorously.

'No. I checked the wood store and the garage. Nothing. He's in the house – maybe a bedroom? I couldn't check it all.' To Ros, his voice seemed remote, clinical; as if he were thinking aloud, nothing more. He was, of course, she realised. He was usually alone. 'Where are they now?'

'Same routine.' She indicated the night-glasses in her left hand, then raised them conscientiously to her eyes, sweeping their grey curtain across the site of Sharmar's bungalow. Nodded. 'Round and round the mulberry bush – they are alert, aren't they?' she added, pulling the shawl closely around her shoulders and breasts. The night was cool.

'Jittery. Maybe Cass tried something. We'll wait until they settle down. A lot later.'

Involuntarily, she looked at her watch. Almost midnight. The party in the closer bungalow was raucous, as if someone had opened a door – yes, a spill of light and somebody staggering happily across it as if treading water. Laughter. Loud Western pop music. There were European cars scattered like pebbles around the place. Its noise and vibrancy made the Sharmar bungalow seem deserted, dangerous.

Hyde was riffling his hands through the equipment he had stationed in the rear of the vehicle. She heard the click of metal, small cold sounds that were immensely threatening. The clinking together of what might have been bottles, but weren't. She distracted herself by watching the drunk lunge back through the door, which was closed behind him. The music dimmed. Ros looked down at her hands clutching penitently at the shawl. Then Hyde was back beside her door, wearing the headphones of the recorder, his face intent and disappointed.

'Bugger's snoring,' he murmured. 'Guard passing –?' He glanced down the long, steep slope, and nodded. A shadow flitted across the large, curtained window at the rear of the bungalow. Hyde appeared frustrated.

'What is it?'

'What? Oh, just waiting – and not knowing where they've got him. I *need* to know that . . .'

She reached down beside her feet and hauled up the thermos flask she had filled with tea at a roadside stall on the poorly-lit edge of Srinagar. Scattered street lighting strung on sagging cables at long intervals, the low houses and shacks crouching in the shadows like penned animals; the spurt of an occasional open fire, the smell of ordure and rubbish and incessant cooking.

'Want some tea?'

'Why not?' She poured some into the cap of the flask and handed it to him. It was as if there was a charge of electricity between them; cold, unerotic, distancing.

He smiled encouragingly as if he, too, had remarked its passage.

'Don't worry. These boys aren't army and they're not any sort of special forces. Just coppers. You can tell by the exact routine –' He paused, aware she was unconvinced. She sipped her tea from the inner cap of the flask.

'Want something to eat?' she asked, determined to be banal for her own nerves' sake. He shook his head.

'Might make me fart at the wrong moment. Could be fatal.' He paused, his grin frozen. 'No, thanks.'

'What – what do we do, afterwards?'

'Can't go back into Srinagar. Sewn up tight by now.'

The conversation, she realised, belonged in an asylum, some special hospital where the inmates had to have their fantasies drugged into submission. She felt colder, despite the tea, which was no more than a tepid trickle of warmth in her chest. They had missed the patrols by taking dirt tracks, crossing the River Jhelum – slowly, very slowly, across a narrow, swaying bridge, the Land Rover in its lowest gear and four-wheel drive. The creaking of the logs and ropes of the bridge like the collapse of a building in a storm. No headlights, the water below rushing, it seemed, in the starlight. It was all mad, insane, perched above Gulmarg waiting for Hyde to risk his life to *kill* strangers for the sake of someone he hardly knew. Crazy that she continued to attempt desultory, in-front-of-the-telly murmurings. Asking about *cups of tea* and remarking the *price of potatoes in Safeway* while half-observing gunfire and bodies in a piece of news footage. Was he as distanced from it as she was?

She shrugged herself away from reflection, as if moving aside from the glare of sunlight through a window.

'What, then?'

'I'll get hold of him first.' There was no impatience in his voice. 'We'll take the track north – like I showed you – up towards Baramula. Then decide. It depends on the state he's in, Ros.'

'I know that –!' she replied too quickly. Then: 'I'm all *right*, Hyde,' anticipating the deception of comfort.

'Sure.' He tugged off the headphones, which he had been wearing askew on his head, one ear listening to the noises from the bungalow. 'Sod all on the radio tonight.'

Ros looked down towards Gulmarg. Occasionally, headlights splashed and bucked towards or away from the resort that had once been a hill station of the Raj. *Cooler for the memsahibs.* The noise of car engines blurted through the night murmurs of the small town. The lights of wealthy houses and bungalows lay scattered like jewels across the sloping meadows. Narrow tracks wound like irregular partings in dark hair. Another set of headlights, spread like two assaulting fingers, swung along the road and stabbed towards the town. Moving quickly. She watched for the sake of another small distraction that promised to last as long as a few minutes. It was past midnight. The headlights splashed hurriedly through the town, emerging from its bowl of light with what seemed renewed urgency, bounding along the track towards –

'Hyde,' she murmured.

'Mm?'

She hesitated; not uncertain, merely reluctant. Then: 'I think –' she began. Hyde still had his back to the headlights and the dark beetle-shape of the vehicle she could now distinguish behind them as it slowed beside the Sharmar bungalow. The headlights disappeared. She thrilled with shock and certainty. 'Someone's arrived – down there. In a hurry –' He had already turned to look, snatching the night-glasses from her lap, focusing them.

'Your eyesight's getting worse,' he murmured with a quiver of excitement. She saw two small figures hurry into the shadow

224

of the building. Hyde said: 'Couldn't make out who they were.' Two of the patrolling guards had followed them into the bungalow. Hyde replaced the headphones and fiddled with the volume control on the tiny recorder. His head was bent, shoulders crouched in concentration. 'Dhanjal,' he murmured in a cold voice.

He began small, jerky, diving movements with his hands and body into the rear of the Land Rover. The clinks and reverberations of metal, the slight, slipper-tread of plastic being moved. She watched him don a shoulder holster and slip a small transceiver into it, then feed a thin lead down the sleeve of his sweater. A small switch nestled in his hand. Under his other shoulder was the pistol. A second pistol was thrust into his waistband.

'Listen to this,' he ordered, handing her the headphones. Then he fitted a tiny earpiece into his left ear. Just as she slipped on the headphones, she heard the slither and kiss of velcro as he adjusted the transceiver's harness. He placed a second transceiver in her lap and she stared at it as at a weapon. 'Well?' he snapped.

'Dhanjal,' she confirmed.

'What's he *want*?'

'He's excited, angry –'

'Where's Cass?' Hyde hissed against her cheek, shrugging himself into a camouflage jacket.

'– bedroom!' she blurted, then in protest: '*No –!*'

'What is it?' His hands gripped her arm fiercely. She shook her head, stunned. 'What? *Ros* – what?'

'Kill him,' she murmured. 'Asking about *you* –' as if that were a more enormous and disabling surprise.

'Shit!' he snapped. She realised he had already known. Instinct. He zipped up the jacket and she saw the smoke grenades go into two big pockets. Then he was at once checking the Sterling sub-machine-gun. 'Made in India – let's hope it bloody works!' He grinned like a savage. Her head whirled with

225

Dhanjal's tinny words and the other voices speaking English. As they debated where to dispose of Cass' body —

'It's an order from Prakesh Sharmar,' she informed Hyde, who appeared indifferent, distracted by the weapon he turned in his hand. A knife, hardly catching the light. Then he gestured her to remove the headphones, which she did reluctantly because even the details of Cass' murder were less terrifying than confronting Hyde's face and the vulnerability of his body. A respirator dangled on his chest from the straps he had pulled over his head. 'No,' she muttered in a strangled way.

He tuned the transceiver after lifting it from his lap, nodded, then thrust it into her hand, indicating the buttons.

'Transmit — Receive,' he said once. 'We'll test it when I get down the hill a bit. Use the night-glasses. I want to know what happens when it happens — *each* of the guards. Got it? Ros — got it?' She could only nod. 'Good.' He snatched up the headphones of the recorder for a moment, listening to one earpiece. 'Still debating the burial plot and who's going to do the digging.' He grinned, then swallowed, before he said solemnly: 'If anything happens — if I *tell* you or if I can't tell you, then get out. Just *go*. Train or bus. Not Srinagar. OK?' Again she nodded. 'It's what I do best, Ros. I'll be back.'

Then, immediately, he was gone, a small, exposed figure seeming to hop, even bounce, down the dark slope away from the vehicle. She swallowed, then sniffed loudly.

'Quiet, they'll hear you,' came a mutter from her lap, as if his head lay there. She stared in horror at the transceiver, then snatched it up with stiff, icy fingers. Clutching at the source of his voice as if to catch his arm and restrain him. 'What's happening, Ros?' She strained to see him, then, galvanised by fear, pressed the night-glasses hurtingly against her eye-sockets. She could see him now, a grey shadow moving like the drunk who had staggered out of the party, dodging from side to side, crouched and apparently irresolute. 'How many still outside?'

'Two — *three*,' she blurted, then pressed the PTT switch and repeated: 'Three – one on your side, two watching the road. Someone's just told them to do it, by the look –'

'OK. Keep it short.'

'Yes –'

The great peak of Nanga Parbat intruded, gleaming like a vast, suspended curtain in the night-glasses. Cold. Ros shivered and fumbled with one hand at the anorak that lay on the seat beside her.

It was narcotic, in a strange and ugly sense, reporting the movements of the men she could see. Twin grey figures beneath the shadows of enormous pines. She could clearly see the sticks of their rifles. She pulled the anorak around her shoulders, clutching it across her chest, which heaved beneath her hand like a quick tide.

'They're talking, still together in front of the house.' In the headphone pressed against her ear, Dhanjal was berating the guards who had followed him inside. He seemed reluctant to proceed, continuing to debate the location of the burial, not mentioning the act of killing Cass. Hyde's grey form was far down the slope now, past the party bungalow which gleamed with light like an explosion –

She controlled her imagination.

'Still there?' the transceiver asked, as if he sat beside her.

'Still here. Can you – can you see the one on your side?'

'Too much shadow. Where is he?'

'Under the verandah, waiting like a servant.'

'OK.' She heard Hyde's breathing. He had halted behind an outcrop of rock perhaps fifty yards or so from the bungalow. A shadow passed across the lighted, curtained window, waving its arms as if pointing towards Hyde's concealment. 'Listen, Ros. Bring the Land Rover down the track to the bungalow *when* I tell you – *if*. OK?'

'Yes,' she replied in a tiny voice.

'Good –' She sensed he had been about to add some patronising endearment and had thought better of it. She might almost have welcomed it, to fend off the immediate, stifling reality of events. 'You're going to have to listen to everything. Understand, Ros?'

'Yes,' in the same helpless voice.

'You'll hear my breathing, especially once I put on the respirator. Keep listening for it, Ros.' Then, more quietly: 'Fucking sub-machine-guns – I don't trust them. Let's get the silencer on . . .' She strained to hear tiny, betraying sounds, but there were none. As if the transceiver had gone dead.

'Right,' he murmured. 'Where and when, all the time, Ros. Any movement. Don't expect me to reply.'

'Hyde –'

There was no reply, only his breathing. She watched him slip from behind the rocks and continue towards the bungalow, now with exaggerated, cartoonlike caution, literally tiptoeing up on them. Christ, *please* let him be all right . . .

'Then get on with it!' she heard Dhanjal snap in the headphone. 'The two of you. Go on!' The voice was strained.

'Hyde, they're ready to –'

'OK.'

His breathing became quicker through the transceiver, like a rush of static. She forced herself to focus on the guards who remained outside, the two on the track still together, one of them smoking, the other scuffing his foot in the dust as if making some mean confession. The solitary third guard – she heard her own breathing quicken to the pace of Hyde's as she glimpsed his ghostly figure converging on the third man, who had stepped out from beneath the verandah and was gazing towards the looming mountain peak. The two together – oblivious . . . the one – unalert. Hyde had paused, his breathing controlled, coming like the background hum of smooth machinery beside her cheek.

Hyde moved closer. Oh sweet Christ –! She was shivering and could not control the spasms. The man turned –

No . . .

Hyde was aware of the six yards of starlit ground between them as the guard turned, bulky in his anorak, the stick of the automatic rifle waving like a wand, conjuring the Indian out of surprise and into action. The moon was nudging over the mountain peak behind the man. Four paces — three, two —

Hyde clashed with the rifle so that it struck his shoulder, numbing it as he thrust his weight upwards, levering the Kalashnikov beneath the man's chin and into his throat, gagging off the voice he had been about to use. Hyde swung the short, folded butt of the sub-machine-gun against the man's head, knocking him off his feet. Then he kicked him heavily on the left temple as he lay on the ground. Glared around him like an animal as he fitted the respirator's mask, its snout jutting into his vision.

'OK,' he announced, knowing she would hear him.

He removed one of the CS smoke grenades from his jacket and weighed it in his hand.

'Hyde,' her voice blurted. 'They've left the room –!'

Now.

There were shadows on the blind at the smaller window to the right, fleeting with ominous purpose. Fifteen yards. The shadows were moving, blurred. Ten yards. Sod the blind, that's going to get in the way. Five yards, then the verandah under his feet, the glass shattering. The blind rolled obligingly up, as if for comic effect. The faces of the two Indians were poised at the bedside, as the pale, frightened features, bruised and crumpled, looked up at them from the white pillows. Then the CS pellets in the submunition burst a second after the grenade exploded. The room was filled with roiling grey smoke within which the blinded, coughing shadows of the two Indians wobbled and gestured like the shadows of hanged men.

Hyde flung the second grenade through the main window and heard it explode, then the pellets burst a second later. He heard cries of shock, warning. He clambered towards the sill of the broken bedroom window as a shadow blundered towards him, arms waving, seeking the window rather than encounter. He squeezed the trigger of the silenced sub-machine-gun. The gases hissed from the casing like a cobra as the Sterling bucked in his hands and against his hip. The body collapsed over the sill as if to gulp air into dead lungs. The second man's shadow was purposeful, looming in the smoke and light over the bed, heaving as it was racked with coughing. Hyde shot towards the shadow, wounding the man, hearing his body hit the floor as he cried out for assistance.

He retreated from the sill as the smoke swirled freshly in a gust from the suddenly opened door of the bedroom. He kicked at the shards of glass jutting from the frame of the lounge window. Something tore at the window frame ahead of the roar of a 9mm pistol.

'Hyde, Hyde —!' It was Ros. 'They're moving towards the front porch, both of them —!'

Hyde fired perhaps ten rounds into the lounge, which was chaotic with smoke and shadows, before he hit the source of the glow from the far side of the room. Larger, dimmer shadows. He ducked beside the window, squatting on his haunches. He heard Dhanjal's voice calling out orders, he thought from the bedroom. The lounge was cavernous with the irritant CS smoke, enlarged too by his sense of imprisonment in the mask of the respirator. He fired in the direction of another glow and immediately there were only the flames of the open fire flickering within the smoke. He heard the front door open and slam shut, and then Dhanjal calling out for it to be left open. The draught of air moved the smoke and began to disperse it. Someone fired towards the window and he fired back at the shadow, hitting nothing except the panelling of the wall. The smoke opened for a moment to reveal the scars on the dark wood. He rolled behind the edge of a long sofa placed at an angle near the window.

The smoke was clearing. There were four — and Dhanjal — unwounded. Someone lumbered from the bedroom and he squeezed off three shots. The grunt was real, not pretended, like the noise of the body slipping on a rug and colliding with the far wall. A gun fell into the firelight. Four in all now. The smoke was thinning. He appeared to be alone in the room. The furniture seemed hunched like waiting men in the flicker from the fire. He fired two more shots – less than twenty left in the magazine now, maybe fewer than fifteen. He fingered the last of the smoke grenades in his jacket, withdrew it, then flung it across the room towards the fire. The ejection charge exploded, flinging fragments of wood and flame into the room, then the CS smoke billowed out of the fireplace.

And then he moved.

Immediately, wood puckered and scarred beside his cheek, splintering him enough to make him gasp. At once he heard in the earpiece:

'Hyde –!'

'OK!' he snarled, huddling into himself as he ran for the bedroom door –

– collision with something soft. Hands tugging more in instinct than purpose at his respirator, heaving on its snout as if to overturn a bullock or a pig. He butted at the man's ribs with the short stock of the Sterling, but his grip did not loosen. His face, as twistedly masklike as Hyde's, thrust itself against the polycarbonate of the facemask, clouding it. Hyde struck again at the man's ribs, making his features snarl silently.

'Hyde – Hyde!' Ros was like a terrified child in a darkened cinema. As he gripped the box magazine of the sub-machine-gun, it pressed against the transmitter switch in the palm of his left hand, leaving the channel to Ros open.

The Indian was reaching into his jacket, struggling with something that would not easily come free, his body thrusting against Hyde, holding him against the door jamb. Then an arm tightened around Hyde's throat, half-blocked by the respirator's bulk. Fingers obscured his vision as the second attacker attempted to rip off the mask. He squeezed the trigger of the Sterling. The

231

hiss of gas like the assailant's surprised last breath. He fell away. Hyde raked his heel down the second man's shin, twice, stamping on the foot. He twisted in the man's grip but lost his balance. The attacker was bigger than he, bulky in a dark anorak. As Hyde was thrust sideways, the man brought his Kalashnikov to bear. CS drifted like incense over a form on the bed, half-propped on one elbow, its pale features sick and stunned.

The Sterling had jammed – or the magazine was empty. Hyde fired through the camouflage jacket without withdrawing the pistol, merely tugging its blunt little barrel from his waistband and squeezing the trigger. The door chipped beside the man's shoulder, then the second shot flung his arm out, making him drop the rifle. He slid into a sitting position in the doorway. Hyde stared at Dhanjal's face, creased with pain, his eyes wide with surprise.

Voices. Smoke that was from burning furniture drifting across the doorway. Someone in the lounge was screaming in agony and terror.

The body of his first assailant lay near his feet as he leant back against the bedroom wall. Dhanjal watched him with hatred from the doorway, as he tore off the respirator. The first to die was still hanging out of the window frame as if vomiting at a party. There was a stillness of shock-response in the bungalow, and the crackling of burning wood. Someone was coughing –

– regrouping? How many? Three dead, one unconscious, two wounded. *Two* others fit – who probably didn't know whether Dhanjal was alive or dead . . . or were cleverer than their panic and would be waiting for him when he came out. Or just waiting for the cavalry.

He moved to the bed and switched off the lamp after a momentary inspection of Cass, who displayed no recognition of him, little sense of time or place. Vacant, drugged shock. The paleness of the features was a false impression. There were bruises and cuts. Blood on the shirt. Needle-marks in his arm. Cass fell back on the bed like an invalid grateful for the darkness.

Smoke drifted through the moonlit room like that from a cigarette left burning in an ashtray.

Hyde crossed the room again, fitting a new magazine to the Sterling. Getting sloppy, can't count. It had been empty. He switched the selector to single shot. Gripped the shoulder of Dhanjal's anorak and dragged him to his feet with a vast effort. The man's eyes were still watering violently from the irritant smoke and something that could only be enraged, impotent hatred. Or the pain from his shoulder. There was nothing else for it, he had to keep the bastards from blowing him and Cass away when they stepped through the door. No sense in shooting your superior officer, Pandit Plod ... Dhanjal struggled until Hyde pressed the muzzle of the sub-machine-gun into his stomach, then moved lamely across the room to the bed.

'Get him up!' he growled.

'Hyde —!' like the sighing relief of the sea.

'Where are they, Ros?' he snapped, remembering her.

He glared back towards the bedroom door, then squeezed off two shots into the motionless lounge. There was no returned fire. Outside, then —

'Three of them —' He hadn't hit the first man hard enough. 'This side of the bungalow — all of them, I think. In the pines to the left —'

'Good girl. I'm all *right*,' to stifle further dialogue. Dhanjal was watching him like a cunning animal, waiting. He snatched the pistol from Dhanjal's waistband as the man's eyes conveyed a sense of advantage, then his features collapsed into defeat. 'Do it. Get him on his feet!'

Dhanjal indicated his shoulder, and Hyde slapped the barrel of the Sterling against his wounded arm, making him cry out.

'Do it.'

Dhanjal struggled with Cass, holding him with his good arm beneath Cass' armpit. Hyde pressed the gun into Dhanjal's side and helped him hoist Cass who protested with the intensity and silence of a dreamer. They got him into a sitting position, then

233

onto feet that immediately parted from one another below rubbery legs. Hyde thrust Cass' deadweight against Dhanjal, then pushed them towards the door. Dhanjal would appear first in the doorway, half-shielding Cass, covering himself. The screams had died, and the fires that had caught at the rugs and the furniture were still hesitant, as if undecided upon destruction.

Hyde pushed them towards the door to the rear of the bungalow. It was open with the hospitality of ambush.

'Tell them we're coming out!' he grunted at Dhanjal. 'I know where they are. Tell them you'll be the first to go – tell them!'

Dhanjal yelled in a pained, frightened voice from well within the shelter of the doorway.

'Do not fire! I am his prisoner! Do not open fire!'

They waited, as if enraged animals trapped together in a sack. Then:

'Yes, sir. We will not open fire!' Shouted from the pines. Good girl.

'OK, Dhanjal – get moving. You're on the right side of our friend to get shot first. Let's go!'

They struggled through the door as in some comic cartoon, then down the verandah steps and across the garden behind the bungalow. The sigh and dribble of water from fountains and the miniature landscapes of pools and rockeries. Their breathing clouded on the cold air. The ground began to slope upwards, towards the –

Bloody kids and their party. The bungalow was brightly lit, people crowded on to its verandah.

'Get on with it, Dhanjal – you're not dying!' Voices called out, questioningly. They struggled up the slope, Cass' left arm draped across Hyde's shoulder, his feet dragging, his voice a continuous mumble now, as if he was imitating the noise of the water in the Sharmars' garden. 'Piss off!' Hyde cried. 'Tell them it's a police operation,' he snarled at Dhanjal.

'Police! Clear the area – we, we require *no* assistance. Nothing has happened here! This is a police operation!'

They were watched by a silenced group from the verandah as they struggled up the slope, leaving the well-lit bungalow behind. Terrorists, drug smugglers – the fictions were too easy for the party-goers to find, too real in Kashmir. As he glanced back, Hyde saw one or two drifting curiously towards the Sharmar bungalow. Spectators, merely interested, excited by the proximity of the covert and dangerous. None of Dhanjal's men had emerged from the pines. No shots – not yet. Couldn't risk killing the officer . . .

'I must rest!' Dhanjal protested.

'Fuck you, sport!' Hyde snarled, forcing them on, stumbling occasionally, dragging either Cass or Dhanjal or himself to his feet again, urging them on, being maddened by Cass' monotone, the dribble of senseless words. Then the noise of music behind them as the party recommenced.

Eventually

'Hyde –!'

Dhanjal, as if recognising their destination before Hyde, slumped to the ground, letting Cass fall into Hyde's embrace. The mumbling had ceased, like a worn-out recording. He lowered Cass to the ground, bereft of feeling – somehow distanced from the slim, now-frail form, as if Cass was a derelict who had slumped against him from the shadows of an alley. Dhanjal nursed his arm as Ros loomed over him, horrified; as if he was the victor about to announce their collective capture.

Hyde looked back down the long slope. Flames flickered behind the broken windows of the Sharmar bungalow, stronger now. Party-goers milled on the lawn, a small knot of people huddled around someone who had collapsed or who they had dragged out of the bungalow. Along the main road leading to Gulmarg, there were no urgent headlights, but there was the distant noise of a siren and a clanging bell from the hill station. Hyde looked down at Cass, feeling the man's weight not as something he had slipped but which insisted into the future. Cass had been beaten –

He opened the shirt and the heart fluttered beneath his hand.

Its sound came clearly through the transceiver Ros held in a dumb hand, and he shook the transmitter switch from his palm. Bruising. Cass groaned as he touched him across the shivery, goose-pimpled skin. One broken rib, perhaps two. He inspected the puckered, punctured arm.

Who gives a sod, anyway, he thought. What could you have told London? Nothing to tell any more . . .

Cass was – a liability, not to put too fine a point on it. Better – dead . . . Dhanjal groaned in a pleading way and Ros' exclamation was pitying.

Hyde stood up and tugged a blanket from the rear of the Land Rover, wrapping it roughly around Cass' shoulders, angry with the purposeless, scrabbling movements of the man's hands and the sick, dead, penitential gratitude that sheened his features. Then he crossed to Dhanjal, the scent of woodsmoke from the bungalow reaching his nostrils, the music of the party in his ears. He stood behind Dhanjal and, like an executioner, so that the Indian's body shuddered itself smaller, more suppliant, thrust the muzzle of the sub-machine-gun against the back of his head. Ros' face abhorred, but he snapped:

'Stick a bloody plaster on his shoulder or arm or wherever.'

Ros quickly, with fumbling inspired by concern rather than nerves, inspected the arm – flesh wound, upper arm, he was in better shape than Cass. Then she brought the first-aid kit from the vehicle and dabbed the wound with iodine. Dhanjal winced back against the pressure of the gun muzzle, then Ros covered the wound with a patch of lint and a crossed plaster like a holy sign on the brown flesh. Dhanjal nodded and pulled his suit jacket and then his anorak over the wound.

Ros got to her feet to confront Hyde, then recalled Cass, his teeth chattering audibly. Hyde shook his head and indicated the Land Rover. Ros followed him. He leant against the vehicle, the Sterling pointed towards the huddled figure of Dhanjal. Ros' breathing might have been a reminder of his own as she had heard it through the transceiver.

'What now?' she demanded.

Nanga Parbat was massive and gilded in the risen moonlight. The bungalow burned as comfortably as a domestic fire. A police car had reached it, and a fire engine was labouring towards it, a second toy vehicle. The party continued, healing over the wound of the interruption.

'Now, we get out.'

'How?'

'Keep your voice down, Ros –'

'Why? What about him?' She gestured towards the squatting policeman. 'Or him?' Cass appeared unaware of his surroundings, his voice once more a continuous mumble.

'Drugged up to the eyeballs. And they've duffed him up.'

'Who? The *late* however many?'

'Shut it, Ros.'

'How the bloody hell do we get out of here?' There were other headlights down on the road now, hurrying into and through Gulmarg. Still had to be local. Srinagar was an hour away.

'I'm thinking. *Not* together – not you, anyway.'

'Why not?'

'I told you. Someone's got to make it.' He scraped the barrel of the Sterling on the door of the Land Rover, making Dhanjal twitch, then subside again into his confinement. 'You –' He looked at her. Then back to Dhanjal. 'There are ways out that I *need* to take, you don't. So, just do as I bloody say for once, will you?' He paused, but she said nothing. 'They'll be looking for us now,' he supplied. 'Not for you. You're incidental, now there are bodies. You can get down as far as Jammu in a bloody *taxi* if necessary, or on the bus. But get there you will.'

'This is the plan, is it?' she sneered. Vehicles had collected like moths around the flames of the bungalow. 'The great-bloody-escape, I don't think!'

He turned his head violently towards her.

'Ros – *don't!*' he warned. 'You have half the evidence. Take

237

it, get to Jammu, then down to Delhi on the train – you've got the bloody guide book, for God's sake! They won't be looking for you in Delhi, you're not connected there. Get a plane to Paris, not London . . .' He was dizzied between Dhanjal's suspect somnolence and her disbelief and silent refusal. He was sufficiently enraged almost to want to point the Sterling at her, move it between her and Dhanjal as he shifted his gaze. 'You have to reach Shelley, meet him in Paris, if you can. You have to *convince* him . . .' He subsided for a moment, shielding his calculation and anxiety from her, then he added: '*You* have to give him the price of the trade, the gold charge card that gets Cass and me out.'

Her breathing in the silence, Cass' mumbling like water, the distant, tiny noises of the fire being put out and the search being organised. There'd be a chopper out at first light at the latest, once Prakesh Sharmar was informed. Dhanjal's absence would slow that process down, but the insistence of those still alive would ensure the pursuit. Kashmir stretched away on every side of him, climbing and falling like a vast mural; a mural he would have to enter, learn, use.

'And you? You're just going to hang about until I can get home, are you?'

'Not necessarily. I can't get Cass out by any respectable route. I've got *him* as some kind of insurance. Otherwise, I've got you. I could get killed, so could Cass. If we're out of the game, then I want someone alive and safe who can screw the Sharmars on behalf of both of us. You're elected, Ros.' He glared at her, then added: 'Ros, you're not going to be able to cope – not with anything that comes after this. I'll take you up the track to Baramula and we'll find a bus station or a taxi rank. Pay the bugger over the odds and his car won't break down before you get to Jammu –' He grabbed her arm and pulled her against him. Her flesh quivered as if with sexual excitement. Her hands were icy. 'Listen,' he whispered, 'just get on with your bit, leave me to do mine. I'll get through to Shelley, if necessary – if I'm

238

desperate. *You* get through and I can get on Air India, first class, out of here . . .' He kissed her.

When she drew back from him, he recognised her compliance. She would not be able to cope, but she did have something she could do. She could try to save him. She knew she was being played upon, but accepted the melody.

'Jammu?' she asked. 'How long, by car?'

He masked his relief. And fear.

'Nine or ten hours from Baramula – I guess.'

She nodded. 'All right,' in a small voice.

'Let's get moving, then.' There were headlights thrusting into the garden of the bungalow, party-goers would be questioned at the other bungalow. They'd already stayed too long. The conversation with Ros had been his post-mission relapse. He felt weary now and shook his head to clear it. 'Let's get Nehru here into the back of the vehicle, tied up like a chicken, and then we'll sort out –' He hesitated, watching Cass, crouched like a mystic, staring at the grass just in front of him; oblivious.

Jesus, he was full of drugs – pentathol or something else, maybe just something to keep him quiet. Now, he was concussed with the immediate; the night, the cold, his rescue.

'Christ, Hyde, he's a bloody liability,' Ros whispered against his cheek.

'I know it, darling – I know.'

But *you're* not, he thought. You're getting out, at least –

into the black

The grey light slipped across the unwrinkled surface of Dal Lake like the wake of a boat. The peak of Nanga Parbat became sheened; the other, receding peaks beyond it. A shikara moved as secretly as a fish. Prakesh Sharmar turned on the verandah of Sara Mallowby's houseboat, away from the slight nudge of the water against the bottom step. Srinagar's noises stirred into audibility, soft as the clash of pots from the cookboat. He slapped one arm against the chilly air as if to dissipate the sense of innocuous peace.

He turned to Sara, her long housecoat wrapped about her, her feet cold and slim in slippers. She seemed to have absorbed the peace of the lake like an affront to his sense of urgency.

Prakesh looked at his watch. Where in damnation was the colonel? Now that Dhanjal had allowed himself to become a hostage – his stupidity would be punished – he needed the colonel here to coordinate the hunt for the agent, Hyde. And the *tape recorder* that the man Cass had become, not only when he'd made love to Sereena but since his captivity . . . because to extract information they had had to supply it, albeit in the form of questions. If Cass retained his mind – they grovellingly admitted that he did – then he now knew much more than he had done. And the search of the houseboat on which that fat Australian woman had stayed had revealed scratch marks on a windowsill consistent with the resting of a telephoto lens. And the bug –

It was the most damnable situation! Every moment that they

240

remained at large, unapprehended, they magnified his danger, the danger to V.K. –

– near her feet – *there* – were the early editions of the newspapers. V.K. and Mehta were neck and neck in some polls; in others, V.K. had moved into a small but dramatic lead. And she sat amid what might symbolise the wreckage of V.K. himself and the whole of Congress, as if she presided over it and approved! He moved his arm again and she flinched, then seemed to despise herself for the reaction. She pulled her housecoat more comfortably about her and gazed sardonically out over the lightening lake, where shikaras now plied in small, busy schools and the noises of ducks and waterfowl rose from the reeds.

It was ready now, everything . . . Poised. In the balance.

Hanging by the merest thread, he admitted. How strong was Dhanjal? What would the British agent do to him, should he need to know more? What would he *promise* Dhanjal? Could Hyde contact Shelley, convince him?

Not over the telephone – he'd never persuade him that way. He had to get Cass out of Kashmir, out of India . . . He listened, his attention suddenly caught and held by the approach of a large-engined car. He leaned like a schoolboy over the rail, feeling her mockery across his shoulders like his father's cane, and saw the black limousine draw to a halt at the end of Sara's jetty. Colonel Rao stepped from it at once. Aides hurried after him onto the houseboat, their heavy footsteps alarming Sara. He saw her look up, as afraid as at a noise that signified immediate arrest. He smiled with deliberate malice and she shivered visibly. Her cheek was bruised and one eye was puffy. Her confidence, all her hauteur, seemed to decline to the condition of her damaged looks. Rao emerged onto the verandah without either pause or knock.

'Colonel,' he acknowledged, stifling his sense of relief.

'Mr Sharmar,' Rao replied formally, with a slight, nodded bow – valedictory, Prakesh sensed. From the moment of his arrival, the operation was entirely his. 'I came as soon as I was able.' It was neither apology nor explanation. The patient piece of machinery who had seemed content to wait in anterooms and back offices was now animate and possessive. 'Your summons explained that they have Dhanjal. That is regrettable. Where are they?'

'There is no trace of them. The helicopters were ordered up as soon as it became light enough.'

'To search what area?' Rao demanded, moving closer to Prakesh, ignoring the tame white woman gazing across the lake. There was something brutally admirable about Rao, something that gave confidence; and discomfiting in its directness, its lack of regard for former niceties, the castes of politics. 'Was that the local army commander in the lounge?' Prakesh nodded. 'Then I must speak with him at once.'

He turned away from Sharmar, and Prakesh had no option, so Sara's mouth and eyes emphasised, but to follow him into the houseboat. The interior still glowed with lamplight, which enlarged Rao's presence, diminished that of his aides and the junior officers who accompanied the army commander. Another colonel was already deferring to Rao's manner and his Intelligence status. He and his aide hovered near a huge map of Kashmir that lay spread on the polished table like a cloth. The soldiers and aides were poised like children awaiting a summons to eat.

Rao began at once, in an interrogatory tone, his hands, joined by other, more supplicatory hands, gliding and gesturing over the map. Occasionally, they appeared tender, as if about to pick up an infant. Rao nodded continually, or shook his head, his large jaw clutched in his right hand, his left arm across his chest. He peered closely at the map like a doctor at the symptoms of a disease; an ailment which had wasted his talents and for which he did not expect payment. The damnable contempt of the *military*. So necessary now, Prakesh admitted. Rao began patrolling the circumference of the table, as if to capture and pen the country portrayed on the map. His power hinted at a dangerous future, even as it made him confident that Hyde and Cass could

242

not escape. The man's disregard for the local commander, his own aides – even himself, unnerved Prakesh.

'Then get equipment installed here – or on another of these houseboats – at once. No, your local headquarters are too insecure, *here* will be best. The centre of the web.' Spiders did build their own webs, of course . . . 'No, only handpicked people involved here –' Rao glanced towards his aides as if to judge their suitability rather than indicate that they were to fill the roles he had suggested.

The telephone rang. The army commander and one of the Intelligence aides looked towards it, but Prakesh felt an irresistible impulse to answer it, if only to prevent it interrupting Rao's concentration. He was no more than a *civilian*, he realised. India's own Raj pertained in the suddenly close atmosphere of the lounge as the day intruded at the net curtains masking the windows. The men in uniform expected, like *England expects* –!

He picked up the telephone. It was V.K., excited and anxious, like a child preparing to come home for his school holidays. He turned his back to the table and Rao, as if embarrassed.

'I am being pressured, Prakesh –' V.K. blurted, then at once: 'What is happening there? Have they been found?'

The connection was secure, there was that fuzz around V.K.'s voice that indicated he had activated the masking unit.

'No, they have not. Rao – Colonel Rao is here and has taken control.' He felt he had had to supply the colonel's rank. He could not subordinate the Intelligence officer. As a result, he added waspishly to V.K.: 'There is no need to panic, brother. Matters are in hand.'

'But your call said that the British agent had Cass!' V.K. protested.

'Is that all you called about?'

'– troops up from Delhi, or units from Pathankot,' he heard Rao announce at the table. The map rustled under his fingers. 'No, your people are *not* suitable, Colonel.'

'No, Prakesh.' V.K. was attempting to win him over with a

child's charm. 'I am being pressured by the party. They want us to go on the results of the latest polls.'

'I know that.'

'How can we?'

'– I don't think they would go north, Colonel,' Rao said. 'That is a bottleneck, up towards the Cease Fire Line. There are too many troops –'

'We must, V.K. We have argued this until it is a dead dog. You must take the tide –'

'I'm not certain, Prakesh! Not while we have these people on the loose.'

'Do it, V.K. See the President and have parliament dissolved. *Call* the election.'

'Are you certain that Rao can contain this?'

'Yes –'

Prakesh glanced towards the knot of men intent upon the map of Kashmir. A comforting, assured bulk.

'I read his file on the way up here,' Rao was explaining. 'This agent is experienced, he is lucky. But he does not know this area. Evidently that is why the woman was sent.'

'Yes,' Prakesh confirmed. 'Yes, it is under control. Only a matter of time –'

Rao had looked up at him, his dark eyes blackly intent. He nodded and returned his attention to the map. Sara was a shadow in the doorway, her face as stunned as if she had opened the door of her home on the wreckage of a burglary.

'No, no – that is not sufficient. *This* size of area – see? In a Land Rover, if they set out at one this morning, they might have reached a point anywhere in this large a radius. That means more helicopters. See to it, Mathur.'

An aide left immediately. Prakesh, absorbed in the minutiae that would bring about the recapture and death of Cass and his rescuer, shook himself back to attention to his brother.

'You can announce the election by midday, V.K. Yes, I'm certain.'

'Get these photographs duplicated and circulated,' Rao ordered. 'Find out about the C31 arrangements. I want the command post set up here in one hour.'

'What the hell –?' It was Sara Mallowby.

Rao turned to her, after a glance towards Prakesh.

'This is the headquarters of an intelligence operation, Miss Mallowby. I take it you agree to cooperate.'

She paused, then nodded dumbly before leaving the doorway. Sunlight spilled warmly on the steps like gold leaf. Prakesh suppressed a smile of pleasure.

'Yes, V.K. I hope to return this evening. What? You have the programme, V.K. No, not *the* speech – you do not need me to arrange your TV appearances, V.K.!' he protested in frustration. 'We have teams of people to do that. Yes, very well . . . Goodbye, V.K. Good luck.'

Prakesh put the receiver down heavily, at once isolated from his brother and Congress and the election, and from the soldiers gathered at the table. An aide entered from the stern of the houseboat, followed by overalled soldiers with the flashes of engineers on their sleeves. They were carrying heavy communications equipment. Leads trailed behind them. He heard a generator start up somewhere, like the purr of a distant motor boat. The whole section of the boulevard where Sara's boats were located would be isolated. There was a comfort in bustle, in the heavy black bulk of the equipment, in the uniforms and Rao's focal, commanding presence. The intimate isolation from the world of a party caucus meeting, any piece of politicking.

It was done, then. The die was cast. V.K. would cope, now that the decision was taken, the necessity of an election obeyed. Parliament would be dissolved, the election announced, the campaign begun.

And Cass and the man Hyde killed –

The taxi had run out of petrol. A shock like a confirmation of cancer. Dread rather than annoyance, a creeping terror that subtly, inexorably increased with each passing minute – with each approaching vehicle, car or bus or truck, until the vehicle passed without slowing or stopping. The dread leaping back into the shallow relief, to create the waves of hot distress and helplessness she experienced.

She obeyed the tic of head and wrist once again and looked at her watch. Nine twenty. They had been on the road for two hours, she had been abandoned in the taxi for another half-hour while the driver walked towards the village of Punch, two miles farther on. He had insisted she not accompany him, had reassured her she was safe . . . The pistol Hyde had given her was in her lap, useless as any piece of machinery she had no idea how to operate. No comfort whatsoever.

The driver had scrambled away down the narrow mountain road as if pursued – more in pursuit of the fare they had agreed. The moment he had disappeared around a twist of the mountain road, the peaks and folds of the Pir Panjal range had threatened her, moving their great shoulders and blank features, already snowcapped, towards her. Dark pine forests, bleak ridges of grey rock, the sheer drop to one side of the road to a dribble of river far below. The isolation and massiveness of the place unnerved her.

Hyde had waved a thick wad of bright notes in front of the taxi driver's nose. The man had been asleep in his seat – his *home*, she had realised. Hyde had given him clear, repeated instructions, pecked at her cold cheek, and waved her off as the first grey light struggled down from the mountains into Baramula. Hyde had issued her instructions with the same measured and distant authority. Dhanjal was trussed up in the rear of the Land Rover, presumably staring at the sleeping form of Cass. A few early workers, children and dogs, the first cooking smells and the drying overnight shower on the deserted streets. There was the scent of snow in the air and a clothing mist on the closest peaks. Even in Baramula's main square, the mountains had seemed to stretch endlessly, disconsolately away, suggesting that there was nowhere to be reached, however far she travelled and in whatever direction. Hyde had instinctively recognised her mood and gripped her hand, but it was nothing but a premonition of this . . .

. . . the sense of unimportance, an imitation of extreme weariness, where nothing mattered. However far the taxi travelled, when its interrupted journey was continued, there would only be more mountains, more dark forests. The landscape anaesthetised like an odourless gas.

The noise of an engine recalled her to her fears. A bus limped past, the driver and the succession of windowed passengers glancing at the taxi while continuing their own journey. Dust from the road rattled against the windows. Then the road was empty again, hemmed by a rock face, threatened by the drop to the narrow river. She fumblingly lit another cigarette and huddled into her anorak.

The train for Delhi left Jammu at six in the evening, arriving in Delhi somewhere around ten the following morning. She had all day to reach Jammu, no more than a hundred and fifty miles away. The pressure of the mountains insisted that it could not be done, and she shivered deeply, the cigarette making her cough. She opened the window and threw it away. The mountain air chilled the taxi, as cloud hovered sombrely along the Pir Panjal. Hyde had been certain she would make the train —

— as certain as she was uncertain of his situation. As she left Baramula, he had made reassuring, empty noises like a relative leaving a terminal sickbed; polite, soothing, finally insulting. If she didn't know anything, she realised, she couldn't tell anyone. He'd reach Shelley somehow . . . or he'd stooge around, waiting for the cavalry . . . he'd hide up somewhere . . . he'd all *all right*, Ros. Then he'd nudged the taxi driver into putting the cab into gear, as if he had slapped the flank of a horse and sent her careering away. She'd watched his retreating figure beside the Land Rover, hand raised as if in warning rather than wishing her well or regretting her departure. Then the creaking, asthmatic taxi lurched around a corner and the rear window was a screen for a travelogue of Kashmir, tiny figures, animals, great peaks watching the town for signals of intent. She had no idea what he would do, where he would go, even though he knew the strain that ignorance would place on her.

She lit another cigarette. The smoke was less rough on her throat, the fugginess of the taxi warm and enclosing. A haze on the windows kept the mountains at bay. The road ahead of the windscreen was empty.

Nine forty . . . two miles there, two miles back, and between them lack of urgency by the driver, except to haggle over the price of the petrol or to pause to eat something. The dread was creeping like cold up through her body again, and once more the cigarette began to nauseate. She persisted with it, however. It was better than opening the window to throw the cigarette away.

She stared instead at her lap, at the litter on the floor of the taxi, at the signs that the driver lived in his vehicle. A portable stove on the rear parcel shelf, clothing, a copy of the Koran, a vase of flowers attached to the dashboard by a large rubber sticker.

Come on, come on, come *on* . . .

A helicopter flashed over the stand of pines and disappeared towards the Cease Fire Line to the north. It wasn't military but that meant nothing. Below him, the scattered village of Kupwara. The road, which had headed due north from Sopore, bent like an elbow as it passed through the low houses and huts, before it slithered like a long brown snake westwards towards Tithwal and the border with Azad Kashmir – and the guards and the Pakistani army.

But it had to be. Had to . . . Didn't it? The faultless logic of his guesswork petered out like the crude huts and refugee tents at the edge of Kupwara. Hindus, presumably, from the other side of the CFL. Moslems from the south the Pakistanis wouldn't let cross into their *free* Kashmir? Pakistanis persecuted for some God-forsaken reason in their own country. It didn't matter. The ragged movements of the tents in the wind were universal symbols of distress and the ignorance or indifference of the world. There was snow in the air, the peaks obscured along the Pangi range. Nanga Parbat was closer, no more than fifty direct miles away. Its bulk was insuperable and unnerving.

But he had to be right . . . this was the route out, the one taken by the heroin shipments from the Sharmar estates around Sopore. This underpopulated part of Kashmir, risky and unsettled, rather than any other route, south or south-west. It had to go out via Pakistan — Pakistan had the experience, the track record. FedEx as far as drugs were concerned, not some mushroom operation only just starting up. And this was the least conspicuous way out of Kashmir — Tithwal and Muzaffarabad — then 'Pindi or whichever distribution centre in Pakistan one had dealings with. He glanced back at the Land Rover. Dhanjal would know. Dhanjal would have crossed the CFL . . .

. . . and could do again.

Frying pan and fire. But the frying pan was hot and getting hotter and the state of the fire was still uncertain, hopefully only smouldering. Crossing the border would give them *time*, the interval of cross-border dealings and collaboration, the spreading of the net until, maybe, it stretched too far. The only way they could even approach the CFL, let alone cross it without papers, was with Dhanjal.

Certainly, Captain Dhanjal — you can cross the CFL with these two Englishmen whose descriptions we have and one of whom has obviously been interrogated . . .

Crazy. But crazier to stay put, let them cast and recast the net, fill Kashmir with the manhunt, get themselves organised, efficient, utterly competent. The Sharmars, through Dhanjal or someone like him, must have the border guards and their Pakistani counterparts on the payroll. It *had* to work — didn't it?

The alternative was down there, the ragged tents between which women trudged to a cold-looking stream, their garments flying in the wind, and men moped on the ground or sulked in tents and children had forgotten everything but hunger. There were no dogs. They'd probably already been eaten. Neither Cass nor he could cope with the mental equivalent of that down there, for however long it took Ros to get back, get Shelley off his bum, get the deal set up — a week? Two —? Before the Sharmars admitted they were on the rack and an exchange was necessary.

Two weeks? They'd find them before that.

In *Kashmir*.

It was already past ten. The helicopter had been the second — or the same one a second time — since Sopore. It had landed briefly on the outskirts of Handwara, but he'd bypassed the village along a deserted track and they'd have received no report of a Land Rover with a pale face behind the windscreen. The search must be concentrated to the south of Sopore, towards Srinagar and south of the city. The city itself would be house-to-housed.

With luck, they'd ignore Ros, even if they assumed she wasn't with him and Cass. It was Cass and Dhanjal they had to silence, and he they had to stop — dead.

He shrugged and hunched against the wind into the camouflage jacket, aware of the ragged hole the two pistol shots from inside had made in the material. His cheeks were blanched and numb. The tents on the edge of the village flapped in distress. He turned back to the Land Rover, pine needles crunching under his hiking boots.

He ripped open the flap of the canvas canopy, startling the Indian, who was tied by his hands to a metal handrail. He was crouched awkwardly on the bench seat. Cass lay in a sleeping bag on the other bench seat, snoring. His features remained as pale and battered and defeated as they had appeared on the pillows of Sharmar's bed. The sleeping bag quivered with the feverish, unregarded movements of his body as the drug-coma receded and the muscles and blood demanded to be returned to silence. That Cass was sleeping through his withdrawal was bad —

Hyde grinned suddenly and alarmingly at Dhanjal, whose anorak, open to the waist, seemed to have breathed in cold air that made him shiver. His eyes were brown and angry. His mouth seemed still aware of the wound to his arm, but there was little sign of real distress.

'Well, Gandhi,' Hyde began insultingly. 'I think it's about time you and I decided your future — don't you?'

Dhanjal was immediately aware of the threat in Hyde's voice, and instantly alarmed. His hands struggled against the rope binding them to the handrail and his left foot stirred against the steel storage box on the floor between him and Cass.

'You've been stupid,' he managed.

'Not bad,' Hyde replied mockingly. 'Not bad. But then, I've left you alone so far, haven't I?' He climbed into the vehicle, his movements deliberate and menacing. Dhanjal flinched as Hyde reached for the rope and untied it. Then he dragged the Indian to the tailgate, gripping the rope that bound his wrists together. Pulled him forward, off balance, and let him sprawl on the rocky ground, stepping back as if to admire his work. 'I'm not leaving you alone any more, though.'

Dhanjal sat up, hunched to protect himself, his eyes watching Hyde's feet rather than his face.

'What do you want with me? I can't help you — as a hostage? I think they want you too much to stop —'

Hyde waited until the self-condemnation brightened like a dark light in Dhanjal's eyes, then he murmured: 'That's it — that's exactly it. You're no fucking use to me, none at all. Are you? You've just admitted as much.' He turned away, hands on his hips, just within the shadow of the pines, staring down at Kupwara. A single wandering cow, a scattering of sheep on poor grass. The few inhabitants he could see seemed slight, insubstantial figures. The weather looked to be worsening to the north, where the mountains crowded beyond Nanga Parbat in what might have been an endless succession.

All the way to Mongolia, given a couple of hiccoughs on the way – Christ . . .

He rubbed his hands eagerly together as he turned back to Dhanjal, whose eyes darted like rats seeking escape from flame. He bent and hoisted the man to his feet, then pushed him more upright against the resinous bole of a pine. He pressed his face close to Dhanjal's.

'Now, you've got nowhere to go unless we cooperate – have you? You can help me, and if you do, I might keep you alive. No one's going to believe you haven't spilt the beans, are they? Prakesh Sharmar isn't known for his generosity or forgiveness, is he?'

Dhanjal was shaking his head.

'They'll believe me.'

'Your first thought was the right one. They want Cass too much – and they want *me* very badly. If the chopper that just passed us by had seen us and was sure who was in the vehicle, what would have happened? Would they have shouted you a warning before they rocketed us or dropped something nicely combustible on the canopy? What do you think, Dhanjal – what do you *really* think?'

He was breathing heavily. The Indian's body against his own was heaving with admissions and denials, with revulsion at his helplessness, at Hyde's threatening pressure against him. He was shaking his head in futile denial –

'Christ –!'

Then the breath was gone from his body and he collapsed to the ground, clutching his groin. Dhanjal's knee had driven between his thighs. Then his hands flew to his head as the Indian aimed out at it with his right foot. Hyde, rolling, snatched at the extended leg but failed to grab it. Dhanjal's shoe caught him in the small of the back, then on the point of the shoulder as he rolled away from the man's frenzied, desperate attack. The breath wouldn't catch in his throat, like an old engine failing to fire, and he was dizzy. His groin stabbed with pain.

You pillock! He's qualified you for the geldings' plate, you overconfident bas –

Dhanjal kicked out again, then turned away, hurrying to the Land Rover and dragging open the driver's door. Hyde, on his knees and still clutching his groin in both hands, stared like a stupefied sleeper suddenly awakened as the engine caught. The vehicle was thrust into reverse and began hurrying towards him, its exhaust pluming smoke, reversing lights gleaming.

He rolled to one side and the Land Rover's brakes were stamped on. The handbrake's rasp. Hyde staggered to his feet, wiping pine needles from his mouth. Beginning to run as he realised the meaning of Dhanjal's hunched shoulder half-turned from the driver's window. Hurried, five paces, three, two –

– jumped for the door, hands outstretched like those of a beggar, fumbled, then grasped the pistol Dhanjal had grabbed from the dashboard locker. Gripped, held on. Explosion. Hyde was deafened, his vision blurred and dazzling from the pistol's discharge into the roof of the Land Rover. Dhanjal grunted in pain, holding onto the gun with his right hand as he worked at something with his left. Hyde jarred his elbows against the sill, his cold hands clammily around the Indian's grip. Then he was jerked off balance as the vehicle was flung into reverse again and rushed backwards. He paddled his legs comically as Dhanjal braked, then flung the Land Rover forward. Hyde saw the narrow pines rush towards him and heaved on the pistol's hot barrel, tugging it free, falling away then rolling on the stone-splintered ground and its carpet of pine needles. He came to his knees as the Land Rover's brakes screeched and the brake lights glowed.

He lumbered to his feet as Dhanjal's wild-looking features stared back at him from the driver's window. Ran as the gears

253

were clashed in desperation and the vehicle rocked backwards towards the narrow track they had turned off to park. He thought he heard Cass groaning in a detached, delirious way from inside. Then the gun was thrust against Dhanjal's temple, hard, as the Indian attempted to swing the Land Rover around to face the track. It teetered as if suggesting the precarious, momentary balance of everything.

'Switch it off! *Switch off the engine!*' Hyde bellowed in a cracked, breathless voice. He dragged the door open and jabbed the gun against the Indian's cheek. 'It's *finished* –!'

A moment, then the ignition was switched off and the handbrake dragged on. Then only their breathing, like challenges between two struggling animals.

'Out,' Hyde managed, gesturing with the gun.

Dhanjal climbed from the Land Rover. His hands were free, his wrists scored from the struggle which had forced one hand from its bonds. The rope dangled from his left wrist. He shuddered, clutching his wounded arm as if only now reminded of it. Hyde gulped in cold air which the wind seemed determined to deny him.

'Sit!' he coughed, his testicles protesting at a renewed surge of pain which all but doubled him up. He sank to his knees, cradling the pit of his stomach. Dhanjal's hatred was virulent, stinging his cheeks like acid. Hyde aimed the gun at him, stiff-armed, until he dropped his gaze into sullen calculation.

'Right, Pandit-bloody-Nehru –! Christ, you've got bony bloody knees, Dhanjal!' He grinned savagely. 'I ought to kick *your* balls into touch, mate –!' Dhanjal rubbed his wounded arm. There was blood on his fingers. 'Right. *Now*, we're going to have a little talk or you won't be able to stop the bleeding with both hands!' He waggled the gun. The wind rushed through the pines above them with a deep moaning noise. 'We're sitting just south of the Cease Fire Line, correct? The road goes west from here to the Line itself. So do the heroin shipments, right?' It was correct, despite the almost immediate blankness of Dhanjal's features.

He was ashen beneath his racial pallor, exhausted by failure. 'Right? Am I *right*?'

He fished in the breast pocket of the camouflage jacket and removed a silencer, which he fitted to the barrel of the Heckler & Koch. Dhanjal's eyes watched him like those of a cat.

'Get the idea?' Hyde asked, then: 'Am I right?'

Without waiting for a reply, he squeezed the trigger and the bullet flicked up dust a few inches from Dhanjal's right leg. The man flinched away.

'Right, am I?'

He fired again, the shot embedding itself in the pine behind Dhanjal's head; audibly.

'Am I *right*?'

He fired again. The bullet flicked stone chippings onto Dhanjal's hand. He stared at it as if certain of the spurt of blood. Then he nodded violently.

'Yes, yes –!' he shouted. 'Yes – Tithwal, Tithwal –!'

'Then Muzaffarabad, in Pakistan?' Dhanjal nodded, his head bobbing like that of a puppet. Inwardly, Hyde felt relief sink through his rage and weariness like a stone through amber. 'OK. Then you've been across, plenty of times – uh?' Again, the defeated, mechanical nodding. 'Then you're about to take another little trip to Pakistan – aren't you?'

Reluctantly – yet with the return of cunning in his eyes – Dhanjal nodded, just once. Hyde got to his feet.

'Stay put, sport.'

He crossed to the Land Rover, walking crablike, the gun always on the Indian. He glanced into the rear of the vehicle. Cass was staring at him like some inmate of an asylum, wide-eyed at surroundings he could not comprehend. He'd been woken when flung from the bench seat by the violent movements of the vehicle. He struggled feebly with the folds of the sleeping bag, as if his survival depended upon it, with the weakness of someone very old, very dazed.

Hyde glanced at Dhanjal, who had not moved. No, he'd wait

now, hoping for luck and a good moment at the border post. A word, a sign, something that would bring guns to bear and save him.

Christ, an invalid and someone who wants to kill you . . . the brochure didn't mention little drawbacks like that when you booked the holiday –

Sara removed one of her earrings and brushed her hair away from her face. She moved to the telephone Prakesh Sharmar, with a smirking, angering kind of amusement, had invited her to take; his long-cherished humiliation of an opponent. She deliberately turned her back to him, staring out across the lake, the cellular phone bulky and unfamiliar against her cheek. She was repelled by the sense of Prakesh's lips having been against the mouthpiece as hers now were.

'Yes, V.K.?' she murmured hesitantly, looking across the water at her own houseboat which had been commandeered by Rao and his uniformed minions, and was now guarded by the army. As if the place had been animate and now disembowelled; cables and leads trailed to the generator truck, and the other trucks whose roofs sprouted aerials and dishes. 'Yes?' She had been billeted on the boat that bloody Ros had used to spy on V.K. and Prakesh!

'How are you, Sara?'

'Fine, V.K.' Prakesh hovered near her like a doctor, his face lugubriously indicating that she lied about her health. She was *not* fine –

'You heard the announcement?'

'Yes. You came over very well.' She had not intended the edge of irony, but did not regret it. 'It's all hell let loose from now on . . .' It was, and the sentiment was too redolent of her own situation and Prakesh's proximity and malice.

'Perhaps. Sara – I think you should talk to Prakesh about this Australian woman. Don't you?'

'What is there to say, V.K.?' she enquired, her voice carrying a vibrato of nerves that were not customary. The sunlight gleamed off the lake as the clouds opened for a moment. Bad weather. 'I'm sorry . . . I *am* sorry, V.K. How was I to know?' She loathed the apologetic tone, like a verbal hand raised to fend off an anticipated blow.

'Yes. Obviously. But, you talked to her, Sara. You *knew* her. I think you could be more helpful.' His voice purred. It was seductive with threat. She felt her balance become unsettled.

'How, V.K.?' she asked hoarsely. Behind her, Prakesh snorted like an eager horse. 'I don't see what —'

'Sara,' he warned. 'I shall be entirely occupied with the election from now on. This matter must be resolved. Very quickly.' She felt the fear well up from her legs into her stomach, then into her chest, so that breathing was difficult. The uniforms on her boat and along the cordoned-off section of the boulevard insisted she was a prisoner. 'You do understand, Sara.' Now the tone was loftily dismissive; disappointment that had become a resolve to disregard. V.K. blamed her, she was the focus of suppressed rage, all his fears. 'I think you should cooperate with Prakesh — tell him everything you can, assist him in whatever needs to be done.' A silence. The connection hissed like a cobra, then: '*Sara?* You *do* understand?'

She turned and glared at Prakesh. Her cheek stung with the memory of him striking her. She was *consigned* to him now, handed over, her status that of . . . prisoner indeed. Even enemy.

'Yes, V.K.,' she replied heavily. 'I understand very clearly.'

She switched off the phone before he could do so and complete his dismissal of her. She held it out to Prakesh, who took it as insinuatingly as if he had begun to undress her. She shivered, her hands clutching at her forearms, which prickled with cold. The earring she had removed fell from her unregarding fingers and plopped into the water, disappearing immediately. She stared after it in what might have been horror.

'Good,' Prakesh announced. 'Very good. Very sensible of you to agree with V.K., Sara.'

'Did I have any choice?' she snapped.

'No.'

'Look, Prakesh – what the hell do you expect me to do? The woman's with the man Hyde, isn't she? Where else could she be? For God's sake, you've appropriated my *home*, you're keeping me here practically under guard –! What the hell do you expect to gain?' There was only anger now, the induced and encouraged heat of argument that kept at bay the cold threatening to well up inside her.

'Sit down, Sara.'

She hesitated, then saw that he wanted her to defy him. She dragged the cardigan closer around her shoulders as she sat down. She looked from him to the lake, and its gunmetal colour under the clouds, now that the sun had once more been swallowed. It now seemed an ominous blank expanse ploughed by small distant boats, a disappointing holiday snapshot of a place that meant nothing. They'd changed it . . . *he'd* changed it. *They*, Prakesh *and* V.K. She shivered and he seemed to enjoy the reaction. His malice was now undisguised. She swallowed.

'I can't *help* you, Prakesh,' she insisted. 'The woman was a guest, I don't *know* her.'

He shrugged, spreading his hands on his thighs as he sat opposite her on a cane chair. It creaked as if the wind was blowing through a dilapidated building.

'Then you must try. For example, Sara, do you *think* she is with the man?'

'How would I know?'

'Think. We know some things about them. They have a long-standing relationship, they inhabit the same house. He, presumably, cares for her – and her safety. Would that make him take her along?'

'I suppose so.'

'But, he has Cass with him –' She shuddered. It was only now

258

that she knew they'd tortured Cass – no, that wasn't true. She'd known they had him at Gulmarg, known *why*, known what the scheme had been from the beginning.

She did not admit as much. Whatever she had gleaned she had been able to lose from consciousness, even from her dreams, even from her bed when she and V.K. inhabited it. She had never admitted that V.K. had had Sereena killed.

'You see,' Prakesh continued. 'Hyde has Cass and Dhanjal with him –'

'He might have killed Dhanjal by now.'

'Perhaps. But, with two of them, would he want the woman, too? Would he risk anything, all his eggs in the one basket?'

'Look, Prakesh, I don't know how a spy thinks. Why ask me?'

'What do you think of this?' He reached into the inside pocket of his jacket and removed a folded piece of paper. Opening it, he passed it across the verandah to her. She took it with an uncertain hand. 'Read it.'

It was a sheet from a message pad, handwritten in English, the letters more certainly and formally shaped than any English-speaker would have produced.

'A woman answering her description paid for petrol at Punch, only two hours ago. The taxi had run out of petrol, apparently. The driver had had to leave a watch, some other things, as a deposit. Then the garage owner agreed only to a full tank at an exorbitant price. Quite scandalous –' He was luxuriating in the description, and in something else she could not discern but which involved her, she suspected. 'It might not have been her, the garage owner's description is vague, a peasant's. He remembers the money more than the payer. If it was her, where would she be heading? Why was she as far west as Punch?'

'It's near Gulmarg.'

'On a very poor road. We haven't located the taxi. The garage peasant remembers nothing about it or the driver.' His features twisted in contempt. 'It may have come from Gulmarg, even from here, perhaps. But from Punch, the taxi continued *south*. What is south of Punch, Sara?'

'Jammu – eventually,' she replied, as if to demonstrate she knew her catechism, or the answers to a geography test at school.

'Exactly. Jammu – buses, trains, aircraft. They couldn't have hoped to get out of Srinagar, so they decided that Jammu was far enough and safe enough.'

Acidly, she remarked: 'See, Prakesh? You didn't need me at all – did you?'

'There you are wrong, dear Sara – very wrong. I have a poor description of a large Englishwoman, nothing more. I did not see her. Colonel Rao has not had the pleasure of an introduction to your *friend*.' He paused. She was bewildered, her head foggy. 'You know her well. *You* can identify her –' She began violently shaking her head, not understanding why she did so. Not merely because he wanted it, nor merely to spite V.K., who apparently no longer required the flattery of her white body beside him . . . she could not comprehend the force or nature of her reaction. Prakesh was nodding. 'Yes, Sara. We will fly you down to Jammu by helicopter – in fifteen minutes. I suggest you prepare –'

'No –!'

'Yes. You will identify her. You will trawl the airport, the bus station, the trains, until you find her.' He stood up. 'I'm wasting valuable time,' he muttered. 'There it is, Sara. If the woman is in Jammu, find her. She will be heading for Delhi, presumably – or Pakistan or Nepal. Delhi, I would think. I haven't time to squander on her, but I would be remiss to forget she might be travelling alone.' He looked down at her. 'I suggest you hurry, Sara.'

He turned away and entered the lounge of the houseboat, murmuring instructions to someone who waited inside.

Oh, *God*, she thought, they want me to point her out so they can kill her . . . and they know I'll do it. I can't do anything else. The grey water surrounding her appeared cold. Nanga Parbat was hidden from view. The mountains to the north and north-west were all masked. Prakesh had removed the veil of self-deception with a single rough gesture. He'd shown her she was their creature, V.K.'s tart and someone to be ordered about at will. What choice did she have? None.

They killed his *wife*, what safety for her?

Or Ros, whom she barely knew. Even though she hoped she was with Hyde, and the taxi passenger was some other fat white woman . . . though she hardly believed it.

The land seemed to have been thrown up into a great barrier across the road, forcing them into the narrowing neck of a valley where Tithwal lay like a small heap of stones fallen from one of the cliff faces. Beyond the village and the border post, the mountains rose again. On the other side of them, north of Muzaffarabad, lay the Kagan Valley and a future he did not want to think about.

He instructed Dhanjal to stop the Land Rover at the side of the road, beneath overhanging rock. There had been little or no traffic on the road, which led only to the Cease Fire Line, the border between Indian and Pakistani Kashmir; a handful of trucks, a couple of army vehicles, two official-looking limousines. The place seemed deserted, quarantined, chilly. Grit was blown off the road by the increased force of the wind, pattering against the canvas hood and the windscreen. Hyde breathed deeply. Dhanjal watched him as a cornered animal might watch a predator. Cass coughed rackingly in the rear of the Land Rover, startling Hyde, encouraging Dhanjal. Leaving the gun pressed into the Indian's ribcage, Hyde turned to inspect Cass.

The face was still vague, like that of a man with very poor eyesight suddenly bereft of his spectacles. White, dead-looking skin on which the stubble of beard appeared like the impregnations of gunpowder. His whole look and posture was that of someone who had been too close to death. He was shivering despite the sweaters and the heavy anorak. He'd drunk a little water and even that had revolted against the drugs still in his system; eaten practically nothing except a few spoonfuls of heated soup. Dhanjal had wolfed his food against some great physical effort he envisaged being called upon to make.

Would Cass pass muster? Could he look *well* enough not to create suspicion?

There'd been no helicopter or unexpected army activity during their journey from Kupwara, just as there'd been no further attempt at escape by Dhanjal. It was just possible that the border guards wouldn't have been alerted. This was the unexpected — wasn't it?

The road wound ahead of them, dropping into the knife-cut of the valley. He raised the glasses to his eyes. The red and white barrier across the road, the guard hut, barbed wire like a fowling net at either side of the dusty, empty road. Bored Indian guards, and a hundred yards beyond them, equally bored Pakistani troops. A parked jeep, a docile army truck. It was as unsuspicious as any trap.

He had no thought but to complicate things for the hunt; confuse them, make them employ a longer, messier chain of command, widen the search area. Talk to Shelley — wait for Ros to get home . . . There were alternatives, but he wanted not to have to choose any of them. Not with Cass, not with Dhanjal, who couldn't be dumped after they crossed the border. He might have to be killed but he didn't want to think about that. Cross-border cooperation to pursue them would have to be carefully conceived and kept secret among the Sharmars' contacts in Islamabad.

None of it made him feel any better.

He lowered the glasses and turned to Dhanjal.

'Your turn now,' he murmured. 'Talk us through those two border posts and I won't kill you.'

'How can I do that?' The disclaimer was almost outraged; nearly genuine. Hyde grinned.

'Oh, you can do it. You've been this way before, and not in

another Hindu life either. You're the Sharmars' *boy*, the drug-wallah –' Dhanjal scowled. 'This is the crossing point and you must know the guards. They know you, anyway. They won't question you crossing over.'

'But who are *you*?' Dhanjal spat back with what might have been childish, playground spite.

'Customers. *Representatives* of clients. Whatever you like. You wouldn't explain to border guards, would you – not Captain Dhanjal!' Dhanjal squirmed with anger and impotence against the barrel of the pistol. 'I shouldn't, if I were you,' Hyde added, nudging the muzzle harder against the ribcage.

'If I take you across – what then?' Dhanjal asked, surprising Hyde.

'I said – I won't kill you.'

'Where will you go?' Dhanjal scorned. 'Where *can* you go?'

The wind picked up, as if to emphasise the isolation and friendlessness of the place. Clouds scurried across the mountains like dark, fleeing sheep.

'I could walk into the High Commission –'

'Do you trust them? After Delhi?'

Hyde grinned savagely. 'Is this to make me keep you alive? Respect your value? You have a deal?'

'No. I will just wait, I think.'

'Suits me, sport.' He caught the hollow bravado of his own voice. There weren't any places he and Cass could safely go. Not until Shelley was prepared to intervene. The proof would get lost down the nearest toilet at express speed, *they*'d be down the same toilet inside ten minutes. Unfortunate accident . . . *No one* wanted to know. 'Suits me,' he repeated carefully.

It didn't, of course. Which was why Ros had only half the evidence. Shelley would have an attack of gastroenteritis as soon as he saw the first frame of film, heard the first voices on the tapes. So would HM Secretary of State for Foreign and Commonwealth Affairs . . . so would everyone. And then Ros would tell them there was more, *just like this lot* . . .

. . . and they'd deal because they had to, to keep the lid on. *After* Ros got back, *after* Shelley was convinced. Until then, he and Cass – and Dhanjal – were on their own.

Cass began coughing again. Hyde whirled around as if to berate him. Dhanjal smirked.

'He is rather ill, I think,' he said.

'Then it'll have to be the fucking food that's got to him, or ice in his gin and tonic – won't it? Let's go, Dhanjal!' He prodded the Indian with the pistol's muzzle. 'You know the deal. You know the details. One word in Hindi or Urdu or anything else I don't understand, and this will go off.' He glared at Dhanjal. It wasn't difficult to appear desperate, wildly uncalculating. That was the problem, it was easy.

Dhanjal studied him for a moment, then started the engine. Hyde turned to Cass.

'Just listen to me, Cass,' he announced. The Land Rover pulled out onto the gravel road and began descending towards the Indian side of the Cease Fire Line. Dust blew across the road as if from a high desert. Clouds raced. 'Listen to him. Just keep quiet and *listen*. If he tries saying something in Hindi or Urdu, tell me. Understand?'

There was only the noise of the engine for a time, and the wind against the canvas hood. Then, through chattering teeth, Cass said weakly:

'All right.' The words seemed dredged from some deep place, a discovery by the speaker of sounds he seemed to have little or no use for. Jesus –

They neared the barrier across the road. There were no other vehicles moving in either direction. The valley closed beyond the scattered village, grey flanks of mountains looming until lost in cloud and the gloomy early afternoon light. The Land Rover slowed. Dhanjal's tension was evident through the divining-rod of the pistol's stubby barrel and plastic grip. An officer strolled towards the Land Rover, an armed guard behind him shuffling in new boots; stunted in growth, it seemed, by the helmet he wore.

Dhanjal looked briefly at Hyde, then slid open the window.

The officer, a captain, recognised Dhanjal with a smile that was both conspiratorial and deferential. The cold wind blew the skirts of his greatcoat about his boots, blew grit into the cab of the vehicle. The captain studied Hyde, who tried to appear indifferent, even impatient.

'Captain —'

'Captain.' The two Indians exchanged ranks like codewords. Hyde felt his temperature begin to rise. Cass coughed in the back of the Land Rover, startling the Indian officer.

There was no other way, except to run into this noose. Only Dhanjal could expect to pass across without the necessary, rarely-granted papers. Hyde saw an anti-aircraft battery mounted on a wide ledge of rock above the road only a few hundred yards away. A wrecked, burned-out, rust-enveloped scout car lay in a shallow grave of land a quarter of a mile away. He suppressed a tremor of nerves. The whole place twitched with danger like the filaments of a spider's web.

'We didn't expect you,' the officer remarked.

'No. My friends here —' He gestured and the captain inspected Hyde, peered into the rear of the vehicle. '— are hoping to understand more of our situation. *Business* friends. Who is on the other side?'

'Husain. No problem. You can go straight through. You're on your way to —?'

'Muzaffarabad, no farther,' Dhanjal replied easily. The voice lied. His body was tense and stiff. His knuckles light-skinned on the steering wheel. 'Not far.'

'One of your passengers seems ill,' the officer remarked. Then spoke rapidly in Hindi, his face casual, even affable. Hyde pressed the pistol against Dhanjal. The flesh was hard as wood, unyielding. The fingers moved on the steering wheel, uncurling as from something he had strangled.

Then Cass mumbled something in Hindi from the back of the Land Rover. The officer laughed and said:

'Your companion is complaining about our food. I apologise. He should be more careful.'

'Yes,' Hyde said. 'Captain Dhanjal, we have a longish journey ahead –'

'Yes,' Dhanjal replied through set teeth. 'We'll go on, then.'

The officer waved his arm and the barrier sprang up. The Land Rover nudged forward beneath it, then accelerated across the no man's land between the two border posts. Hyde felt relief choking in his throat. Dhanjal's features were twisted with rage.

The noise of the engine, the wind, the clunking of the suspension across the rough, pitted gravel – and the other noise. A military helicopter blazoned with green and white and the crescent of Islam dropped like an olive-coloured stone out of the cloud, its downdraught swirling the dust as it settled to land at the Pakistani border post.

TWELVE

the road to the north

The wind tugged open the cloud and sunlight fleeted on the slowing rotor blades of the helicopter as its wheels skipped, then settled. Then the light whisked across the border post, the soldiers and the Land Rover as it came to a halt. Rifles gleamed for a moment before the afternoon became dull and grey once more. Dhanjal's face seemed to retain an illuminated cunning that shone like hope.

A Pakistani officer hesitated between the Land Rover and the Puma helicopter, the sliding cabin door of which remained closed. There was an unhurried certainty about the machine as Hyde heard the upspring of the wind once more. Clouds pursued each other across the grim flanks of the mountains. Then the door opened and two uniformed men jumped down. A few moments later, an officer clambered gingerly from the interior. The border post commander moved towards the Puma, his hand raised in greeting. Hyde nudged Dhanjal, who switched off the engine.

Four more soldiers climbed out of the helicopter, their movements neither urgent nor alert; bored and reluctant, rather. Then Dhanjal said:

'I don't know the officer. They're changing the guards. It happens every two weeks.' Further confirmation as the hut door opened and two soldiers humped with kit and weapons hunchbacked into the wind. 'We won't be allowed through.' He smiled a grim, nervous smile, newly aware of the pistol nudging against his ribs.

'Pity for you,' Hyde managed.

The two officers were conferring, their troops huddled together in greeting and commiseration, the hands of the new-comers flapping arms against the chill wind. The two guards who remained at the barrier seemed eager to be gone, scowling at the Land Rover as if it were a customer banging at the door of a shop that had just closed.

'Get out – *now*!' Hyde hissed. 'Do it. Call him – what's his name, Husain? *Call* him, make sure he knows it's you. They'll let us through. *English.*'

He thrust Dhanjal against the door of the Land Rover and the Indian twisted the handle angrily, as if killing a chicken, then stepped down. He followed the indication of Hyde's gun and came round to the passenger window. Waved to the officers, called out Husain's name.

The man looked up, and appeared startled.

'Cass?' Hyde whispered hoarsely.

A few moments of the wind, into which Dhanjal called again, then:

'Yes?' The croak of a hermit.

'Get the bloody gun out, will you? Get back among the living instead of the undead. We might have a small problem here.' He checked that Dhanjal had left the key in the ignition. If it began to explode, he'd reverse, handbrake turn –

– and go where?

They were stranded between the two border posts, amid a dozen uniformed Pakistanis, all armed.

Husain gabbled something to the relieving officer, then scur-ried towards Dhanjal, his face pale, his coal-black eyes burning with distress and compromise. This was a small link in the chain, just baksheesh for Husain. His commanding officer might be on a tiny percentage, then *his* senior on a bigger one, then a general or two, like the ones Ros had photographed on the houseboat, lining their pockets – however many it took to keep a nice clear open road for the Sharmars' heroin. Hyde studied Husain and then the relieving officer, who was lighting a cigarette as he hunched against the wind, his troops stamping with cold and silent protest; rifles slung on their shoulders, kitbags at their feet.

'What are you doing here, Captain Dhanjal?' Husain asked in English. 'There was no warning, I did not expect you – you know the guards are changed today!' His knuckles were white as he gripped the windowsill of the Land Rover, his face puzzled by Hyde's unfamiliarity. Dhanjal had known – hoped. All that was needed was that they be turned back.

'A small emergency,' Dhanjal explained levelly, his voice consciously under control. 'Let us through before you go off duty.' There was nothing deceptive about the voice, no sign or gesture to create suspicion.

Because Dhanjal didn't want the other Pakistani officer to know . . . Hyde felt the relief drain him, make his hand quiver as it held the gun out of sight. So, come on then, let's get on with it.

'I can't – you have papers?'

'No,' Dhanjal replied. Then he reached into his breast pocket and removed his wallet. Fictitious papers. 'Pretend to inspect them,' he instructed. Oh, you're good, Dhanjal. You're really good. 'Hurry, Husain – let us through.'

The man looked dubious, and glanced towards the new arrivals. His own men appeared uninterested, eager to collect their kit and climb into the waiting Puma. Then he nodded, and stepped back, gesturing that the barrier be raised. The other officer seemed casually observant, smoke being snatched away from his mouth by the wind. His greatcoat billowed like a skirt. The barrier climbed slowly upright like an arthritic, warning finger. Dhanjal stared for a moment at Husain, as if he had been betrayed, then hurried around the Land Rover and clambered into the cab, slamming the door behind him and switching on the engine with a snatched, enraged movement.

'What shall I tell him?' Husain all but pleaded.

'Intelligence – just say Intelligence. I outranked you!' Dhanjal snapped angrily, as if a child was pestering him.

The Land Rover lurched forward. Husain waved his men towards the hut and they scuttled away to collect their kit. Hyde glanced back. The relieving officer had ordered two of his men to man the barrier and they reluctantly moved forwards as it dropped into its rest.

Dhanjal was grinding his teeth in a fury of frustration. The cover story was thin, but it ought to hold. Back and forth, diplomats, trucks, traders, Intelligence people. No questions asked . . . it should hold.

It had better –

– and Dhanjal? He'd have to be watched like a hawk.

One in the afternoon.

The road dropped away beyond the scattered, gritty-looking village towards a narrow river. Mountains thrust up again ahead of them. Mountains surrounded them. They were in Pakistan, without papers and with no good cover story. Smart move.

It was the heat and dust of another world. Jammu was hot and crowded, alien after Srinagar and the cloud and wind that had seemed to be hurrying her down from the mountains to the plain. The afternoon sun burned through a haze of dust as she looked along the cramped, struggling platform of the railway station. The old town sat on its hillside, its fort and temples lacking identity against the warm sky. She felt her balance go again and leaned her leg against the suitcase beside her, lowering the travel bag to the extent of its strap as she did so. She was exhausted.

The taxi had deposited her at the main railway station in the new town, amid a sudden flurry of bearers and touts and police and passengers. It had been a gauntlet of rucksacks, backpacks, suitcases, tickets offered at cut prices for trains already full, beggars and bright frocks and shirts. She was unprepared for it and without reserves. The station had crowded against her as if to indicate her presence to the uniformed soldiers and policemen.

Then she had queued for an hour for a ticket to Delhi, only to find that there was no sleeping accommodation, no ladies' compartment – just second-class ordinary, as they called it. The long-distance express was as much a chaos of caste and class and confusion as everything else in India – second-class ordinary, second-class sleeper, first-class sleeper *without* air-conditioning, first-class *with* air-conditioning and de luxe with carpets on the floor and the best loos. *Nothing, no, I am so sorry, nothing but second-class ordinary, I am so sorry . . .*

It was not so much disappointing as frightening. She wanted a small, four-berth compartment around her, the comfort of no more than *three* strangers . . . instead, she would have wooden slatted seats, the crowd, heat and halitosis and sweat, luggage racks swaying on chains suspended from the ceiling, iron bars across the windows, the gloomy, soupy air hardly distressed by two inadequate fans. Four or more to a bench –

– why are you worried, you've done it before. When you were eighteen there wasn't any other way . . . It brought back her younger self, the innocent from Melbourne passing around the funny fags with people she hardly knew; sleeping with some of the strangers, sharing food and money with others –

Ros shook her head. She couldn't afford to be that girl any longer. She needed concealment. She was afraid of a crowded carriage filled with strange faces, hers probably the only white one over the age of twenty.

She shook her head, dizzying herself, and remembered she had not eaten since mid-morning; a snatched lump of spicy bread and some vegetable curry from a stall in Rajauri's one shabby street. She glanced towards the rows of cookstalls, then towards the retiring rooms. She should have paid for the use of one, lain there in the hot gloom until it was time to board the train. But that was something you couldn't do if you were travelling second-class ordinary. You had to perch on the

271

platform waiting to pounce on a seat as soon as they blew the whistle to board. She needed luggage space.

Beyond the old town across the river, the mountains of Kashmir were pale, gold-flanked mirages. She swallowed. She was hungry, *that* was the something wrenching at her stomach, she told herself, not the distance between herself and Hyde.

Dragging her suitcase by its dog-lead strap – it moved through legs and bustle like any reluctant animal – and hefting the travel bag, she crossed to one of the cookstalls and chose something unlikely to upset her or cause her to use the loos they provided in second-class ordinary. She chewed on the papadam that came with the *thali* vegetarian dish on its battered metal plate. Her stomach rumbled as she tasted the fruit and nuts rolled in a leaf. Ignoring Hyde was only possible when her own anxieties were inflating in her mind.

She shook her head as another tout offered her a seat in first class – air-conditioning of course – at a discount price. First class was already full. Someone pressing towards the cookstall nudged the travel bag on her shoulder and her temperature jumped for an instant, as she thought the tubs of film and the tapes were being snatched away. The Indian apologised profusely. Longingly, she watched bearers wheeling luggage towards one of the first-class compartments behind a well-dressed Indian and his saried wife. She looked at her watch, balancing the metal plate awkwardly as she rotated her wrist. Another forty minutes before the train left. The lowering sun burned along the platform, its light falling heavily through the dusty glass roof of the station. Pigeons and bright, sparrow-sized birds flicked and waddled around her feet amid the crumbs of dozens of meals.

She finished eating. She must wash. The edge of the platform, along the rank of second-class carriages, was becoming more crowded. She was again aware of herself, white, looked-for, endangered, then she shook her head and hoisted the travel bag to greater comfort. Sod it.

'Ros!' She whirled, unnerved, the travel bag banging a boy, who scuttled away. 'My God, *Ros!*'

Sara Mallowby.

Unbelievable – and immediately threatening, despite the broad smile. Nervousness in her eyes, even though the hand that flicked the blonde hair aside was steady.

'I –'

'You left without a word!' And then she knew it was something acted. The words were uttered in the tone of a chiding hostess welcoming a belated guest. 'What happened?' The eyes were lascivious, mocking. 'Was it your friend? Was he *that* persuasive? But what are you doing in Jammu, of all places?' It was a performance she must have rehearsed over and over, but it still failed to carry conviction. Or was she just over-suspicious, her nerves jumping like fleas between a dog-pack of fears?

'Sentimental journey,' Ros managed, and Sara's glance hesitated between suspicion and what seemed to be pain, as if she had caught a stitch while running.

'Oh. Oh, yes, of course – retracing old steps, I see . . .'

'You've got it. Silly, but there you are.' She hesitated, then added: 'But you're here, too. *Train?* I wouldn't have thought that was you.'

Sara shrugged.

'One has to fill in time somehow.' She sighed. 'I'm on my way down to Delhi for a few days.' Again, the expansive shrug, and something in her expression that indicated there was a bitter taste on her tongue. 'Are you on your way down?'

'Yes. Just thought I'd do it this way.' Ros gestured with self-mocking ingenuousness. Don't overplay it. She doesn't think you're stupid. 'I should have booked. Second-class ordinary was all they had left!' She forced herself to laughter, waving her arms with the gesture of any memsahib confronted with India.

Sara would know about Hyde by now, know about everything. She must have been *sent* –

273

'God, how awful!' Then, at once: 'But you don't have to! I've got a whole four-berth to myself.' She grinned. 'Wonderful to have friends in the highest places – sometimes.' She moved her hand towards the suitcase, as if to appropriate it. 'Come on – I was just getting a last breath of fresh air before the air-conditioning!' Ros hesitated. Yet there was no alternative. No one turned down de luxe for second-class ordinary! Even if the de luxe was a carpeted, Western looed, shower-cubicled, strip-lit trap. 'God, what a piece of luck. I thought I was going to be bored out of my mind for the next fifteen or sixteen hours!'

The suitcase slid behind them, one of its wheels squeaking like a tiny, warning voice. Ros gripped the travel bag deliberately close to her side. At the corner of eyesight, she felt rather than witnessed a man detach himself from a newspaper stand and flit across the crowded platform on a parallel course. Sara's hand companionably cupped her elbow.

Don't let them get close –

– something from one of Hyde's few audible nightmares as he had struggled in sleep beside her.

Sara's manner, even if forced, began to envelop her as they moved along the crowded platform towards the carriages where bearers were deferential and luggage was boarded as gently as the first-class passengers. Sara, the slanting afternoon light, the warmth, the smells of food and pressing bodies, all a conspiracy that was narcotic in its effect. She was tired, she didn't want to feel on edge, fearful. Surely Sara was there by accident –?

No.

But there was nothing she could do, so she allowed herself to be guided towards the carriage. Her luggage was taken from her by a smiling bearer and she was assisted up the steps into the interior where she felt the air-conditioning bathe her like cool water. She glanced back in a moment of fear and Sara smiled encouragingly.

There was no sign of the man she had felt was shadowing

274

their progress like a shark whose interest had been aroused by movement in the water.

'You all right?'

Hyde brought the Land Rover to a halt. The late afternoon gloom made the Kundar River appear like a bed of flint as hard and pocked as the narrow, twisting road that climbed ahead of them towards the Babusar Pass. Behind them, the long valley descended through the massed, indeterminate darkness of pine forests towards cultivation and the activity they had abandoned. Scattered villages, hamlets and isolated, dotted houses lay on the valley floor beyond the road.

'What — ?'

'Are you all right?'

Cass was quietly, continuously shivering inside his sweaters and anorak and gloves, like a very old man dragged to some inhospitable place where harm would undoubtedly be done to him. Hyde knew that if he could choose, he would ask to be returned to the bungalow in Gulmarg and the intermittent assaults of his captors. Now, all he had was the continued interrogation of the weather and the slowly fading daylight. He'd awoken only briefly from the trance that seemed to hold him to tell Hyde — after being bullied — not to join the Karakoram Highway at Mansehra but to take the narrower, slower road up the Kagan Valley to Chilas. Because of the checkpoints along the KKH and the necessary travel permits they did not possess.

'Yes,' Cass replied, wearily lying.

Dhanjal stirred in the rear of the Land Rover, but Hyde did not turn to look at the Indian, tied to a metal handhold, and gagged.

'Will we make Chilas before dark?'

'No.'

'Why not?' I got you *out*, he wanted to yell into Cass' abstracted, dumb face. *Do* something to help.

275

'Too far. The pass is difficult, even without snow.'

'Great.' He reached into the door pocket and withdrew a thermos he'd had filled at a stall in Muzaffarabad. 'Drink some tea,' he ordered.

With exaggerated caution Cass took the thermos cap and grudgingly sipped at it. His upper lip trembled around the plastic. The constant wind rattled the canvas hood of the vehicle and fingered through the closed windows and doors into the cab. Hyde felt his determination fading. Nanga Parbat was all but obscured by cloud, but it was still *there*, that same bloody mountain dominating his horizon. It was a huge upthrust gullet with the teeth of countless other, lower peaks in front of it. A slanted, narrow fir jutted optimistically out from the cliff face above them.

'Where are we heading?' Cass asked suddenly.

'Chilas — I told you.'

'And after?'

Hyde was aware of Dhanjal behind them, his breathing had been hoarse, but was now controlled. He was listening, but it didn't matter.

'It depends.' He leaned towards Cass, his hand gripping the man's thinned wrist hard. Cass appeared intimidated, but attentive. He whispered fiercely: 'We have to stooge around, *Phil.*' Cass' features brightened. 'We have to *wait.* Shelley's going to get us out —' Difficult that, since he didn't trust Shelley to do *anything* until he'd been shown what Ros had. 'He doesn't know *where*, yet. I have to talk to him —' He studied Cass' face, which blinked in and out of attentiveness like a revolving light in a lighthouse. 'I'll do that. But you say we won't get to Chilas tonight?'

Cass shook his head with the vehemence of denial of a child. 'The pass is so *slow*,' he enunciated angrily. Then, shockingly, he giggled like a drunk. 'The natives aren't friendly!' he burst out, subsiding at once into moroseness. 'Have to camp this side of Chilas, sleep in the vehicle . . .' The lighthouse was going out.

Dhanjal had all but stopped breathing in his effort to overhear. Hyde turned and waggled a pistol towards the dim features that hated him from the rear of the Land Rover.

It was all too oppressive, he realised. Cass and Dhanjal crowded him into identifying with the lassitude of the one and the impotent hatred of the other. A redoubled gust of chill wind thrust against the vehicle, emphasising its smallness, its status as a tin box on wheels, liable to fail at any moment.

He rubbed his face. The action did not wake him. And there was the need to sleep. Cass couldn't drive, and he wouldn't let Dhanjal do it. Anyway, they wouldn't make Chilas and the highway tonight. Tomorrow, then. It didn't matter . . . Ros must have made Jammu by now. She'd be in Delhi tomorrow morning, Paris tomorrow night.

He had to tell Shelley to meet her there.

Another twenty-four hours, thirty-six, two days – three? There *was* one way out – but when he glanced at Cass studying the empty screw-top cup of the thermos with blank intentness, he realised that it didn't really exist. To emphasise the impossibility of it, Cass stirred half-aware in his seat and immediately winced with pain and clutched his ribcage with his wool-gloved left hand. His white face was drawn with pain. The top of the thermos rolled on the floor near his feet, unnoticed.

'The strapping too tight?' Hyde asked. Cass shook his head, his breath coming like a ragged wind in and out of a small cave; lonely and lost.

Cass had two, maybe three broken ribs. His whole left side was darkly bruised. Strapping was outdated, but Hyde had done it almost viciously tight, because somehow he had been holding the man together, or what was left of him.

It wasn't good – it wasn't *any* good. He glanced back at the straggling hamlet of Battakundi, lying like splinters from a dead log beside the cold river. Malika Parbat loomed out of the clouds, closer than Nanga Parbat. The other mountains, a wilderness of knife-sharp rock faces or snow-covered flanks, reared all around the valley. The cold they suggested reached to his marrow, freezing him.

He glanced again at Cass, who had sunk into some recollection that made his lips move quickly and fearfully, as if muttering prayers against an approaching storm.

He had to call Shelley, from somewhere.

He started the engine with cold-numbed fingers. Dhanjal growled in the rear of the Land Rover like an animal that must, sooner or later, be confronted.

'Magazines!' Ros blurted, getting up from her seat.

Sara was immediately startled, possessive.

'It's too late, Ros. The train's about to leave –!'

Ros snatched up her travel bag, empty-seeming apart from the tubs of incriminating film and the cassette tapes. She blundered into the corridor, sensing that Sara's hand reached out for her. She felt hot, desperate. It was like an attack of fever, or the bloody change, a hot flush that had been mounting irresistibly as she sat opposite that bloody woman she couldn't trust any more.

The platform was all but empty. The bookstall was fifty yards away. She glanced back, to see Sara framed in the doorway, but no one else watching her except an incurious gaggle of bearers in railway uniform. She hurried towards the bookstall, seeking the glossier, subtler covers of English language magazines scattered amid the violent colours of Indian titles.

She fumbled the magazines, perspiring freely in the smoky dusk light streaked along the platform and burning on the glass of the station roof. What was she doing? She couldn't get away –

– whistle. She started as at a gunshot. There was a man in a cream suit on the platform now, competent but undecided, glaring at Sara Mallowby, who stood beside the carriage steps. A bearer waited to remove them. A second whistle. She snatched money from her purse to pay for a month-old copy of *Vogue*. The woman who served her was smiling inanely. How could she not get on the train? Hyde had told her she had to get to Delhi, and out of India.

She whirled around, to see Sara's skirt billowing her across the platform. The man in the cream suit was speaking to the bearer, who seemed suddenly to regard the steps as immovable, something reverent. Sara's features were flushed with effort and something that could have been anger.

The travel bag was clutched against Ros' side as Sara reached her. They both seemed preeminently aware of it. The guard's whistle was continuous now.

'Ros —!'

She cowered back for an instant, surprising Sara, her eyes darting towards the train, along the platform, at the man in the cream suit, at the platform signs that arrowed the only exit. She'd *meant* to get away from Sara and the trap she represented, yet now, as Sara touched her arm, almost with solicitation, she knew it was impossible.

Sara guided her towards the train, hurrying her. The man in the cream suit had vanished and the porter was once more impatient with the steps. Ros climbed awkwardly into the carriage and, almost at once, the train jerked and began to move.

The last of the light was slipping back across Dal Lake as if it had been spread like a cloth for the duration of the day and was now being removed. Colonel Rao stood at the front of the houseboat, his chin cupped in one hand, his arm folded across his chest to support his elbow. Behind him, there was murmured activity around the big dining table and its maps and, farther away, the noise of cars and 4WDs as reports were received or despatched. Everything was being coordinated, refined, reassessed. His head was dense with detail and prolonged command. The cool air off the lake helped. The clouds had glanced aside from Srinagar, and Nanga Parbat loomed golden-flanked. The lower slopes were already dark, as if they had sprouted new forests.

There was a quiet coughing noise behind him, and he turned.

One of his aides was holding out a telephone, its lead stretching back into the houseboat's crowded lounge. Cigarette smoke moved heavily in warm lamplight. Spotlamps glared on flip-charts erected on easels towards the far end of the long room.

'Mr Sharmar,' the aide murmured. Rao reluctantly accepted the receiver.

'Yes, Mr Sharmar?' he enquired. 'What may I do for you?' However enunciated, it was the remark of a damned shop-keeper. His political master —

The line was clear, crystal as the lake. The stars were beginning to emerge from the darkening sky, large and glittering as diamonds.

'Have you news for us?' Did he use the plural because his brother, the Prime Minister, was present? 'What news is there?' There was a kind of post-coital elation in the man's voice. He had just come from the bed of his mistress, politics. Images of Mehta and V. K. Sharmar were already being erected all over Srinagar, there were loudspeaker vans on the streets in the unaccustomed lack of violence and riot.

'There is nothing definite yet, Mr Sharmar — I would have informed you had there been anything.'

'Do you need more people? Send for them if you do.'

'At present, there are sufficient.' He had effectively under his command, units of the Parachute Brigade, of a Mountain Division, the Border Security Force, air force helicopters and all the C_3I backup and input he required —

— *but you have not found them*. The thought was as clear and stinging as if it had been voiced by Prakesh Sharmar. It was almost inconceivable to admit that there was no trace of the Land Rover and its driver and two passengers. Two Englishmen and an Indian. The net had been cast, again and again, the search organised like a whirlpool's ripples spreading out from Gulmarg. But still they had not been seen. 'There are sufficient forces here,' he repeated.

'Then where are they, Colonel?' A pause, and: 'Why are they

not in custody or disposed of, if manpower is not a problem?' The politician's insinuating threat, the stick always behind the back.

'We have not been able to locate them. It is simply a matter of *time* rather than men.' His teeth closed together in a bite.

The water of the lake was dark now, cold-looking, with a mist beginning to curl off the surface like the smoke from a stubble fire.

'How much time? It must be dark there by now.'

'It is. They will rest, they will have to. Your people – *tired* the man Cass, and Dhanjal is not to be trusted by them. There is only the agent to drive.'

'Presumably. You were informed of his peculiar efficiency, Colonel. Don't underestimate him.'

'I do not.' The reply was ground out. He felt angered. Not with Sharmar. He could deal with politicians. He and others like him were entirely necessary to them. No, he was angry at the light Sharmar's condescension shone on his apparent failure.

An army transport, by its navigation lights and bulk against the stars, dropped low across the lake like a black pigeon towards the airport. He turned. An aide, as if posted, saw his impatient gesture and, interpreting it correctly, immediately brought him a folded map. He shone a torch on its colours, mountains, scattered towns and hamlets. A ravined, heaved-up, jagged landscape, few roads, fewer hiding places . . . if the man Hyde had gone north.

'Are you there, Colonel?' There was an edge of anxiety in Sharmar's voice now, satisfyingly. Rao flicked the map over. It dropped its folds open as if he were a fumbling conjuror who had let slip a pack of cards. Could he have gone south, out of the mountains and down towards the plain – Jammu? The woman had been heading for Jammu, after all –? He shook his head.

'Yes, I'm here. I'm checking something, Mr Sharmar.'

'What?' he heard blurted in the tone of an eager schoolboy.

'A moment, please.'

He handed the receiver to the aide and took the torch and then gathered up the dangling folds of the map. South —? No. Not in the same direction as the woman. To the east, the Zanskar Mountains were all but trackless, a few scattered villages and hamlets amid peak after peak . . . It had to be north, because to the west was Pakistan and the man Hyde would not have provided — *could* not have provided — himself with the appropriate papers to move freely on either side of the Cease Fire Line. He couldn't pretend to tourism up there —

Revelation, or merely feverish imagination? He suspected the insight that had suddenly sprung on him like a tiger from the lake. It could not be —

'Mr Sharmar,' he snapped, 'how do your irregular cargoes leave Kashmir?'

'*What?*' Sharmar was winded by the question, his subsequent breathing that of a stranded fish.

'It is not directly my business, nor has it been, Mr Sharmar. But it was Dhanjal's —?'

There was a silence, except for Prakesh's sharp inhalations, and heavy sighs. Rao pondered the notion that had come to him as if picking over rags that might conceal gems. Dhanjal was the key, if there were a key at all. Border guards would be on the Sharmar payroll.

'Mr Sharmar?' he enquired softly, firmly; cajoling a secretive child that had done wrong.

'Muzaffarabad —' followed by a throat-clearing noise, which recaptured confidence. 'At Tithwal, there are people —' Then he dismissed his confessional mood and snapped: 'Dhanjal would have *known*, Colonel —!'

'Could they have crossed the Cease Fire Line with Dhanjal's help?' The *Cease Fire Line* . . . it rankled still. It was inadmissible and yet inevitable, this *surrender* of Kashmir. And the Punjab . . . The Army had been mollified with promises of money, new weapons, greater influence, but there was still the surrender of

Indian territory to the Moslems. He shook his head. Old habits of thought, dying very hard.

'Depending on whoever was in command at the border posts,' Sharmar admitted. There had evidently been no expected shipment. Sharmar's voice sounded hollow.

'Then I suspect that that is what has happened to them, Mr Sharmar. They have crossed into Pakistan.'

'Damn! What do we *do*?'

'There are requests to be made, contacts to be established. I shall need your authorisation —' That, too, was difficult to admit, but necessary.

'Very well. Of course. What do you need?'

'For the moment, I must make certain. I suggest you remain near a telephone — perhaps the Prime Minister, too?'

'Yes, that can be arranged. I need to talk —'

'Yes. But not until I have made certain, Mr Sharmar.'

'Hurry, Rao! Call me as soon —'

Rao replaced the receiver, then barked at the aide:

'Get me contact with Tithwal — the border post. And get through to Islamabad. You know who to call in the ISID — quickly, man!'

The aide, like a hornet, seemed to stir the group around the table into hurried movement. Rao returned his attention to the lake, which was blank except for dotted lights and the glow from the urban sludge of Srinagar creeping along its western shore. It must be the case, he thought, clearing his head of buzzing angers. He'd *know* within ten minutes, but already he was certain. Hyde had used Dhanjal to get them into Pakistan.

But not to escape. Their escape was illusory. Islamabad would cooperate in the only area that mattered, men on the ground, machines in the air. They'd do that because of the Sharmars. Their overtures to the Pakistani army and members of the government would assist now.

He'd have them — soon.

*

The Land Rover hiccoughed over the last of the ascending track, its nose bucking down as if it sniffed Chilas in the distance. Food and warmth and lights that Hyde still could not see through eyes bleared with weariness and the obscurity of pine forest and mountainous twists in the road. They'd passed a cheerful, waving, solitary trekker climbing up towards the Babusar Pass, his raised hand diminishing in the mirror.

He rubbed his eyes again. The headlights bounced and weaved along the rutted track, whipping rock faces, drops, thin, leaning trees before his eyes. His wrists ached and his hands and fingers were numb on the steering wheel. The temperature had dropped like a stone and the wipers flicked light, flurrying snow away from the windscreen. There seemed to be snow in front of his eyes, closer than the windscreen. He knew he'd have to stop soon.

And the journey kept coming back like an ill-digested meal; the scattered villages, the narrow pines stuck like abandoned arrows in alpine pastures or bare cliffs, and the jade-green lake he had glimpsed just before the sunset lit it an unreal orange. Solitary farmers, thin sheep with muddy coats, the glimpses of sky with high eagles or hawks turning.

Cass was asleep in the passenger seat, sprawled like a drunk. Even Dhanjal dozed wearily in his awkward, trussed posture in the rear of the vehicle.

He blinked for the hundredth or thousandth time, and tried to focus, the rising of the offside wheels alerting him. The track was slushed and gleaming already, but he didn't know when the snow had begun. Time meant nothing any more, only the time of year that was already making whole villages deserted as people and their flocks drifted urgently down to lower pastures and shelter. He'd been held up for forty minutes by one flock of bemused-faced sheep and surly drovers, and the donkey-carts that had come behind, carrying the masked women and the dishevelled belongings.

He slammed on the brakes: the sheep were so real, jumbled

and bucking like snowflakes in front of his eyes. The Land Rover halted. The road ahead disappeared around a hairpin bend and the headlights strayed off into blank darkness. No, there were lights, miles away. Chilas —?

Cass woke briefly, touched his broken and bruised ribs, rubbed his arm where the memory of pentathol lingered even now, then slid rather than fell asleep once more. Hyde listened. Dhanjal was snoring. Warily, scenting the inherent danger of his weariness, he slipped the vehicle into reverse and climbed away from the drop that lay at the side of the road. Then he eased around the hairpin, one rear wheel nibbling rather than biting at the track. Then the darkness dropped away on every side, making him begin to panic before the track gleamed in the headlights again. Nose-down, the vehicle seemed to be carrying him effortlessly into the night — he jerked awake once more.

The trees were close to the road now, like a crowd of spectators. Another hairpin, but he got round it without backing up. He saw the flash of something furred and quick, across the track and into the trees. The descent continued . . .

He awoke, terrified. One wheel was spinning. The radiator grille was against the earthen cliff at the roadside as if it nuzzled for food. The vehicle was still in gear and his foot was on the accelerator. Dhanjal shouted in panic. Cass awoke slowly. End of journey.

Rubbing his eyes, he strained to see beyond the halo of the headlights. Darkness, flowing like velvet. Chilas' lights were hidden by another twist of the road. Thin firs were stuck in the corpse of the landscape.

He opened the door and the chill struck him awake. An alpine meadow, with soft lumps like the forms of sleeping cattle, spread around them. He felt grass crunch under his feet. There was snow in the wind, but nothing settling. The nose of the Land Rover was thrust into earth, some road-repair gang's spoil, he thought as the torchlight flicked over it. The meadow and the track bumped away downwards to another twist and another hairpin that lay beyond leaning pines. The wind rushed through a clump of pines no more than twenty yards away, their branches swaying obediently, softly clashing together as if in welcome. Hyde touched the gun in his waistband, then clapped his hands against his upper arms as the wind bit. Cloud swirled seemingly only feet above him.

When he tried to speak, he sounded hoarse and rusty.

'Cass – *Cass*, you idle fucking *bastard* –!' he managed to bellow, and the echoing noise of his voice and the momentary exhalation of his weariness delighted him. 'Move your arse!' The wind and the night carried his words away, but not before they had invigorated him.

'What –?' from the Land Rover.

Hyde hurried to the passenger window, banging on it with a wind-numbed hand. Cass wound it down in surreal slow motion.

'Let's get the tent up – unless you want to go on sleeping in the vehicle? No? Right, move yourself, then – I'm bloody tired and bloody hungry –!'

His weariness came back with his next breath and he was too bone-tired to care about the tent . . . or food, even. He was cold now, very cold. *Food* –

'We'll sleep in the Land Rover,' he growled. 'But I want something hot! Understand? Something hot to eat.' He slumped against the vehicle. Cass was nodding vigorously as he looked up at him. Hyde held onto the door as Cass opened it.

He . . . remembered Cass' face, still behind the smeared window, then – later? – soup or something else, thick and hot, then someone – Cass again? – zipping him into a sleeping bag . . .

The bag that enclosed him now. There were crumbs in his teeth as his dry tongue traced across them. He remembered the biscuits now, Cass forcing him to eat them when all he wanted was to sleep.

Someone was snoring in the muffled, windy darkness. It was the tone of Cass' snores, coming from a small distance. *He* was in the rear of the Land Rover, wasn't he? Yes . . . the trees creaked like a chorus beyond the rattling canvas hood. There was a dim gleam of whiteness on the sleeping bag where snow had thrust through the canvas. *He* was in the rear of the vehicle *with* – that was the point, *with* someone . . . A bulky figure in an anorak –

Dhanjal must be the shadow that breathed hotter than the surrounding air and loomed over him. Touched him, searching for –

The sleeping bag was all around him, hampering, imprisoning. He struggled one arm free of it, and it came out rubbing against his unshaven cheek, alerting Dhanjal so that the Indian clamped a hand across his mouth. He could taste the man's palm.

Bit it, like an animal reacting.

Dhanjal cried out in a stifled way, then jerked away from Hyde's grip. He struggled away, holding something that Hyde felt dragged out of his waistband. He heard Cass cry in alarm. The canvas hood opened and the wind came in, throwing a handful of snow ahead of itself. Then the loosened flap dropped back as Hyde struggled free of the sleeping bag and lurched to his feet, his head spinning only for a moment, then clearing –

– so that he fumbled in one of the metal lockers and drew out a pistol and slid the first round into the chamber with a loud rasping noise, then ducked his head through the flapping canvas. Lighter, snowblown darkness after the interior of the Land Rover. He saw a figure shambling away across the dimly gleaming meadow, bulky in its anorak. He fired twice – to warn rather than hit, but the shapeless figure continued without pause. The gunshots echoed eerily around the meadow, deafeningly loud. Then the sighing of the trees was restored. He jumped down and collided with Cass.

'Has he gone?'

'Yes. Stay here while I –'

'I tied him up!' Cass protested.

'Yes,' Hyde replied. 'Stay inside the Land Rover — get yourself a gun, he'll want the vehicle.'

'You?'

'If he doesn't want the vehicle, he'll want to tell someone where we are. Sit *tight*.'

He knelt for a moment, catching one glimpse of Dhanjal's gorilla-like image before it disappeared into a thick stand of pines. He rose like a runner, and lumbered towards the pines. Dhanjal looked as if he was following the track, heading for Chilas to raise the alarm. Hyde did not want to kill him — Dhanjal might be as useful again as he had been at Tithwal — but knew he would probably have to. He reached the pines. They straggled away on all sides, a miniature forest moaning in the wind. Snow pattered on his upturned face. There was no sign of Dhanjal.

He waited in the darkness, listening. He heard Cass moving inside the Land Rover, the wind, the creaking of branches, the cracking of high ice . . .

. . . they were almost noiseless, but they were there, he realised. There were *others* — not Dhanjal, *others* — sifting through the pines almost as silently as the snow. *Who — ?*

THIRTEEN

strangers on a train

A flash of light – from a station? Yes, she could hear the train's noise echoing back in an enclosed space. The light gleamed at the edge of the drawn-down blind and showed her Sara's white hands hovering over the compartment's table. Ros held her breath, then began to breathe calmly, regularly . . . still asleep. The tapes and film lay on the table in a second gleam of light. Sara's hands were possessive, certain. Her blond hair hung forward, masking her face, as she bent over what she had managed to remove from Ros' travel bag. As the noise of the train died away in openness once more, she was oblivious to Ros leaning out of the upper berth.

Christ, everything's there . . . She waited, certain there would be a muffled, polite tapping at the door of the compartment, that the Indian in the cream suit would be there, to be given the tapes and film. Her breath caught and made her cough before she could suppress the strangled noise. Sara looked up, startled out of her intent distraction. Her features were bland in the moonlight that seeped around the edges of the blind, pale and staring. Ros' hand gripped the edge of the bunk, the sheet clenched into creases.

Then Sara said in a hoarse whisper: 'You did do it, then. Spied on me –' The voice and the sentiments it expressed both possessed the peculiar suggestion of a gramophone record being started, then gathering speed until it created a coherent impression. 'You – and *him*, I suppose? The man you hardly *knew*? Christ –!' She flung her hair aside from her face with a rough, dismissive gesture. The noise of the train flowed away across the emptiness of the plains of Punjab south of Jalandhar.

Ros glanced at the table, which was sheened with moonlight. As was the pistol lying beside the tapes and film. Sara had found the gun Hyde had given her. Ros' breath came and went with asthmatic difficulty, her chest tight. The pistol loomed with more menace even than Sara, or the thought of a soft knocking at the door.

'I –' Then she was angry, expelling tension rather than outrage, so that her words came breathily. 'What are you bloody doing in my luggage?' she hissed.

Sara seemed nonplussed. Just for a moment.

'What the hell are these?' she retorted, her hand gesturing towards the table where the blind flapped idly with the rolling of the train, letting in more moonlight. 'You bugged my houseboat!' The outrage was genuine. Ros rose onto her elbow and forearm. Sara's face was only a matter of inches below her own. 'What were you doing? for whom?' But she knew the answers already, that much was obvious. The pistol insisted its presence and potency.

'Look, I'm sorry it had to be you!' Ros yelled. 'At least, I was. But you're in it. That's why you're here, isn't it?' Then she added: 'You *work* for the Sharmars.' Sara flinched as if struck, her mouth stretched into a rictus of anger and admission.

'No,' she murmured, her hands pressing downwards at her sides, as if to quell nipping, importunate realisations. 'No, I don't – not as you mean it.'

'You know what it's about, don't you?'

'Do I?'

It seemed hotter in the air-conditioned compartment, but the noises from the carriages on either side seemed inexplicably loud, as if transmitted on frosty air. Ros nodded.

'You do. The poor bugger they had blamed for the wife's murder. Who *did* do it? Do you know?'

290

Sara shook her head in a childlike, intense way. Then she looked up.

'I – don't know.' The words seemed forced from her.

'Christ!' Ros exclaimed. 'What are we going to *do*?' She had no idea why she had included Sara, as if both of them were threatened. And yet the woman responded, even if only to ask:

'D'you want some coffee?'

'Might as well,' Ros answered in a surly, grudging tone as she swung her legs over the edge of the bunk and slid down to the floor. They were suddenly cramped in what remained of the space between the seats. Ros thrust her bunk back to its upright position. Then she collapsed onto the bench seat, her forehead slick with perspiration. Sara busied herself with the thermos of coffee the attendant had brought an hour earlier. 'We'd better talk – hadn't we?' Ros announced belligerently.

Jerkily, like a nervous trainee, Sara thrust the cup and saucer towards Ros. Then she sat hurriedly and heavily opposite her, her own cup cradled in her hands. Her eyes were angry as they glared through a sweep of blond hair.

Their breathing. Nothing else for some time except the noise of the train quickly being lost in the spaces of the Punjab night and the occasional clicking of a set of points beneath the carriage wheels. Someone coughed loudly in the next cabin, startling them both.

Sara fidgeted. She was enraged at being discovered, enraged too at Ros and the evidence of the film. There seemed to be conflicting pressures thrusting her on. The train listed as with tiredness as it followed a long curve of the track. Then Sara stood up with a robotic jerkiness and switched on the light.

'What's the point of sitting here in the dark,' she muttered, 'since we're both wide awake!'

She returned to her seat.

'While we are awake,' Ros began, swallowing her throat clear of nerves, 'we'd better decide where we go from here. Apart from Delhi. I take it you weren't planning to throw me off the train?' She was surprised at how levelly the words came out. Sara appeared deeply affronted. 'Hadn't you thought about it?'

Sara shook her head vehemently while she stared in the direction of the film and the tapes – and the pistol. Her thumb and forefinger plucked mechanically at her lower lip.

'Christ, you *hadn't*, had you?' Ros breathed. The situation was more dangerous because more unpredictable. 'I know you County Set females aren't supposed to have any minds to speak of, but what did you think you were doing here?'

Sara merely pointed at the table beside them. The blind's cord moved its small wooden acorn-like grip amid the tubs of film and the tapes. It seemed to be inspecting them like a large, inquisitive insect.

'Look, Sara – they're trying to kill Hyde and Cass, the man they had prisoner. Don't you understand that?' Ros leaned forward, the cup rattling softly on its saucer, her face intent. Sara adopted a posture more appropriate to a leisurely dinner party. 'They're not going to let *me* just bugger off, either – are they? Can't you see that?'

'What the hell were you doing interfering in my life!' Sara suddenly snapped back, her eyes glaring, cheeks high-spotted with pink. She snatched at her handbag as if reaching for a weapon, then fished inside and withdrew a packet of cigarettes. She lit one and puffed angrily. 'I'm supposed to have given these up!' she growled accusingly. 'You started this, Ros. You *intruded*.'

'All right! But while they're trying to kill Hyde, I'm not going to just stand back.'

'Are you trying to kill V.K. – kill India?' Sara asked with virulence.

'What?' Ros was bemused.

'Now it's you who understands nothing, isn't it?'

The woman was suddenly transformed. There was no languor, even if there was a regained superiority. She was calmer, certain. The look, the confidence, the intensity, were all too familiar to be misinterpreted. She'd seen it before, on charity committees, from activists. Idealism . . . *the cause, my soul, the cause.* He wasn't just her lover, he was her hope.

'I'm not trying to kill anyone,' Ros offered lamely.

'Then why interfere?' She snorted, then threw up her hands in a large, dismissive gesture. 'Why did you come? You must have come to spy – *why*, for God's sake?'

Ros knew she must remain aware of her surroundings as she glanced at the door. The man in the cream suit, or maybe others, might knock at any moment; expecting Sara to hand her over to them.

'Hyde is a friend of Cass. He didn't believe he killed Sharmar's wife –' A complementary doubt appeared like pain on Sara's face for a moment, before she shook her head.

'He did it.'

'Whatever – the situation is as it is. We have to decide what can be done about it.'

'Why did you ever come here?' Sara accused bitterly, stubbing the cigarette into the ashtray beside the table with a furious, intent, grinding motion of her fingers.

Jesus –

Who? And *where* – ?

He remained with his back pressed against the bole of a narrow pine, the wind soughing through its branches above his head, listening to the human noises of the night. Where was Dhanjal? There was no sound of him blundering through the trees or crunching across the frosty pine-litter. No noises either, of the other footfalls, which had been quieter and more dangerous. *The natives aren't friendly,* Cass had said. Hyde glanced back towards the shadowed bulk of the Land Rover. He could hear, distinctly on the wind, so they could hear it too, Cass' movements. The man coughed, helpless and inviting. He slid down the tree until he was in a seated crouch.

The pistol was pressed against his cheek, both his hands gripped around it. He strained to catch movement against the faint, backcloth sheen of mountains and the lights of Chilas. A figure flitted, minutes later. His thighs and feet felt cold and stiff. Too small to be Dhanjal, a loose jacket flapping like a cloak. He waited, his eyes moving back and forth between the Land Rover, isolated amid the pallor of light snow on the meadow, and the thickening obscure perspective of the trees. Another figure, small and huddled, fled from the cover of one tree to another. Were they looking for Dhanjal?

Dhanjal, eventually. At least, he thought so. A bulky figure, moving with exaggerated and unpractised caution, perhaps fifty yards further into the trees. The wind moaned and, somewhere high and distant, ice cracked again, rumbling like an empty stomach. A harshly whispered word, then the movement of the two figures towards where he thought he had seen Dhanjal. How cautious were they, whoever they were? Afghan refugees, the local Kohistanis, bandits – troops? No, they weren't soldiers. More voices, then. Closer. They'd located him by a process of elimination. He slid upright against the tree. Then Dhanjal, unnerved, detonated the situation.

'Hyde!' he heard. 'Hyde –?' It was querulous. Not to tempt him out of cover, just to confirm that he wasn't alone amid *their* soft noises.

One shot. Automatic rifle. The noise cracked away beneath the pines, pursued by a command in a language he did not understand. Not Afghans, he thought. Two shots in reply, towards the calling voice, the small barrel-flickers from a pistol visible beside a tree. Running footsteps. Another shot from a rifle, a big, old-fashioned noise.

Then someone blundered against Hyde in the darkness. Dark, bearded features, winded and surprised and quickly malevolent. Hyde struck out with the flat of his hand across the bridge of the hawklike nose. The Kohistani staggered against the tree, a knife's blade gleaming near his middle as he unsheathed it. Hyde struck again, plunging his fist at the opening mouth. The man's head struck the bole of the tree with a small, cracking noise and he slumped into a drunken, unconscious position at Hyde's feet. Hyde whirled round at the noise of footsteps, but they were hurrying in the direction of Dhanjal. Two more pistol shots, their gleam betraying Dhanjal's position.

'Hyde —!'

He hurried. Dhanjal was suddenly to be stolen from him, and was therefore at once valuable, indispensable.

'Patrick!' he heard from the direction of the Land Rover. He glanced back. Cass was standing forlornly beside the vehicle, a betraying torch in his hand.

'Put the bloody light out!' he roared, before sliding quickly sideways, then in another direction, zigzagging away from his betrayed position, towards which two rifle shots were fired.

Leave him, leave the bugger, his thoughts repeated. Two more pistol shots — how many's he got left?

He came up behind one of them, his outstretched hands all but colliding with the man's form before seeing him. He struck at the back of the head, that was beginning to turn, with the barrel of the pistol and jumped the body as he might have done a log. Then skidded to a halt beside a tree, scraping his hands and cheek on its icy, rough bark. Assessed, saw, aimed. One shot, and a form crumpled, only wounded but out of the game for the moment. How bloody *many* of them —?

Two shots digging into the tree above his head. Just above. Then a third, from another direction, leaving a white scar beside his hand and fragments of bark clinging to his skin. He slipped away from the tree, body crouched, moving nearer to Dhanjal, from whose direction there were no more shots. No clicking, either. Hadn't run out of bullets, not yet . . . being sensible, is he? Saving his —

He stumbled over the humped obstacle of bodies, all three of them alive. He plunged forward, off balance, and landed on gritty pine litter and sharp ice. Slid to a halt on his stomach, like a child thrown from a toboggan. Then rolled away onto his back, but only in time for one of them to throw himself down on him, his filthy sleeve across Hyde's face, the man's clouding breath noxious. A knife had hovered over Dhanjal's form as he had blundered into them. Then he saw the knife again and grabbed for the wrist holding it. Thin, wiry, strong –

He fired into the man's body, which bucked coitally, then was still. He flung it aside, rose onto his elbow, and fired again. The man kneeling over Dhanjal toppled away with a groan. Not dead. Voices, not too close. He crawled to Dhanjal and pulled at the skirt of the anorak, hoisting the man to his feet.

His head flopped. Throat wet and dark. The gun was missing. Dhanjal seemed to assault him, pressed against him by the impact of a bullet. He dropped the body and ran, skipping from tree to tree, thrust forward by the cold, reliable panic that had saved him before. Pause, run, pause. Zigzag, dodge, pause, run. For the moment, they'd be looking for the dead and wounded. He had to be sure of their numbers before they had a go at the Land Rover . . .

. . . squatting isolated and shadowy in the meadow as he emerged from the trees. Thank Christ for smaller mercies. He hesitated, then clumped towards it across the meadow, slush and frozen grass soaking his boats and trousers, restraining him like thick mud.

'Cass!' he bellowed in a hoarse whisper. 'Cass!'

His face at the flap at the rear of the vehicle. 'You all right?'

Hyde nodded. 'Dhanjal isn't – he's dead!' He shook his head, drawing in great, relieved breaths of icy air. 'Get in the front – rifle! Let's bloody get out of here.' He dragged open the driver's door and lumped into the seat, his hand at once fishing for the ignition key, turning it. The engine barked coldly. Cass clambered into the cab, the rifle as awkward as a long-handled broom in his hands. He turned the ignition again, then a third time – figures were coming out of the trees, stirred by the violence and deaths and the lack of money and valuables on Dhanjal's corpse – and the engine caught and roared. He let off the brake and skidded out of the ruts. A bullet careered off the Land Rover's side.

Cass wound down the window and poked the rifle through it with all the aggression of a meteorological instrument. The Land Rover lurched forward like a charging bull, elating Hyde.

'Keep your bloody head down!' he yelled, gripping the recalcitrant steering wheel.

The vehicle bounced over the rutted, frozen grass and skidded in slush as he struggled for the road against their tension and without the comfort of headlights. A black shape jumped aside, then another stumbled backwards out of their path. His side window shattered and the bullet spent itself against a metal upright. The trees enveloped them as he felt something collide against the flank of the Land Rover and the back wheels jump like pounding feet on what had to be a body. 'Head *down*!' Cass fired twice, probably into the air, then the road was illuminated as he switched on the headlights and followed its violent curve and drop, all four wheels leaving the ground for a moment.

Then he skidded on a bend, following the descent of the track, rutted and prickled with ice like cold sweat, down towards the distant lights of Chilas. Cass was firing blindly and uselessly out of the window, back behind them, but it didn't matter. Cass was awake, they were both alive, even if they'd lost Dhanjal. It would be minutes yet before the adrenalin evaporated and left Hyde exhausted.

'Look, look here —' Sara was saying. It was as inveigling as a remembered song. The bench seat on which she sat was littered with newspapers in English and Hindi. The one held out towards Ros was the Jammu and Kashmir regional edition of the *Indian Express*. During the early hours of their journey, Sara had done no more than leaf aimlessly through them, just as Ros had flicked the pages of *Vogue*. Now, the newspaper was thrust at her with the intensity of a copy of a religious tract on a Sunday-morning doorstep. '*Look!*' Sara commanded.

Ros looked down. A page-broad photograph of Mehta, the leader of the Hindu fundamentalists, the BJP, Sharmar's principal opponents, standing in what appeared to be a decorated chariot, waving his arms in the midst of a huge crowd. The headline proclaimed, *Star's pilgrimage from Delhi to Srinagar*. Ros looked up, to Sara's evident contempt.

'You don't understand, do you? It might as well be in Hindi, for all the sense it makes.' She gestured at the paper before flinging it back onto the seat beside her. 'He'll appear at various points on that so-called pilgrimage, that's all. If you bothered to read the article, you'd realise why he's so dangerous,' she added. 'He's calling – the BJP's calling – for an end to the secular state. This pilgrimage is to call for unity, to prevent any hiving-off of Moslem Kashmir and the Sikh Punjab – V.K.'s *plan*!' She was leaning forward now, her hands twisted together in her lap. 'He just wants more trouble in Kashmir – Hindu immigration, a stronger Hindu presence in the Punjab, the army everywhere, putting down everything that moves!' She sighed. 'I don't know why I'm bothering to explain all this. It doesn't matter to you, does it?'

Her eyes challenged. Ros eventually shook her head, a gesture confronted with another glare from Sara's pale eyes. She didn't believe in anything, she'd left nothing behind in England she didn't have contempt for . . . Sharmar offered a grail.

'It's a wonderful ideal, V.K.'s,' she added unnecessarily.

'What?'

'Letting Kashmir and the Punjab secede –'

'What happens to his bloody heroin afterwards!' Ros snapped back, angry at herself immediately.

It was as if she had introduced the subject of abattoirs at a dinner party as the guests stared down in sudden shock at their lamb or beef, disguised with herbs and sauces and the impersonal cuts of the blades. She had done that once. Hyde had laughed, but the dinner party had been ruined and though their hostess had murmured agreement they had not been invited again. Now, she might have prompted her demise rather than mere ostracism from a dinner table.

'What would you know about it?'

'Enough.' She was impelled to be angry. 'He kills people or has them killed. For his ideals!'

'He sometimes has to do it for the general good –!' She glanced towards the table and its contents, amid which the little acorn-shaped wooden insect still hovered. There was a flash of lights from some buildings the train hurried past.

'*You* can't guarantee he won't have Hyde killed.' Then, again impelled against sense: 'You can't ensure they won't kill me. But this time it won't be far away and out of sight. You'll have to watch them take me –' Sara was shaking her head.

'No –'

'Who's the guy in the cream suit?'

'What?'

'The guy in the cream suit. He's the one who'll do it, or take me to the place where they'll do it. You'll at least be able to wave me goodbye!'

'Look,' Sara countered, everything except the flicker of her eyes oblivious to Ros' words, 'you know what's going on in Kashmir. It's been happening for years. Do you want that to go on getting worse and worse? Do you? It's been happening everywhere – bloody *religion*! – ever since Partition! It will get worse, make no mistake, if you help to bring V.K. down! He's the only damned hope for this bloody marvellous country!' Ros' wrist was grabbed by a cool, fervent, long-fingered hand. 'Ros, please – you can't hand over that stuff to someone and just forget about it – please!'

The noises of the train in the ensuing silence. The clatter of points, then the resistance of a slight gradient.

Ros said, eventually: 'I can't just forget about Hyde. Walk away and not think of him.' She shrugged herself more upright in her seat. 'I can't pick up the gun and shoot you, Sara. But

I'm not giving you the film and the tapes either. Not willingly. So, you'd better decide what to do.'

There was a fleck of saliva at the corner of Sara's mouth, which her tongue, as it darted across her lips, ignored. Her eyes were troubled, filled with conflict. Ros was, now she had become silent, newly aware of the compartment, the movement of the train, the flimsy sliding door on which a knock must come, soon. She'd done it all wrong, cocked it up. The woman opposite her had been seduced by the man's dream more than by the man. She was dreaming open-eyed. She was dangerous to anyone who threatened the cubs of her ideals, which had come late in life and all the more precious for that.

Sara wouldn't let them go for Hyde's sake, not even for hers —

Prakesh Sharmar watched Singh, their Finance Minister, being interviewed on TV. One of their media analysts had had it recorded, so that Prakesh and V.K. — if V.K. could be bothered with it — could check the quality of the performance. Singh was competent, lucid, enthusiastic. It was a good broadcast and would have its effect with the educated classes . . . *In three years, the rupee will be fully convertible . . . there will be accelerated privatisation of state assets . . . a new climate of deregulation has been brought into being* . . . strictly for the cultured and business classes, Prakesh confirmed. But necessary. It gave Congress a real power; the impression that the economy, and a record that had looked bad, was beginning to look up . . . *foreign investment, our talks with the IMF* — IBM, Ford, BMW and Shell were all involved in huge joint ventures — *we will cut income and corporation taxes, and reduce interest rates . . . overhaul the banking system . . . much of this work has already been begun by the Congress government* . . .

'Yes, that's fine. Congratulate the Minister,' Prakesh murmured. He walked away from the monitor and the media analyst, to the window of the high office which looked towards Connaught Place and the government buildings.

Yes, it *was* fine. It would cut a swathe through the urban

business communities, even please the wealthier farmers, please the educated. It all sounded responsible, sane, *secular*, something for the next century . . . while Mehta and his damned fundamentalists cut another swathe through the countryside with this ridiculous Pilgrimage of Unity, impressing the peasants, the poor, the Hindus! No one could win without the countryside.

The dawn was leaking into the city, outlining the India Gate at the far end of Raj Path. He could see the rows of streetlamps, Edwardian and so British, along each pavement. And the mock domes and columns, the Anglo-Indian temples of power. Everything that was at stake was there. Near India Gate — would they vote for the past or the future? He shook his head. Such speculations were more in V.K.'s cloudier line.

He turned away from the window. It would not be politic to appear to be brooding. And it was time to talk to Rao. He'd made the necessary calls to Islamabad, involved the Pakistani army units that would now be required. They would — ironically — be seeking fleeing drug smugglers, who might also be terrorists. Cooperation was another glimpse of the future . . . the man Hyde could not be allowed to snatch it away with a few photographs and bugged conversations! He clenched his fist as a drying thong seemed to constrict around his temples. An aide approached carrying a sheaf of clippings from the early editions of the regional newspapers, which had been faxed to them. He waved him aside with a flick of his fingers. A few minutes, he thought, as he looked at his watch. V.K. would be on breakfast-time TV from Calcutta in ten minutes, knee-deep in the homeless and beggars. Offering *them* a future. He must be back in the room to watch it, so that his aides and the party workers could watch him for his reaction.

No one succeeds in Indian elections without carrying the countryside, the peasants. Mehta and his bloody pilgrimage! His head ached. As he closed the door behind him, he soothed his temples with the long fingers of both hands. He must talk to Rao. It had become an irresistible need for his confidence to be bolstered by conversation with the Intelligence officer. It must happen now, they must be caught and eliminated today.

Sara had inveigled the woman into her cabin on the train. That, at least, was secure, since both women were being watched. He flicked his wrist to look at his watch again. In a few hours, the Jammu express would arrive in Delhi, where his people would be waiting to whisk the woman into oblivion the moment she stepped unsuspecting onto the platform. Sara would then have repaid some of the debt she owed the Sharmar family. V.K.'s bed had never been sufficient gratitude.

'Get me Colonel Rao,' he murmured to the Intelligence officer who sat in front of the bank of communications equipment. As if to mock him, the man was, even before he spoke, fiddling with the monitors, flicking switches.

Rao would have crossed into Pakistan by now. The hunt would be underway . . . again, his confidence sagged like lead in his stomach. Damn these people – there were only *two* of them, and one of those ill and exhausted from interrogation!

Imperturbably, the dawn was making the stone of India Gate lighten, gleam brighter than the dimmed neon and the early car headlights that were closer to Connaught Place. The Rotunda and the North and South Blocks, all at the far end of Janpath from his vantage, became the most real things in the lightening city.

It had been light for more than two hours now. The Karakoram Highway had allowed them to make good time. Out of the creeping dawn, rock carvings appeared at the side of the road east of Chilas. The town had been sombre, foggy with the smoke of fires. Then the carvings. A Buddhist monk holding an incense burner, a pilgrim with a water jar – a Bodhisattva offering his body to a lioness who, along with her cubs, devoured his flesh. Later, in almost full daylight, the reassuring Buddha seated above the wheel of the law. The Indus was strong and brown beneath the Thalpan Bridge. As the road turned north towards

Gilgit, the massif of Nanga Parbat seemed closer than ever, over-whelming Hyde. There was no sense of progress or escape, that same dominant feature always there, its morning peak gleaming with ice through drifting, dark cloud.

They crossed the Rakhiot Bridge, the Indus Valley like a moonscape of barren, decayed glaciers and ice-peaks, that same mountain always persisting in the rear-view mirrors, as if pursu-ing them. A high desert, heaped like mine-spoil or gleaming, metallic wreckage. The wind was icy, the clouds ragged and rapid, threatening snow.

At Jaglot, Hyde halted the Land Rover, totally weary and dizzied with the encirclement of the mountains. Cass had dozed beside him after the elation of their escape had left him spent. A small remission of the exhaustion which now ate at him again. The mountains hung above them like planets – summits, snow-fields, ice walls, rock, high pastures, alpine meadows and firs, dotted villages. So vast. Hyde shook his head. They were an hour from Gilgit, less than forty miles. He felt drained. He glanced at Cass, who stared unshavenly back, his eyes chilly as the land-scape, his expression defeated.

An ancient donkey-pulled cart eased past them along the KKH towards the village. The driver was incurious, hardly glancing at them from within his wrappings of cloth and sheepskin, mummified against the cold. Below them, the dark ribbon of the Indus was joined by brighter, clearer water from the Gilgit River. The Indus swallowed the clear water. Hyde sighed emptily and leaned his head on the steering wheel.

'You all right?' Cass asked solicitously. 'I could drive, if you –'

'With two broken ribs?' Hyde scoffed. Some parody of a domestic quarrel seemed in the offing. Ridiculous.

He knew he had to ring Shelley from Gilgit, from a hotel lobby or the post office. It *couldn't* – he swallowed – depend on Ros, not entirely; not their lives. A bus tottered up the highway towards them, enveloped in the dust it raised. It was rendered small as an insect crawling on a brown grass-stem by the

303

mountains behind it. Gilgit was an administrative centre. It had police and army, and an airport that linked it to Islamabad. The Sharmars would have Pakistani generals in their pockets like small change. The bus enveloped them with dust and noise, then dragged itself away and out of sight around a bend in the highway. The dust settled on the Land Rover to suggest that it was immobile, had been abandoned.

Something could happen to Ros . . . Shelley might not listen to her, at least not in time. Jesus. He felt resolve sink into the muddiness of his speculations, the silt at the pit of his stomach.

'I could try,' Cass replied sulkily.

'Sorry.'

Then his head swung up as he glimpsed something tiny as a speck on the windscreen, but moving high up against Rakaposi's flanks. A helicopter or a light aircraft, making for Gilgit. It could be anyone or no one. It could be someone like Dhanjal. Dhanjal – but his death was caused by the *natives*, not the army. Not Pakistani units – the Frontier Force Regiment, the Azad Kashmir Regiment . . . there was an airforce installation in Gilgit, wasn't there? They could easily fly in special forces, helicopters like the one on which the fugitive sun flashed for a moment. The weather wouldn't hold them up. There'd be plenty of resolve, plenty of motive.

Cass passed him a water bottle and he drank the icy liquid hesitantly, then gratefully.

'Want something to eat?'

'Only something hot.'

'What do we do after Gilgit?' Cass asked.

'What? Christ knows . . .' *I could get out, with difficulty. I could make it . . . so long as Shelley knows what I'm doing!*

But he doesn't and you couldn't . . .

His resentment of Cass remained unfocused, lacked any sharp edge.

'We'll get something in Gilgit.'

'Are you in touch with Shelley?' Cass asked pointedly, after gazing at the mountains. 'I mean – there is a plan, isn't there? You didn't just stumble across me?'

'There *was* a plan. Delhi Station was necessary to it, and you know Delhi Station. They'd all rather you were dead – Phil,' he added almost gently.

Cass nodded. 'Not surprising, in the circumstances. The Sharmars have got it sewn up then, haven't they?' His features were bleak in sudden cold sunlight.

'I'll call Shelley from Gilgit. *Make* him do something.'

'He'll probably be too busy sorting out the colour scheme of his new office for when the service moves to Vauxhall Cross!' Cass snorted.

Unconvincingly, Hyde said: 'He's not a complete tosser. He did send me –'

'Then chickened on the decision.'

'Something like that. They all want to believe the Sharmars.'

'They actually have the only sensible solutions. Pity about the drugs and the murder of Sereena –' His face crumpled into horror and genuine grief for a moment. Then he added: 'Pity I ever took a bloody interest in them really!' He slapped the dashboard with his gloved hands, shaking his head repeatedly.

'Shelley won't leave us out to dry. He daren't. Ros has got some of the evidence, I've got the rest. And *you*. If I phone him, I could call the *News of the Screws* at the same time. Or some Hindu rag that supports Mehta . . .' He grinned fiercely and clicked his fingers dully inside his gloves. 'Jesus, Mister-Bloody-Mehta the film star! That's *it*! The lever. They'll have to get us back to shut us up – won't they?'

'Bit thin, isn't it?'

'It only needs to be a cloud on the horizon. If I convince Shelley that we'll give it to the BJP, then Shelley will run round to the Foreign Office and wet himself all over the best Persian carpet!' He switched on the engine, as if he needed the warmth and noise of it and the heater to keep the idea nourished.

'What if you convince him – what then?'

Hyde stared at Cass.

'Then they'll have to get us out, won't they? *Trade* us out — or come in and get us!'

Sonipat. The Jammu express' last brief stop before Delhi. The carriage jerked slightly, just once, as the train halted. Ros stared at Sara, unable to breathe. The travel bag bulged at her feet. The tubs of film and the tapes made two separate heaps, like gamblers' chips, on the table between them. The day was already hot and the air-conditioning grumbled audibly. Beyond the window, the light hurt the eyes. Ros squinted as she looked across the tracks, beyond other platforms, towards sidings, rusted rolling stock, a steam engine shunting empty carriages. Then she turned her head. Their platform was on the corridor side.

She looked back at Sara. There were bruiselike stains under her eyes and her skin appeared to have the pallor and texture of parchment. There were tiny lines around her swollen mouth that seemed more confidently etched by time, or nerves.

'Well?' Ros managed to say.

Eventually, Sara nodded, swallowing.

'Yes. *Yes*.' Her anger was undirected. She brushed her hair aside and looked at the table. Had they been chips, she would have been the more successful. 'Oh, yes . . .' she sighed.

Ros had retained one roll of film, two of the tapes, forcing herself to remember their contents, remember beyond the numbers she had scribbled on each roll, each tape. She reached for them as for something that might bite or poison her with its sting. The numbers had been erased on the winnings close to Sara's hand. Ros shuffled the one tub and the two cassettes into the travel bag, which she then kept on her lap like a school satchel. Being sent away to school, the sense of being bereft. Through her anxiety and her mistrust of Sara, she felt the isolation of the hours ahead of her.

'I — I'll talk to him, then,' Sara said. 'The train only stops for five minutes here —' Someone passed their compartment along

306

the corridor, easing something heavy along the wall. Sara thrust film and tapes into her handbag and zipped it shut. 'I'll keep him occupied, they won't discover you've gone for as long as I can —'

'There's not only him —!'

'He's the one in command. The others don't matter. I'll give him what he wants, then —' Her eyes narrowed. 'The rest is up to you. I can't do anything more. Wait until the train's left, then find a taxi. Then do what the hell you like!' she ended.

'Right.' It was ridiculous, but she could not avoid adding: 'You'll be all right?'

'I'm his bloody *mistress*, aren't I? What could happen to me?' Ros remembered Sereena, who had betrayed Sharmar — then shook it aside. 'You're wasting time. I'll go and see our friend —' Sara stood up violently, as if to assault her.

'Thanks,' Ros said.

'I couldn't let them kill you. That's all it is. I couldn't let his people — not him, but some of the others, even Prakesh . . .' She admitted it reluctantly, again trying to avoid the unpalatable implications. 'Look, I don't want to do this, but I don't want you on my conscience! That's all —' She hesitated, then mumbled: 'Good luck,' and slid the door open, then slammed it shut behind her.

Ros began shivering uncontrollably, gripping the bulging travel bag against her stomach and breasts as if to smother it. Her mouth filled with saliva and her eyes blurred wetly, even as she berated herself. *Pathetic, snivelling, get off your backside . . .* The hot sunlight seemed to infiltrate the window, nullifying the air-conditioning. She was hot, then chilled, hot again. The day glared outside, the tracks weed-strewn and gleaming beyond the end of the opposite platform. A bearer dozed against mailbags in the mid-morning sun. A locomotive whistled and churned steam somewhere out of sight —

She jumped to her feet and scrabbled the table into its folded position, clicking it roughly home. Fiddled clumsily with the door and then swung it open, almost over-balancing out into the hard glare of light that seemed to assail her. The tracks beside the train doubled and then redoubled, as if she was drunk. The step wavered as she felt for it with her right foot. Then she leaned her weight on the door and awkwardly clambered down to the track. It was clear except for an empty Coke can between the rails. The opposite platform was sparse with idlers. The gravel was hard and penetrating through the soles of her shoes. She stumbled to the platform end, then ascended its slope. Hurried, because that had been the plan before the panic had begun and her disorientation increased. Out of sight to the far side of the suburban platform. Found a bench because she had to, and sat down heavily. A child's huge eyes watched her from its mother's squashed, milk-supply breast. Ros' heart thudded in her chest and her head felt as if it would split open like a dropped melon.

Then the noise of a peremptory whistle which had no meaning except to startle her. The baby went on feeding from its mother's breast. A bearer passed by, bent as if chained behind a luggage trolley. An announcement over the tannoy in Hindi. The whistling ceased and a train moved.

She turned her head. The tracks slid away, polished and dazzling. The Jammu express curved into view, heading out of Sonipat towards the hazy sky above Delhi. Ros swallowed, a sense of being abandoned, as if she had unintentionally missed the train. She lifted her head to the platform roof, exhaling like a stranded fish.

What was it she was meant to do now? What was it Sara had told her?

Eventually . . .

. . . taxi. Get a taxi. She looked along the platform. The station seemed quiet, the town beyond it somnolent. A white board, the blue image of a car emblazoned. EXIT, in English and Hindi. A taxi —

*

He could see, from the bank of telephones along the wall of the lodge's dining hall, the Gilgit River and the long, delicate structure of the suspension bridge across it. In the distance, where cloud was lowering on the mountain slopes, the bigger bridge over the Hunza River. Early lunches were being eaten by trekkers and 4WD tourists – a busload of Japanese were noisy in the other window corner. The thermoplastic tiles on the floor clattered with bootsteps or squeaked with trainers. Normality enveloped him in the Riverside Tourist Lodge, easy peace and a sense of the openness of the Gilgit Valley seduced from the windows that ran the length of the noisy room. Cass was seated at one of the long tables, still eating, hunched intently over the food as if counting hoarded wealth.

There were terraced fields of rice across the river, other terraces palely-green with new grain. The ranks of apricot trees, still full-leaved, too, as if they had descended thousands of feet to another climate.

The telephone connection was risky – open and operator-placed from the local exchange. Any call from Gilgit would be, unless he asked the army if he could have a secure line to call the D-G of British Intelligence . . . or unless he tried calling from one of the plush new hotels in Gilgit, and he didn't really look the part and anyway the army and the local officials and the police hung about places like that. Nevertheless, his own nerves seeped back down the unconnected line to him like the breathing of someone stalking him. He looked at his watch. One o'clock. They'd seen more helicopters, large military transport choppers, Russian-made and Pumas, heading towards Gilgit. A couple of fly-buzzing Alouettes scouting the KKH. No military transport on the highway, yet. It looked not quite normal, not quite an operation – hovering between the two. The helicopters were parked on the military airfield by the time they reached the town.

The operator informed him, once more, that she was trying to connect him.

His stomach rumbled. Food, not nerves, he told himself, tasting the spiciness of the meal on his breath. The Land Rover was parked on the campsite: they had hired a tent to preserve a very thin cover story. They'd be expected to report to the Foreigners' Registration Office before evening, or hand their papers in to be inspected by the police. They'd be gone by then . . . smiles and enthusiasm and tourist naivety ought to last another couple of hours. He'd bought the gear they might need – were going to need, if the phone call worked –

– phone ringing out, distant and hollowly unreal as if in an empty house. Not his bloody answering machine, he pleaded silently, please . . . It was eight in the morning in London – in Surrey, to be exact, where Shelley lived in stockbroker Tudor splendour, master of all his mortgage surveyed. The phone went on ringing beyond the four of five summonses an answering machine required.

Alison's taken the kids to school and Shelley's driver's already collected him –

'Yes?' A very distant, impatient female voice.

'*Alison!*' he shouted, turning his face into the helmet of the booth. 'Can you hear me, Alison?'

'You're very faint,' he heard. 'Who is it? I was just leaving with the kids –'

'It's Patrick – Patrick *Hyde*,' he called distinctly. *And that's stuffed it if the operator's been told to listen.*

'Patrick –!' He could hear the catch in her voice, the shock and relief, even though her words remained distant and whispered. 'You're *alive*!' *So far.* 'Peter's left for the office. Do you want his car phone number?' Then: 'God, this line's awful!' Worse followed. 'Is Ros all right?'

Christ, I hope so, I really hope so.

'Yes. Fine! Don't give me any numbers. Just listen. Then tell *him*. OK? Alison – OK? You *understand*?'

After what seemed an inordinate silence: 'Yes. Got you.'

Bloody ridiculous, this – ET, phone home. He and Cass were an alien life-form, playing the games of the 1970s in the wrong decade. No wonder he was ringing Shelley at home. Who would even want to remember how to pull off an extrication operation?

'Just listen. Ros will call you. He has to talk to Ros. Got it?'

'Yes, I'll tell him. She isn't with you?'

'No.' His forehead was damp, the helmet of the phone booth hot as an old-fashioned hair-dryer clamped over his head. 'He has to be ready to meet her.' He all but added, *Not London*, but told himself not to say where, when or how. At this end of the phone they're in a time warp, they still play the old games. 'Tell him it's *utmost* —'

'What's wrong?'

'Almost everything. Tell him —' He didn't need to threaten Shelley, especially through Alison. Just the buggers Shelley would have to convince. '— he *has* to help. If he's prevented, in any way, then I'll go to the BJP — the Hindus. If he's blocked by *anyone* then the B-J-P will get everything we have. I'll ruin the Sharmars.' Even if anyone was listening, they already knew that. They'd expect him to sell them to Mehta.

'I'm writing this down, Patrick — Sharmars. Bloody hell!' It was the comment of a housewife, half-amused, half-shocked, at the name of a local adulterer; an unexpected, unlikely neighbour. 'Have you got — *him*, Patrick?' No names, no pack drill. *She* should be the new D-G, not Shelley.

'Yes. Tell Peter that Ros will know where.' Involuntarily, he glanced at his watch once more. Her plane hadn't yet taken off, and he couldn't place her in more danger — surely? He had to tell Shelley *something*. 'It has to be —' He looked at the valley, shadowed now as the sun once more disappeared. To the north-east, Rakaposi was gloomy with snow-heavy cloud. '— twenty-four hours maximum. No more than twenty-four. He *has* to do it, Aly —' Even if only for old times' sake.

'He will, Patrick.' She understood. No fuss, no outburst, no equivocation. She wasn't even torn. No wonder Aubrey had always liked her, the old bugger! 'He will. Inside twenty-four hours. Good luck –'

'Have to go, Aly!' he burst across her wishes, and put down the phone.

Two soldiers, by their stripes a havildar and a naik, had entered the dining hall of the lodge. Their eyes slowly, methodically, scanned the clumps of diners, as if studying unfamiliar and probably dangerous terrain. They scrutinised each group, each couple, each individual face.

FOURTEEN

business class

He willed Cass not to become startled or alarmed. Willed himself, too, to remain casual, possess the slightly dazed perfunctoriness of a tourist at high altitude, dizzied with mountains and a strange language and customs. The corporal and sergeant stood close to the doors of the dining hall, their hands on their hips as if about to mimic some acrobatic circus trick. Then, as someone attempted to skirt them, they at once requested the Japanese woman's papers. Slowly, she comprehended and obeyed. Their inspection was cursory, but not necessarily without intent. The river valley beyond the window, trees and terraces climbing towards the mountains, seemed incongruous and very distant.

Hyde crossed the room slowly, hands in his pockets. Even so, the havildar's head turned to watch his progress. Was there greater interest? Yes . . . the corporal beside him was nudged into attentiveness, and both soldiers studied him as he slouched absent-mindedly to a vacated table where plates and cutlery remained littered. *His* meal, already eaten, before he made a telephone call . . . Cass was twenty feet away, puzzled and staring. Hyde glared from beneath his narrowed eyebrows and Cass seemed to understand. If they were looking, then they'd be alert for two Europeans travelling together. If they were *really* looking, then they might not be fooled. They'd have descriptions, even photographs . . . He held his breath as the havildar reached into the breast pocket of his greatcoat – the wind seemed to rattle the long window just at that moment, so that coat and noise emphasised the inhospitable landscape. He removed . . .

cigarettes. He did not offer one to the naik, merely lit one for himself. Hyde shivered, then suppressed his involuntary reaction to the immediate and to the day and night ahead. If they got out of this – the wind against the windows again, flexing the feeble glass, cutting off his thoughts.

The sergeant exhaled smoke while the naik moved towards Cass. There were elderly Americans in a small party on the other side of the dining hall but the soldiers had shown no interest in their accents, their age. They had descriptions, then. Hyde reached behind him, touching the gun in the small of his back. Cass buttered hard bread, apparently oblivious. Hyde was aware of the deep stains beneath his eyes and the dead pallor of his skin; aware of the bruises that still marked his jaw and temple. The corporal halted beside him and Cass looked up incuriously. Hyde's eyes moved between the two soldiers. The havildar was idly observing and occasionally glancing with parochial contempt at the Japanese and the Americans. Cass muttered something to the corporal – in Urdu, Hyde thought, not understanding it. Cass shrugged expressively and the corporal glanced towards the senior NCO, but only for a moment. Cass was nodding, then he pointed, looked at his watch, indicating the time – another time, the future?

The corporal nodded and moved away. Cass appeared to slump with relief in his chair, his eyes feverishly bright. Sunlight flashed blindingly into the dining hall as the sun came from behind chasing clouds. Shadow and gleam pursued each other across the landscape, then the mountains darkened as the brightness once more disappeared. Cass glared at him. The naik had moved a little away from him, hands on his hips, attracted yet reassured by Hyde's unshaven, unwashed swarthiness and small frame. Just another bloody wog.

Cass got up, nodded imperceptibly towards the doors, and left the dining hall without hurry or delay. The corporal, attracted by the laughter of the Americans and the loud voice of their courier – high-pitched, assured, dismissive of the food they were eating and of Gilgit's hotels – followed his sergeant towards the group. It was, perhaps, the volume and indecorum of the female voices rather than the disparagement of Gilgit, that provoked the two Islamic soldiers. They approached the tables around which the Americans were gathered . . . *the scenery is fantastic, don't you think, but that* road! *And they call it a highway* . . . with an enhanced swagger of authority. *You have to put up with* some *discomfort to see all this* . . . *Can we help you?* The last phrase coming from the travel guide or courier or whatever she was, greying blond hair spilling from beneath a woollen hat, as Hyde rose carefully from the table and moved inconspicuously towards the doors. *Papers? Which papers?* The voice was impatient. Then Hyde was through the doors.

Cass was hovering in the foyer, close to a party of Europeans debouched from a bus parked outside the doors of the lodge. Luggage littered the foyer as did the voices of the French tourists. Cass grabbed Hyde's arm and Hyde felt the tremor of relief and weariness. It was as if the small incident had been a marathon.

'What did you tell him?'

'My papers were at the Registration Office. I was waiting for a fishing licence. I paid someone to queue at the Bureau of Fisheries – he thought I was stupid, letting my papers out of my hands.'

'Come on, let's bugger off before they get through with the Yanks.'

Hyde bullied them into the gritty, flying air outside. Cass shuddered with the bite of the cold. A military transport plane dropped towards the airfield, to join the huddle of helicopters. Troops moved away from one of the big Russian transport choppers, small as insects, numerous as ants, too, it seemed to Hyde. His gaze swung towards the mountains to the north-west. Up there, sport – up yours, more like. Cass grabbed his arm and attention before they reached the car-park and the Land Rover.

'Where are we going?' he demanded, as if Hyde had attempted to abduct him; an outrage of weariness. His eyes were feverish again. 'Where the fucking *hell* are we going?' His arms waved at the enclosing mountains, the ragged, streaming rag-bundles of cloud, the airfield and the scattered trees and dwellings of the narrow valley in which Gilgit sat like a thin, twisting snake above its shadowshape river. 'What the hell were you doing while I was parked like your granny?' Cass was shouting now, expelling some of the tension of his narrow escape. He leaned over Hyde as if in threat.

Hyde shrugged.

'You won't like it –' He glanced back at the doors of the Riverside Tourist Lodge. Its pennant cracked in the wind and its buildings seemed small, huddled beneath the mountains – so many bloody mountains.

'Why not?'

Hyde turned away and moved closer to the Land Rover. Cass trailed after him like a shambling idiot child.

'You won't like it because *I* don't like it!' Hyde snapped, as if challenged over some incompetence he had shown. He turned back to Cass, his hand on the door-handle of the 4WD. Cass' anger was blunted by the expression in Hyde's eyes; a flat, hard glare. 'Look down there,' Hyde said. 'They're not here for the fucking polo, Phil! They want us – *just* us. Sharmar's arranged things. Pakistan isn't safe for us.' He knew it never was, that's why they were here in Gilgit, on their way to . . . I shouldn't tell him, not just yet. 'We have to – *walk* out. Trek it.'

Cass seemed winded. His frame sagged, like wet washing dragging down a line. 'I *can't*,' he breathed at last. He leaned against the vehicle, his glazed look drawn hypnotically across the mountains to the north and west, moving as regularly as an old-fashioned typewriter carriage.

'Come on,' Hyde said, guiding him to the passenger side of the Land Rover. 'It's not *all* walking – but let's get on with it, before –' Too late.

The havildar and his corporal appeared in the hotel's doorway, the glass sliding its reflected images into place behind them.

Reflections of mountains. At once, their attention seemed to be on the Land Rover and the two Europeans standing beside it. Cass hadn't seen them . . . then he turned, before turning back to Hyde with a shocked, blank fear on his face.

'Just get in,' Hyde said.

One of them shouted in Urdu, then in English. Merely calling for their attention, almost polite. Then more peremptorily as Hyde closed the door on Cass and moved with apparent unawareness to the driver's door and began climbing in. The voice issued a command. The two soldiers had begun hurrying – not quite running, but scuttling as their hands unbuttoned their greatcoats to get at their pistols, the coats flying behind them like threatening cloaks.

The transport plane had landed and begun to taxi. One of the helicopter's rotors was whirling like a gleaming shield in sudden, brief sunlight. Gilgit glinted and retreated. The river was cold, hostile. Hyde started the engine. The naik had drawn a pistol but seemed undecided. The sergeant, too, seemed self-conscious, as if they had over-reacted. Hyde accelerated. The havildar's face, its moustache like an emphasis of surprise, loomed close to Cass' window, then the tyres screeched them out of the car park, jolted them onto the road. In the mirror, the two soldiers were still, bemused. Then the sergeant fumbled something from his greatcoat and pressed it against his cheek. Hyde swerved the Land Rover away from collision with a cart heaped with vegetables and dried fruit as strange as countless tiny lungs. He lost sight of the two soldiers who were evidently summoning assistance. But they wouldn't have been fooled a second time, not by two of them without papers. Cass lay back in his seat, his face white and thin. They were paralleling the airfield.

Two or three small private aircraft or tourist carriers dotted like boiled sweets amid the olive-drab of the military transports. Mostly Russian and French helicopters, a couple of recently arrived Hercules transports. Then the road swung into Cinema Bazaar, which stretched the length of Gilgit, and he could no longer see the airfield, or the Hercules, or the troops filing out of the open cargo doors into another fugitive gleam of sunlight. The Sharmars had got their act together. They had enough Pakistani generals in their pockets to make sure that what they wanted to happen happened. And *that* was he and Cass dead.

The Land Rover raced through an endless corridor of shops and stalls, dodging between stray animals, moving carts, gaudy buses, military trucks and jeeps. Hyde swung right then left across a crowded square, easing the vehicle through the countless pedestrians, all heading along the Chitral road as if hurrying to become spectators for the pursuit he knew must occur. Cass went on staring through the windscreen as if watching a landslide, the ground opening before him. He isn't going to make it, he isn't going to make it, Hyde heard his thoughts repeat.

The restored mosque, then the crowds fell away, leaving the road ahead clear, against which the mountains pressed. The polo ground was all but full. Blurs of movement, the roaring of the crowd like an uninterrupted crashing of surf. Then, quickly, the dusty town straggled away into the tents and petrol-can lean-tos and mud shacks of the Afghan refugees, displaced, lost, listless in the wind. Huge-eyed children, one limping, his left foot vanished, a couple of thin dogs, demoralised men, patient, burdened women. It was a scene of drab clothing and habitation, as if dust had settled thickly on everything over a period of many years. The minaret of the mosque faded in the mirror. The road was empty behind them.

Ahead of them, too. The buses had already deposited spectators for the polo. They'd run on time, for once. The river ran alongside the road, the colour of cold mud. Then Cass said:

'I can't, Hyde. I *can't*!' He seemed disappointed in himself, but also accusing; as if he had been misled, deceived. It was as though he expected a prize, something almost for nothing . . . Yet he could not condemn Cass. He had two or three broken ribs, he was exhausted. Couldn't cope. Hyde had been there, he *knew*.

Hyde slowed the Land Rover, the view in the mirror obscured by dust. His hand gripped Cass' wrist as it lay idly on the man's thigh.

'There isn't any other way, Phil,' he coaxed, the effort at gentleness almost genuine. He spun the wheel as he avoided a fallen jumble of boulders that littered the side of the road, then replaced his hand on Cass' wrist. 'Believe me.'

'Where the fuck is Shelley, then?' Cass wailed like a child.

'He'll be there. It's arranged . . .' I called his wife, she promised to pass the message on! 'Ros knows where we need to be by tomorrow. I've got Shelley by the balls, he has to show up.'

'How – where?' Cass demanded, sniffing loudly.

'Afghanistan,' Hyde said quietly, after a pause. Cass turned his death's-head features towards him, the eyes glittering but dead.

'Where?'

'Across the border. They can't come in.' Or won't. 'We have to go out. Look, it's ten, maybe twelve miles from where we'll have to abandon the Land Rover, no more than that. We can do it. Up the Ishkuman Valley, the road goes as far as Chillinji – at least, it does for one of these. From there, it's just a hike, not a trek. We'll make it –'

'I just can't,' Cass replied at once, with utter, final certainty.

It was only one of the Sharmar family's various properties in and around Delhi, but it was the one she always chose to use. Not hers, but then no one else stayed there; no one at all lived there. It was, of course, a spacious Raj bungalow on the edge of the Chanakyapuri enclave, looking towards the scrubland forest of the Ridge marooned within the vast concrete sandbanks of the city. The bungalow was close enough for the noise of peacocks to be heard above the traffic on the Sardar Patel Marg, and the breezes had always seemed illusorily cool. Occasionally, from one of the long windows in the lounge or breakfast room, one could catch glimpses of a bright flash of birds or the bulk of a blue bull antelope. The seeming distance of the city, the proximity of wildness, her own and V.K.'s nudity at the windows, sipping champagne after copulation . . . the images repulsed her now.

As Prakesh did . . . The past frightened her, too, as he stood at the dusk-glowing window of the lounge, staring absently at the Ridge.

Sara swallowed, careful to avoid the slightest noise. The sigh of the air-conditioning was all but inaudible, as if absorbed into the silence; as her own noises had been during the long after-noon as she waited for V.K. – more likely Prakesh – to arrive and to begin questioning her concerning Ros . . . damn Ros! The gesture she had made, helping her to leave the train, seemed not merely futile now, but incredibly stupid, romantically naff. Prakesh remained at the window, his figure haloed by the sun-set, the glasses in his hand glinting. Beyond him, she thought she caught the flick of an eagle or a large kite, scouting for prey. The image disturbed; there was a sense of a lost and self-deluding past. The place had staled on her tongue like unwanted liquor as she had stared at the Ridge through the afternoon.

Then he turned. She suppressed her nerves.

'Why didn't you come to the offices?' he asked silkily.

'Was there anything to come for?' she replied. 'V.K.'s in Cal-cutta. The details of the election I find boring. Sorry.'

His eyes, even in the shadow of his face, glittered. Beyond him, the Ridge ceased to exist, and she saw only office blocks and high-rise flats in the smoky, golden dusk.

'You should have come to report to *me*!' he snapped. 'You were responsible for that bloody woman!' She realised how her mind had slowed matters. He had not been in the room more than a few minutes, he had poured the drink angrily, quickly, spilling some of the whisky on the trolley's lace mat. Had stormed to the window, hovering there as if to recover his breath before he spoke. Only minutes. Her mind had been trying to avoid him, change him into a casual, diffident visitor – as Prakesh had once been, when in his brother's shadow. 'You let her get away! I had you telephoned – here – but you were *too tired*!' He crossed the room with a venom that suggested he would fling the drink into her face, and she flinched against it. If he once suspected . . . Then he paused. 'Where the devil is she?' he raged.

'How should I know? Prakesh, I have apologised already. I got you the film, the tapes. There was nothing else that I could find in any of her luggage. I assure you I searched it thoroughly. Does she matter?'

Prakesh Sharmar was indecisive, somehow adrift, at the mercy of something not of his own making. Which meant they didn't have the two men; Sereena's lover, and Ros' lover, she added. They were still loose, as was Ros. For some reason, Prakesh was afraid of that continuing freedom. They couldn't be that much of a threat, could they?

'It may very well matter. Yes, you did *part* of your job well enough, Sara. But you should have watched that woman until she left the train in *Delhi*. We were ready for –' He broke off and turned away. 'She would have been taken care of,' he added in a murmur.

'She isn't anybody. She can't hurt you, surely?'

He turned on her.

'You simply walked away from our people at the station, Sara – why?'

'I was tired! Do you think I slept on the train, knowing what you wanted me to do?' She brushed her hair aside from her face. One of the bruises he had inflicted in Srinagar seemed to prick with pain.

'I wasn't able to come here,' he growled. 'Not until now. I haven't been able to concentrate on the search for the woman. Do you understand the problems your carelessness has caused? Do you?' Again, the two small, pouncing dangerous steps towards her; again she flinched back on the sofa. The elegance of the room seemed to retreat into insignificance, as she did herself. If Prakesh ever so much as . . .

321

'I'm *sorry*,' she replied with ironic defiance. 'Your people didn't do much better. They didn't even see her get off the train.'

'They've been made to understand their failure,' he announced. 'But time has passed and the search has been in the hands of idiots!' he burst out, his arms rising and falling like those of a windmill. 'Where would she have gone?' he demanded. 'Did she say anything? Does she have friends, help here in Delhi? The British High Commission has been watched, the various offices their spies use are under surveillance. Who was she intending to see in Delhi?' It was as if his voice had hold of her and was roughly shaking her.

She shook her head. Strangely, he accepted that Ros' escape was from Srinagar, not from India. Perhaps it was merely bureaucratic of him to assume that. She must be seeking help from people here, going through channels – ? Perhaps it was because the man Hyde was still at large. They were both still in India, and he made the assumption that they would remain. What would Ros do, anyway? Run out on him? No, she wouldn't do that . . . so she must still be in Delhi, trying to obtain help.

'I don't know. If her lover is a spy, then it's to other spies she would go – surely?'

'*I* don't know.'

There'd been no travel tickets in Ros' bag, not that Sara had seen. She had plenty of money, travellers' cheques, credit cards – but nothing to indicate a plan of escape.

'Well *think*!' he bellowed.

'I *can't*!' she shouted back at him. 'I have no idea what she's likely to do – what goes on in her head. She's a stranger!'

His eyes seemed to gleam with nursed and hitherto concealed suspicion. Yet he made no further movement towards her. He *was* undecided. He couldn't imagine Ros, she didn't fit any models. He returned to the darkening window. The Ridge was a lumpy, colourless mattress now, above which a last few specks

322

of birds soared and glided. The city's neon glow was brighter than that of the sunset.

Then there was a discreet knock at the door of the lounge which startled her. Prakesh whirled round.

'Yes?' he called.

His driver appeared in the doorway, his manner hurried, excited.

'Sir —'

'What is it, Menon? What is it?' Prakesh crossed the room as if to embrace the man or strike him.

'Sir — the airport, Indira Gandhi, sir —!' Prakesh was prompted, for a moment, to turn triumphantly towards Sara.

'What?' he yelped like an excited dog.

'There is a report, sir — the woman has been identified —'

'What flight?'

For an instant, Sara was intensely disappointed at Ros — disillusioned was a more accurate description. She was running out on . . . no. She was *getting* out, she still had film, tape, *evidence*. She was on her way back with it. A trade-off.

'She is in the Air France first-class lounge, sir.'

'What time is the plane due to —'

'Fifteen minutes, sir!'

'What —? Why haven't they —?'

'She was identified only a few minutes ago, sir, they assured me of that.'

'Get me airport security — *no!* Get me Rao's man at the party offices. Quickly, Menon, quickly!'

He moved about the room as if panicked by a fire, blinded by smoke and with no sense of the location of the doors and windows, his body desperate with energy. Then he came and stood in front of her, his face flushed.

'Sir!' the driver called, holding out the receiver.

'Sara!' he snapped. 'I hope you didn't know anything. From this morning until now, I hope you knew nothing!' Then he all but ran to the telephone, blithe as a lover.

Sara felt her stomach revolt, then weaken as if with an enteric disease. When they caught Ros, she'd tell them she had help to get off the train, that they'd *agreed* it together.

And V.K. would leave her to Prakesh . . .

She had stared at the detritus of Delhi, hazy in the distance and through tinted glass, for most of the afternoon. Now, through the thickness of the Boeing's small porthole, next to her seat in business class, there were only the pricks and flares of airport and runway lights; Delhi was an indistinct haze, like a shout muffled by an intervening wall. Ros leaned back in her seat. The safety video flickered on its screen, the artificially loud commentary meaningless. She closed her eyes, the 747 jolting and clumping along the taxiway towards the main runway, to queue patiently behind other aircraft. Her breath came raggedly, the relief evident in it startling her; as if she had breathed for the first time since she had been ushered into the Air France lounge.

Delhi had rushed against the window of the room, Indira Gandhi airport seeming small, a tussock in which she could not conceal herself with any hope of success, with the city massed against her just beyond the tinted windows.

Green lights, red, white . . . running away in diminishing lines, sliding past the porthole window as through oil. The night flared with the rush of an aircraft retreating down the runway before staggering like a dark, huge bee into the air. Her breathing calmed.

Book upendedly open on her broad lap, her feet out of her shoes, the headphones thrust beside her, the menu and the untouched glass of champagne on the armrest. The seat next to her was empty, which made her concentrate on Hyde's absence – for the first time without blaming him for the raggedness of her nerves, the wearing hours she had sat in the first-class lounge. The aircraft was on time – now time seemed normal, sliding away in whole, unnoticed minutes. A little after seven as she glanced at her watch in the dimmed lighting of the cabin.

Business class was restfully two-thirds empty. A stewardess passed, glancing mechanically at her with a mechanical smile. The inexpressive look acknowledged a rather worn-looking, middle-aged, fat woman, and Ros embraced her usual self with relief.

Even embraced the eight-hour flight, because at the end of it Shelley must be waiting, there would be activity, there would be whatever was required to pull Hyde and Cass out of Kashmir . . . she had the tiny piece of tissue paper folded in her compact. She hadn't looked at it, not once since Hyde had put it there. She knew only how to demonstrate its use, rather than convey its information, to Shelley. Who *had* to be in Paris . . . Her head ached, her temples were thong-tight. She glanced at the champagne and dismissed it before turning again to the window. The safety video ended its vain plea for attention and the screen went blank. Lights sliding past . . . more slowly –?

The 747 slowed on the taxiway, and the lights stilled, to stretch away as individual, unmoving points. Another airliner roared down the runway, suggesting that her flight had been left stranded. The heavily-accented English of the captain was badly amplified in the cabin.

Delay . . . slight . . . apologise for the inconvenience . . . only a few minutes . . . Ros felt bemused rather than alerted, already institutionalised by the cabin, the subdued lights, her vast and draining relief. Seven fifteen.

Passenger steps, climbing like a small crane from the back of what might have been a beach-buggy driven by a turbaned Sikh in a white shirt, approached the side of the Boeing like an opened jaw. There was a black limousine with blank windows behind it. Behind her, the cabin door was opened and the warmth of the darkness outside at once bullied into the air-conditioning. She turned her head, curiosity no more than an itch. Some local bigwig who'd arrived late . . . they'd hold the plane for a diplomat or some fat-cat businessman. Other business-class passengers were smiling, complacent at the delay, diverted by the prospect of who'd climb the steps and appear flurried and hot and apologetic.

Two men on the tarmac, a third ushering them to the steps with waved arms and an instructive, commanding commentary. The two men at the bottom of the steps were nodding, then they hurried — hardly baggaged, no suitcases, one small bag between them — up the steps and into the plane. A French stewardess was respectful, reassuring, though neither of them seemed apologetic to any degree, and showed them to two seats opposite Ros, on the other side of the cabin. The door closed, the steps and the limousine pulled away, vanishing almost at once behind the aircraft.

She turned away from the window and made as if to settle, closing the book on her lap, steadying the champagne flute as the aircraft jolted slightly as the brakes came off . . . until she realised she was being studied by the newcomers. Two slim, young Indians in well-cut suits, both of them all but oblivious to the casual enquiries of other travellers in the seats around them. They were looking at her as if precisely matching her face to a photograph they had been made to memorise. Identifying her.

As the aircraft swung onto the runway and the airport terminals slid distantly back into place in the frame of the porthole, they seemed satisfied. One of them removed his jacket, then rebuckled his seatbelt.

They were sure. They were on the right flight — the one she was on. They were *with* her . . .

The last gleam of light on the highest peak winked out like a bulb being switched off — sudden, complete darkness. The headlights sprang out at once, as if it was the Land Rover reacting rather than his hand, because the thin dusting of snow no longer reflected sufficient light for him to steer by. Navigation by snowfall. Hyde glanced at Cass, who dozed, drugged with painkillers because his broken ribs were now intolerable. Hyde realised it was like the aftermath of a tragic accident. The cassette player he had wired to the battery droned on, trying to get through to Cass, as if he were in a brain-damaged coma. *Don't walk away, Renée . . . What a Wonderful World . . .* Tapes of hits of the '60s and '70s, all appearing not to reach him.

Cass had retreated from the future because it had frightened him, coming at him like an unavoidable accident through the windscreen . . . but part of it was because he *couldn't* do it, anyway . . . Another part was sheer exhaustion and disorientation. *Carry no passengers*, they always said. The tape Hyde had picked up in some narrow Delhi sidestreet, while keeping Lal's house under surveillance, was pirated and poor. *Twenty-four hours from Tulsa*, coming through hiss and fog. Perhaps Cass would have preferred Brahms or ragas, but he couldn't have either –

– neither can you any longer. He switched off the tape and the quiet of the Land Rover was immediate and confining. Then the strain of the engine, the creaking of the suspension, and the grind of the wipers against the now heavier snow. By his best guess, they were half an hour away from Chatorkhand in the Ishkuman Valley. The narrow track following the river was accessible only to 4WDs and walkers and donkey carts. Trees crowded over it and the wind jolted against the vehicle like a continuing series of minor collisions.

Cass seemed to have hypnotised himself into remaining oblivious . . . your time's coming, sport, don't worry about that –

A lake spread out like black glass beside the road. The narrow, twisting river had scuttled away somewhere, as if to hide itself, leaving this dark mirror. The headlights glanced across snowy rubble and stiff sedges and the occasional bent and sullen tree. Hyde stared at the road, its surface all but vanished beneath the snow. His night vision had adjusted to the glare of the headlights, though his awareness remained just as suspicious of their betraying gleam as the moment he had switched them on. He'd seen the helicopters in the fading daylight, seen them come in close to hillsides and high meadows and riverbanks, always depositing a group of tiny figures before whirling away into the cloudy, rushing sky again. From Singal along the road to Gakuch. Then he'd turned north, more dangerously and therefore unexpectedly. The sky had been clear for almost an hour, then the first high dot, then another . . . swooping, hovering, laying the little black eggs of troops, then whisking away again. He knew with certainty there were troops ahead of them now; troops behind. There'd be roadblocks along the one road, the track that finally petered into a trekking route at Chillinji, still inside Pakistan.

The rifle was to hand on his right side, beside the seat like another brake handle. One pistol in his belt, another in a pocket of the parka he had been forced to don by the plunge of the late afternoon temperature.

A thin moon slid like a lopsided, sardonic grin above the mountains, and he switched off the headlights, halting the Land Rover as he did so. The tyres crunched, then skidded slightly – he'd changed one rear wheel that had blown east of Gakuch. The snow was thickening. He opened the door and descended from the vehicle. His boots creaked eerily. He looked down. The toecaps were whitened. His breath steamed before being snatched away by the wind. His cheeks were at once numb. Cass dozed on behind him. So far, the electrics and mechanics of the vehicle had held up. He wouldn't run out of petrol, either – just out of time and road. He rubbed his icy face with gloved hands, as if washing or distancing grief. His ears rang with the cold. There were no other sounds in the night. Round one bend or the next or the one after, there'd be a patrol of cold, bored, suspicious soldiers – and that would be that. Stop. Dead end.

He kicked the front offside wheel angrily. Sod it.

The relief from the chilly fug of the Land Rover, the imminence of Cass' presence, the depressing weight of the immediate future, were all like emotions he might have felt walking out on a quarrel in a soured marriage. The trapped helplessness he felt invested him like an ague. He continued to rub his face, but nothing was erased from the tired, continuous tape-loop his imagination had become. He banged his back against the door of the Land Rover, as if to irritate a disliked neighbour. The wind soughed through firs and the cold black surface of the lake was wrinkled like ancient skin. The sedges crackled.

Up ahead somewhere, within the next few hours, it would come to an end. *He*, not just it. This time was different, too different to survive. Even Afghanistan had not been like this; at least, not in recollection. Here, there was no *warrant*, he wasn't official. He had slipped through a crack in the Whitehall pavement, to become casually employed, without importance, without backup. And there was no one, not even Ros, who knew where he was. And he was carrying a passenger he would have to abandon, when not to do so had been the whole point.

He opened the door of the Land Rover dispiritedly. Cass stirred from his doze and his white, empty, drawn features stared at Hyde, the bruises like the atlas of an ancient world, the eyes black gleaming holes.

'You all right?' he asked. Hyde tossed his head, clearing his throat in a growl.

'What do you think?'

Cass' gloved hands were pressed against his sides, as if he were suffering acute indigestion. His head hung forward, his breath in the now-colder vehicle smoking against the windscreen. The snow melted on Hyde's hair, running in icy trickles against his neck and ears. The windscreen was opaque with it, the lake lost to view. He suddenly realised how much snow had fallen on him during the few minutes he had been standing outside.

'I – I'll try,' Cass offered, his voice filled with foreboding.

'You're right you will,' Hyde began, then added more softly: 'Yes, sure. Just take it easy.'

He switched on the engine and reached for the headlight switch.

Headlights glared against the snowblind windscreen, bouncing wildly in a ghostly parody of lamplight inside the Land Rover. A vehicle approached them down the narrow track.

'Shit.' Cass' features were in wild disorder, the muscles slow to deflect the fear. Hyde felt his forearms quiver as his grip on the steering wheel tightened.

'What —?' Cass began.

Hyde turned irresolutely in his seat as if seeking a bolthole. The headlights closed, tossing up and down as if mounted on a wild horse. He could make out nothing behind their glare. The lights washed the sedge. As the Land Rover's wipers cleared the windscreen, the snow flew across the challenge of their headlights and those approaching them.

Hyde tossed the rifle into the rear of the Land Rover and covered it with a heavy backpack. Then he pressed the air in front of him with his hands, staring at Cass as he did so.

'Just play along,' he announced. 'And be ready.'

Cass fumbled at his parka, as if to locate the pistol Hyde had given him, seeming inordinately pleased as he did so. God —

Hyde opened the door and stepped out of the vehicle, slamming the door behind him. The approaching vehicle's headlights swept across him like a gleaming arm. Then it drew to a halt at the edge of the lake, almost beside the Land Rover, pressing Hyde vulnerably between the metal flanks of the two vehicles. It was Russian-made, a UAZ-469, looking like a cheap imitation of their own vehicle. The Russian Federation, the Ukrainians, every bugger and his mother were selling off anything they could turn into cash. The family gun room rather than the family silver. Hyde waved, his mind as cold and contracted as his face. There could be up to six men behind the driver. The canvas flap at the rear of the Russian 4WD crackled with frozen snow. Hyde stamped his feet and flapped his arms in protracted innocence as a greatcoated shape detached itself from the darkness of the vehicle and the night. Two other shadows clambered without complaint from the interior of the UAZ. The snow's gleam displayed their upright black sticks of automatic rifles. The driver grinned from behind his half-opaque window, his lips pressed around a cigarette.

'Good evening,' Hyde called, extending his right hand. His left hand was behind his back, waiting to snatch at the pistol. The extended hand was aware of the other pistol, a pocket away. 'Does anyone speak English?'

The first figure, tall, hawk-nosed and gleaming-eyed beneath the Russian-style fur hat, wore the epaulettes of a major. The snow poured into and through the splash of the UAZ's headlights. The origin of the vehicle was somehow comforting, less empty and unknown than the landscape and the immediate future. It was a vestige of the old game.

'Yes.' There was a medal ribbon on the greatcoat, the *Hilal-i-Juraat. For Valour.* 'I do. Who are you? Where are your papers?'

The wind was hollow, as if a cloak of sound had been dragged aside to reveal the vast emptiness of the place.

'Geomorphologists – yes?' Hyde replied with an edge of insult, his head cocked to one side in the arrogance of all experts. 'Taking seismic readings, checking our stations, instruments –' He laughed. 'People round here keep pinching them!'

Again, the slight insult. He had heard Cass' window creak down against the silted snow. Good, he was listening to the sudden cover story there hadn't been time to inoculate him with.

'Seismology? The Karakoram Project was many years ago,' the major replied. 'There has been no new expedition.'

Hyde shrugged. 'Ah – some funding that came along. We're just scouting the old sites, preparing for new work.' His voice had already become bored with his explanation.

'There is to be another project, of the same kind?'

The two soldiers, a corporal and a private, stamped rhythmically behind the major, rifles held across their chests. Snow thrust itself between Hyde and the major; the Pakistani officer, assured and even amused, loomed over Hyde. The water of the lake rustled like paper being screwed into a ball.

'Might be. We're checking it out. Costing, you might say. University of Sussex, England –' Again, he thrust out his gloved right hand, which the major ignored. It retreated again to the warmth of the parka pocket and the location of the second pistol. 'Mean anything to you – er, Major?' *Blow the bugger away*, something prompted in a hectic, unexpected whisper in his thoughts. He knew he didn't have himself under much control.

'Perhaps. Your papers would mean a great deal more. Sir.' The irony was palpable, like a metallic taste at the back of Hyde's throat.

'Pete!' he called, turning to the blind windscreen of the Land Rover. 'Papers, mate! The major doesn't believe we're who we say we are!'

'Your assistant?'

'Senior lecturer, actually. Almost my boss,' Hyde demurred. 'Hurry up, Pete – it's cold out here!' Start inventing *now*.

'I thought you had them,' Cass said. Hyde could not make out any more than a dull and shapeless shadow behind the windscreen. He prayed he'd got his gun at the ready. 'They're not in the dash or the side pockets, I've looked. Christ, *Bill*, you had them last in Gupis – or was it Pingal?' Travelling from the other direction, west to east, the fiction established. Well done, Cass.

'Are you sure?' Hyde persisted, moving to the driver's window. He opened the door and winked at Cass. 'I thought *you* showed the papers last time? I remember you putting them in *your* door pocket, I'm sure I do –'

'That was the map!'

Hyde patted his parka in bemusement, shutting the door behind him. He grinned apologetically.

'Look, I know this is stupid, but we can't find our papers!' He laughed. 'Christ! Oh, sorry – look, I know how important it is to show our papers whenever, but we really are engaged in scientific work, we are who we say we are . . . why *else* would we be up here? With all due respect, it's almost the most God-forsaken place on the entire planet!' He laughed once more, with forced and embarrassed jollity.

'Really?' the major replied. He hesitated for a moment, then moved to the passenger side of the Land Rover and opened Cass' door, flicking on a small torch at the same moment. The interior of the vehicle glowed with an artificial, ghostly light. 'Would you step down – sir?' Then, as Cass did so, the major added, 'You seem to be in some discomfort – ?'

'Nothing. Just a few bruises. Slipped and fell.' Then Cass all but shrieked. The two soldiers appeared electrocuted into jerky movement. Cass' breathing was audible, as was the slump of his body against the Land Rover. The metal quivered under Hyde's hand. Cass was doubled up, nursing his ribs. The major had jabbed him just where he expected a pained response. Identity confirmed.

He was luxuriating. Confident of his own perspicacity. Smilingly superior.

'A very bad *fall*, Mr Cass – ?' Then he began to realise that cleverness was sharply two-edged and at once turned towards Hyde –

– who fired twice, three times because the corporal failed to fly back and fall at once.

'Kill that bastard!' Hyde roared at Cass, then he turned and fired across the small distance of the Land Rover's bonnet.

The major decorated for valour flinched away and dropped out of sight behind the vehicle. Two shots at once, together like a sonar's instantaneous echo. Hyde turned and fired into the cab of the UAZ, at the driver's alarmed face. It disappeared from the side window. Another shot from beyond the bulk of the Land Rover – *Christ, no* – then Hyde was shielded by the vehicle from the rear of the UAZ. Noises of alarm from inside the 4WD, almost of panic rather than response. He didn't look around the Land Rover, preferring not to know. Instead, he fished beneath the backpack and hauled out the rifle, switched to automatic fire and squeezed the magazine empty in an elongated, terrifying cry.

The silence came back, wrapped in the wind, hollow and suggesting great distances. Swallowing, Hyde rounded the bulk of the Land Rover, his boots creaking on the hard snow. The two bodies lay together, all but entwined, greatcoated and parkaed, two shapeless and unmoving lumps.

Quiet inside the wind, the blowing snow, the rippled blackness of the lake, the creak of wind-bent firs. And the two bodies lying in the slushy, disturbed snow beside the Land Rover.

Christ, *no* —

V.K. sat across the coffee table from her, the settee and floor near his feet littered with press cuttings, faxes curling like cheap parchment, digests, estimates, open-mouthed folders. While Prakesh spoke, he merely studied Sara; as if he were attempting, after a long absence or a sexual betrayal, to accommodate himself once more to a domestic charade. There were no emotions on his features. His sole change of expression lay in the slow disappearance of the glow he had worn on entering the room, and which had been sustained and even heightened by the reports from his aides and senior party workers — all of whom had now been dismissed, leaving just the three of them in the smoky, lamplit lounge. Delhi bellowed with lights beyond the long window and the Ridge lay in darkness, except for the occasional flash of headlights. Almost Central Park.

And the bungalow almost like an hotel, and herself certainly like a houri, registering the minutiae of a man's moods towards her. She was frightened, self-contemptuous, unanchored between the immediate past and immediate future.

'Then they are on that flight?' V.K. asked suddenly, himself uncertain. Prakesh nodded.

'Two of them. The woman boarded the flight — we managed to get them aboard.'

'Paris, Prakesh?'

'To throw us off the scent. She's simply fleeing, V.K. There is no alarm on her behalf, there are no suspicions in London.'

'The man?'

'Will be found, V.K.'

'You're certain?' Sara responded, like the sensitive insect she had become, antennae waving for every disturbance of the smoky atmosphere. Regretting what she had done . . . that bloody, *bloody* woman –! It was as if she had been mesmerised or infected with something. 'You are *certain*, Prakesh?'

It was all up in the air, falling in slow-motion, the priceless porcelain of his dreams and ambitions . . . which she shared, for God's sake, had done for years, unlike that sexually-motivated cow he had married.

And she had stuck out a foot to trip the smooth progress of the porcelain in safe hands. What had she done?

And what would they do if they knew?

'I'm sure. It's a matter of time, nothing more. Be certain of it, V.K. The news is good!' He gripped his brother's forearm as it lay on the arm of the settee and shook it encouragingly.

'What of the woman, now?' A pause, then: 'When?' he all but whispered, his eyes still on Sara but secretive; perhaps embarrassed that she should witness his ruthlessness.

'Any moment that offers itself. During the flight, even afterwards . . . No violence. A heart-attack –'

V.K. was nodding quickly, accepting and at the same moment dismissing the detail. Prakesh looked at her then with hard interrogation. She blanched inwardly, but remained outwardly calm. Even sipped at her whisky. Prakesh's suspicion seemed deflected.

Ros was to be executed. Not brought back – not questioned, just killed –

– then good luck to them, whoever they were. Ros *had* to be killed. There was no other way *she* would be safe . . .

*

335

'You OK?' Hyde asked at last.

His shoulder ached as he gripped the steering wheel. They were between Bohrt and Chillinji and the track was worse. Narrow, climbing, twisting like something alive always trying to shrug them off, obscured by still-falling snow. Almost a blizzard now. He had bruised his left shoulder heaving the bodies of the major and the two soldiers into the back of the UAZ. There'd been two others inside, and the driver. All dead. Ribboned by the automatic fire. A lot of blood, smelling sick-sweet even in the icy cold. He'd bruised the shoulder then, or minutes later when, after searching the vehicle, he'd jumped from the UAZ after sending it roaring down the slight slope to the water's edge. He had the food and thermoses of hot tea and coffee and the ammunition they could adapt. He'd watched it, lying prone, the pain of impact shuddering through him, as the vehicle had sunk with a drowning flurry of bubbles beneath the thin ice and dark water at the edge of the lake. The black water had closed like a mouth on the last stream of noisy bubbles.

'What?' Cass replied, groaning as he roused himself. 'Sure.'

He looked like someone staring into a high wind, enduring its force. No longer expecting change, diminution or relief. Less than twenty miles from the border, it was the best that Hyde could hope for . . . and the bleeding seemed to have stopped. The major's bullet had passed through the muscle and fat just below the ribs, on Cass' left side. Powder burns on his parka, his shirt reddened as Hyde had pulled open his coat to expose the wound. The UAZ's emergency medical kit was better than theirs, he'd used that to patch Cass up. The major's face was a mess. Cass' second bullet must have caught the Pakistani as he turned, and entered the base of the skull, exiting at the front.

'Good,' Hyde muttered.

They were skirting the vast bulk of Koz Sar, nearly twenty-two thousand feet, beyond which was the Chillinji Pass across the border into Afghanistan. Maybe no more than eighteen miles away . . . fifteen of which they'd have to *walk*. The pass was seventeen thousand feet up. They'd been climbing steadily up the narrow river valley ever since Chatorkhand. The weather had worsened, like some animal sure of its prey and prepared to wait for the kill. A snowstorm a day keeps the choppers away . . . The headlights betrayed them, but darkness would tip them into the river within a hundred yards. Snow flew across his eyesight, even seemingly behind his eyes.

How far could Cass possibly walk? His thoughts quarrelled and debated the inevitable.

The Land Rover's rear wheels squeaked and slid, then the four-wheel drive righted the vehicle and it turned slow as a tortoise around a sharp-edged cliff and climbed again. The blackness where the river valley dropped away beside the road seemed to run like dark water at the edge of the headlights. The occasional stunted tree, then clumps of firs as if gathered for mutual safety. The wall of Koz Sar's western flank heavier and more threatening than the cloud, glimpsed through wind-gaps torn in the curtains of snow.

They'd seen nothing, no one, after Chatorkhand. Imit had been silent, the occasional glimpsed light, the tiny gleam of a fire. Low, squat houses huddled against the weather. Bohrt had been the same. No soldiers, even though by now they'd know the major's patrol was missing or in trouble because they wouldn't have answered their radio or called in their position. They'd be looked for, and there was only the one road, going north to the border. The Chillinji Pass, unless they supposed them to have branched north-west, to Ishkuman. No, they'd know a 4WD was better heading directly north.

Have you prayed tonight, Desdemona? . . . Too bloody right, sport. He glanced aside at Cass, once more slumped in his seat, his body moving painfully in the troughs and peaks of each lurch of the Land Rover. Bugger that. *Othello* reminded him of Ros and her cultural outings, his programme of improvement – and Ros now, wherever she was, and the frail cord he and Cass were holding –

– blinked it away, but the snow-rush remained, speckling his vision. In half an hour they'd have to abandon the Land Rover and go out there, in that weather. The interior of the vehicle was already colder, the inefficient heating coughing small puffs of warm air that had no effect. And how the hell could Shelley get anyone to them, anyway, along the thin finger of Afghanistan that stretched between Tadjikistan and Pakistan, pointing towards China? There wasn't *any* way – was there? You've really buggered it this time, really *fucked* it up!

A frozen waterfall beside the track glittered behind the snow as the headlights slid across it – then wobbled, then slid. The lights were wiping a smear of light across the waterfall which they were not passing but turning to confront even as the Land Rover backed away from it like an animal startled yet attempting to defend itself. He juggled his foot on brake and accelerator, used the handbrake. Its rasp awoke Cass.

'What –?'

Goodnight, Vienna . . . The vehicle was sliding across a sheet of ice beneath the snow and he couldn't prevent its gradual, inexorable retreat towards the edge of the track and the drop to the river. Not a long drop, quite shallow really, we might even survive it . . .

'Fuck off out of it!' he screamed at Cass. '*Jump!*'

Whitefaced, clownlike incomprehension, then the survival mechanism. A blast of icy air as the door was opened, then a gap where Cass had been, then his body rolling in the headlights as they swept lazily across the waterfall, Cass, their tracks in the snow, the black and white snowladen arms of the trees, then the blackness of the gap of air above the river. The vehicle pirouetted delicately on the unmasked ice, then the front wheels roared over nothing. The headlights dived over the edge of the track, illuminating the black river, narrow and far down, it seemed. Then the lights gobbled at the slope as the Land Rover left the track and leaned out into air.

the undiscovered country

It was midnight in Delhi — and wherever *he* was now. She looked at her watch, perhaps for the hundredth time. The inflight movie flickered with grinning, vacuous, soundless images on the tiny screen set into the back of the seat in front of her. She didn't dare use the headphones, cut herself off from the murmur of the engines or the noises of the cabin — or from any movement either or both of them might make towards her. Didn't dare sleep. Ate in snatched nibbles from the tray she hadn't allowed them to clear away, like a harvest mouse anticipating the rush of the white wings of a hunting owl. In Paris it was seven in the evening, just getting dark. She had to endure another two and a half hours of this —!

At times, the tray opened across her lap seemed to suggest safety, like a child's high chair, at others it trapped her. The stewards and stewardesses were now casual, patrolling occasionally and perfunctorily, like warders not expecting a disturbance. They could cross the cabin at any time they chose. It would be a needle, a pill, something silent and not even discovered until the autopsy. Fat woman dies of heart-attack during flight. *We found her when we removed her tray . . . just as we were about to land — how awful . . . she seemed to be sleeping.* End of story. Her travel bag might be missing, but who'd ever connect its disappearance with those two Indian diplomats who boarded the aircraft while it was on the taxiway?

No one.

Two and a half hours.

She was not even certain that Shelley would be at Charles de Gaulle to meet her. She'd rung from the Air France lounge, but Shelley was unavailable. Alison had relayed a message from Hyde, that much she knew. But – *I can't reach Peter again, he told me not to. Don't call here, he said. Nor you*, Alison had added.

So, what the hell did he intend? Anything, or nothing? It had to be nothing. His little unofficial operation had disgraced itself at the dinner table. He'd pinch his nostrils, and hope the smell would go away. He'd ignore it –

Then how do I get away from them? In the tunnels of Charles de Gaulle airport, in the baggage hall, Customs –!

If you get that far!

She looked across at them. One of them seemed to be asleep, the other, in the aisle seat, intent upon the film. Some feminist buddy movie – oh, *buddy*, do I need one now. Occasionally, the one watching the movie, headphones masking his profile, glanced across at her. He seemed to be content to wait while she remained alert. *He* was assured of her future. Certain.

Ros swallowed drily. She'd ring for a glass of mineral water, display she was awake, parade the stewardess like a bodyguard.

She reached beside her and pressed the button, her hand shaking.

'Are you all right?'

The constant need for reassurance seemed to be the only communication between them. Cass' words lost their impetus against the force of the wind, reaching Hyde at the bottom of the slope as dissipated as the snowflakes that numbed his face. He stared up through the rushing whiteness towards the top of the slope down which the Land Rover had plunged, to end nose-down in the river.

Two, three times he might have jumped before the impact. Instead, he had controlled it. There were skewed and violent wheel tracks and a disturbance of pebbles and rocks on the riverbank. The vehicle was finished, but it hadn't caught fire and hadn't spilt their supplies into the black water. Now, having clambered the slope and staunched Cass' renewed bleeding, then descended again by means of the rope rescued from the back of the vehicle, he was ransacking it like any local bandit. The two backpacks – one too bulky for Cass but he'd *have* to carry it – the tight bundle of the tent, a second rope, ice axe, crampons, compass, torches . . .

'Yes!' he yelled back at Cass.

Set fire to the bloody thing or leave it? Leave it. Get going.

He struggled the two backpacks across the narrow fringe of pebbles to the end of the rope he had let down, anchored to a thin, strong tree that whined with foreboding as the wind distressed its branches. He'd got everything. He looked up as he struggled his sodden parka into one of the backpacks and adjusted the weight on his hips. Right –

Finger of light, tiptoeing at the edge of vision. His head turned stiffly. A crawling white finger of light moving along the surface of the black water, a finger whose hand was black, a bulk against Koz Sar, all but obscured by the snow. Helicopter. Searchlight stabbing down, flicking in and out of the snow and dark wind, following the course of the river. It was seventy, eighty feet up, slipping as elegantly as a slow-motion dancer along the valley, parallel with the track. It must have some kind of terrain-following radar or be flying by computer map. There was a square of light, a welcoming window, on one side of the dark bulk. IR binoculars would be scanning the road through the open cargo door.

He felt leaden with the weight of the two backpacks, the rifle across his chest and the ammunition. Handicapped, tethered like a goat. Then he began to clamber up the rope, his boots scraping and slipping, yelling to Cass:

'Keep your bloody *head* down!'

The second backpack trailed from his bruised shoulder, seeming to drag him backwards. The rifle jolted against his stomach. The finger of light had become a thicker, more discernible walking leg now, stamping martially towards the Land Rover half-drowned in the Ishkuman. His arms ached with the strain of hauling himself up the slope with frantic running motions against the loose scree and jutting rocks. Then he tumbled wearily over the lip of the slope onto the edge of the track. Cass' hand reached him at once, seeking reassurance. Hyde shrugged it away, turning onto his stomach to watch the light walking, walking . . . hesitating, stepping backwards, scrabbling as if to squash a cigarette-end, then locating the Land Rover. The light caressed it, nose-down in the river, as if stroking a dog, the noise of the rotors and engines of the big Russian helicopter banging back off the rocks of the narrow slit of the river valley. *Déjà vu* all over again, he thought, chilled and panting for breath. The cargo door was open, he could see two outlined figures squatting in the window of light. The motionless beam now telescoped as the helicopter dropped down towards the Land Rover.

'Will they land?' Cass bellowed in his ear; a whispered noise.

'I don't think so –' he began.

The eruption of flame from the open door of the MiL startled him. The Land Rover was engulfed as the missile detonated. Almost at once, the flame was itself swallowed by the wind and snow, dying down to aftermath. He thought he heard what might have been a cheer from the MiL. Then there was a second explosion as the debris from the first rattled against the slope below them and he smelt petrol, metal on the wind. The glare blinded Hyde for a moment, then, out of the glare, the MiL dropped lower, hovering beside the flickering bonfire, its landing wheels down but not choosing to settle on the pebbly margin of the river. Two men descended on a rope ladder that trailed across the bank, then cautiously approached the wreckage. The fuel had already burned, but they were nervous. He heard shouts, saw waving arms. A loudhailered reply.

The two men climbed back up the rope and into the lighted opening in the side of the helicopter. Then, after a minute or so, the rotor noise changed pitch and the walking leg of light extended once more, then proceeded as if tiptoeing away from the wreckage, north along the river, its foot splashing on the black water, its noise retreating.

Eventually, he heard the wind again, unadulterated and icy and filled with thousands of miles of emptiness. He shivered, the reaction seeming to displace organs, make his heart quail. He looked at Cass, who was staring after the retreating light, which had become a finger, then a smear, then an illusion.

'Jesus,' Cass exhaled, 'you were down there!'

'I wasn't. I was up here, *watching*.' He glared at Cass, who nodded, then swallowed. 'Want a drink?'

'I think I'd better, don't you?'

The coffee was still warm in the thermos. The major's thick, sweet coffee. Missing patrol, all hell let loose. 'Here.'

Cass grasped the cap of the thermos gratefully, swallowing at the coffee as if he had found an oasis. Hyde felt exhausted, squatting in the slushed snow, his lower body and legs numbed by the cold. He swallowed the thin trickle of warm liquid, tracing its reluctant progress and lack of effect down to his stomach. He threw the remainder of the coffee away. Cass, almost guiltily, handed back his emptied cap. Hyde screwed it onto the flask and thrust its shell-case back into the pack. Two packs, two rifles, the tent, the rest of their equipment littering the zipped pockets of their parkas. Map? US Army Map Service U50J Series . . . Like Hillary and Tensing. He wondered if Cass had got the flag for when they reached the summit!

He rose to his knees, them clambered upright like a very old man. Cass looked up pleadingly, then, childlike, licked snow from his lips. Hyde tossed his head.

'Let's begin.'

He pulled Cass to his feet. The pain in his side and ribs doubled him up, making him cough and groan. Hyde rested his weight on his knees, gloved hands gripping them, feeling their quivering weakness and reluctance.

Eventually, he inserted Cass into the embrace of the backpack,

343

handling the equipment and the flesh as gently as he could. Cass' continual groans of protest and pain unnerved him. He was relieved when they became a torrent of expletives. They rested again. Time was slipping away, it was after midnight – tomorrow morning –

He stood up. The wind howled angrily.

'Fifteen miles – maybe twelve. Maybe less!' he shouted, knowing it was all uphill. 'Let's *begin*.'

He walked away from Cass, following the track, suddenly struck that he had been driving along it half an hour earlier . . . along this narrow, treacherous snake of a thing. The snow crunched under his boots. He paused, but did not look round.

After what seemed like minutes, he heard, through the wind, the crunch of Cass' boots behind him; slow, reluctant, but coming on. He nodded fiercely, then bent his face aside from the flying snow and continued walking; knowing there were other, unheard footsteps, close behind Cass and getting closer.

At first, it wasn't Paris, just somewhere laid out in light like a vast circuit board. Then, as the 747 settled lower over the city, she could make out the black snake of the Seine and the garishly illuminated specks of the Arc de Triomphe and the Eiffel Tower. Other landmarks she left unidentified, her glance flicking again and again across the cabin to the two Indians, apparently absorbed like her in the city. Roads rushed with processions of glow-worm lights, then the countryside was present for a moment as scattered suburbs and clumps of darkness, before the glow of the airport.

Oh, Hyde –

The ground was somehow his element – she needed him especially after the plane landed. She glowered at the two oblivious Indians, who were trying to lull her, their silence assumed.

Her travel bag was zipped, her coat returned to her and lying across her lap. The click of a seatbelt as the sign came on startled her. Neither of the Indians had moved. A businessman drifted past her, refreshed with expensive, cloying aftershave. His shirt was creased across the small of his back. The stewardesses had reassumed their smiles with their makeup, and she felt crumpled and jet-lagged. She dismissed the sensation; she'd managed to stay awake so far – she would now.

Should she dash for the door? Be first or last out? She mustn't get stuck in a crush in the disembarkation tunnel. The fear of needles, one slight, quick nudge with something and she wouldn't fall over until they were thirty yards away, innocently separated from her. First out of the door, then.

The airport was suddenly near, looming up underneath the aircraft as if climbing to meet it. Lights and traffic on the road, then the runway lights – she tensed, her palms wet – and the jolt of touchdown. Roar of deceleration. The lights coming out of their oily blur, separating, slowing. The irritating jingle of muzak and the landing announcements in French, English, Hindi – *en Paris, l'heure est* . . . nine thirty by her watch. On time. Wherever Hyde was, it was two thirty tomorrow morning.

The Boeing turned off the runway onto the taxiway, and the terminal wobbled ahead of her, glimpsed through the porthole which streamed with condensation. She tried to remember the complex hub-and-spoke layout of Charles de Gaulle, but memory came from a Paris weekend with Hyde and that merely confused and unnerved. Baggage claim lay at the end of the spoke, down one floor, she thought.

The 747 slowed. She watched the two Indians, one of them struggling into his jacket, the other adjusting his tie then putting on his shoes. Just like the other businessmen and the few women in business class. All normal, nothing awful could happen now, they'd landed. Relief all round.

She saw the tunnel's mouth extending to meet them, closing like a gourmand's against the door. French kiss, she thought, but there was no giggle inside the image, it was a husk drained by her growing, quick fear. She got to her feet, hefted her bag, and moved down the aisle to the door. The stewardess reproved,

345

then became absorbed in opening the cabin door. Paris was cooler than the cabin, just for a moment, then her own temperature overtook her again. She looked behind her. The two Indians had their bags in their hands, almost standing to attention — faces frustrated as a couple pushed colonially past them. She thrust past the stewardess the moment the door opened, hurrying at once up the carpeted slope of the tunnel, listening for the first hurried footfall behind her. The murmur of passengers pursued her. Her bag was heavy. She looked round. The couple, she fur-coated, he polo-necked and cashmere-sweatered, remained ahead of the two Indians as if determined to reach some sale bargain first. But the Indians were still confident. They saw her only as a fleeing, lone female, their contempt casual and assured. She turned into the long, bright tunnel with its whispering moving walkway. The plane lay beached beyond the windows, a catering truck already nuzzled against it.

She stepped onto the walkway and hurried herself along it, her footsteps spongy on the moving rubber. Then they were on the walkway, too, having elbowed the couple aside or dodged around them. They were hurrying, but not running. They'd needle her, do something, spray something in her nostrils and mouth as they passed her. Were there others to meet them? She looked ahead, into the diminishing perspective of the walkway. Just a blur of lights, people, shops. She passed a lone French policeman, small and armed beneath his Foreign Legion cap. How could she explain? They were twenty yards behind her and catching up quickly. Her legs felt weak, her body heated and trembling. Oh, *bugger*! she wailed inwardly. Christ, Shelley, where are you?

Ten yards behind now, the taller of the two slightly ahead of his accomplice. The walkway was more spongy under her heavy, stumbling tread, the policeman now fifty yards or more behind them. Seven yards, six strides. The taller one increased his pace. Would anyone remember that they weren't met like diplomats,

346

would anyone connect them with her anyway? Five strides, four . . .

There were people at the end of the walkway. A luggage trolley with flashing lights and a wailing horn passed her. An invalid woman sat on the back of it in her wheelchair. Too potent. A hand reached for her sleeve, grasped it. She swung the travel bag and missed the Indian, who side-stepped without losing his balance, and smiled. The man behind him pressed forward, too, so that they blocked the walkway. Ros' hand gripped the moving rail. A poster of the Eiffel Tower, another of the Place de la Concorde, one of a tiger's face through greenery – *Magical Kashmir*.

The tall couple in their elegant clothes were strolling twenty yards behind, a gaggle of first- and business-class passengers trailing behind them. The policeman was invisible far down the perspective of the tunnel. The Indian darted his briefcase forward, as if to spar with her travel bag. Something gleamed at its edge, she was certain. A needle. She backed away, losing balance, everything happening with frightening speed except her reaction. She stumbled. There *was* a glitter at the corner of the briefcase as it darted at her again. She fell away from it with terrible slowness, her heel caught by something, her body accelerated as she tripped against the end of the walkway. The Indian was immediately above her and bending towards her with mock solicitousness. All she could see was the briefcase, filling her vision. Blood rushed in her ears like people shouting –

Hyde rose above the rock and fired twice. The shadow disappeared behind the blown snow; random gusts now. Stars pricked out in a ragged, clearing sky. His breath smoked and he dropped into cover again. A bullet whistled away, puffing snow from the rock behind which he was hidden. The thin, lopsided smile of the narrow moon was high in the sky. The stars watched like surprised, inert eyes.

There were four of them, perhaps six. Not knowing was bad

347

enough. Almost tripping over them was worse. The wind swept snow off the rocks around him, and ice cracked somewhere with a groan. Where was Cass?

He sat, the Kalashnikov pressed against his chest. Where? Cass had tumbled to the right, unhit he was certain, and he had scrabbled away to their left, at the first shot. Ten minutes ago. The straps of the peak ground into his shoulders, the harness pressed into the small of his back.

Moon, diminishing snow, a clearing sky, and they were a thousand feet above the timberline, close to the pass. The wind howled, asthmatically angry. The peak of Koz Sar gleamed out whitely through a pause in the snow. Ice shone on its flanks; everywhere, it seemed. Another planet.

He heard someone moving, after a muffled order. He raised himself above the parapet of rock, the lichen scarred into exposure by ricochets, and fired. The greatcoat lost form and volition, becoming merely a lump of rags on the snow. Ducked down again. The returned fire whistled away wildly off the rocks.

'Cass?' he called. 'Phil?'

'Yes!' he heard, all but lost in the fire directed at himself and the location he and they guessed was that of Cass. Away over there, across the narrow track, closer to the grumbling little tarn locked into the embrace of the mountains. They'd been resting, looking down at it, or just staring at nothing, when the first shot had been fired. 'Yes!' Cass bellowed again after the gunfire, in ragged defiance. He was holding up – just.

Until they call in a chopper . . . The moonlight cast shadows now and there were great, torn gaps in the cloud. The river was a dark-silver ribbon away to the west. The wind was still fistlike in its repeated buffets, but it wasn't too strong for a gunship, just difficult.

He listened, head cocked. Nothing inside the wind. Then a muffled groan and a shuffling noise. Cass moving. Two shots, which whined away. The mountains stretched everywhere

348

beyond Hyde, the Hindu Kush to the west, the Karakoram to the east. There was nothing other than endless mountains. The thought crushed. He looked for navigation lights against the glaciers and snowfields, but saw nothing. The wind made his eyes water. Around him the land fell away in a delusion of space, except up ahead. It was nothing more than a scratch in the mountains, this track and the slight gap of the Chillinji Pass.

Three in the morning. They'd made reasonable time, trekking up towards the border. They'd managed to skirt Chillinji — there'd been a patrol there, gathered around a truck, the glow of cigarettes visible. The tiny hamlet of scattered, snow-gripped huts was silent, except for one invisible dog barking at imaginary disturbance. The place might have been long deserted, except for the patrol. Three in the morning. They'd eaten once — soup, tinned meat, rice, coffee. Chocolate and biscuits. Cass had seemed a little refreshed, though that might have been illusory.

Again, he listened, and thought he caught the crackle of a radio, the whisper of voices and ether and the tiny clicks of switches or buttons.

'We have to move!' he called out — in Russian. What else did he speak they wouldn't understand? He couldn't remember whether Cass spoke Russian or not. 'We have to move!' A desultory shot whined away above his head, not even striking the rocks behind which he was hidden.

That made it certain.

'OK, comrade!' Cass called back. More shots towards his position, but again, without enmity or aim. Just restraint. Hyde gritted his teeth.

'They must have called up choppers — gunships!'

'I understand,' Cass called back in English. It seemed to provoke more intense fire. He heard someone scrabbling — not Cass — leaned to one side and fired off three quick shots. The noise was louder, possessing an echo. The wind was dropping. The clouds moved more slowly. The anoraked figure — Frontier Force — ducked out of sight thirty yards away. They weren't closing

349

in, just closing the gaps. There were at least two of them up ahead, farther along the track, the others would be half-encircling them. They just wanted to keep them where they were.

'Wait till I move!' again in Russian.

'Two – up there!' Cass called back in Russian.

'*Kak pozhivayete?*' Hyde called. What state are you in, tourist version.

'OK!'

Good. But they must know Cass is in difficulty, know the background? He *sounds* bad. He heard the crackling of the radio, but they'd retreated with it, so that he couldn't hear what was being said. The cavalry's on its way, they want reassuring that we're still pinned down. Easy targets, precise references. They might even send this lot down the toilet with us, for the sake of surprise. He listened again, as intently as he could. The night was calmer, almost silent, the sky bright with hard stars. He couldn't hear the sound of engines, just the scrape of metal on rock as someone moved.

Five, ten minutes – an hour? The border region was littered with temporary and permanent army bases. All of them were supplied by helicopter. It wouldn't take long to put up a couple.

He had to move up the track, keeping to the shelter of the rocks as best he could, try to take out the two men up ahead of them.

Someone snapped out an order in Urdu. At once, Cass shouted:

'They're dropping back!'

'Out of range!' Hyde called back, his voice high with an onset of nerves.

He moved on his haunches, like a Cossack dancer skittering across the ground. Then he saw the flicker of a darkened knife-blade as the man leapt from the rocks at him. He raised the blunt Kalashnikov and the knife clashed on the barrel between Hyde's hands. Then the barrel was under the man's arm and Hyde

350

heaved upwards with it. The Pakistani's assault knocked him off balance, but carried the man's bulky, anoraked form over the top of him. He turned onto his stomach and fired two shots. Immediately, shots from the left, and from up ahead. The Pakistani got to his feet and fumbled his own rifle from behind his back. Hyde squeezed the trigger again. Nothing.

Empty or jammed.

The noise of engines, the chilling mutter of rotor blades, very close, masked until that moment by the —

— it sprang up like a huge spider, over the lip of the scree slope. The Pakistani soldier was startled by it, his attention distracted. Hyde, lungeing from his haunches, struck the man across the cheek with the butt of the rifle. The rock ten yards away roared with flame, and the concussion of the explosion threw him off his feet, struck him with sharp shards of rock. He was deafened by the noise.

He was right, he realised, they hadn't waited. Surprise was everything. They didn't care who they killed, so long as they got them.

His mouth was filled with snow, it was difficult to breathe. He realised it slowly. The explosion still roared in his ears. Then there was a second flash of light and a rain of debris on his back and head. The rotor noises were distorted and distant and yet filling his head. He thought someone was screaming, but it might even have been himself. He couldn't think, there was only the noise.

Two more explosions in swift succession. He could hardly hear them, his hands pressed too late over his ears. The continual bellow of noise was already inside his head. Someone was screaming. He could see only the faint glimmer of the snow in front of his face through the retinal dazzle. Something heavy landed on his leg.

He looked up. The MiL was hovering in a mist of updraughted snow just where the slope fell away to the grumbling tarn. Its insect-eyed cabin was blind. The updraught wobbled it like a spider at the end of a long, invisible thread. Retinal spots danced around it like small flares. He dropped his head, exhausted. Then the noise in his head subsided and he began to hear the rotors.

Something dragged at him, something that screamed. A shadow above him, leant over him, a shadow that screamed.

'Get up, *get up*!' it kept bellowing, like a child discovering a dead parent. 'Get moving – *move*!' Panic, desperation.

Hyde turned his head sideways and looked up. It was Cass, his hand gripping Hyde's backpack, pulling vainly at it. Behind him, the gunship loomed like a dark moon through the mist of snow. Then the helicopter danced away.

Hyde struggled to his feet. Cramp in his calf. He looked down. His trousers were torn, flapping wetly. The pack weighed like a great stone. Cass was still screaming at him, his voice hoarse and high-pitched.

Then they were stumbling up the track, hauling themselves along the fringe of boulders and rocks, slipping on hidden ice, their breaths clouding round them. There was someone, a shape no more, ahead of them, waving a gun, confused as to their identity. Cass shot it from a distance of five or six yards and stumbled over the body as it fell. There was no sign of anyone else, no shooting. Hyde turned. Cass fell rather than leaned against him, almost unbalancing him. The snow-mist was settling now and the MiL was moving back towards it, its dark snout thrust forward, the rocket pods visible beneath its stubby wings.

Come on, Hyde waved, when no sound would emerge from his throat. He half-pulled, half-jostled Cass ahead of him. The taller man was bent double as if by age, his legs struggling through his total exhaustion. Twice, Hyde hauled him to his feet, looking back each time. The snow was being drawn up again by the rotors. Then someone must have moved and there were two more bright explosions, followed by a concussive wind that reached them like a hot breeze, then the noise of tearing rock.

The third time Cass fell, Hyde fell with him, stumbling into a snowdrift that was suddenly shoulder high around him, sparkling with frost, numbing his body and his check. Cass lay on the hidden track, his chest heaving. Hyde struggled out of the drift. They had rounded a bend. There was nothing behind them now.

Hyde crossed to Cass.

'Come on,' he said hoarsely. Ominously, Cass was pressing his hand to his side. 'It isn't over. It's just begun. Act Five. Come on – on your bloody feet!'

They were above fifteen thousand feet. The air's cold hurt his lungs. Cass' chest seemed on the point of eruption as he fought in the thin air. There were four, perhaps five miles to the border –

– and to what? Nothing, probably.

The needle, bright-tipped, was jutting through the corner of the briefcase – rich brown leather, gold clasped. People shouting as if encouraging the swing of the needle towards her. The legs of the taller Indian, the bent-down face of the other. She was entangled with her travel bag, couldn't get her legs to move – one shoe'd come off, one leg was twisted under her. Oh, *Christ* –!

No police whistles, no one near enough. But someone kept shouting and shouting in French, then English, the voice distorted through effort and panic. Surely it was a yell of alarm, a warning – ?

Then arms were pulling her along tiles that were still wet. She collided with the notice that declared such to be the case and it collapsed on her. Someone swore in French. The smaller Indian raised his gun at her and she cowered away from it against blue-serge trousers, striped like a uniform down the outside leg. Then there was a noise, a sharp twig-crack of sound, and the Indian fell down, as if he, too, had tripped. Then there were people screaming, panicking to run backwards on the moving walkway, yet being propelled towards the fallen body.

The Indian with the briefcase bent slowly, carefully, and placed it upright on the gleaming tiles. A policeman removed it, another inspected the Indian lying down and shook his head. Took the pistol from a dead hand. The passengers on the walkway were being channelled to one side with brutally shouted orders and the occasional thrust or gesture of a sub-machine-gun. They streamed away in a gabbling, semi-hysterical troupe, staring back like excited schoolchildren.

Then Shelley was kneeling beside her, holding her upper arms, looking into her face with genuine concern and relief.

'Christ, Shelley – where have you *been*?' she screamed at him. Then pulled him against her, holding onto him, feeling her whole body shudder against his. There were suited legs standing behind him, the drape of long overcoats. Police uniform trousers, too. Eventually, she pushed him away, shook his hand free of her hair. 'That's enough of that,' she announced with a mock brusqueness that came out with a peculiar inflection, as if she were losing her voice.

Shelley was openly grinning. His eyes were still moist with relief.

'Thank God!' he sighed. 'Thank God . . .' Then: 'I got in an hour ago, I thought I'd have more time, but something blew up. It's taken me until now to put the squeeze on Claude –' He glanced behind him, as at someone he expected Ros to recognise. The Frenchman, elegant to the point of provoking irritation in a long camel-coloured overcoat and a Burberry scarf, nodded as if they had been formally introduced. Ros sat up, legs splayed unselfconsciously, and brushed her hair from her face and eyes.

'Who's Claude when he's at home, Shelley?' It seemed the only thing that might reasonably be asked. It was, at least, prompted by a desire for normality. Her hands were shaking violently.

'DST – their MI5. I couldn't do anything here without their supervision.' Then his eyes clouded, his brow creasing. 'You're all right? You're sure? I couldn't really take it in for a moment – luckily, Claude realised . . .' His voice trailed away and he shrugged.

354

Claude Whoever was bending over the dead Indian, then murmuring to his companion, who at once appeared to protest some form of diplomatic immunity. The Frenchman smiled thinly, shaking his long dark hair. He was taller than the Indian who had tried to murder her —

— hands shaking again, stomach turning over. Jesus.

Then the DST officer gestured to two uniformed policemen and they placed themselves at either side of the Indian. Then Claude Whoever walked swiftly towards her and Shelley. He all but clicked his heels as he nodded to her.

'I am Claude Rousseau, DST. Welcome to Paris, M'selle Woode.' He reached out his hand and she shook it. He helped her gently to her feet. She brushed her clothing into some kind of tidiness and modesty, then her hair into a semblance of order. Then she was bent double by stomach cramps, having to catch at her breath and swallow the sweet nausea that threatened.

Rousseau held her arms as she straightened up, wiping the moisture from her lips. Thank Christ she hadn't thrown up! Then someone pressed a bottle of Evian water into her hand and she sipped at it.

'Something stronger?' She shook her head. The water was dizzyingly strong, invigorating. Rousseau nodded in satisfaction.

Immediately, she sensed the fictitious paint of the situation begin to peel and fall away. Shelley stripped the remainder of it as he said, low and urgently:

'Where is he, Ros? Is he still alive?' Adding almost at once: 'You don't know, do you — you can't tell us?'

As if exposed in some humiliating failure, she shook her head. Then blurted: 'I know where he was aiming for, that's all.'

Shelley glanced at Rousseau, who nodded, then snapped out a stream of orders to those around him. Then he said:

'Come with me, both of you. Somewhere more private, I think.'

Shelley took her arm.

'Do you know if he's alive?' she asked, turning on him.

Shelley looked lugubriously at his watch. 'He was, twelve hours ago – a little more.'

'I know *that*!' she snapped.

'Sorry. That's the last news of him.'

Then they were hurrying through the clotted passengers, then down a narrow flight of iron stairs to a corridor that echoed with their footsteps, to an unmarked door. Rousseau closed the door behind them. The room was cramped, sparsely furnished. Rousseau locked the door. The place seemed designed to intimidate and disorientate. Rousseau indicated a stiff-looking armchair.

'Some coffee?' he asked solicitously. She shook her head.

'Patrick said you'd know where he was heading. Right – where?' Shelley asked. He appeared uncomfortable.

'I just have something . . . you need a map. The US Army Service map . . . ?' Rousseau was nodding. Shelley opened his slim briefcase on a low coffee table and riffled through its contents.

'Which one, Ros?'

She fished in her handbag and found her powder compact. Her urgency made her fumble and the powder spilt onto the stained cord carpet and over her skirt.

'Oh, *shit* –!' she bellowed, ridiculous tears clouding her eyesight. Then she shook the folded piece of tissue paper and held it out to him. 'There's a reference written on that,' she said, sniffing. Shelley unfolded it with delicate movements of his fingertips. 'You place that over the right map.'

He continued searching in his case, then unfolded a map with unnaturally loud cracking noises. He spread it out on the floor. Rousseau knelt beside him. Shelley shuffled the powdery sheet of paper across the map. The landscape was nothing but mountains, she realised. He made finer adjustments, as if finishing a jigsaw. There was perspiration on his brow.

'There,' he sighed. 'The – er, Chillinji Pass.' He looked up, shocked. 'He's crossing into *Afghanistan*.' Then, to Rousseau, he murmured something like: 'Tomorrow, he said,' and glanced at his watch. 'It's almost four over there – *tomorrow*.'

'What are you going to do?' Ros asked as she saw Rousseau shake his head, then shrug.

'I – I'm not sure –' Shelley began.

'Get him out!' she heard herself growling, leaning forward on the narrow, uncomfortable chair, her hands clenched into fists.

'Where's your evidence?' Shelley asked urgently.

She clutched the travel bag. 'In here. I've got it – so has he. Get him out.'

'You're *sure*?'

'I'm sure. It would ruin them. The Sharmars.'

Shelley nodded, and turned solemnly to Rousseau. 'Claude, there's one way. Medicins Sans Frontières. They'll have a helicopter, more than one, closer than anyone else –'

'I can't arrange that, Peter. Not even for you.'

'You have to, Claude. The lady insists. I *know* SDECE people fly with or even *fly* some of those medical helicopters. They have to, Claude, just to protect the doctors! *Please* speak to someone senior in Intelligence. I'll regard it as being in the Big Favour class. *Grand obligation*. I will reciprocate in kind and degree.'

The room was hot now, with the tension of all three, and with her impatience. Hyde's situation had drowned her own and her only fear was for him. Shelley seemed pained by her demands and those of what might have been his conscience. Rousseau weighed advantage against the risk to valuable pawns, but seemed drawn to study her.

Eventually, he nodded, his dark hair falling across his forehead. He flicked it away from his broad, pale brow. He smiled at Ros.

'Very well, Peter.' He wagged his long index finger. 'I want to know – everything.' He pointed at the travel bag, which Ros at once clutched against her as if he intended a mugging. Shelley made to protest, then he, too, succumbed to the delicate adjustment of scales.

'Agreed.'

Satisfied, Rousseau crossed to the telephone in a corner of the room and snatched it up from the grubby carpet. Ros sighed as he began, without hesitation, to dial.

'I'm sorry, Ros,' Shelley murmured, watching the travel bag as if it were a small animal that might, at any moment, jump from her arms and flee. 'We'll do everything, of course . . .' He shook his head. 'We'll do everything we can.' He already seemed to partly regret his bargain with the Frenchman. His tone was bereft of optimism, and his attention remained on the bag – its contents. They were forfeit to Rousseau – for *nothing*.

'You think he's dead already, don't you?' she challenged.

Shelley nodded. He had, evidently, made a bad bargain and regretted it. Wanted to breach the contract. Then he said:

'He put the phone down in a panic, Aly said. They were on to him twelve hours ago and more! Look what a risk they took in trying to stop *you*, Ros.' He spread his arms. Genuine regret flickered like a flame of exotic colour, burning differently amid the calculation and negotiation. He had wanted to do good, the proper thing, but the mood was dissipated by a chill breeze of pessimism. He murmured: 'I don't know if even he can make it this time, Ros.'

She shook in the force of her own brush with death, which now raged like a gale.

And neither do I, she admitted. Neither do I . . .

Cold, now. Snow had become ice crystals, needles in his skin. The weight of Cass' laboured progress dragged on the nylon rope that bound them together. The rifle slung across his chest was frozen to the parka. The weather had surged into the pass, thrusting them back towards their pursuers. The wind howled as it circled and buffeted them.

Hyde could see little. The path was treacherous with ice beneath the newest snow, and he stumbled often, bringing Cass down – Cass bringing him down or at least to a grudging halt

358

each time he fell. The flesh wound in his leg was now no more than a numb ache.

The Chillinji Pass wound unseen ahead of them, clambering its way towards the border. He had begun to sense they wouldn't reach it, simply because his perception of what was beyond that border had diminished into a single faith. There'd be no one, nothing on the other side, just the same appalling weather and the slow process of freezing to death. Or survival until morning and a clearing sky brought anyone following them at the run to finish their task. A few rounds of automatic fire into two already-stilled bodies.

His internal temperature had dropped. He was certain of that. Beneath the layers of thermal clothing and the icy skin there was a sluggishness about his blood that was echoed by his thoughts. *You're not going to get out of here* . . . The thought repeated itself, as on a tape-loop, and he no longer had the energy, the *warmth*, to fight it. It was the bloody-fucking weather that had caused that. Landscapes he could deal with; desert, mountain, forest, scrub, tundra. In *good* weather, so that men were still the only real danger . . . but not here. The bulky, armed shapes would rush in only to find the job already done.

Cass stumbled again.

His mind reached back like frozen fingers along the nylon rope to realise the reason for his having been dragged off-balance. In a moment between driving snow, he saw vast glaciers and frozen sheets of water gleam like crumpled tinfoil. He turned awkwardly, his feet lacking purchase, and saw Cass lying in the hard snow, a whitening lump. He'd have started to bleed again, if the temperature allowed bleeding. He stumbled back towards the prone form, collapsing onto his knees, shaking Cass at once because he dared not believe this was something final. He screamed at him, the curses all but soundless, as the air required to expel them burnt in his chest.

Cass, turned onto his back, stared up at Hyde's ice-lidded eyes through a bushy, frozen rime on his own lashes and eyebrows.

His stubble was frozen, his lips cracked and approximate as he attempted to reassure. His mittened claw gripped Hyde's sleeve, tugging at it. Hyde hefted him into a sitting position, growling against the frozen collar of his parka:

'Ready?' He had to bellow. *'Ready?'* Against both the wind and the cold burn of his throat – and against the black heaviness that had begun the moment he halted. To impel Cass was as burdensome as to carry him – it might come to that. He seemed content to lie staring up into the blowing snow. *'Come on!'* Hyde yelled, dragging him once more into a sitting position, then roughly turning him onto his stomach, hoisting him then onto all-fours, as if arranging a dog for inspection at a show.

He bullied him upright. Cass pressed his hand against his side, then bent double as if to vomit. Hyde wanted to leave him, let the rope slacken from around his waist, as if Cass would drift off on black water to drown out of sight. He couldn't. It would make it purposeless, it would be admitting that he couldn't win. Cass was the necessary luggage that suggested there was a destination to his appalling journey. He leaned Cass' weight against his body, in a loose embrace. The howling wind rocked them, his parka was thickly whitened, seeming to crackle into ruts and folds as he moved. There must be a patrol close behind, had to be. He pulled Cass forward, felt his freezing breath against his cheek as he leaned their faces together.

'Come on, sport! All in a bloody day's work!' he shouted. Cass nodded dumbly. 'They can't catch up with us as long as we keep moving!' Two steps, the third, fourth, fifth and sixth; stumbling upwards to where Hyde's own footprints were busily being covered by the falling snow. 'Moving, moving, *moving* . . .' he grunted, as much for his own encouragement as for Cass.

'Where are they?' he heard.

'Back there. Behind us. Must be!' Cass paused in new snow – up to their ankles now – dizzily righted himself and flapped his arms like a drowning man. His face was grizzled, weak. Then he turned and bellowed coughingly:

'*Bugger* off! Bugger *off*!'

Hyde grinned. His lower lip split. He dragged Cass after him as he prodded ahead. The river was somewhere out of sight beside them, like something dangerous tracking their progress, its icy grumblings heard in the small gaps between the gusts of the storm. The cliff face alongside them loomed and danced closer then farther, like an assailant always threatening to hurl them into the river. It was insane to be there, insane to continue their futile movement. He looked back. Slowly, woodenly, Cass came up with him and at once slumped against him. Yet within the icy fringes of his lashes, his eyes seemed more determined. Hyde nodded, and turned to continue.

The shot was almost silent, no more than a flat, hoarse whisper. As were the two shots that quickly followed. Hyde fell to one side, dragging Cass with him – who groaned on impact with the snow-covered ice.

Hyde could see nothing. Nothing at all. Snow raced across the track behind them, obliterating whoever had fired at them. He listened, but the wind swallowed all sounds other than its own. Except where ice cracked and thundered distantly.

'Where?' he heard from Cass. Hyde merely shook his head. Back there, somewhere. They'd been glimpsed through a ragged hole in the curtains of snow. Lost again now, though.

He staggered to his feet, climbing against the steep staircase of the wind. Dragged Cass upright, too, and bullied them both on. He shuddered with more than the cold. They were too close, maybe only a hundred yards or so. Hours yet to daylight. It wouldn't take that long, not anywhere near. There were a couple of shots, which made him crouch, but he heard no ricochet or whine of a bullet anywhere near them. They turned a snake-twist of the track and Hyde pulled them into the inadequate lee of a jutting shoulder of rock. He could hear their breathing like a revelation. Cass was still aware enough to be gripping the rifle with frozen hands.

You're not going to get out of here . . . It came back, then, into the relative lull of the rock's shelter. *You're not . . .* Eventually, the hypnotic whisper of defeat would shut out everything else from his thoughts. Freeze his mind.

'Let's go!' he growled against Cass' ear. He nodded in exhausted reply.

A shadow on the track, a bulk that struggled through the snow.

Hyde fired without thought, feeling a wild exhilaration. The bulk slipped, stumbled, flung itself outwards and disappeared, as if the snow and wind had digested it. Something clattered down towards the river. He heard no splash.

'Come on!'

There seemed no one else, only perhaps a faint shouting, a sheeplike and inconsequential noise amid the storm. He couldn't be certain. He might be imagining it. They lumbered together up the track — twenty yards, thirty even, before they stopped to drag in freezing air, bent double with effort. The track dropped away, and they slithered after it. Clumsy, shifting pebbles suddenly under the snow. The noise of the river, water threading between the plates and banks of ice that grumbled together, quarrelling with the river's momentum.

'Where's the track?' Cass wailed.

'Christ knows!' Hyde yelled back.

The river, narrow and black except where fringed with ice, lay across their progress. Hyde, on one knee, traced it to either side of them. To the right, it rushed away, swelling and lessening in gradient. To the left — upwards — it vanished into a narrow crack in the rocks, followed by no discernible track. They were stranded on the bank of the river. The route up the pass had disappeared.

'Where is it?'

It had to be on the other side of the narrow river. He strained to see through the flying snow and ice crystals. No larger perspective, no sky or mountain peaks. Just the black, narrow defile from which the source of the river emerged.

The rustle of moved pebbles, grating icily together.

Dark figures within the storm.

'Get down!' he yelled at Cass, dragging at his sleeve. The first shots went wide. The approaching figures — two of them — became smaller, closer to the ground. Prone. 'Get across the river, Cass!' he whispered urgently against the man's ear. 'Get moving — get across the river! Cover me!'

Cass shrugged away, slithering across the pebbles like a wounded animal. Two more shots. IR nightsights. Cass' movements would have made him light up just enough in this weather. He raised his own rifle. The nightsight was old-fashioned, ineffective . . . except that the two of them lay in prone firing positions close together. He heard Cass stumble into the shock of the icy water. He squeezed the trigger of the Kalashnikov, three times. The blurred, partial IR image did not fade, but he heard a groan of pain. The returned fire was sporadic, disorderly. He slid away on his stomach, across the snow-covered pebbles of the riverbank towards the water.

'You all right?' he heard from somewhere ahead of him.

'Keep your head down!'

'The track's here! I'm sheltered —'

The river was a couple of feet deep, the rocks and pebbles slippery, the close farther bank obscured, then there, then obscured again. He couldn't feel his feet or ankles or calves. His knees and thighs worked by memory rather than volition. No more shooting, just the noise of raised voices.

Hyde collided with the bank of snow-covered rock. He clambered thankfully out of the freezing water, ice jolting against him with the malice of knives. He lay on the bank, shuddering with intensified cold.

There must be a bloody rope bridge across the river, probably no more than thirty feet away! He crawled like the first amphibian towards Cass' voice, into an alien element.

'Over here — *here*!'

Then his mittened hand was gripped by another hand, his arm pulled unmercifully. He rolled awkwardly behind the rock litter

363

where Cass crouched, the backpack skewing sideways as if to separate from him.

Their voices echoed immediately. The wind was quieter. There was rock all around them, hemming in the river at this point. But the track continued on this side of the river, Cass said it did. He needed to believe him. He listened to the soldiers' voices again, then raised himself behind the rock and rested the rifle on it. The nightsight gathered what light it primitively could. He fired again, three times, but believed he hit nothing.

He stood up, stamping his sodden boots. They couldn't halt long enough to change socks, never mind light a fire. There'd be others, soon, close behind them. They had to keep moving.

He shrugged Cass ahead of him and they located the track. Narrower now, winding away from the river between high, sheer cliffs, a litter of snow-covered rocks and gravel. The storm whisked aside, as if to encourage and then disabuse them. Peaks reared like the great heads of wild horses around them as the track climbed more steeply. A vast ice sheet glimmered. The track seemed to slip furtively beside it – or perhaps had been swallowed by it, he thought, before the snow obscured the scene once more. If the track had disappeared beneath the glacier or whatever it was –

– it hasn't. You can't afford to believe that.

It was after four thirty. The border was somewhere less than a mile ahead now. A last mile.

He was jolted into a shiver of admission. He had no idea what kind of border post or fence there might be, none whatsoever. But there had to be something, some barrier to the smugglers and separatists and bandits and refugees. Some paranoid outpost in this vast nowhere that claimed that *here* Pakistan ended, *there* Afghanistan began, however much the high peaks and the snow-fields and the glaciers mocked the idea. Soldiers.

They were clambering exhaustedly towards soldiers, not away from them.

*

'Peter, they say it's impossible –'

She caught the whisper, shook her head at it as at maddening flies. *'No –!'*

Shelley seemed afraid; genuinely concerned. 'Claude, they *must*,' he insisted. 'They must *try*.'

Rousseau was lugubrious. 'The weather is impossible. They have *one* helicopter, an old Chinook. They need it for *everything*. They can't risk it.'

'They have to.'

But, Ros realised, Shelley's eyes were already back on her travel bag. Some of the gold was inside it. Enough of the precious metal, even it wasn't to be used as a ransom for Hyde.

'No! Do something – *do* something!' she protested out of deep anguish, the tears blinding her, scalding her cheeks. 'You *must do* something!'

Colder now. Frozen. Hands and feet totally numb, even in the shelter of rocks and the storm blown out as suddenly as it had begun. So cold . . .

The noises of the soldiers thirty feet below them. The occasional, distant noises of their pursuers, coming up quickly, knowing where the border post lay and certain they were trapped between the border and pursuit.

They were. Hyde knew they wouldn't hurry, knew they were confident that this would be their last border with anything, that only death lay ahead.

The sky was filled with high, icy stars, scraps of glinting glass. The moon had gone down, having mocked them enough; satisfied it was over. He rubbed a frozen mitten over his face. Its shock failed to wake him. Cass dozed, roused, dozed beside him. His determination had fatally weakened him. Even if he got him moving, just once more, then the next time they halted, he'd roll over and die. Hyde had seen it in his eyes. And he was too exhausted to carry him. It was a vast effort even to keep nudging him awake when all he wanted was to sleep himself. The storm had retreated into Afghanistan like an apparition they couldn't follow. It obscured the more distant peaks. Beyond the border post, the track fell sharply away down a snow-covered slope towards the timberline. Seventeen thousand feet. The air was thin, debilitating. The chocolate was almost too hard to break in clumsy fingers, too cold to chew and swallow. He could smell harsh coffee being brewed below them.

The border was marked by obligatory, casual barbed wire, rolled out at either side of the track, across which lay a barrier. A hut stood beside the ridiculous painted pole. A larger barracks hut – from which most of the occasional noises emanated – lay immediately below them, smoke curling from its single tin chimney. Its roof was thickened with snow. Two guards sat in the smaller hut. There might be another half-dozen or more in the barracks hut.

He studied the scene again and again, concussed by it as he might have been by collision with the rocks around him. Dead end.

You're not going to get out of here . . .

He sat with his back against a rock, the Russian rifle cradled in his stiff arms and numb fingers, Cass nodding again into icy unconsciousness beside him – he nudged him awake once more – staring down at the smoking chimney of the hut, smelling the woodsmoke. In the other hut, the two guards were playing cards, or hunching over something else that lay interestingly between them. The snow on the roof was a faint sheen in the starlight, the chimney's skein of smoke only slightly less dark than the night.

He looked down at his hand. It was shivering, either because his eyesight was affected or his numb hand retained the capacity to register cold. It was gripped like a claw around something larger than a cricket ball and not quite round that it had found in one of his pockets. Very slowly, he relearned its nature. Weight, two-fifty grammes, the ring was a safety clip, there was the lever, the plug . . . weight of explosive, sixty grammes . . . nine hundred tenth-of-a-gramme fragments around the explosive. Lethal radius, nine metres. Four-second fuse. It was a fragmentation grenade. Now, he knew all about it . . .

The chimney smoked above the glimmer of the snow-covered roof. The barracks hut was perhaps forty feet long, but the cots or bunks would be as close to the fire as possible. Lethal radius, just about twenty-eight feet. The hut was narrower than that.

There were subdued noises from the guard hut, a startling, clear mutter from the barracks hut with its iceblind windows. Nothing from the track behind them, no sign or sound of pursuit. Not yet —

He nudged Cass awake once more. The man groaned softly, hardly protesting. It had to be now, before they both fell asleep for the last time. The roof sloped shallowly. The chimney was less tall from the peak of the roof than a standing man.

He leaned against Cass' dull face.

'This — ' He held up the grenade. ' — is going down the fucking chimney — understand? *Understand?*' Eventually, Cass nodded. 'When it blows, there'll be casualties *and* survivors. Mostly, there'll be panic — understand?' Again, the robotic, concentrated nodding. '*You* have to be down *there* — ' He pointed at the guard hut. ' — to take care of those two.' Cass looked at the smaller hut as if for the first time. Nodded slowly, deliberately. 'Don't fucking fall asleep on me.'

'I won't.' He shifted his bulk. Ice crackled as the landscape of the parka changed. 'I won't,' he promised earnestly.

'OK.'

Cass would be awake as long as he was moving. If he stopped and fell asleep immediately, Hyde could kill the two in the guard hut from the roof of the barracks. He brought the coil of nylon rope that had bound them together out from beside him, then looped it about a sharp thrust of rock. He lashed it tight, tested it, then moved away from the cliff to lean out against the rope's tautness. The roof was directly below him. He scrabbled gently

367

over the edge of the narrow ledge and began walking carefully backwards. His body was heavy against the air beneath him, dragging at his arms and shoulders.

Then, almost at once, he was squatting on the roof, close to the chimney. He heard gruff laughter from the guard hut. He loosened his hold on the rope and left it dangling. Dug into the snow like a small, crouching bear. Maybe two or three inches of snow, then a layer of ice – shit. Cautiously, he began moving up the slope of the roof, his frozen fingers curled into claws, his dulled feet pushing gently inside the ice-stiffened, unyielding boots. He slid forward softly, mechanically. Weight thrown forward, not looking up. There were quiet noises from beneath the roof. He glanced once towards the guard hut. Two faces in warm light glimpsed through the window's closing pupil of ice. He leaned his weight further forward as the angle of the roof increased, a frozen wave repelling him. With relief, he heard Cass moving, the scrape of his boots on frozen rock. Bugger hadn't fallen asleep, then –

He began sliding, his feet losing purchase, hands unable to grip, everything happening slowly. He dropped flat, spread-eagling himself on the snow, toes digging in, hands searching for the edges of wooden tiles, finding, finding – *one*. His body skewed to a halt, then, scrabbling with his right hand, he found a second tile that wasn't flush. He stopped. Incredibly, his body was hot.

He listened. Began again, easing himself on his stomach, sloughing himself through the snow, making more noise. At first it would be snow falling from the roof, then the noises would be too regular and suspicious to those awake. He wriggled up the angle of the roof, finally slapping one hand over the ridge, then the other hand. Shimmied sideways towards the chimney. Someone muttered from inside now, drawing attention to the noises he had made. He gripped the blackened tin chimney. The smoke leaked out of it, reluctant to leave the barrack hut's warmth. He eased himself upright, one foot planted uncertainly on either side of the apex of the roof. More murmuring below now, and an angry response from someone newly disturbed. He reached into his pocket and brought out the grenade. Pulled the pin, released the lever with a relaxation of the clawed right hand, and dropped the grenade down the chimney. It rattled like a stone.

Three – four.

Smoke and soot erupted over him as he slid away from the chimney. Snow grumbled down the roof. Windows shattered. Screams. The glare of the scattered fire blazing on the snow – no, the place was catching alight. The chimney belched smoke and screaming. The door of the barracks hut opened – door of the guard hut was banging open, too. Something fell on the snow beside the track, burning and torn. The screaming was louder, tormented. Nine hundred fragments. A spirally bound steel wire, pre-notched, which the explosive charge metamorphosed into splinters. Lethal radius, nine metres. Eyes, face, arms, legs, organs.

He slid down the roof, reached its edge and dropped onto the blind side of the hut, his boots crunching on fragments of glass buried in the snow. The screaming just went on, helplessly. Firing from the guard hut. He raised himself and looked into the burning interior of the barracks hut. Two bodies still in their bunks, bedclothing ripped as if by savage beaks or claws. A torn body, lying on the floor. Something that had once been human must have been crouched near the fire, for warmth. It had been shredded by the steel splinters from the grenade. Then he moved, clumping heavily through the snow that had drifted on that side of the hut, towards the guard hut, where fire was being returned through the broken pupil of the window. *And* from the door.

There'd been four in the barracks hut –

– *officer?* Separate quarters. He whirled round, but the figure with a heavy greatcoat flung over a nightshirt was already fumbling with the safety of the rifle. Hyde dropped to one knee and fired. The Kalashnikov, on automatic, emptied itself in a fraction of a second. The greatcoat fell leadenly into the snow beside the track, lit by flames as the wooden barracks hut really caught and flames gouted above the roof and through the windows like desperate, pleading arms. He dimly felt the warmth of the fire on his face.

Jammed a new magazine into the rifle, turning on his knee. He couldn't see Cass. Saw one figure at the window and fired two shots. Hit nothing, was almost glad. Except that they had to pass the hut. Fired again as a shadow moved.

'Where are you?' he called in the silence that crackled with unreal flames. Warmth on his neck, seeping into him.

'Other side!' he heard.

'All right?'

'– not much more help!' he heard, fainter. Cass was blown out, shuddering down into silence like a rackety machine.

He looked up at the night sky. Grey was leaking into it somewhere over China, beyond the closer peaks. No navigation lights, but it wouldn't be long, and they wouldn't be friendly either –

He could hear nothing from the pass beyond the barracks hut, just its cold, crackling fire. He raised himself into a crouch, as if carrying a huge rock. His legs were quivering as weariness buffeted him. Then he lurched towards the guard hut, watching it joggle in his vision, watching the window, the window, watching –

– *one*. Fired. Window empty. Watching, watching –

– blundered against the wood of the hut, making the structure quiver. Glanced through the shattered window. Nothing at first, then a leg stuck out from beyond the crude table. A shadow slumped over its edge. Moaning softly. Wounded. The scene blurred and then was gone as he left the window. He ducked heavily beneath the pole – the *border*, welcome to Afghanistan. It didn't work because he had no good memories the country's name could dredge up.

He found Cass beside the road, kneeling on the ground as if praying. Slumped beside him, heavily on one knee. Weariness was at once paralysis.

'All right? *Phil* – all right? Bugger you, all *right*?'

Cass looked up blankly.

'There's no fucking more of this, is there?' he growled.

Hyde shook his head.

'Let's get moving . . . come on, Phil,' he coaxed. 'There's no one alive, no one following –' For the moment anyway. Hyde got to his feet, one stiff, weak arm around Cass, hoisting him. They leaned together like saplings in a gale. The grey was staining the eastern sky with cautious optimism. The barracks hut was diminishing into a smaller fire. 'Come on.'

The track remained narrow, but sloped downwards. They stumbled along its twists until they were out of sight of the border post's ruins.

Cass stumbled, fell spreadeagled as if staked out on the snowy track. Didn't move. Hyde knew he wouldn't get up again. They were both finished.

Then he heard the rotor noise. Saw the navigation lights blinking against the stars, coming on fast from inside Pakistan. Pakistan . . . Cass was right, just lying there. He was making the right choice. There were two sets of lights, two helicopters. They emerged around their lights as black, bulbous-headed shapes, hovering like great insects over the dying flames of the barracks hut. Hyde sat in the snow, dumbly fascinated by the instruments of his defeat. He couldn't see the fire, but it flickered on the bellies of the two helicopters. Snow drifted in the updraught, the rotor racket banged back off the walls of the pass. Then they dropped out of sight, and their noise nosed ahead of them as they began following the track. Only moments now. Two Alouette IIIs. The dying firelight had flickered on wire-guided missiles slung at each flank of both helicopters. Eight missiles, two cannon – minimum armament. *You won't feel a thing . . .*

The rotor noise boomed ahead of the invisible Alouettes,

becoming louder, deafening him. Snow began to pucker and lift at the last twist of the track, then become a tiny blizzard blowing ahead of the two helicopters. The noise and power of the engines throbbed in the rutted, gravelly track. The finger of a searchlight moved into view. It was hypnotic, mesmerising, so that he wished to bring it to an immediate conclusion by running back up the track towards them. The light splashed on the beard of a frozen stream.

'Oh – *shit*!' Cass yelled, his voice tiny and hoarse. He glared wildly as the first of the Alouettes drifted into view, shadowy behind the smoke of snow its rotors threw up. Nose down like a hound.

Cass struggled to his knees, grimacing with pain and exhaustion. Pushed himself, but couldn't stand, then began scrabbling on all fours away from the helicopter. Hyde watched him, motionless. The blunt, blind nose of the Alouette stared at him as he sat in the snow, cross-legged like a Buddha. It paused. The second chopper lifted out of the snow and swept up and over them, then dropped into position farther down the track, nose up in the hover. Cass was blindly crawling towards it.

Hundreds of feet below them, the pass opened out into a narrow valley. Now that the sky was almost half stained with the pre-dawn, he could make out the distant timberline, even the faint spot of a frozen lake. And the mountains stretching away. You weren't – ever – going to get out of this . . . not ever.

Cass had stopped crawling. He remained on his knees, staring at the Alouette that had blocked the track below them. Hyde stared at the other helicopter as it studied him.

Snow drifted down on his shoulders and head. On his arms, hands, the rifle. The snow crept forward from the updraught. The helicopter was diminishing inside its own created snow-storm, like the miniature scene in a glass ball turned upside down. It lost feature – *he* lost feature. From shape to shadow to indeterminate something –

– he crawled to Cass, nudged him, shivering with anticipation. Gestured upwards, behind them. A gleam of frozen water. A slit in the rocks, big enough for two of them?

He braced himself against the rock, half-thrusting Cass into the crevice behind the narrow, frozen dribble of the waterfall. The Alouette lifted out of its own snow-fog, disconcerted. Hyde watched it. The other one did the same. They buzzed together like pedagogues discovering disobedience to their authority.

Then, a third set of navigation lights.

All remaining resolve collapsed.

The lights dropped lower as the two Alouettes stared at each other, then turned, looking in different directions, bemused but still ultimately assured. A big troop carrier, by the look of it. Chinook?

At once, the Alouettes flipped upwards like fleas towards the bigger, two-rotored helicopter. They entered the hover on either side of it. A light splashed down from the Chinook, spraying the frozen track with droplets of silver. The light raked back and forth like a finger locating a word amid a page of text.

Red cross on the belly of the Chinook, illuminated by the light from one of the Alouettes.

Swallowing icy air, he stepped out onto the track, arms raised above his head, waving feebly. The light moved towards him, then beyond, then flicked back, surrounding him. The two Alouettes remained peremptorily in the hover. Then the Chinook dropped towards him.

'Phil!' he bellowed hysterically. 'Phil – *get out here, for Christ's sake –!*'

Cass was heavily beside him, blundering into him, to be contained in the blinding, magic aura from the Chinook's searchlight. The Alouettes remained stationary –, they needed orders.

Medicins sans Frontières. He could read it blazoned along the flank of the Chinook. An arm waving, near the open cargo door. The Chinook fitted itself into the narrowness of the pass like a matron settling into a small chair. The arm beckoned.

Cass and he stumbled forward together. French helicopters, French doctors, *French* . . . untouchable, never know when you might want arms or aid from the Frogs. God *bless* the bloody Frogs —!

Hands and arms lifted them gently into the interior of the Chinook. Into safety.

POSTLUDE

'Change is not made without inconvenience,
even from worse to better.'
Richard Hooker: *Ecclesiastical Polity*

Hyde looked out across Bennelong Point, where the Opera House glittered almost as fiercely as the wrinkled, yacht-carved water. Then he looked towards the Harbour Bridge and then the ferries waddling like the pigeons in and out of Circular Quay. The sun was high and hot. Almost Christmas, in Sydney. He chewed on a burger and sipped at the frosted can of Foster's. Tourists and office-workers drifted past him, luxuriating in another almost endless day of sunshine and heat. He wriggled his feet in his trainers.

The burger bun was tasteless and dry and he put down the remainder of his lunch on the bench beside him. The light on the water hurt. Ros was with her lawyers. Her uncle's estate was becoming like Jarndyce versus Jarndyce. She'd get through it though, and be wealthy, he had no doubt. He turned on the bench and looked, as if with irritation, at the massed soldiery of the business high-rises, over-shadowing Government House and the Botanical Gardens. The sun heated his back now. He smiled when he remembered that he thought he might shatter like a cartoon cat when Ros had first grabbed hold of him and almost squeezed the breath from him. He tossed his head, amused.

The Chinook hadn't bothered to argue with the two Alouettes, merely challenged them to follow it into Afghanistan. All the *élan* the Frogs could muster, and they were home free, wrapped in crackling foil like oven-ready turkeys . . . drugged, chafed, debriefed. Rubbing them back to life in the Chinook had been more significant than Shelley's endless, patient questions.

He looked down at the copy of *The Australian* he had bought to read while he hung about for Ros – in her best suit, like a uniform with braid and buttons. She'd soon have plenty of cash, own a sheep station, property in King's Cross and Paddington – *Sydney* not London, and that struck him like indigestion. Good old Uncle Bruce.

Third headline, front page. *Congress Party squeezes home in Indian election.* The Sharmars had done it – just. Mehta, the film star and fundamentalist, had been edged out after six weeks of neck-and-neck.

And Shelley and the Foreign Office – and the French, he suspected – knew all about the drug-smuggling. They had a *lever*. Already, Sharmar had had *very* nice things to say about European investment in India. The Foreign Secretary himself had appeared briefly in Hyde's life. His bespectacled features and quiff of white hair had been sufficient warning, even without the reminder of Hyde's obligations towards the Official Secrets Act. Don't tell the *Sun* was what it amounted to. Or *Private Eye*.

He finished his beer and spread his fingers on his thighs. A happy ending. He'd survived, he'd got Cass out, saved his life. Cass had been patched up but had taken longer to recover than he had. He was now on extended leave, Florida or somewhere warm, and Tony Godwin had promised him a job on his return. He hadn't got Ros killed by dragging her into it – thank God. He was a wealthy woman's lover . . . a woman who, he was certain, wanted to stay in Oz. Didn't want either of them to go back . . .

Hyde sighed, frowning. A tiny sense of betrayal in his chest.

He attempted to ignore everything except the flexing of warm muscles in the sun, entertain nothing but the darts and glides of small sailing boats. Every detail would disappear into that glitter of light if he so much as squinted.

Everything except the letter he'd had from Aubrey. The one he'd crumpled into his pocket, unopened, suspecting Ros' reaction. The letter he'd read after leaving her at the lawyers'. The letter he'd just finished re-reading.

Aubrey needed his help. Unofficially, since the old man was as retired as he was himself. He was offering him a job, *work*.

He'd ring him, soon . . .

All the Grey Cats
Craig Thomas

The Spider
From his new position of eminence within the KGB, the traitor Andrew Babbington, allied with General Brigitte Winterbach of East German Intelligence, seeks to determine the future of Nepal.

The Web
Kenneth Aubrey, untrusted by his masters, bungles the defection of an East German civil servant, Brigitte Winterbach's only son. By a tragic irony Aubrey's former ward. Timothy Gardiner, at the same moment stumbles upon the Soviet plans for Nepal . . .

The Fly
Tim Gardiner becomes the prey of an unremitting manhunt while Aubrey desperately tries to uncover proof of Babbington's plot, in London, Malaya and finally Nepal itself . . . where Brigitte awaits him . . .

ISBN 0 00 617726 3

Emerald Decision
Craig Thomas

A compulsive thriller from the master of the genre

Emerald Decision

A British agent uncovers a secret nest of Nazi submarines. German agents multiply in Ireland. A massive Nazi parachute drop is imminent somewhere in the British Isles.

Code Name Emerald

is put into effect – a secret plan so lethal and so illegal that all traces of it must be obliterated and all evidence buried.

Code Name Emerald

One of the best British intelligence agents lost his life in this secret action. The war over, a top American author seeks information for his bestseller. His quest spells death, danger and violence, and at the heart of it all, lies the mystery of his father.

'The great strength of his books lies . . . in the presentation of powerfully exciting bouts of action in authentically realized settings.'   Reginald Hill, *Books and Bookmen*

ISBN 0 00 617440 X

Winter Hawk
Craig Thomas

A World in Jeopardy
A laser weapon is about to be launched. Once in orbit, it will be used, destroying the world's balance of terror.

A Man With the Proof
The CIA's Russian mole is the only man who can prove the weapon's existence.

A Man in Trouble
The US President needs that proof within four days, before he signs an arms agreement banning all nuclear weapons.

A Desperate Remedy
Major Mitchell Grant, hero of *Firefox* and *Firefox Down* must bring the proof out of Russia. Unless he succeeds, the next and final war is imminent.

ISBN 0 00 617434 5

HarperCollins Paperbacks – Fiction

HarperCollins is a leading publisher of paperback fiction. Below are some recent titles.

- ☐ RED SQUARE Martin Cruz Smith £4.99
- ☐ THIEF OF ALWAYS Clive Barker £3.99
- ☐ BELLADONNA Michael Stewart £4.99
- ☐ NIGHT OF THE HAWK Dale Brown £5.99
- ☐ MORNINGSTAR Peter Atkins £4.99
- ☐ DEEP BLUE Gavin Esler £4.99
- ☐ THE TIGER OF DESIRE John Trenhaile £4.99
- ☐ THE ANIMAL HOUR Andrew Klavan £4.99
- ☐ EVIDENCE OF BLOOD Thomas H. Cook £4.99

You can buy HarperCollins Paperbacks at your local bookshops or newsagents. Or you can order them from HarperCollins Paperbacks, Cash Sales Department, Box 29, Douglas, Isle of Man. Please send a cheque, postal or money order (not currency) worth the price plus 24p per book for postage (maximum postage required is £3.00 for orders within the UK).

NAME (Block letters)_____

ADDRESS_____

_____